Doocey Half-Sees Whodunnit

Detective Doocey Mystery Series, Book One

Tom McAndrew

CAVEL
PRESS

KENMORE, WA

A Camel Press book published by Epicenter Press

Epicenter Press
6524 NE 181st St.
Suite 2
Kenmore, WA 98028

For more information go to:
www.Camelpress.com
www.tomcwriter.com

Library of Congress Control Number: 2025945200

ISBN: 978-1-68492-330-4 (Trade Paper)
ISBN: 978-1-68492-331-1 (eBook)

Cover design by Scott Book
Design by Melissa Vail Coffman

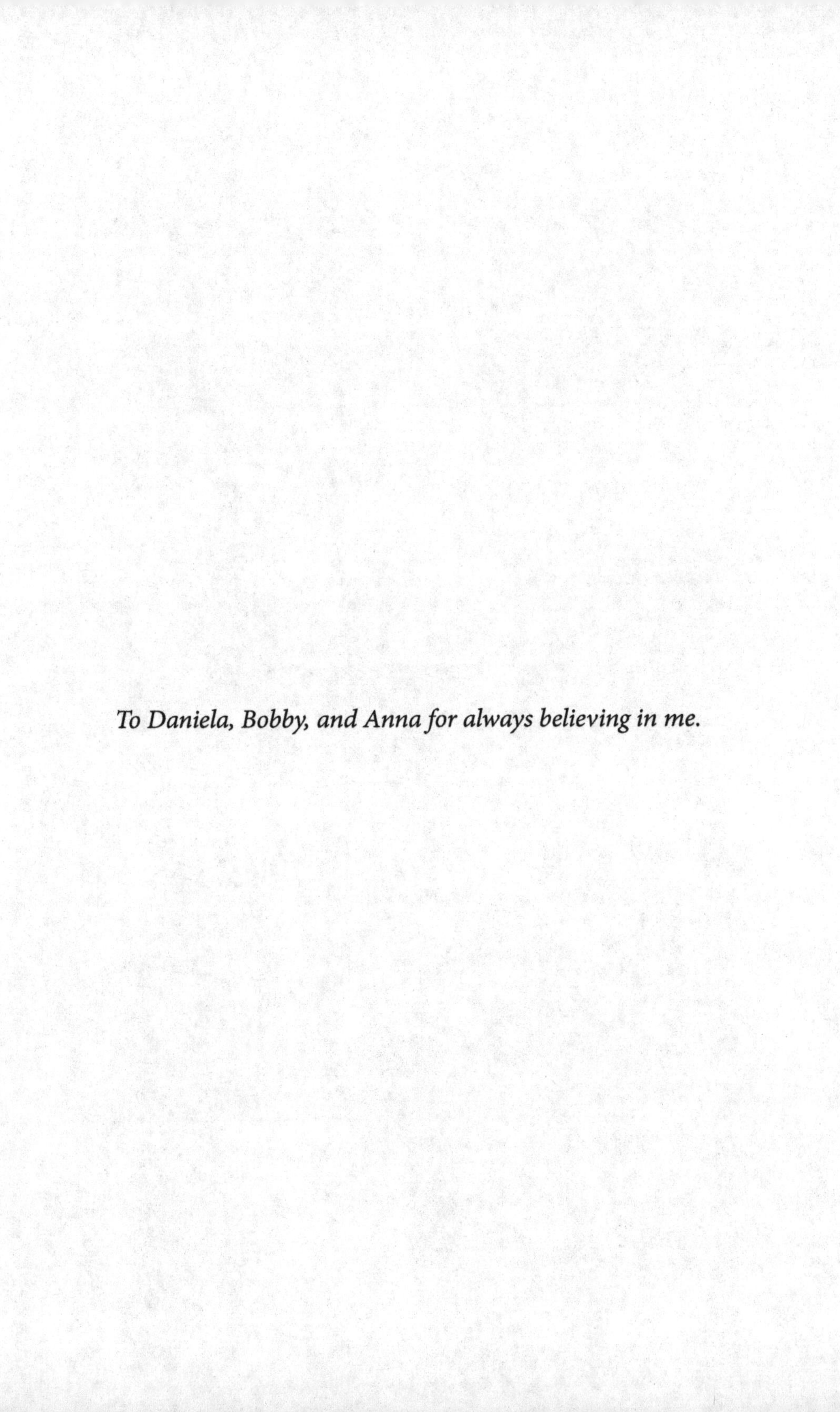

To Daniela, Bobby, and Anna for always believing in me.

ACKNOWLEDGMENTS

THANK YOU TO JENNIFER MCCORD for her invaluable input and making my dream of publication come true.

ONE

"WHERE ARE WE HEADED FOR, buddy?" the taxi driver asked, peering into his rear-view mirror.

"Can you drop me off at *The Eye and Ear Hospital* on Adelaide Road?" Shamie Doocey replied. Then after finally succeeding in buckling his seat belt, added, "At the entrance to their Accident and Emergency Department, please."

With a loud groan, the taxi driver heaved his ballooning belly around to eyeball his scruffy passenger. "Everything all right?" he asked in a breathless voice. With his bobbed black hair and seventies sidelocks, the man reminded Doocey of Elvis Presley. Albeit a bloated Presley in his latter days.

"Oh, I think so . . . It's just when I woke up this morning, I wasn't seeing the sharpest." He forced out a chuckle. "Like my glasses were dirty or a bit fogged up." He waited for the nosy fecker to get on with giving his diagnosis, in the vein of your typical, *seen-it-all, know-it-all,* Irish taxi driver, and then to drive the hell on.

But Elvis just kept gawking back at him. Obviously in need of his full fecking medical history.

Doocey gave an irritated wriggle of his small shoulders. "I went to my local optician but they told me, just to be on the safe side, to head into *The Eye and Ear.* They said not to bring my own car because the hospital ones would probably need to put these drops in my eyes which make everything go blurry, and I wouldn't be able to drive myself home."

Now, is that enough information for you?

The taxi driver fixed his gaze on Doocey's brown-rimmed glasses. "You're sure it's not the old specs? Maybe you got dirt on them?"

"No," Doocey snapped. "It's not the glasses." Cleaning and recleaning the blasted things—a hundred times over—gave him the confidence to be at least sure of that. Plus, the fog was there when he took them off. Though harder to see on account of how everything turned so much fuzzier without his glasses.

"Ah . . . I wouldn't say it's anything to worry about," the taxi driver reassured, finally turning back around. However, contradicting his words of reassurance, he pressed hard down on the accelerator, and the car shot forward.

Doocey took to gazing out his passenger window as they joined heavy traffic. The waters of *The Royal Canal* looked extra black this morning, and raindrops, like tears, trickled down the car door's glass. It was almost as if he were an actor in some—over-sentimental—Hollywood film and the whole world was his set. Except no casting director would ever consider Doocey for any soppy film. Not when his upbeat disposition and quirky looks made him perfect to play a comedic or light-hearted role.

His ninety-plus mother always maintained that he was far too easygoing. According to her, the world could be ending and he'd still be as cool as a fecking cucumber. However, at this particular moment, he couldn't help but feel worried, and he knew his mother—of all people—would understand exactly why.

"Yeah, I'm sure it's nothing," Elvis, unprompted, piped up again.

"Yeah, I don't think it's anything either," Doocey echoed back.

"No . . . I'd say . . . you're . . . safe enough," the taxi driver persisted but in a faltering voice. Then after a pause, "Though I heard of this fella once who one morning noticed something wrong with his sight, and by the very next day, he was stone blind." Elvis gulped in some air. Air that Doocey had noticed smelt of pine forest air freshener, masking a faint scent of vomit. "Yeah, the poor chap couldn't see a thing, for the rest of his life." He looked into his rear-view mirror, "Imagine that for a nightmare. Sure . . . if you can't see, you can't do anything."

"Well . . . I wouldn't agree there at all," Doocey whipped back. "My own mother has serious sight issues, and they never stopped her from doing things."

'If you're not growing, you're dying,' she would always say and in fairness, these were not just airy-fairy words on her part. She truly lived by that mantra. That was because even after she'd developed her sight issues, you name it and she'd done it. Chess, poker, running, tennis, karate, football, cycling. Not to mention the charity fundraisers, the skydives, the parachute jumps, the sea swims.

Yes, lately she'd cut down on the more physically demanding activities, but that was just because of her getting older and frailer. Even so, she remained the busy bee and still did some physical stuff. Like playing drums in a heavy metal band called 'Old Iron Maidens.' Though the racket she and her three golden oldie pals made would make an ear-splitting jackhammer sound soothing in comparison. And his mother knew, herself, they sounded rubbish—but what Doocey thought fantastic about her was the way she was prepared to keep going with things as long as she was enjoying herself, not bothered about what anybody else thought.

Most recently she'd set up a visually impaired darts team and according to her, it didn't matter that they couldn't properly see the dartboard because they used this electronic one that sounded out their scores. She was even determined that they were going to beat the local pub's darts team—Paddy's—who all had perfect sight.

Elvis speedily moved on from arguing blind people were basically helpless and asked that question every Irish taxi driver (or at least the ones Doocey ever encountered) loved to ask, "What is it you do for a living yourself, bud?"

Doocey momentarily considered answering, "Take a guess." Confident that even if he were to give the buffoon a thousand tries, he'd never hit on his occupation. But not being in the mood, at this precise moment, for playing goofy games—he just spat it out, "I'm a detective."

"You're a detective?"

How gobsmacked the taxi driver sounded came as no surprise whatsoever to him. It was always the same old story. Irish people, he'd found, had a certain image ingrained in their heads of what their detectives ought to look like. They expected them to be tall, smartly groomed and have the eyes of a hawk. Not to be this scruffy, five-foot-nothing, little fart with mad white hair and glasses.

"Working on any big cases?" The taxi driver followed up.

Doocey heard the sneering undertone in the question which said loud and clear, *Don't think you've me fooled for a second. I know you're no detective—I'm just playing along.*

Working on any big cases? The very same question his mother had been asking all his career—though, of course, she'd been genuine in asking—and his disappointing answer back had always been the same. "No." He'd often wished his mam could've been more like his departed dad who never used to ask about whether the cases he was working on were big or small. He couldn't care less. Just so proud that his son had made it to becoming a detective.

As a small boy, he and his father would sit on the sofa, watching classic detective shows, trying to tease out together the murderer's identity before the TV detective beat them to it. Nearly always—his dad guessed wrong, sparking a grinning shake of his head and him christening the TV detective to be a "pure genius." His young fella qualifying as a detective had then made him so proud. There wasn't a person he met that he couldn't resist talking their ear off about how his son was this hot-shot detective up in Dublin.

Whereas when it came to his mother, he felt she set the bar far higher. His making it to being a detective wasn't enough for her. She had much bigger expectations and a much bigger opinion of her son's capabilities than just that. As if from her perspective, he would not be living up to his potential until he was solving the biggest of big cases but he'd yet to be assigned one of those.

His mother also loved to listen to crime fiction audiobooks and, having listened to so many, she reckoned she was up to being a detective herself—but she really wasn't. He'd explained to her so many times that real-life murders were very different to those to be found in her crime fiction audiobooks which—with the clue being in the name—were after all only 'fictional.'

In crime fiction, the crime writer held all the clues (or pieces of evidence) to catch the murderer and it was just a matter of them chucking out those clues, one at a time, like breadcrumbs—knowing with certainty they would lead their fictional detective to the murderer. Whereas real-life detectives had to unearth any clues there were for themselves and there was no guarantee of them finding or even identifying the right ones.

However, Doocey just could not get this logic into his mother's otherwise logical head. Her mind was fixed. There could be no persuading her that her son (and even herself if she only got the chance) wasn't more than capable of solving any big murder case.

And up until such a big case landed on his desk, to her, he was really only an administrator, a paper shuffler. Someone who tidied up the paperwork on smaller cases. Something any nincompoop was capable of doing which sadly was more or less the truth.

Sadly too, Doocey's work colleagues hadn't ever viewed him as a real detective either—but more as a clown. In the end, he came to realise that instead of forever battling to persuade them or anybody else otherwise, it was easier to let the world think him that clown.

There were, however, some upsides to constantly playing the eejit. Suspects, he'd discovered, were much more open with you when they thought they were just chatting to some little shabby halfwit with specs and not a legit well-dressed, sharp-eyed detective.

It's just a pity that he only got to hoodwink small-time offenders seeing as he only got to work on smaller cases that involved less serious crimes. He'd love to see how he got on hoodwinking a more serious offender—like say a murderer—but any of the big cases that involved major crimes such as murder got dished out to more conventional-looking and acting detectives. To the likes of his boss, that pompous ass, Ed Dickson who'd been assigned the latest big case. The case that had everybody in the country talking. The Nolan case.

Oh, how he'd regretted, given the earbashing to come from his mother, ever mentioning in passing to her about Dickson nearly having every other soul in the station working on the Nolan investigation. *Him and his big mouth!*

"I just don't understand why you don't stand up for yourself more," she'd lectured. "I mean, it's all well and good being easy-going but that doesn't mean you have to be anybody's doormat. You need to march into Dickson's office and demand to be put on that Nolan case. Do you hear me? Demand to be put on it!"

In the end, to placate her, he promised he would do just that. But, of course, he never did storm into Dickson's office to speak up for himself, knowing that his superior—donkey that he was—would have only laughed in his face. Instead, he lied about Dickson saying he had him working the smaller cases because he was so good at them and how his work on those was just as important as any work he might do on any big case. *Yeah right!*

Although, not long before this, there had been that one case that he supposed could've been categorised as being genuinely important. He'd been assigned to find a tearaway teen named Indigo Armstrong who had a fondness for illegal drugs, especially crack cocaine and ecstasy, and whose daddy was a bigwig politician. Not only that, but Daddy Armstrong hung out with Assistant Commissioner Mike Ryan—Ed Dickson's boss. The man who was effectively second in command of the Irish police force, known in Ireland as The Guards or The Gardaí. Within the force, Ryan was widely respected for doing a good job of getting himself constantly on the telly to waffle on about what a great job he was doing as assistant commissioner.

It hadn't been initially copped how high-profile the missing girl was. Explaining why the case got ditched off to him. When his superiors realised their cockup—in no doubt, double quick time—Doocey had fully expected the case to be reassigned to a 'proper detective.' But almost miraculously he'd got the thing solved within a few hours, managing to get key information as to the teenager's whereabouts from Nick Sweeney. A man deemed to be Dublin's number-one drug dealer and a crook with an extensive network of underworld contacts across the city.

The lowlife had sworn though that he'd sooner fling his beloved mother off the balcony of her fourth-floor flat than ever squeal to The Guards or in his words, "The Filth." A promise that in a successful criminal career spanning thirty years, Sweeney had held firm to—until that is Doocey, just this once, had got him to talk. But because the girl's rich and powerful daddy, with the help of Assistant Commissioner Ryan, hushed it all up, the story of Indigo Armstrong going missing never made it into the public domain. Doocey's dream then, for his mother to read in the national newspapers about some big case her detective son had cracked—went on.

Not that Doocey would even have categorised the Armstrong girl's disappearance as a proper big case. His idea of a proper big case, and he was sure his mother's too, was one where there were all these intriguing twists and turns. Not a straightforward case that only took a couple of hours to solve. That any numbskull could solve.

Sometimes Doocey would wish that as a younger man, he'd had the get-up-and-go to have struck it out on his own. Set up his own detective agency. To have been his own boss. Then he could've chosen which cases he investigated and—with any luck—they'd have been big interesting cases like the Nolan one.

Now in his fifties, he'd missed that detective boat. Plus, his mother was seriously old now and could be heading for the pearly gates at any moment. He'd more or less accepted that he'd never be able to prove to her that he was a proper detective. However, Doocey was not one for dwelling on regrets. There was always that buzz he got when he wrapped up—even a routine—little case. He still loved being a detective. His work was his whole world.

"No big cases," Doocey answered back to the taxi driver with a fake little laugh. "I'm afraid . . . I only work on run-of-the-mill stuff."

"I thought you might be working on that Nolan lady's case," the taxi driver said, even more sneeringly.

'No," Doocey replied, wondering, not for the first time, what it was about that particular case that so fascinated the Irish public. As, down through the years, many other Irish people had vanished without a trace, and there hadn't been half as much fuss about them. What then made Harriet Nolan's disappearance so different? From his previous meditations on the question, three possible reasons for the Irish public's huge interest in the case had come to mind.

First of all, he supposed there was how Harriet Nolan was such an incredibly beautiful woman. The mainstream media stereotyping her as a 'blonde bombshell.' She was exactly the kind of stunning woman a plain Joe Public or Jane Public or even a taxi driver with delusions of being a reincarnated Elvis would naturally take an interest in. She was so photogenic or to put it more tabloid press crudely "so sexy" that all the newspapers loved taking every opportunity to plaster her picture over their front pages.

Then there was her being married to Markus R. Nolan, a man almost twice her age—who just happened to be a multimillionaire—and who also professed himself to be a crime writer. Though not a cent of Markus R's millions came from book sales, as he'd yet to be published. All his wealth had come from his father, the late Mick Nolan, a dodgy builder who'd made his millions from bribing politicians and planners to build shoddy housing estates on green belt lands.

Another intriguing factor was the bizarre circumstances of Harriet Nolan's disappearance, causing people to speculate like crazy about whether Markus R. had secretly murdered his wife.

Two

Doocey dodged some traffic to get across to *The Eye and Ear* Hospital, this lengthy, three-storey structure punctuated by countless tall windows. A building well over a hundred years old. Inside was a rabbit warren of corridors and small rooms, forcing a red-faced Doocey to finally ask a porter for directions.

He queued to register with an abrupt receptionist, who barked questions at him and typed his answers noisily into a computer. Then she growled for him to take a seat in a waiting room located around the corner. On spying the packed, noisy waiting room, Doocey stepped back out into the hushed corridor, deciding he'd better ring work.

This was the first time he'd ever had to ring in sick and he hated the thought of doing so, especially when it meant having to explain himself to an ass like Ed Dickson, who, many years back, had somehow managed to get himself promoted to being his direct boss.

Though Doocey could see how that promotion—on paper—looked well-merited. Seeing as how Dickson had solved every big case ever assigned to him. Except—all of Dickson's success came down to just one thing.

Him being a first cousin to the commissioner, the overall boss of The Guards. Meaning Dickson had his pick of what cases to investigate and, of course, he only ever chose the open and shut ones. Cases with a confession or a dozen eyewitnesses or it was all caught on CCTV. Yet, Dickson excelled in convincing you that he just might be the greatest detective since

Sherlock Holmes. He had always considered himself a class above Doocey, if not to belong to an entirely superior detective species.

Doocey feared that Dickson, as his boss, would make his life unbearably difficult but instead, he'd made it almost unbearably easy. He just dumped the unglamorous, routine cases, the likes of car collisions and small burglaries, on his desk. Cases that didn't challenge him in the least. But with Dickson having this cast-iron view of Doocey as being an imbecile, there was never the slightest chance that he'd let him work on any big case.

It delighted Doocey then to hear those rumours, circulating about the station, that things weren't going according to the usual open-and-shut plan when it came to Dickson's investigation of the Nolan case.

As he listened to the dialling tone, he pictured Dickson in his mind's eye. A man with oily, backcombed hair and a nose taking up most of the real estate of his face. A particularly ugly man by all accounts. Yet, an ugly man who dressed impeccably. Doocey had to, at least, give the blighter credit for that.

He would always remember what had happened when—taking a leaf out of Dickson's dapper book—he'd tried to smarten up his own appearance. Buying himself a nice dark suit that unusually came with a free white shirt, free red tie, and even free shiny black shoes. Straightaway—and making a nice change—he got tons of compliments on how well he'd scrubbed up. He even got loads of compliments from Dickson, who usually was such a dickhead to him.

Dickson must have sauntered past his desk a dozen times, saying in so loud a voice that everybody on the station floor could not but hear, "Oh, I love your new rig-out, Detective Doocey."

Only then for the snake to slither desk to desk with a stack of pictures of his ugly ten-year-old son, Ricky, who was the spitting image of his big-nosed father, and who'd just done his First Holy Communion. Shoving picture after picture of his Ricky into everybody's faces as his free hand pointed to Doocey and his big mouth loudly explained, for fear, people were too dumb to notice for themselves, that Detective Doocey was wearing the exact same bloody navy suit with the exact same red tie and exact same shiny shoes as his little boy. Dickson paraded about with those pictures for weeks.

From that point on, Doocey kept away from swanky suits, knowing that Dickson would only love the chance to make a show of him again. "Oh, is that another new suit, Detective Doocey?" he could easily imagine him asking. "Did you pick that one up in the children's department, too?"

Instead, Doocey regressed to his trusted anorak that he'd been wearing ever since.

He heard Dickson's voice on the other end of the line and got straight down to telling him how he would need to take the day off, lying about having some sort of respiratory virus, not wanting the knob to know there might be something up with his sight.

Dickson's voice became louder as if he wanted those sitting outside his gigantic office to hear, "I hope, Detective Doocey, it's not one of those sexually transmitted viruses. Did I hear you say . . . you're very itchy?"

Then he started to laugh at his own stupid wit. "Well, I'm sure we'll just have to somehow struggle on without you," he continued at last, without even an attempt at sounding sincere.

Doocey reckoned that the pig wouldn't give a hoot if he never came back. He'd easily find some other clown to look after the small, unimportant stuff. He took a seat in the packed waiting room, squashed between a smelly builder on his phone and a skinny girl in a hoodie who was struggling to hold onto her child, a spiky-haired boy in a school uniform.

The builder, still in his high-vis jacket, was relaying in loud whispers to his pal at the other end of his phone all about how he'd pretended something had gone in his eye to get the day off work and how he even hoped to squeeze a bit of cash from the boss in compensation or as he put it, 'squeeze a nice bit of compo out of him.'

Meanwhile, the spiky-haired boy had broken free of his mother's half-hearted grip and was now roaming about the waiting room, free to torment everybody else. Leaving his mam to browse her phone in peace.

With so many people ahead of him, Doocey settled himself in for a long wait and was thrilled then, just minutes later, to hear his name being called. He followed after a smiling man with an Indian accent, who had introduced himself as Doctor Akshat, into a small room, and was directed to take a seat facing an eye chart on the opposite wall.

"Okay Mr Doocey, what seems to be the problem?" Akshat, standing to his right, asked.

Doocey duly told him the situation and ended his reply with a question of his own, "Yeah, it's only this tiny bit of fog—you don't think it sounds like anything serious—do you?"

"Oh no . . . I shouldn't expect so." Another broad smile. "Don't worry."

Doocey smiled back, feeling better already.

"Any history of this kind of thing in the family?"

"No . . ." He answered after a lengthy delay, naturally having considered telling him about his mother's sight issues but then he'd reckoned it might be better to keep quiet about those. Let the young doc come up with his own standalone conclusions. A bit like not wanting to prejudice a jury by telling them about a defendant's past criminal history. Anyways, his mother had been nearly seventy when she'd started having her sight problems. What happened with her eyes was just some degenerative thing that much older people got. He was only in his fifties. Too young for him to get it.

"How long have you worn glasses?" the doctor followed up.

"Only since my mid-forties. About ten years."

Akshat proceeded to examine Doocey's eyes by looking through this instrument with a dazzling light. Then pointing to the eye chart, asked, "What's the lowest line of letters you can read?"

Doocey's gut clenched with terror on realising a lot of the letters were too blurry for him to recognise. His thoughts automatically sped to the annual medical that Dickson forced all his staff to take and which included an eye test. How was he going to pass that eye test if he couldn't properly see the bloody eyechart? How was he going to stay being a detective? After calling out the lowest line of letters he could make out, he said, "Sorry . . . I normally can read down much further."

"Oh . . . no need to worry," a smiling Akshat reassured. "I think you may have a minor eye infection which can often cause the vision to cloud."

Doocey felt his whole body let out a sigh of relief. He must have been more worried than he'd wanted to admit. Which was only to be expected, he supposed, considering his mother's sight issues. Neither had that damned taxi driver helped matters.

Akshat asked Doocey to follow him into another room with clunky machines for taking 3D scans and this one that shot unnerving puffs of air into your pupils—to check their pressure levels.

After quickly studying the resulting on-screen scans, the young doctor, again with a broad smile, reassured, "The scans seem fine too." Before finally declaring, "Okay, Mr Doocey . . . as I thought, it looks to me like you just have a minor eye infection. I'll prescribe you some eye drops which, within a few days, should have your vision back to normal."

"Thank you, Doctor," Doocey said, through an involuntary giggle of huge relief.

"No problem at all. If you can please take a seat back in the waiting room, I will get the prescription for the eyedrops organised."

A full forty minutes passed before Doocey heard his name being called again, but he hadn't minded the wait for his prescription—still over the moon that it was just a minor eye infection.

He sauntered over to Doctor Akshat who in a whisper said, "I have reviewed your scans with Miss White, the senior eye consultant on call, and she would like to see you."

The detective felt his heartbeat gallop. "Does that mean it's not just an eye infection—after all?

"Ahhh . . . we'll know more after Miss White examines you," Akshat replied, and this time round, there was no broad smile, just a worrying shrug of the shoulders and Doocey just about resisted the urge to give the youngster a good clip around the ear.

"Miss White would like your eyes dilated so I just need to apply some of these drops," Akshat continued, holding up the vial containing the dilating drops for him to see. The dilating drops that Doocey's local optician had warned him would make everything go blurry but had failed to mention about them stinging like hell.

When Doocey walked through to White's examination room, he found her studying on-screen images of what looked like two giant orange moons, crisscrossed by countless delicate lines. "Please take a seat Mr Doocey," White said, turning her gaze away from her computer screen towards him. She was this square-bodied, masculine-type woman who spoke with an attractive South African accent. "I just want to have another look here at the scans we took of the back of your eyes." A minute or two later, she came over to stand beside the high-backed leather chair, he was sweating in. "Pop your glasses off for me and let's see what's happening," White directed.

She proceeded to examine his eyes, using a dazzling light instrument of her own and spent ages doing so. All the while, Doocey inhaled her harsh deodorant and felt her minty breath on his face. He tried to convince himself again that there might still not be any reason to panic but failed.

Setting her torch device aside, White announced in a solemn tone, "I'm afraid the scans we took of your eyes have shown up some issues. Unfortunately, the visual anomalies you've been experiencing are not due to a simple eye infection, as per Doctor Akshat's initial assessment."

Doocey felt again the urge to clip that same Doctor Akshat around the ear.

White continued, "There have been some degenerative changes at the back of both your eyes." She paused. "And I understand from Doctor Akshat that there is no family history of sight issues. Can I just double-check that is correct?"

"Well . . . actually . . . my mother is partially sighted . . ."

White pressed a finger to the centre of her forehead and nodded. "Do you happen to know the condition that caused your mother's partial sightedness? Would it be wet macular degeneration by any chance?"

"Yes . . . I think that's what it's called." He inhaled through his nose. "But that's not what I have—is it?"

"I'm afraid it is."

"But I thought you had to be much older to get that . . . I'm only fifty-five."

White pursed her lips. "Unfortunately anybody over fifty can develop the condition though it is more common in people of a higher age."

As Doocey felt himself exiting his body, White continued to speak, getting into the particulars of his wet macular degeneration. "The macula, as you probably know, is a very tiny part of the eye, little more than a millimetre in size or say about the width of the tip of your average writing pen, but despite its tininess, it is crucial when it comes to a person's ability to see well. In your case, haemorrhaging at the back of both your eyes has caused bloodlike fluid to pool very near your maculae. This fluid is effectively the green fog that you've been seeing. Such fluid also accounts for the use of the word 'wet' in 'wet macular degeneration' and the degeneration part of the name refers to the fluid being damaging to the macula, causing its 'degeneration' over time."

The eye consultant fell silent, and Doocey got to ask the only life-changing question he wanted answered, even if—going by his mother's experience—he feared he already knew the answer would be a negative one: "Can something be done to fix it?"

White replied, "Not . . . to fix it." Adding, after a momentary pause that had felt to Doocey like a hellish eternity, "But there is a treatment that will hopefully prevent it getting any worse. It involves injections, on an ongoing basis, of a special solution that would effectively wash away the blood resulting from the haemorrhaging."

Doocey cut in, "Are these injections a new thing? It's just that I never heard my mother mention anything about injections. She told me that there was nothing that could be done for her sight."

White nodded. "When did your mother get diagnosed with having wet macular degeneration?"

"Oh . . . well over twenty years ago."

"Yes . . . back then injections would not have been an available treatment option for the condition in Ireland."

Doocey inhaled deeply, "I suppose . . . I'm lucky in a way . . . that there's now these injections." He forced out a little chuckle—longing to believe with all his heart that there wasn't then any problem and spoke rapidly, as if not wanting to give White the chance to contradict what he was saying. "I don't even think my sight is that bad at the moment. The only thing is . . . I can't see as many of the letters on the eye chart as I would normally . . . And for my job—I'm a detective—"

White cut in, to question in a surprised tone, "You're a detective?"

Doocey smiled, "Yeah, I know it's hard to believe but I really am."

Sounding embarrassed, she protested, "Oh . . . not at all . . ."

After an awkward silence, Doocey continued, again speaking rapidly, "Anyways, for my job, I need to pass an eye test as part of this annual medical I've to do. But I think I should be fine with passing that eye test. The injections should make me see clearer again. Shouldn't they?"

White frowned. "I'm afraid, given the quite severe retinal haemorrhaging that has already occurred at the back of your eyes, it's unlikely that your vision will improve substantially from how it is now, even with the injections. The injections are just to stop matters from getting worse."

Doocey felt the walls of his detective world collapsing in upon him. He clutched a chunk of thick hair at the back of his head and pulled it hard, hoping to wake from this nightmare, but no matter how hard he tugged—it was no use. The nightmare continued.

As unexpected tears flooded down his cheeks, White plucked some handkerchiefs from a noisy cardboard box for him and placed a hand on his shoulder. "I'm sorry for being so direct, Mr Doocey, but I always find it best, in the long run, to be upfront with patients." Her tone became much more upbeat. "But that's not to say that I don't believe in the importance of my patients' maintaining a positive attitude. With so many exciting medical breakthroughs happening these days in the field of vision, I'm really hopeful that very soon there will even be a way of reversing the condition. The other thing to say is that with wet macular degeneration, there is no real danger of you ever losing your entire vision." Her tone turned more sombre. "I appreciate all this must be so difficult to take in." She removed her hand from his shoulder. "Perhaps, it might be a good idea for you to speak with the hospital's counsellor, to explore what supports are available. Would you like me to check if she's free to talk to you?"

Doocey shook his bowed head. "No thanks. I'll be okay."

White's voice again, "Or maybe there is someone you'd like us to phone?"

Doocey though had nobody to phone, except, that is, for his mother, but he'd no intention of telling her anything—and not because he reckoned, with her having her own sight issues, it would be too much extra for her to cope with. No—but almost the very opposite.

He just knew if he told her, she'd instantly start wrecking his head. She wouldn't give him a minute's peace. She'd be at him all the time about all the proactive things that she did when she'd found out she'd sight issues, the life skills she'd learnt and he now needed to learn and how he would have to start doing his bit to help fundraise for the organisations who'd teach him those life skills. She probably wouldn't be happy until she had him jumping out of aeroplanes like she'd done. Anyway, there was no need for any of it—at least not yet and hopefully never—when his sight was fairly alright.

All the same, he would've liked to have someone to phone and for them to come there to be with him. If only he had a wife. How nice, how comforting, it would be, in this terrible moment, to have her wrap her reassuring arm around him and whisper in his ear, "It will all be okay, darling." But alas—no such wife existed. For most of his life, he'd never been brave enough to approach any girl he fancied. Held back by a belief that no one could be so desperate to want an ugly, little oddball like him.

However, he'd been wrong. There had been one girl, Amanda Holmes, who'd worked on the deli counter of this shop close to his station. When he'd pop in to buy a sandwich, they'd get chatting, and he would always manage to make her smile. *She had such a gorgeous smile.* At last, he got the bottle to ask her out and—amazingly, crazily, wonderfully—she'd said yes.

Then after eighty-one and a half days of them going steady, Amanda ran off with some other, much taller, and much more handsome, son of a gun. Last he'd heard, the two were happily married down the country and were parents to four beautiful children. After Amanda Holmes, there were lots of false starts but he never really let himself get close to anybody again for fear of having his heart re-smashed.

Neither had he much going on in terms of platonic relationships. *Though God knows*, he'd tried there too.

At one point he used to go for pints with the lads at work, even with the likes of Ed Dickson and they used to have a real laugh. Until he realised that Dickson and his buddies weren't laughing with him but at him.

He only then had one real friend. The only one living person in the world who gave a genuine damn about him, and pathetically that one friend was his mother.

White's South African voice broke into the silence. "If you agree, I think it would be best if we begin your injections today and decide a schedule for when you will return to the hospital to receive them going forward."

"Okay," Doocey replied in a resigned tone."

White nodded. "I will get that organised. Just some other points I wanted to mention. There are vitamin supplements specifically aimed at improving the health of the macula and I would recommend you start taking these. You should be able to pick them up at any pharmacy. There are also saffron pills you can find online which are thought to be of benefit. But more generally, a healthy diet is very important, especially eating lots of green veg and salads which studies have shown to improve eye health."

Fantastic! Doocey thought. He was more a burger and chips man than a green veg and salad one.

Doocey emerged from the hospital to dazzling sunshine and a bright blurry blue sky. Not at all the right type of weather for how frantic he was feeling. Where were the whirling black clouds and the crackle of lightning? His vision was now even more blurry after having had the injections but White said this extra blurriness would be gone by, at the latest, the next morning. Even so, he still could see plenty well enough to get about fine without any fear of falling over and breaking his neck. *What did that White one know, anyhow?* An angry inner voice questioned. Sure his sight was more or less fine. It was just this tiny bit of fog. Nothing to worry about.

Yet by the time he'd negotiated the short distance to a queue of awaiting taxis and had got into one, he'd gone from being angry with White to pleading with God. Promising he'd never whine to him again if he'd just let him have his good sight back. He would—*happy as Larry*—go on working one nothing little case after another. It didn't matter if he never got to work some big case—like the Nolan one—if only he'd let him have his good sight back.

THREE

As Doocey was trudging up to his apartment building, he heard someone call his name and recognising—with dread—the voice to be that of a neighbour, a Mr Muldowney, he squeezed his forehead with a hand, thinking, *Have I not suffered enough today!*

He turned back to see a blurry Muldowney. A man he knew—even if he wasn't able to see him clearly at this moment in time—looked much fitter and younger than himself, even though he was a good few years older. Not a single grey rib in his full head of curly brown hair or wrinkle on his boyish face. He looked athletic too—not an ounce of fat on him—and always so well togged out. Today, Doocey could blurrily see he was wearing a smart navy blazer, blue shirt, and cream-coloured trousers.

Doocey was certain the reason Muldowney always looked so well came down to the fact that the man was bone idle. Always complaining of very questionable poor health, trying to collar people's pity and to have them do everything for him. He silently cursed himself for not being a few seconds quicker in getting into his apartment. After the bad news he'd got, the last thing he wanted was to be forced to hear your man endlessly droning on about health niggles like that *debilitating* patch of dry skin on his right elbow.

"You wouldn't mind, would you, carrying this sack of spuds up to my apartment?" Muldowney asked as he dropped, with a thud, the said sack of potatoes at Doocey's feet.

Then dramatically bending his back as if about to touch his toes (which Doocey reckoned the sod could do without the least chance of bending a knee) he explained with a groan, how his old gluteus maximus—or in layman's language—the muscle in his arse was giving him fierce bother.

Doocey picked up the sack of potatoes and opted to take the stairs, seeing as Muldowney's apartment was only on the first floor—and as bad luck would have it—next door to his. Not wanting to risk the lift, just in case—*God have mercy*—it broke down, meaning he'd be stuck in there with misery guts for hours. The only added complication, with his sight being blurry, was that he'd need to take the stairs extra slowly.

"How are you anyway, Shamie?" Muldowney enquired as they started up the stairs.

"Oh, I'm grand, thanks," Doocey lied, determined not to mention a word about the breaking news of his sight troubles. Though even if he had done so, he'd bet his bottom euro that in less than a minute Muldowney would've steered the conversation around to some health concern of his own. To talk more about that pain in his arse or about how his own eyes— all of a sudden—were not great.

"Yeah, I'm not so bad myself, only for my old gluteus maximus muscle is playing up big time," his neighbour suddenly blurted out, triggering Doocey to squeeze the bag of spuds he was lugging even tighter in an effort to vent his frustration. "It seems to get worse later on in the day . . ." Oh how Doocey longed to be able to take the stairs two steps or even four steps at a time but he just couldn't risk it, not with his blurry vision. Of course, Muldowney, so caught up in his own troubles, didn't even notice they were climbing the stairs at a snail's pace. Finally, Doocey deposited the sack of potatoes at his neighbour's door. Then quickly said, "I'll see you so . . ." and made a mad dash for his apartment door, frantically rooting for his key in his trouser pocket.

"Thanks very much, Shamie," Muldowney called after him.

"No bother."

"I wonder if you wouldn't mind though . . . bringing up my few other bags of shopping. I'll come down with you to unlock the car."

By the time Doocey finally made it into his apartment, he'd been fully versed as to the complete history of Muldowney's arse muscle troubles and how he believed they stemmed from, years back, standing up from the toilet too speedily.

Doocey headed into his stale-smelling bedroom, trampling over a sea of clothes, to pull the curtains closed on the remainder of that day's sunshine. Then after placing his glasses on his bedside locker, he collapsed into his unmade bed, shutting his eyes. Naively telling himself that maybe in the morning—after some rejuvenating sleep and because he'd received those injections, his sight might be back to normal.

Hours passed and though further from falling asleep than ever, he kept his eyes firmly shut, hoping that in the absence of sleep, just letting them have a break from seeing might in itself be enough to make the fog go away.

When the usual alarm on his phone buzzed for him to get up to go to work, he plonked on his glasses and leapt out of bed, pulling back the curtains with force. He waited a few seconds for his eyes to adjust to the searing daylight and hoped against hope for the fog to be gone.

But, of course, it was still fecking there, interrupting his view of the other apartment buildings. Maybe this morning it might even be that bit thicker. *So much for those injections!* Although the hospital ones did say it could take a few days for the injections to fully do their work.

He glanced at his bed and wondered if he should get back in, to have another go at sleeping or just to try resting his eyes some more, but it only took a second for him to categorically rule out a return to the old scratcher. He'd already had enough: enough of not sleeping, enough of resting his eyes, enough of worrying himself crazy. There was just no way he was going to let his sight diagnosis turn him into some bedridden wreck of a human being.

He had to believe White's predictions that a medical breakthrough to fix his eyes was just around the corner—or by some miracle, they would just fix themselves up, to believe that his sight was still good enough to keep on working as a detective, to keep doing the job he loved—the only thing he knew how to do.

What other alternative had he but to go back to work? Lock himself away in his apartment? *No.* Drive himself mental—worrying? *No.* Become like his layabout, pain in the arse (literally) neighbour? Muldowney. *Definitely not.*

What did that White one know, anyhow? His angry inner voice chipped in, again. Sure his sight was more or less fine. It was just this tiny bit of fog, no biggie. When the time came, he'd pass his medical just fine, but no point even worrying about that now. *Just get on with things. Keep going.*

He speed-showered, threw on a crumpled shirt, tie and trousers, and his manky anorak, and stepped into some untied, unpolished shoes before slamming his apartment door shut behind him.

FOUR

SITTING INTO HIS CROCK OF a car, apprehension pulsated through Doocey. What if his sight was already not good enough to drive? When he'd looked out his bedroom window, only half an hour or so ago—hadn't he thought the fog thicker? He hadn't asked White if it was *definitely guaranteed* that the injections would stop his sight from getting worse, fearing that no such guarantee would be forthcoming. That as with life in general there were no definite guarantees.

Only after he'd survived traversing those first few tense kilometres did he somewhat relax. Finding he could still drive just fine—which was when it happened. Seeing too late some old biddy—who'd wandered out into the middle of the road when he'd a green light—or so he'd thought—he'd slammed hard on his brakes. Then came a terrifying succession of thuds as he saw her wrinkled face pressed up against his windscreen.

It took a hellish eternity for him to realise the woman was unharmed. Those terrifying thuds had just been the battleaxe fisting his bonnet as she vented her rage.

"Are you bloody blind or what?" she howled, coming round to his driver's window. He reached for the door handle, about to step out to try to explain himself.

Then thought better of it, and with his heart hammering out of his little chest, he sped off. Praying his hit-and-run victim hadn't memorised his car reg number and worryingly wondering if he might not have properly seen the traffic lights.

When he'd gone a few kilometres, he pulled into a countryside road lined with wild hedgerows. This voice in his head roaring for him to turn the car around for home. It was all well and good him wanting, with all his heart and soul, to go on being a detective, but that couldn't justify him knocking down pensioners.

In the end, he decided to keep going on, but he drove much slower than he ever would've normally and kept twisting his head about, on the lookout for other foulmouthed old biddies. A good hour later he drove into the town of Blackstones, population 8,000, on the Wicklow, Dublin border and two minutes after that turned into the car park of the place he considered his real home.

Fittingly from the outside, Blackstones Garda Station also resembled a private home. This large three-storey white townhouse with window boxes containing flowers in an array of vibrant colours, red, pink, yellow, orange, purple. Vibrant flowers which were ideal in distracting the eye from the depressed state of the building they adorned, distracting the eye from the cracks in the walls, the missing roof tiles, and the rotted window sills. A blue lantern hanging near the door with the word 'Gardaí' printed on it— the only clue to the building's true identity.

Inside more decrepitation—rooms with tall, damp-stained ceilings and mouldy walls. Ed Dickson's workspace stood out as the extreme exception. His hundred-square-foot palatial office—all bright and airy with quadruple-glazed windows, sandalwood floors, and sleek furnishing.

As he headed for his desk, Doocey glanced in the direction of that office now, disappointed to spot Dickson was in and was holding a meeting with what looked like everybody who worked for him. The old shyster looked angry—judging by the way he was shaking his fist—though with his office door shut, you couldn't hear what he was ranting on about.

"Morning Shamie," a voice called out, causing Doocey to look over to the middle of the office floor and see Bernadette Willson, or just Ber, waving at him. He felt a pang of pity, seeing her sitting there alone in a wasteland of empty desks. The only one not invited to Dickson's meeting. If he hadn't driven so slowly, he wouldn't have been so late getting in and she would've at least had him for company.

Technically, Ber was also a detective but Dickson had her effectively working as a junior administrator, in charge of handling mileage expense claims and making sure the canteen was stocked up with tea and coffee and most crucially—the toilets had enough bog roll.

Dickson would openly remark that he considered Ber 'to be a bit slow' and wasn't up to doing regular detective work. However, Doocey reckoned his stupid boss was all wrong about her. He'd always found Ber to have a brain that was as sharp as a knife. He thought Dickson, by now, might even have realised this, especially after his multiple failed attempts to sack or move her on. Ber outwitting him with HR fine print legalities every single time.

Doocey reckoned then that Dickson incredibly hated the woman even more than he hated him: hated her extremely direct nature, hated how she refused to lick his arse like all the others and hated how she was so slow at completing her work (not appreciating that she was just being methodical).

He even hated how she looked. Doocey had often overheard Dickson loudly joking to his closest work pals that only for that long fiery red hair down to her "fat arse," you'd mistake Ber for a fella, "a very ugly fella."

Doocey waved back. "Morning Ber. What's going on in there?"

Ber turned her chair to glare over at Dickson's office. "Just another meeting about the Nolan case. He wants more progress in closing it off as an accident or suicide." She shook her head and sniggered. "More progress from those boneheads, what a joke—and sure don't we know Dickson is the biggest bonehead of them all."

Doocey chuckled back and, not wanting to catch the eye of the man Ber was slagging off, hurried over to his desk at the opposite end of the ground floor. Unlike all the other desks which were out in the open, his remained largely hidden behind partitions as if his colleagues needed to be shielded from such an embarrassing eyesore as him.

With having to do with only four crammed square feet of space, his chair and tiny desk were squashed right up against the station's mouldy back wall. Doocey now sat down at that tiny desk and after powering up his computer was relieved to find that he could read the text on its screen almost as well as normal.

However, after skim-reading through just a couple of emails, he found that his eyes were already feeling tired. He tried zooming up the text size and found that this gave him some relief. In the background, he soon heard loud chatter and took this to mean that Dickson's meeting had finished up.

Doocey was continuing to go through his emails when he smelt pungent after-shave and looked up to see Ed Dickson leaning over his partition. "Oh, I wasn't expecting to see you in today," his boss said with a smirk. Then, almost in a roar, asked, "Have you got over that virus of yours, already—Detective Doocey? You're sure you're not contagious?"

The man was so pathetic, so childish. Doocey, however, just smiled back in response which seemed to annoy him.

"Well, now that you've decided to grace us with your presence, you might take care of the paperwork on a couple of Naughton's smaller cases. Minor road collisions mainly. With him helping with the Nolan investigation, he hasn't got the time to work them himself."

Maybe if the lazy sod didn't take twenty lengthy smoke breaks a day, he might have a bit more time, Doocey ruminated but just answered aloud, "No problem." Anyway, he was okay with taking on the extra work. He liked being busy and this kind of scenario made him feel useful, even feel a tiny bit like he was working as part of a team.

"I'll get him to drop them over to you," Dickson said in a tetchy tone, seeming to have also taken offence at Doocey's 'no problem' reply. He was probably irritated that he might think there was ever an option for him to say, *Sorry, but I can't take those extra cases, I've already got too many of my own* (which he really had).

He waited for Dickson to piss off back into his huge office, but the donkey just kept standing there, and then Doocey felt cold sweat trickle down his back as he realised what was happening. Dickson was gawping open-mouthed at his computer screen, zoomed up to a humiliating two hundred percent.

"God, can you make that blasted text any bigger?" Dickson now exclaimed. "Is there something wrong with your eyes or what?"

After a second of stunned speechlessness, Doocey stammered, "Ahh . . . no . . . I don't know . . . why it's gone so big." He tittered, "I must have pressed some wrong setting by accident."

Dickson shook his head as if to say, "You're some moron," and sauntered off.

Less than a minute later, Tony Naughton strode into Doocey's work cubicle. Naughton, this fool in his fifties, was Dickson's number one skivvy and, trying to emulate Dickson, liked to wear expensive suits. Though regrettably for Naughton, the first thing you noticed when you saw him was not any expensive suit, but his unfortunate face, a face plagued with countless freckles.

Looking as pleased as punch, Naughton deposited a massive pile of files on Doocey's desk, many of which, as Doocey would later discover, dated back years. "I believe you are taking these over," he declared with a broad yellow smile. "Sorry, but I don't have the time to go through them with you. I'm just too busy on the Nolan case. Anyway, I'm sure even you will be fine with them. They're all simple stuff." A look of puzzlement passed over his face before another big smile. "Whoa . . . the size . . . of the text . . . on your computer. You must be as blind as a bloody bat."

Before Doocey even got the chance to reply, Naughton had walked away, chuckling to himself.

As weeks went by, Doocey was mightily relieved to find that his sight issues weren't stopping him from doing his detective work as normal. He even reckoned the cursed fog had receded a lot. He barely noticed it anymore. He wondered if it was down to the injections or all those horrible-tasting vegetables and tasteless salads he'd taken to eating, or maybe the jars full of vitamin supplements and saffron pills he'd gone through had done the trick.

However, in a scheduled follow-up visit at *The Eye and Ear Hospital*, for his next round of injections, White explained that the fog hadn't actually receded. His brain had just gotten used to seeing it. She cited the example of how people, after wearing a pair of scratched glasses for a while, often don't notice how scratched they've become. Complicating matters further, patients suffering from his condition could experience good days—when they could see very well—and bad days when seeing well was a real struggle.

Naturally Doocey was disappointed at hearing his sight hadn't really improved but did take comfort in the fact that at least it hadn't got any worse and he was still getting on with his detective work just fine. Although his eyes continued to be a lot more tired than usual—but he could live with that.

Then, exactly seven weeks after a delighted Tony Naughton had dumped all those files with him, the lazy swine again marched into Doocey's work cubicle but this time round he looked rightly cheesed off. With a childish stomp of his foot, he mumbled, "I've been told that I've to take over all your cases."

"What?" Doocey shrieked, jumping to his feet. "Why?"

"The hell—if I know," a teary-eyed Naughton blared back. "Ask Dickson?" Then taking a few deep breaths and large sniffles, he half composed himself. "I'll need you to do a proper handover. I'm going on my smoke break now, so call over to my desk with your *stupid* files in forty minutes."

Before a gobsmacked Doocey had a chance to ask anything else, Naughton had scarpered. He stood up and gazed over at Dickson's office. Ready, in line with Naughton's suggestion, to stomp over there and find out what the hell was happening—but the glass-paned office was empty.

Not that he needed to speak with Dickson anyhow to know what was up. Because wasn't it obvious? Dickson had found out about his sight issues and that's why all his cases were being taken from him. He flopped onto his chair, his stomach doing Olympic-style somersaults. *But how had he found out?* Had someone in the hospital tipped him off? Maybe that eye consultant, White, was a pal of his, or, however unlikely, had Dickson managed to figure out for himself that something was wrong after spotting his zoomed-up computer screen? Not that it mattered how he'd found out. He knew and that's all that mattered.

The phone on Doocey's desk, like a shrieking fire alarm, started to wail—and he just knew it would be confirmation of the worst. "Detective . . . Shamie . . . Doocey," he managed to utter.

A woman's voice, he recognised as belonging to this Human Resources one, Becky, who worked on the second floor, icily instructed him to head immediately upstairs to interview Room 2C and without a word of explanation just hung the phone up. With legs of jelly, he wobbled to his feet, knowing now why Dickson wasn't in his office. He'd be sat up in interview room 2C, looking forward to giving him the sack.

As he entered the gloomy stairwell, Doocey began rehearsing his defence. *It's only this tiny bit of fog. I can still see perfectly fine. I can still drive, still read, and still do my work.* Though the logical part of his brain knew full well it wouldn't matter a damn what he said. When it came to being a detective, it was cruelly black and white—you had to be able to see clearly. No fog in your eyes allowed. Not even a tiny bit.

FIVE

W**ITH A QUIVERING HAND**, D**OOCEY** knocked on the interview room door, prompting somebody from inside to shout "Enter" and it wasn't Dickson. Yet, somehow the male voice sounded familiar. *Probably some HR henchman who'd been about the place before.*

Instead, on stepping inside, a now rightly gobsmacked Doocey saw it was no HR henchman that was waiting for him. Sitting at the head of the interview room table was none other than Assistant Commissioner Mike Ryan. Someone he had never met in person but who he'd seen and heard lots of times being interviewed on television boasting about how he, single-handedly (or so he made it sound) had been responsible for solving one case or another.

At six foot two, the black-haired, broad-shouldered Ryan was *Superman* handsome. This morning, bedecked in a dark silk suit, pristine white shirt, and sky-blue tie. His ultra-sharp appearance contrasted with the ultra-shabbiness of interview room 2C and its threadbare grey carpet and worn-out white table and chairs. It all contrasted more dramatically still with the ultra-shabbiness of the man who'd just skulked in.

Doocey tightened his drooping tie—and wondered how to discreetly pull up his trousers a little more—whilst also naturally pondering the bigger question. *Why someone so senior as Ryan would be sent to sack him?*

Politically savvy, Mike Ryan, at the age of thirty-nine, became the youngest assistant commissioner in the history of the Guards. Word also had it that he was ruthlessly ambitious to take over from the current, elderly commissioner, due to retire any day now.

However, notwithstanding that ruthless ambition of his, it was not thought that Ryan would be successful—this time around. He was just a bit too young yet for the top job and his brash CV was lacking when it came to showing a high-profile case he'd cracked all by himself. Doocey had even heard that Dickson—who reported to Ryan and who had ambitions of his own, however deluded, of one day becoming Commissioner himself—was also not helping matters, by always scooping up the easy-to-solve big cases and not letting poor Ryan share the credit for having "solved" any of them. And, of course, Ryan couldn't do a thing about this as Dickson had the ear of the commissioner—the ear of his first cousin.

Rumour also had it that beneath his polished, posh-sounding exterior, Ryan on an intellectual level was at the bottom of the class. Whereas on a crafty political level, the man was a genius and his skill at heaving himself up the career ladder by piggybacking on the successes of his subordinates was legendary.

The assistant commissioner shot an angry look at Doocey as if annoyed that some scruffy idiot, maybe a handyman, had got the wrong room, and when the scruffy idiot showed no signs of leaving, snapped, "Can I help you?"

"Ahhh . . . you asked to see me? I'm Detective Doocey."

"You're Doocey?" Ryan mouthed back. Then after taking—nearly a full minute of silence—to get over his shock, commanded, "Take a seat."

Doocey, feeling as if he were about to be shot, collapsed onto a chair to Ryan's right which faced a window looking out onto a jumble of ugly buildings.

"Okay, let me get straight to the point. I was very impressed with your recent work in tracking down the missing Armstrong kid, and how you managed to get information from that dirtbag Sweeney. I figured you might then be of help to us on the Harriet Nolan case."

Doocey felt himself go dizzy at what he was hearing.

"As you will be aware," Ryan continued, "Detective Ed Dickson has been overseeing the investigation into the Nolan woman's disappearance."

The assistant commissioner gave a kind of grunt. "I can't say, however, that I've been at all impressed with his handling of things to date. From the outset, he has been trying to convince me that Harriet Nolan either committed suicide or just slipped from the cliff path she'd been walking on, and got swept out to sea."

Ryan put a hand to his smooth forehead. "But what if, after we closed off the case as that suicide or accident, Harriet Nolan's corpse showed up with say . . . I don't know . . . a knife sticking out of her back. How embarrassing would that be for us?" He gave no time for Doocey to reply. "With Dickson being under my command, ultimately, I'd be the one in the damned doghouse."

He inhaled deeply. "So before I let Dickson close off the case as an accidental drowning or suicide, as he's still—more than ever—bugging me to do, I want you to cast your eye over things. Review his investigation and interview whoever you need to interview for yourself, especially Harriet Nolan's husband. I think interviewing him is your best chance of coming up with something. You see, I'm not at all sure he hasn't murdered his wife."

With the shock of hearing all this, Doocey was feeling even more dizzy and had to hang on tight to the armrests of his chair to stop himself from falling to the floor.

Ryan frowned. "I'm afraid though there's a bit of an issue with you doing your . . . ahh . . . review." He eyed Doocey warily as if unsure he could trust him with what he was about to disclose next. "You see . . ." he continued at last, "as you'd expect Dickson is kicking up an almighty stink about getting someone else to mark his homework. But what has especially got his nasty goat up is that the someone is you. He's taking that as the biggest personal insult of all." The assistant commissioner grinned. "He doesn't seem to be your number one fan."

He stopped grinning, "If I was dealing with just any other report of mine, I wouldn't give a toss. I'd gladly have told the numpty to f off for himself, and long before this. Except Dickson—as I'm sure you're aware—isn't any ordinary staff member, with him being first cousins to the commissioner, my boss, and the two of them are like two poisonous peas in a pod." He threw Doocey a stern glance. "Obviously—all that I'm telling you here is in the strictest confidence and not to go outside the walls of this crappy meeting room. Understand?"

"Of course," Doocey firmly replied and fervently nodded.

Ryan rubbed a hand along his chiselled jawline. "So I played it all down—said your review would only be a tiny one and would only last four weeks and not a day longer. Still, I wasn't expecting Dickson to agree to it. However, amazingly he has. I've also got him to reassign your current cases and he's going to get someone to lend you a helping hand with your . . . review." He consulted his notepad, "A Ber Willson who he says he rates very highly."

Ryan looked to Doocey again. "I would have liked to have given you more people, but doing that would only be sure to make Dickson go running off to his first cousin." He imitated the whinging of a young child: 'Ryan said Doocey was only supposed to be doing a little review—so why does he need a big team when I've investigated it all already.' The assistant commissioner, wolf-like, showed Doocey his dazzling teeth. "I'm sure you get the idea."

His smile faded. "Just so you know though, the only reason I think Dickson is playing any sort of ball is because of how confident he is that you are going to be an absolute disaster. Giving him the chance to go running again to his cousin, crabbing to him how I must've been crazy ever to have brought you in—calling into question my good judgment."

He paused as if to emphasise the gravity of what he had to say next. "If this goes belly up, I wouldn't be at all surprised if the commissioner demoted me or got rid of me altogether." Looking deadly serious, Ryan stared into Doocey's smudged glasses. "You can see how I'm putting a huge amount of faith in you. Risking my career. I'm counting on you to come up with something concrete. Something strong enough to convict Mr Nolan of murder." He grinned. "Such as finding out what he did with his wife's body."

Ryan's mobile, which he'd placed down on the interview room table in front of him, began to delicately ring, playing this chime that sounded to Doocey like the tranquil music you'd hear in one of those beautiful Buddhist temples that he'd only ever experienced via television. "Excuse me, I need to take this," the assistant commissioner explained, having first checked to see who was calling him. He gestured that Doocey needn't leave the room and whispered, "It's only the wife."

Pressing the answer key Ryan put the phone to his ear and growled, "What is it now?" He briefly listened. Then in a low, stressed voice, "No, no, I haven't changed my mind. We don't need it. The one we have is perfect . . ." Their conversation, or more argument, continued for some time. Eventually, it sounded like the call was nearing an end. "Listen . . . I'm in a meeting . . . We'll talk about this when I get home." His wife said something back and Ryan raised his voice, "How many times! We don't need a new bloody kitchen." His wife said something else back which caused her husband to raise his voice even louder. "Don't you dare go ahead with ordering it! Do you hear me?" But there was then only the sound of the line going dead.

The assistant commissioner glanced over to Doocey and said, "Women, they'd drive you bonkers." Not waiting for a reply, he flung a cardboard folder, full of paperwork, across the table.

"That's a hard copy of Dickson's investigation. It should contain everything you need, statements, forensics . . . the lot." Then Ryan asked the question that Doocey reckoned he might have been wiser to have asked from the outset, before sanctioning everything with Dickson and the commissioner, "Are you okay so with taking over the investigation or . . . I mean . . . doing a review?"

Doocey with his little heart pounding, answered, "Yes, Sir." *Oh yes, you bet I'm okay with it.* There's no way he was going to turn down the chance to investigate his first big case. And just maybe, if by some miracle, he managed to solve the thing, Ryan would let him—despite his sight problems—stay working as a detective.

"Of course," Ryan continued, "Nolan might very well refuse to let you interview him. He might be stubborn—say he has already given his statement . . . refer you off to his solicitor . . . which might well be the wiser move for him. And if that happens, I'd say you're more or less goosed before you even get started."

"Yeah, you're right Sir, if he won't speak to me that would make things tricky alright." Doocey glanced down at the copy of Dickson's investigation file. "But hopefully I still might be able to come up with something."

"I doubt it," Ryan shot back. "It's not like there's any hard evidence lying about the place to show that Harriet Nolan was murdered. If there had been you can be sure—no matter how much an idiot he is—Dickson would've had to have stumbled across it. But I suppose you can only try. A fresh pair of eyes and all that . . ."

Doocey gave a solid nod, and as his own little private joke, said aloud, "Yes Sir . . . a fresh pair of eyes might be all that's required."

Doocey exited the meeting room, proudly clutching the Nolan folder, just happy to have been given the chance to investigate his first big case, regardless of how hamstrung a chance it might be. He thought about phoning his mother to let her know his enormous news. However, he first had something to sort out or that is someone to sort out.

"God, almighty!" Tony Naughton shrieked, gawking at the big stack of files that Doocey had just plonked on his desk. "How are there so many? What have you been doing?"

"Oh, just scratching my little arse . . ." Doocey answered with a smirk and started to walk away.

Naughton shouted after him, "Where do you think you're going? You need to do a proper hand-over. Update me . . . about exactly where you're at with each case."

Doocey returned a smiling shake of the head. "Oh, I'm sorry Tony, I won't have time for that. I'll be too busy working on the Nolan investigation. Anyways—most of those cases were yours originally and like you said to me, they're all simple stuff so even you should be able to handle them."

Stepping into his partitioned work area, Doocey eyed his desk phone and thought about now ringing his mother, to tell her his exciting news. But he resisted the urge, calculating it would be best to save that treat for later when back in the privacy of his apartment. Thereby avoiding the embarrassing risk of some nasty piece of work, like Dickson, listening in and using what he'd overheard to mock him, even to go around telling everybody about what a "Mammy's boy" he was. Not wanting to acknowledge that all he had to do—if he was so concerned about privacy and nobody overhearing—was just to step out of the station and use his mobile to ring his mother.

Even more so, he didn't want to acknowledge this tiny feeling of foreboding that he might have been too hasty in taking on the Nolan case—that he might have bitten off more than he could chew and might yet be going back to Ryan, detective tail between his legs, to tell him he'd made a mistake.

He sat down at his desk and opened up the cardboard folder Ryan had claimed should 'contain everything he needed' when it came to the Nolan investigation—a claim he very much doubted held true—considering who the lead investigating detective had been. His skim reading of the file confirmed to him that his lack of confidence in Dickson's capabilities seemed well justified, as he saw there were lots of lines of inquiry he had either been too stupid to see or too lazy to follow up.

It truly amazed him that Dickson, a supposedly trained detective, would just accept at face value the account Markus R. Nolan gave of his wife's disappearance—an account with more holes in it than a piece of fecking Swiss cheese. Right off the bloody bat, as Ryan had said, Dickson, the tunnel-visioned donkey, seemed positive that Harriet Nolan's disappearance was simply down to an accidental drowning or suicide.

He'd probably only taken on the case in the first place because of his certainty that it had to have been either one of those two straightforward enough scenarios. Never foreseeing that he might have on his incapable hands, the altogether more complex challenge of solving a covered-up murder.

A one-line note Doocey had come across in the file concerning Nolan's daughter, Jennifer—written in Dickson's own slanty handwriting—summed up for him the man's stupid single-mindedness and the lack of any proper investigation on his part: *'Nolan's daughter Jennifer (who was Harriet Nolan's stepdaughter) wasn't there—has own apartment—and anyways couldn't have been involved.'*

The note had caused Doocey to naturally wonder—besides her not having been about—why exactly Dickson reckoned Jennifer Nolan couldn't have been involved. Fat chance of him finding that out—from Dickson's file though—because there wasn't a record in there of any interview he'd done with her. It wouldn't surprise Doocey if Dickson hadn't even bothered to interview Jennifer Nolan, because why would he want to interview her or anybody else when he was so convinced there'd been no foul play involved in Harriet Nolan's disappearance?

Two hours later, Doocey was still reading documentation from Dickson's file, mulling over every inadequate sentence, and his eyes were feeling so sore—much sorer than they'd ever felt before. He'd avoided asking the eye consultant whether too much close work like reading would speed up any degeneration in his vision. Afraid of hearing it would, because how was he to do his job if he couldn't read?

He was considering taking a break and making himself a good strong cuppa when his mobile started to ring. He put the phone to his ear—startled to hear who it was. "Ryan filled me in about you doing some class of a review into the Nolan case," Dickson burst out, without even a hello. Then the sound of him sighing heavily. "With you not being used to handling investigations on this scale, you best call over to me so I can help you out."

Hearing Dickson offering to "help" him made Doocey smile inside as he knew what such help would involve: browbeating him into believing, as he was so desperate to believe himself, that there was no foul play involved in Harriet Nolan's disappearance. Still, Doocey calculated the wise move, on his part, would be to leap up from his desk and race into Dickson's office, to listen to him bullshitting on. No point making a total enemy of the sod. "Oh, that's very good of you, Sir," he said aloud, "but I think I'll be able to manage."

There followed a few seconds of what Doocey presumed to be stunned silence. He could almost hear Dickson thinking, *I don't believe this fool! I'm offering him my vast expertise and he has the gall to say no.* "Well . . . if you're sure," Dickson muttered.

It surprised Doocey how well his thin-skinned boss seemed to be taking the rejection. He'd been bracing himself for a right tongue-lashing, except in the very next second, as if Dickson could no longer hold himself back, he started into that tongue-lashing.

"I think it's ridiculous anyway that the likes of you should be reviewing a big investigation. I mean . . . you've only ever worked on *Micky Mouse* cases. It's a complete waste of time. Plus, there's nothing to investigate. Harriet Nolan just slipped from that cliff path or threw herself off. But if you don't want my help, that's fine by me." He tittered. "Don't forget, after this four-week fiasco, you'll be reporting back to me, not to Assistant Commissioner Ryan. Though . . . I'm not sure if I will still even have a position for you."

On having issued his threat, he promptly hung up, leaving Doocey more fired up than ever to solve Harriet Nolan's disappearance and to show Detective Ed Dickson up for the gobshite he was. As if God was doing everything to make this dream of his happen, when he went back to reading the Nolan file, and a section relating to Harriet Nolan's medical history, something immediately sprang out.

It seemed that just a month before her disappearance Mrs Nolan had visited her doctor to seek treatment for severe bruising to her neck, but mysteriously no explanation was given about what had caused the bruising.

There were no notes either from the dumbass Dickson as to whether he'd followed up on the matter with Harriet Nolan's doctor—a Doctor Bullock. This left the major question unanswered, at least in Doocey's mind, about whether Nolan had tried to strangle his wife—just a month before she disappeared.

A few file pages later he also came across another—potentially—very useful snippet of information. Up until three months before his wife's disappearance, Nolan had employed the services of a housekeeper, a Mrs Nelly Boyle. And who better than a housekeeper to know a household's secrets or in every sense of the phrase 'their dirty washing.'

Back in his apartment that evening, Doocey sat on his sofa to make the call he'd been itching to make since his meeting with Ryan or even itching to make all his detective career. That inkling of foreboding, however, remained.

With the phone pressed to his hair-covered ear, he listened to a dialling tone for many long seconds, and pictured his—frailer by the day—mother, in her usual pink tracksuit and pristine white runners, tottering out to the porch where the phone was plugged in. During the winter months that porch was even more Baltic than the rest of the house. Growing up, he remembered it often being warmer outside, even with an icy Atlantic wind blowing. Oh, how he used to love to retreat to the warmth of his bed and cuddle up to a hot water bottle.

His first detective wage packets went to having central heating installed. That, though, hadn't made much of a difference to the chilliness of the porch on account of its enormous windows that looked out at the neighbouring houses and fields of Castleglen, this little village on the West Coast of Ireland where his mother now lived alone. After his father's death, many years back, Doocey had rented their tiny farm out and he'd stayed living on in Dublin, over three hundred kilometres away. He'd never wanted to be a farmer, only ever a detective.

Finally, an "Hello" and in a voice loaded with excitement, Doocey told his mother all about being summoned upstairs to see the assistant commissioner and exactly what he had to tell him. His mother must have congratulated him a hundred times over on his fantastic news. Every single time, his heart gave a little leap of pure joy.

Her tone turned more businesslike. "From what I've been listening to online, I think it's the husband, Nolan himself that's done her in. Sure in these husband-and-wife murders, isn't it always the husband? Though, of course, no one is publicly coming out and saying this—too scared of being sued by him. Do you think he did it, yourself?"

Going by what he'd even already learnt, Doocey would be fairly confident in answering that question with a "Yes." However, he chose to be more circumspect in giving his actual answer, afraid of having to later eat his words if Nolan were somehow proven to be innocent. So he pronounced with an orchestrated chuckle, "Ahh give me a chance . . . I've only been on the case for a minute . . ."

"Oh yes, of course . . ." Then in a stronger tone, "Tell me this, am I right in thinking that Mr Nolan is a crime writer?"

"Yeah, he writes crime novels but he's never been published."

"All the same, I'd say if anybody could come up with a good way to murder someone and cover their tracks, it would be a crime writer—published or not." There was an awkward pause, after which his mother's tone turned much more upbeat. "I'm still positive you'll be able to pin it on him though . . . I believe in you, son. The assistant commissioner wouldn't have let you take over the case if he didn't believe in you too."

The following morning, sat at his desk reading once more through the Nolan file, Doocey continued to try batting away that persistent thought, of throwing in the blasted towel before he'd even stepped into the ring.

For, no matter how heartfelt his mother's proclamations of believing in him were, to his mind they just didn't count for a whole lot. She hadn't the professional detective background to tell if he really had what it took to solve a big case.

However, the assistant commissioner did have such a background. Yet this fact didn't reassure him either; Ryan's belief in him being able to solve the Nolan case had only come from how impressed he'd been with how he'd managed to find that runaway, Indigo Armstrong, so quickly.

Doocey worried though that it might've been a mistake for Ryan to have been so impressed seeing as his finding the girl so quickly only came down to that drug lord, Sweeny, taking pity on him by telling him where exactly to find her. Taking pity on him because probably he saw that he wasn't the regular gorilla of a detective, like Dickson, to come hammering on his door. On another day, depending on Sweeny's mood, he might not have taken pity on him. His solving of the Armstrong case could then be said to have come down to just pure potluck.

Anger started to build within him. What the hell was he playing at? This was no game. A woman was missing, likely murdered and he, the detective taking over her case, had never investigated a murder before and not alone that but had something wrong with his eyes.

If he'd any shame, any decency, he should ring Ryan that second to offer his resignation. The assistant commissioner was bound to have loads of better detectives to replace him with, or at the very least, detectives with their full sight.

A ping of a new email cut into his thoughts and as he clicked on it, more panic set in. The email was to notify him of his next work medical, scheduled for just over four weeks. Doocey pressed his head into his high-back chair and squeezed his tired eyes shut. *God, what was he going to do?*

"You've no time for snoozing!" he half heard someone say and opening his eyes, he saw Ber Willson looking down at him with a grimacing face.

He attempted to reply, "Oh yeah, sorry . . . just—"

"I heard you're going to be working on the Nolan case and that I'm supposed to be your dogsbody . . ."

"Well . . ." he began, but again she cut him off.

"And don't worry . . ." she reassured with a smile, "I'm going to make sure I'll be the excellent dogsbody. Because nobody in the world wants you to solve the thing more than me. It's past time that dunce Dickson got taught a real lesson."

"Yeah, I'd love that . . . but . . . the thing is . . ."

"Now . . . don't tell me you're having second thoughts?" Ber let roar.

"Well . . . kind of . . ."

She jerked his chair with one hand, causing Doocey to judder as much as if a massive earthquake had hit.

"Will you cop yourself on! You've already said yes to the assistant commissioner, so it's too bloody late to back out now. Anyhow, if you did, he'd just give the case back to Dickson and then there'd be no chance of it ever being properly solved."

She ran a hand through her fiery red hair. "Plus, I can't see Dickson being too delighted to have you back—the bloke that Assistant Commissioner

Ryan thought could do a better job than him. Yeah . . . I'd say he'd either end up sacking you or end up making your life so hellish that you'd have to resign. So your only real chance is to get somewhere with the Nolan case and hope Ryan might sort something out for you."

Doocey had to admit that Ber seemed to be talking a lot of sense, and Dickson had already issued that threat about how, after he'd finished his 'four-week fiasco,' on the Nolan investigation, his old job might not be there for him to go back to.

There was also that impending medical scheduled for the very week after the four Ryan was letting him have to work the Nolan case were up. *God, what bad bloody timing!* Though, he wondered again, if by some miracle he managed to solve the Nolan case—if Ryan might turn a blind eye to his sight issues and any failed medical and let him stay on working as a detective.

"I know you're a good detective," Ber stormed on. "Though you'd hardly be able to tell from the scruffy state of you . . . And with my help, I know you can solve the bloody thing."

"Well . . . I . . ."

"Anyways isn't this your big chance to prove yourself? Unless you're happy working shitty little cases for the rest of your life. Letting your detective brain rot."

In other words, 'If you're not growing, you're dying.'

Ber pulled up a chair as if *discussion over.* "Right, what's our plan of action?"

Despite all his self-doubts and the fact that he'd never investigated a murder case before, for whatever reason—call it pure, crazy intuition—Doocey felt he had a good handle on what that plan of action should be. For starters, he reckoned he should not meet with Nolan until he'd compiled as much information about him and the case as possible. To give himself the best chance of catching the prime suspect out. It made sense then that he should speak to people who might have relevant info or even dirt on the man. People that Dickson didn't look to have properly followed up with.

The first person he wanted to speak with might even provide a big early breakthrough: Mrs Nolan's former doctor, Doctor Bullock. By testifying those injuries Harriet Nolan sustained to her neck—just a month before she disappeared—had come from her husband's efforts to strangle her.

Six

DOOCEY TEETERED INTO A ROOM so bright, it almost felt like he'd stepped back out onto the swanky street he'd come in from. Except, courtesy of the heat-conducting glass roof above his head, the day had transformed into a scorcher. Beads of sweat broke out on his forehead as he moved towards Doctor Bullock who was this brown-bearded man with an enormous head—way out of proportion with his teeny body.

Happily, he'd been able to get Ber to see that it was better he did any interviews alone and it really hadn't been that hard to persuade her. She seemed to have the self-awareness to know, on account of her blunt disposition, that questioning people might not be her strength. He could well imagine her literally jumping down a witness's throat if she thought they were lying to her. Ber's interviewing style would be akin to taking a hammer to force juice out of an orange. Whereas his normal modus operandi involved gently squeezing the truth out of people.

Doctor Bullock cast a look—somewhere between confusion and revulsion—towards Doocey. Some madcap vagabond, he must've been thinking, had barged his way in, ahead of the serious, smartly dressed detective he'd been expecting. Even when Doocey introduced himself and presented his official identification, Bullock continued to look dubious.

At any rate, Doocey lowered himself into a chair that, like the desk Bullock was sitting behind, had a modern sculptural look to it, and he imagined any modern sculpture, even the most angular, would feel more comfortable to sit on. He rested his briefcase on his lap. The Italian leather briefcase he'd picked up for a fiver in a local charity shop.

"I'm sorry but we'll have to make this quick," Bullock declared. "I'm afraid there are just such great demands on my time. Would you believe, I've got a fortnight's waiting list of patients?"

"Sounds like you're very popular," Doocey said, with a half-smile.

"Yes, yes, very much so," Bullock answered in a serious tone to what had been intended as mere banter.

Silly arrogant twit, Doocey inwardly noted as he removed from his briefcase his copy of Harriet Nolan's medical file—a medical file that revealed she had only visited her GP three times in the previous five years. The first two of those visits arose from nothing more unusual than bad cases of the flu. The third visit then was the only one that interested him, extremely interested him. Doocey said aloud, "I'd like to hear what you can tell me about Mrs Nolan's last visit to see you in April. The file notes mention something about 'severe bruising to her neck,' but there's no other detail."

"Yes," Bullock said, glancing towards the documentation in Doocey's hand. "One has to be tremendously careful, these days, about what you write concerning a patient. There are all manner of privacy and defamation legalities to consider. Thus, my policy is to write down as little as possible, and it's a policy that's worked splendidly in keeping the many litigation wolves out there, from my doctor's door."

Bullock smirked, and Doocey longed to punch the giant head off him. The doctor's dumb arse-covering looked to have banjaxed any hope of that early breakthrough.

"Nevertheless, let me see," Bullock continued, "I may have, as happens on the rare occasion, made some notes just for my private reference. Please call out to me the file number on the cover page."

Doocey ran his eyes over the cover page of the medical file he shakily held but—for the life of him—he couldn't make out the file number. Even though earlier that morning, he'd been able to see the same file number perfectly clear but now it only resembled a faint line of black dots. *Fecking hell,* his sight had suddenly gotten a lot worse. *What now?*

He blinked like mad and blinked like mad some more and *phew* started to see a bit better. It must have only been that his eyes had gone very dry, probably on account of the heat of the room. He was just about to get on with calling out the number when Bullock—fed up of waiting—stood up and whipped the medical file from him, and began hitting computer keys. Meanwhile, Doocey zipped down his anorak, feeling like he was soaking in a bath of his own sweat.

After one last noisy key tap, Bullock announced, "Nope, I've made no other notes, just treatment of severe bruising."

Well f-you again anyhow, Doocey thought. "Can I ask . . ." he began aloud but suddenly stopped as if just realising the silliness of his half-aired question, and said all formal, "Thank you very much for seeing me, Doctor Bullock." Taking back Harriet Nolan's file, he began packing it into his cheap, fancy briefcase.

Bullock, with a puzzled expression, asked, "Was there something else Detective?"

"Ah no . . . no . . . It's ridiculous to think you'd ever be able to answer what I was going to ask."

The doctor leaned his weighty head to the left and said, almost as if spoiling for a fight, "Try me."

"Ah well . . . I was just wondering if aside from any notes, anything stood out in your memory about Harriet Nolan's April visit but I don't see how it would. Not with the hordes of patients you get coming through your surgery door. You'd need to be some sort of genius to recall individual patient visits."

Bullock's reply came quickly. "I actually have remarkable powers of recollection and despite the vast volumes of people I see, I've been known to remember patient interactions going back years. I personally believe I've got a photographic memory."

"You're not serious? I've never met anybody with one of those. To be honest . . . I thought the likes of you only existed on the big screen."

"Oh no, we very much exist in real life," Bullock replied, stroking the top of his enormous head and gazing up at his glass roof. "Now let me see . . . if I can recall anything of Harriet Nolan's last visit."

After a substantial silence, he suddenly smiled a smug smile and stuck out a dinky finger. "Ah yes, I distinctly remember, she'd been wearing a white scarf to hide the bruising to her neck, and I have to say, the severity of her injuries shocked me. Her neck was quite badly bruised."

With his heart beating a kilometre a second, Doocey kept going with his plámásing of the doctor. "Gosh, you really do have a marvellous memory!" prompting Bullock to nod solemnly. "Did Mrs Nolan say at all . . . how she'd got the injuries?"

"I believe she loosely referenced something about tripping whilst out walking and falling into briar bushes."

"You didn't believe her?" Doocey probed, picking up on the significant scepticism in tone.

"No, I didn't. The injuries might have been the result of such a fall but they might equally have been caused by . . ."

Bullock stalled, as if not sure whether he should go on but seeming unable to keep his supercilious trap shut, burst out, "Frankly, I thought the bruising may have been the result of an assault. Though, even if I were the greatest doctor in the world, I couldn't have been certain of this."

Doocey's whole body became one huge knot of tension as he held his breath in anticipation of what *Doctor Arrogant* would say next.

"I tried to get Mrs Nolan to confide in me," Bullock continued, stretching out an open-palmed little hand. "I told her that there were organisations that could help. That no one should have to endure physical—"

"Were you able to get her to talk?" Doocey cut in, eagerness getting the better of him.

Bullock returned a blistering stare, obviously offended by Doocey daring to interrupt such an esteemed person as him. In his own good time, he eventually resumed. "Actually . . . Mrs Nolan became rather agitated at my attempted interventions. Told me quite categorically she needed no such assistance. How she simply wanted her wounds treated." He leaned back in his steel-framed chair and folded his weedy arms across his flappy belly. "Given my significant professional experience, her angry reaction did not, in the least, surprise me. It's typical of how victims of domestic violence usually respond. Their anger is simply a defence mechanism, masking a fear of facing up to their abuser."

"Did Mrs Nolan give any indications about who that abuser might be?"

Bullock, with a frown, replied, "No."

No, Doocey silently repeated. The word, like a piercing arrow, sent his inflated expectations of a big breakthrough plummeting to earth.

Bullock suddenly continued, "Though, in a husband-and-wife scenario, the husband usually turns out to be the abuser."

When Doocey debriefed Ber about how his visit to Bullock had gone, her first reaction was that the doctor sounded like "a right pillock." As for Bullock's assertion of how—in a husband-and-wife domestic abuse scenario—the husband usually turned out to be the abuser . . . well . . . she didn't think such an assertion on his part was worth a damn, maintaining: "If it ever came to prosecuting Nolan in court, that kind of testimony by the pillock would be dismissed as just his pompous speculation."

"Yeah, I agree," Doocey had responded. "Unless that is we could find someone able to back up Bullock's theory. Someone . . . say . . . who had the most opportunity to witness Nolan beating up his wife—say for instance an ex-housekeeper."

SEVEN

DOOCEY OPENED A RUSTY GARDEN gate hanging precariously by one squeaky hinge, and trampled his way through an overgrown garden of weeds, to a cottage with another healthy crop of weeds sprouting from its roof. Even though not the tidiest person himself, as evident from the constant bombsite mess of his apartment, the untidy condition of this property nonetheless came as a surprise to him—especially considering the owner's profession was to tidy other people's properties. Maybe, though, only the outside was a disaster zone and the inside would be tidiness personified.

The cottage door was opened by a woman who—astonishingly—was even shorter than himself but what she lacked in height, she certainly made up for in width, possessing the body shape of an over-pumped beach ball. After confirming herself to be Mrs Boyle, Nolan's ex-housekeeper, Doocey got out his detective ID and explained about him investigating the disappearance of Harriet Nolan. Boyle let out a barking laugh as if he was pulling her stocky leg.

Down through the years, Doocey had found that fellow shorties, like Boyle, were always the biggest sceptics in believing him to be a genuine detective. However, Boyle eventually allowed Doocey to step inside. As his host closed the creaking door behind him, the ancient adage that you 'should never judge a book by its cover' leapt into his thoughts.

Except, if Boyle's house had been a book, it would be perfectly fine to judge it by its awful external cover as the inside looked just as awful. The hall's yellowed wallpaper looked like it had been stuck up not long after the invention of the printing press. The missing floor tiles and cracks in the ceiling added to the sense of neglect, as did the stench of dampness.

They went through to a cramped kitchen with all its condiments, from sauce bottles to bowls, to loaves of bread sloppily squeezed onto two long shelves that ran around the room.

Catching the whiff of something burning in the oven, Doocey risked faking a compliment about the delicious aroma of baking. This led to him being invited to pull out a chair from a tiny pine table and pretend to enjoy a weak cup of cold tea with—an allegedly fresh from the oven—rock-solid scone and a rock, he reckoned, would've probably tasted far better.

Boyle silently monitored his every mouthful, looking as delighted as a mother watching her little darling devouring all his veg. Doocey reflected that after putting him through this, the woman had better properly blab about Nolan. "Delicious, absolutely delicious," he exclaimed, and using the stained paper napkin he'd been handed—wiped sticky strawberry jam, that had come from a disposable plastic container, from his mouth. "I only wish my Mrs could bake so brilliantly."

Hearing of his bad baker of a wife prompted Nelly into letting fire at him, in mind-numbing detail, her tips for making scones, as well as all her other—presumably equally unpleasant-tasting treats—from rhubarb tart to black forest gateaux to lemon ice cream. An exasperated Doocey felt he only had himself to blame. In trying to get in with her, he should never have gone so far as lying about the nice smell of baking or about a wife who couldn't bake.

Multiple times, Doocey strived to nudge her off the subject of her fictitious baking expertise, but without success. He began to daydream about wedging his remaining piece of scone into her gob, although he doubted even its granite hardness would succeed in shutting her up. As Boyle started reciting her secret recipe for custard pudding, Doocey succeeded in cutting in, "If you don't mind me saying so," he said, eyeing her plump face and rosy cheeks, "you seem a very young woman for retirement?"

With a stern stare, Boyle wiped her hands in her filthy pinafore. "That's what Nolan told you—is it? That I retired?"

Pretending this to be the case, Doocey firmly nodded.

"Well, let me tell you the truth of the matter," a frowning Boyle proposed. "I didn't retire. I resigned. The man was a nightmare to work for. If he found one speck of dust, and I do mean the tiniest speck, he'd go berserk. Flat-out berserk." She pushed out her beachball belly. "I wouldn't mind, but I'm a very good housekeeper."

"You're looking for another job then?" Doocey impulsively asked and instantly thought, *Now, why go asking such an effing stupid question, ruining everything.*

"I certainly am," she said, in exactly the defensive, pissed-off tone of voice, he'd feared. She might as well have said, *I know it's been months now since I worked in Nolan Manor, but that doesn't mean I'm so bloody useless that nobody wants to hire me.*

As if to show some solid evidence of her housekeeping fabulousness, Boyle now started belting out unoriginal cleaning tips: salt's superbness in getting rid of red wine spills and vinegar's excellence in cleaning stubborn toilet stains. She shook a finger, "You should see the job—"

"Sounds as if he's very house-proud," Doocey interjected.

For a second, Boyle looked confused, before it dawned on her that he'd gone back to talking about Nolan.

"No, no," she finally exclaimed, "It's more than that. Have you not seen what he's done with Nolan Manor?" She gave him no chance to answer. "How he's gutted it, turned the house into this horrible empty white box. His father, the one who hired me originally, God bless his soul, must be spinning in his crypt. The crypt he built with his own builder hands. To see all his precious antiques flung out."

She gave a sad shake of the head. "And all because his cracked son is afraid of a little bit of dust. The man's not right in the head. I tell you . . . he's not right. You should've seen the way he'd chase after me with his white glove checking for dirt. Sure, just before I walked out, didn't I catch him watching me on those cameras of his. Playing back my every move. Have you noticed too—how he's shaven off all his hair? The same story there." Another sad shake of her head. "Afraid of the tiniest rib of hair. If you ask me, he badly needs to see a psychiatrist. I'd say he definitely has that OCDC thing."

"Obsessive-Compulsive Disorder?" Doocey stipulated, just to one hundred percent rule out that Boyle really wasn't on about an aged rock band.

"Yeah, that's the one," she said and let out a hearty laugh. "Hard to believe someone as stuck-up as him could be obsessed with, of all things, cleaning."

"Yes, it's a strange one alright," Doocey acknowledged and wondered if some sort of trauma might've triggered Nolan's OCD because any time he'd encountered, as part of his work, someone with mental issues they usually had a traumatic background story to tell.

"Anyway," Mrs Boyle ranted on, "whatever his problem, I'd a bellyful of it. I told him to stuff his job." She grimaced. "How poor Frankie sticks him, I don't know. I just don't know."

"Sorry, who's Frankie?" Doocey interrupted, wanting to be certain that the Frank Murphy—Nolan's gardener—who he'd seen mentioned in Dickson's investigation file, was one in the same person."

Boyle's tone became more cautious. "He's my brother's lad. He does the gardens in Nolan Manor."

"Yeah," Doocey said, regressing to her previous point, "I don't know how anybody could stick him when he's so particular and so posh. Sure, that would get up anybody's goat."

Boyle rattled down her cup. "Oh, you don't know the half of it. Working for him was like stepping back in time. The Irish peasant servant waiting hand and foot on the English Lord except this cursed Lord wasn't a Lord and wasn't English but Irish."

Doocey pulled a disgusted face to demonstrate his empathy and bravely bit into more scone, feeling sure that he'd chipped a tooth in the process.

Boyle tutted, "Sure he even plays cricket with the British Ambassador to Ireland, and he and his other fake Brit pals get invited to all these big galas at the embassy."

That might be a useful little piece of information, Doocey considered. The vague shape of a related plan already forming in his mind.

"It's sickening," Boyle ranted on. "Oh yes, he's a pure snob and herself is even worse."

"You mean Harriet Nolan?" Doocey asked, rocky crumbs falling from his mouth.

"Yes *Harriet*," she scoffed. "That's not even her real name. Would you believe she's my own namesake? But of course, Helen, or God forbid Nelly, wasn't good enough for that madam!"

Doocey joined with her in giving a look of exasperation to the heavens.

"I might at least understand himself being snobbish, him coming from such wealth." Boyle's face contorted, "Though as for your one. Not that I wish anyone harm, but you should've seen the airs and graces of her. You'd swear she were royalty—instead of being the offspring of Peadar Reilly. A poxy bin man's daughter—for goodness' sake!"

"She's a fair bit younger than him too," Doocey remarked, reaching for his cup, and somehow managed to topple it over.

Tepid tea streamed everywhere. *Damn it!* he silently shouted, *and just when I'd got her all revved up. God, I'm turning into a real blind klutz.*

Boyle swung into action as if her big chance had arrived to practically demonstrate her superhero capabilities as a housekeeper. Dirty dishcloth in hand, she got mopping.

Looking chuffed with herself for a job well done, she dumped the drenched dishcloth into a sink of grimy dinner plates. Next, she poured Doocey a fresh cup of cold tea, plonked a second stony scone on his plate and to cap it all horribly off, asked if he knew what was great for removing tea stains.

Pretending not to have heard the question, he said, "With such a huge age gap between them, I can't see what they could've had in common."

Boyle, once more, took a few seconds to get up to speed before replying in a sour voice, "Nothing. They hadn't a thing in common. She just married him for his money."

Doocey, crouching in towards her, sank his voice to a whisper, "Were the two of them not getting on?"

Boyle lowered her voice now too. "I wouldn't think so. My guess is they hated each other's guts. Though they were great at putting on this all rosy in the blasted garden show."

"They never argued?"

"No . . ." Boyle said slowly with an air of major disappointment.

"Or he never hit her?"

"No . . ." Boyle repeated, sounding even more disappointed. Then she added as if all wasn't entirely lost, "Well, not in front of me, anyhow."

Reckoning there was no point prolonging the inevitable awfulness, Doocey got stuck into devouring his second scone. A smiling Nelly Boyle cautioned, "I know they're delicious but take your time. You don't want to get stomach ache."

Doocey managed a smile back and after a marathon of hard chewing, got to ask his next question. "Was it the old silent treatment then between Mr and Mrs Nolan?"

"No, not even that . . . the two of them were always chatting," and again that major disappointment in her tone.

She straightened herself. "As I say though, I think it was all a show, and it wouldn't surprise me one bit if he murdered her. Our Markus R. has a terrible temper. You should have seen how mental he'd get with me over something as silly as a couple of old cobwebs. His face would go fire brigade red and he'd be clenching his fists like he wanted to punch me."

"But he never did?"

"No . . ." Boyle said sombrely, almost as if she deeply regretted the fact.

Doocey pressed a hand to his forehead. "If the two of them weren't getting on, I don't understand why they didn't just divorce?"

"That's down to money again. Nolan wouldn't have wanted a second costly divorce."

After managing with a struggle to down the last lump of scone, Doocey asked whether Harriet was the reason Nolan split from his first wife.

"Oh she was," Boyle replied, nodding zealously and wiggling about in her pine chair. "Tempted him away with skirts up to her tiny arse. Such a shame . . . and the original Mrs Nolan was so lovely. A nicer woman, you'd never meet."

"Am I right in saying she died of cancer?"

"Yes . . ." Boyle mouthed and repeated in a whisper, "Cancer."

She gripped the edge of the table as if to anchor herself. "The poor thing passed away not long after her divorce from Nolan. I've no doubt the upset of it all brought on her illness in the first place. She was an actress, you know? Wasn't in anything big, only small plays. All the same, she was supposed to have been brilliant." Spotting Doocey's empty plate, Boyle urged, "You'll have another scone. I've any amount of them there."

"Ah no . . . no . . . thanks . . . I'm only after the breakfast," Doocey said, patting his chest frantically as if he were performing CPR on himself. "Those two though were delicious, absolutely delicious."

Boyle proudly grinned.

"With the big age difference between them," Doocey went on, "I wondered if the current Mrs Nolan might have been seeing other men?"

"Oh, you can bet your life on it. I'd say she's been with a whole bus-full."

"You wouldn't happen to know any names?"

For a few seconds, the ex-housekeeper looked truly terrified, as if it had just dawned on her that she'd said something she ought not to have said.

Theatrically throwing up her hands, she proclaimed, "I'm afraid, Detective, I'm a woman who likes to keep herself to herself. I'm not one for gossip."

Doocey nodded neutrally, not giving voice to his puzzlement that an obvious busybody like Boyle (despite her laughable denials) would all of a sudden go coy.

He said aloud, "I'm surprised Nolan would put up with his wife seeing other men?"

Boyle tossed her head backwards. "Ah, sure, he just turns a blind eye."

"He must really not have wanted the expense of a second divorce."

"Herself didn't want one either. She enjoyed swanning about too much as Lady Muck."

"I understand Nolan has a daughter from his first marriage, Jennifer. What's she like?"

Boyle's tone thawed. "Ah, Jennifer's a lovely girl. She is so like her late mother." Her tone became sharper. "You do know she's blind?" Boyle glared unnervingly at Doocey's glasses.

He stuttered back, "Ah . . . what happened there?"

"Some defect at birth—nothing to be done."

He hadn't known about Jennifer Nolan being blind as there had only been the briefest mention of her in Dickson's investigation file.

Just that one hand-written one-liner from him: *'Nolan's daughter Jennifer (who was Harriet Nolan's stepdaughter) wasn't there—has own apartment—and anyways couldn't have been involved.'* The note made a lot more sense to Doocey now. As per Dickson's prejudiced mindset, he believed Jennifer Nolan couldn't have been involved in her stepmother's disappearance because she was blind.

"Ahh, she's a great girl," Boyle continued as if only talking to herself, before looking back to Doocey. "She's a professional singer, you know? Very successful too."

It struck Doocey as peculiar, considering his own recent sight issues that his very first big case should involve (however indirectly) a blind person. He would wonder later—when he had more time to think or over-think—if it might be more than pure coincidence. If just maybe, his dead dad had a word with the big man upstairs and told him he wanted his son's first big case to be one where the main suspect's daughter would be this successful blind singer. As a kind of inspirational reminder to Doocey that his own sight issues should not stop him pursuing his dreams.

No matter how much this otherworldly theory of his stretched credibility or sounded frankly bonkers, it didn't stop Doocey from wanting it to be true. *Sure, as they say, God works in mysterious ways* and probably worked all the more mysteriously when he'd the likes of his dad whispering in his ear.

Boyle supplemented in an unsure tone, "Yeah, she's supposed to be a brilliant singer."

"You don't think so yourself?"

"Oh no . . . it's just that she sings all that opera stuff. You know those songs where you can't make out a word. It all sounds like a dog screeching to me."

"To me too! I can never understand how some people love it so much. Tell me this—how does Jennifer get on with her father?"

Boyle winced as if the mere act of attempting to answer the question was causing her to feel sick and then spat out sourly, "They get on fantastically and she regularly stays over in Nolan Manor."

"When it came to Harriet, her stepmother, how did she get on with her?"

Boyle's tone became cheerful. "Jennifer couldn't stand the cow, and who'd blame her? Considering how she'd stolen her father from her mother. Even if she's blind, I swear the girl knows more of what's going on than a sighted person would."

"She's clever then?"

"Very—and she has the acting skills of her mother. I always remember how as a little girl she'd cry fake tears to get her loony tune father to give in to her childish demands."

Doocey stood up. "Well, Nelly, it was lovely chatting with you."

"Not at all. It's been my pleasure," she said, also getting to her little feet.

Doocey sauntered out into the decrepit hallway, stopped, and turned back to the ex-housekeeper. "Oh, one last question. Did Mrs Nolan have any close friends?"

"Only the one main one," Boyle replied with her head arched upwards to the hall's cracked ceiling. "This Miss Penelope Powell. Another right madam." She snorted. "Every week, they met for *coffee*. If there is anybody who'd have a good idea of what happened to herself, I'd wager it to be that madam."

Even a good idea of whether Nolan had been secretly beating Harriet up, Doocey pondered. Because maybe, just like Boyle had maintained, things weren't so 'rosy in the garden' when Mr and Mrs Nolan were by themselves. Plus, when Harriet Nolan got those injuries to her neck, Nelly Boyle was no longer working at Nolan Manor. She'd left, or more likely was sacked, two months earlier.

Sat in his car across the road from Boyle's tatty cottage, Doocey took out his phone to make his daily call to check in on his mother. When he told her all about his chat with Nelly Boyle—the ex-housekeeper instantly replaced Nolan as her new number-one suspect, on account of how Boyle hated Harriet Nolan so much. Doocey had to stop himself from pointing out that Boyle seemed to hate Mr Nolan just as much, if not more. Why then murder his wife and not him?

"It's nearly always the one you least suspect," his mother maintained. A cliched insight, no doubt, she'd got from listening to too many cosy whodunnits.

The one doubt Mrs Doocey had, owing to her son's descriptions of Boyle as a small, beach ball of a woman, was whether she'd have had the physical strength to dispose of the body. "Though she might've had help," she hypothesised. Only to concede, after a pause, "Or maybe not." Until finally, in an altogether firmer tone, "No, I still think it's Mr Nolan who's our murderer." Then excitedly exclaimed. "I know too what he did with the body."

After asking if he'd remembered "your man in Slovakia," she wasn't at all impressed with her son not instantly grasping which specific man in Slovakia she was on about.

"Don't you remember the story doing the rounds, not so long back, about that Slovakian serial killer?" She heaved an impatient sigh. "Anyway, this Slovakian fella, like a hawk, had been watching his local graveyard for any freshly dug graves. And before the funeral of the next person up to be buried happened, he would—during the night—dig the empty grave down deeper, plonking in his latest victim and covering them up with the extra clay he'd removed. The officially dead person would later be buried on top and nobody ever would be the wiser to there being two bodies in the one grave. Clever, ha?"

"Very clever," Doocey conceded, and he found himself being pressurised into promising to investigate whether Nolan might have disposed of his wife's body in a similar fashion. It was a promise that he'd no intention of keeping. Did his mother seriously expect him to head off to Nolan's local graveyard and arrange for any recently buried souls to be dug back up? Just on the off chance of Harriet Nolan being in there with them.

Because even if (which was very doubtful) families would allow their loved ones to be exhumed, it would also take months to get all the proper paperwork . . . and he hadn't months—plural. Now, he didn't even have one full month.

More to the point though, he also thought it'd be a total waste of time. It would have been much easier for Nolan to dispose of his wife's body within the grounds of his huge, isolated estate or in the vast surrounding sea than to go carting it off to some graveyard with locked gates and the public coming and going.

Later though, Doocey would not think his mother's idea, or a version of it at least, to be so ridiculous, after all.

It disappointed Ber to hear that Nelly Boyle, or as she'd speedily labelled her, "the old yapper" hadn't witnessed Nolan harming his wife."

"Well . . . at least she gave us another lead on the matter," Doocey had proffered.

"What lead?" Ber snapped back. "What are you on about?"

"I'm on about Penelope Powell. What if Harriet Nolan told Powell about Mr Nolan trying to strangle her, and there should be a good chance of her having done so, with Powell supposedly being her best friend and them meeting up every week."

EIGHT

Miss Penelope Powell stood in the doorway of what from the outside more resembled a cow shed than a house. She glared down upon Doocey—a puzzled expression stamped on her face. A face that had this rigid quality. It almost looked as rigid as her jet-black hair which she had squeezed into an ultra-tight bun.

Cocking her chin, she declared, "I never make charitable donations on the doorstep."

"No one's asking you to make any charitable donation," Doocey whipped back and before he'd the chance to say anything further, Powell went off on one.

"Don't tell me . . . you're another one of those wretched journalists. How many more times does one have to tell you people—I'm not giving interviews about Harriet Nolan."

She went to close the door but Doocey stuck out a little blocking foot.

"Now, look here," Powell burst out, "If you don't get off my property this instant, I shall call the police."

"There's no need to do that," Doocey coolly replied, holding up his detective ID. "The *police* are already here."

To his inquiry as to whether he might come in, Powell, with a frown, replied, "If you must."

Turning her back on him, she marched inside, muttering, "It's astonishing for what passes as a detective these days."

Slamming the door behind him, Doocey trailed after her through a narrow, dark hallway. In his rush to keep up, his elbow touched a glass sculpture of a savage lioness—triggering it to violently tremble but mercifully not crash to the floor.

He followed Powell into a small room with brown wallpaper. The sound of sheep bleating and the strong scent of fresh manure from nearby fields encroached through a half-opened window. With a few agitated waves of the hand, Powell piloted Doocey to this rigid wooden chair as she opted for a lavishly upholstered cream sofa. Doocey got out his notebook and pretended to read, taking his time, determined to yet show who was boss.

Two seconds later, Powell exclaimed, "What is it you need to ask of me?" and flicked a speck of microscopic dust from her steel grey trousers. "I've got a large luncheon to organise."

"Good for you," Doocey mumbled. Then in a clearer voice, "I'd like to ask you about your friendship with Mrs Nolan. Were you close?"

Powell looked uncomfortable at the question. "I wouldn't say we were that close, more acquaintances."

"Yet, according to my information, you and Mrs Nolan met up weekly."

Powell's face twisted even tighter. "If you already know the answer Detective, why ask the question? It insults one's intelligence."

Putting on a mock posh voice of his own, Doocey replied, "Well, *one* simply wants to check that *one* has their facts ship-shape. That's all." Reverting to his authentic accent, he asked, "Can you tell me—before the Tuesday Harriet was reported missing—when the two of you last met?"

Powell touched her lip with a purple-painted nail. "I think she might have called over for a coffee, the week before, on the Wednesday."

"How would you describe her mood? Did she happen to be feeling down?"

"No, not at all, she seemed in good spirits." She gave him a stern look. "You're not possibly suggesting that Harriet might have taken her own life?"

"Well at this stage I'm ruling nothing out. Did Harriet ever mention anything of the sort?"

"Certainly not."

"She never was depressed?"

"Well . . . like everybody, she sometimes got the blues. Nevertheless, I really can't imagine Harriet killing herself."

"Yeah, I'm finding that hard to imagine too," Doocey, with a rub of his pot belly, muttered as if only speaking to himself—but Powell instantly leapt on the comment.

"She therefore simply slipped and fell from the cliffs?"

"Well, it might not have been that simple either."

Powell's narrow eyes widened in wonderment. "You actually suspect she was murdered?"

"It's too early to be sure," he said, keen to give as little as possible away to the unhelpful piece of work.

"Did Harriet confide in you about any marriage difficulties?"

"No," came the swift reply, but in a feeble tone.

"So she and Mr Nolan were happily married."

"Yes . . . I believe so." Again, there was that feebleness to her reply as if it were no stronger than eggshell. "Whenever I had occasion to meet them, together as a couple," she continued, more confidently, "they seemed to get on wonderfully. They were forever teasing each other."

Doocey tried looking confused. "That surprises me because I understood Mrs Nolan had been seeing other men."

Powell swept away another microscopic piece of dust, this time from her jacket's padded shoulder. "I'm not sure of that but even if it were the case, perhaps—Mr Nolan, as a much older husband was not very bothered about his wife seeing other people."

"Did Harriet ever mention any names?"

"No," Powell tersely declared and stood up. "Now, I really must get back to organising my luncheon."

Doocey remained seated. "If I might just have a few more moments of your time, it would be very much appreciated." He put on his posh voice again. "It would also save *one* being dragged down to the station."

Powell, looking furious, flopped back onto her cream sofa.

"Miss Powell, you, too, would be insulting my intelligence, if you expect me to believe that you don't know the details of Harriet Nolan's extramarital activities. Given that you were friends that met weekly, it defies credibility that she didn't open up to you."

Powell folded her arms. "There is such a thing—you do know—as not betraying a confidence."

"Yes, whilst I can respect that—I'm sure you'd agree that the priority at this present moment must be in locating Mrs Nolan and I'd hate to see you being charged with withholding information."

The stiff features of Powell's face quivered before she finally gave a disgruntled shake of the head. "I think, most recently, Harriet may have been carrying on with—of all people—her gardener. He may have been called Murphy or had some such ubiquitous name."

Jackpot, Doocey silently yoo-hooed, now understanding why Nelly Boyle had been so coy in naming any of Harriet Nolan's fancy men. Nolan's ex-housekeeper hadn't wanted to get her nephew Frank, or Frankie as she called him, into bother. He remembered also Boyle's scathing speculation that Harriet Nolan had likely been with a whole 'bus-full' of men.

Doocey eyed Powell. "Do you remember if she'd been seeing anybody else?"

"Well, before . . . *this gardener person* . . . I believe she had also been seeing a married man . . . but she never told me his name. She was much more secretive about him, presumably scared of his wife finding out." Making to stand up again, Powell declared, "That really is all I can tell you."

Once more, Doocey remained seated. "Harriet's medical records show that she visited her doctor a month before her disappearance. To have bruises on her neck treated. Did she confide in you about how she might have got those injuries?"

"No . . ." Powell replied in a perplexed tone and, as if in a daze, fully resumed her seat. "Harriet hated us talking about anything to do with doctors. They terrified her."

"Any idea why?"

Powell put a hand to her hair bun and squeezed it, looking to be agonising over how to reply and then speaking at pace as if she really would prefer not to be asked any more on the subject, "I believe as a young girl, a doctor may have attempted to molest her." Powell's voice became a whisper. "Goodness, Harriet's injuries must have been very serious for her to have visited a doctor."

"Yes, I think they were, and her doctor suspects that she may have been a victim of a domestic violence incident." He paused, looking towards Powell's inky-black eyes. "I'd have expected that Harriet might well have confided in you, her best friend, about such a harrowing experience."

"No . . ." she replied, sounding unsure. "You say this all took place a month before she vanished?"

"Yes."

"Well . . . the only point leaping to mind is that Harriet got a new BMW about that time, and she told me Mr Nolan paid for the vehicle." Powell pursed her lips. "Even though Harriet never uttered a word, I wonder in retrospect if the car may not well have been some sort of bribe, on her husband's part, to buy her silence."

Interesting theory, Doocey reflected before asking aloud, "You personally hadn't noticed the bruises to her neck?"

"No, I can't say I had."

As a follow-up to what Doctor Bullock had told him, Doocey suggested, "Maybe she used a scarf to cover them?"

Powell's tight face seemed to loosen. "Yes . . ." she said slowly as if thinking back, "I'd actually teased Harriet about her sudden penchant for scarfs."

As if the true horror of the situation had just dawned on her, she exclaimed, clasping her mouth, "Oh, my word—it's dreadful to think that Markus could've been harming her."

Arriving back at the station, Doocey asked Ber to join him in meeting room 2C. After listening in silence as to how his interview with Powell had gone, Ber had lamented, "God, it sounds like it was real hard work to get anything out of the snooty cow."

"Yeah, it was," Doocey agreed and wondered if there might be an easier way to extract useful information from any more snooty pals of the Nolans and particularly from any close pal of Mr Nolan.

NINE

That Saturday evening, Doocey did something he hated doing—looking at himself—in his full-length wardrobe mirror. Unable to see his reflection clearly, he told himself this was only on account of how dusty and scratched the mirror must be and not because the fog in his eyes had grown denser.

He stepped right in close to the mirror and managed to smile at the figure he blurrily saw. He gave a wriggle of his bony shoulders and adjusted his silk bow tie. Although not so silly as to believe a tux instantly transformed him into James Bond, not unless 007 had shrunk by two feet and had started wearing specs. All the same, he reckoned he didn't look too terrible.

He couldn't recall the last time he'd worn a tux. He definitely hadn't needed one for—decades ago now—his school ball, seeing as how the last unspoken-for girl, Rose Madden, with her impressive moustache, had even turned him down.

After a final—happyish enough—check of his fuzzy replica, he rang for a taxi to take him to the British Embassy. His stomach began to churn as he pictured what lay ahead of him. All those snobs nibbling canapes, sipping champagne, literally looking down their la-de-da noses at him.

At the entrance to the embassy, a doorman wearing a swanky donkey-style jacket greeted the couple ahead of him. "Good evening, Lord Godfrey," and with a respectful nod, "Lady Godfrey. Good to see you both." The scraggy Lord Godfrey stood back to let his wife go ahead of him which Doocey respected as good thinking on the man's part—considering that his Mrs's large gold-gowned arse required the full breadth of the door.

Doocey carefully inched his way up the external steps of the embassy, as the steps were slippery from a recent shower, but careful and all as he was, he still managed to go flying head over heels. Bolting to his feet, and with everybody staring, he pretended to laugh off his clumsiness and swooped out his party invite. The invite he'd wrangled from the British Ambassador to Ireland, Sir Charles Chapman.

"Wrangled" mightn't be the right word though, considering the Ambassador's overzealousness to be of assistance. Doocey had feared that the fecker would not go along with what he'd planned because of his friendship with Nolan or being the high-minded sort. However, the Ambassador made it clear from the outset that though he played cricket with Nolan, he wouldn't classify him as a friend, and it was more out of a sense of obligation that he invited him to parties at the embassy, seeing as how he invited the entire cricket team.

From their previous phone conversations, Doocey had got a definite wannabe-spy vibe from the Ambassador. He'd even come up with his own crude code name for the night ahead: "Operation Nutcracker" which he kept referencing.

Doocey had feared from the outset that it would be like pulling posh teeth to try to get any friends of Mr Nolan to openly confide in him, expecting they would be ultra cautious about what they would say to the detective investigating the disappearance of their pal's wife, for fear it might contribute to Nolan being mistakenly charged with murdering her, or because they simply wanted to distance themselves from the dastardly business. Hearing Nolan's ex-housekeeper, Nelly Boyle, mention about how Nolan and his pals regularly got invited to big galas at the British Embassy had then spawned Doocey's idea for "Operation Nutcracker." He would get the Ambassador to invite pals of Mr Nolan to one of his galas. Then posing as a fellow uppity guest—he hoped those pals would be more inclined to talk freely with him and that he might get them to give him the true lowdown on Markus R. Nolan and his missing wife.

The doorman rechecked his invite for the third time, causing Doocey to have second thoughts about whether he truly had spruced up all that well. He swept a hand over the top of his head, no longer convinced that the near bottle of gel he'd deployed to keep his rebellious hair in check was doing such a decent job.

With a forced-looking smile, the doorman finally relented, "Oh good evening, Sir Cornelius," (Doocey's undercover name for the night).

To which Doocey replied in someone else's posh voice, "A *very* good evening to you, my good man," and with a swivel of a finger, he appended, "I do like your donkey-style jacket, it rather seems to suit your personality."

As the taken aback doorman struggled for words, Doocey swaggered on inside.

The British Ambassador stood, greeting people at the doorway to the main reception room. When it came to Doocey's turn to introduce himself, the Ambassador seemed just about able to muster back, "Good evening."

Doocey felt as if he ought to apologise for not looking more like the handsome movie star spy the Ambassador had been expecting. To look more, in fact, like the Ambassador himself, who with his tall, broad-shouldered figure, dark complexion, piercing blue eyes and slightly silvered black hair could easily pass for a middle-aged movie spy.

Sir Charles cleared his throat which also seemed to have the effect of clearing away some of his initial shock. "Sir Cornelius, I must introduce you to some friends of mine."

To even his own annoyance, Doocey heard himself once more reply in someone else's posh voice, "That would be delightful," and he followed the Ambassador through a sea of raven black tuxedoes, glittering ball gowns, and deafening conversation. A jazz band played in the distance. The scent of sizzling steak in the air.

The Ambassador whispered to Doocey, "Nolan's main pal is over there—Tyson Tidd and his wife." Without further elaboration, he hurried over to the couple with Doocey trailing behind him.

Mr Tidd was an ancient dinosaur of a man with incredibly bushy eyebrows, whereas Mrs Tidd was a much younger woman who sported a strapless purple dress that showed off to the full her flat chest.

As Sir Charles enquired about how the Tidds were enjoying the evening, the couple eyed Doocey with blatant repugnance as if to silently question, *Why doesn't that little weirdo move on? Can't he see we're speaking to the Ambassador?*

Sir Charles turned back to Doocey. "Mr and Mrs Tidd, may I have the honour of introducing you to Sir Cornelius O'Connor."

Seemingly super-impressed that the heretofore *little weirdo* had a title, the couple's aggressive eye contact instantly fell away and they could not get hold of Doocey's teeny hand fast enough to fervently shake it.

The Ambassador, as he retrieved two glasses of champagne from a white-jacketed waitress for him and Doocey, added, "I'm sure you must have heard of all Sir Cornelius's great philanthropic work."

One of Kenneth Tidd's mammoth eyebrows shot up his wrinkly forehead and when it eventually came back down, he mumbled, "Yes . . . yes . . . of course."

Mrs Tidd, looking as if she might be too excited to speak, enthusiastically nodded her head.

Doocey gulped some champagne. It tasted sweet and strong and went straight to his head. "One does what one can," he heard himself say and cursed again his mouth for having taken on a bloody upper-class life of its own.

Mrs Tidd pushed herself forward. Her tiny eyes frantically twinkling, she mouthed breathlessly, "What was Her Majesty like?"

Doocey took another gulp of champagne to buy some time. Then began, "She was a very nice lady to talk—"

"You . . . had . . . a conversation . . . with her," Mrs Tidd interrupted, in a hyperventilating voice.

Her husband too looked suitably impressed, one of his incredible eyebrows rising once more.

"Oh yes, we had a good old chat."

"What did you talk about?" Mrs Tidd burst out, now making the full transformation into a giddy little girl about to open what promised to be her best birthday present ever.

"Oh, this and that," he said casually whilst racking his brain for inspiration. "The poor lady suffered with a lot of health niggles," he continued at last, thinking of his mother, another elderly woman, and her many aches and pains. "Not a lot of people know this but she was tormented by ingrown toenails."

The Tidds gave a loud laugh, followed by a belated one from Doocey.

The Ambassador tried to move the conversation away from Buckingham Palace but Rebecca Tidd would have none of it. She wouldn't be satisfied until she'd heard every minuscule detail about the day of his imaginary knighthood. How did the sword feel on his shoulder? Heavy or light? Did Her Majesty wear perfume? Strong or weak?

Dear Lord, all these pathetic, piddly questions, Doocey silently blasted. He prayed that he could just hold up the pretence given Mrs Tidd's encyclopaedic knowledge of royal matters. Though, the woman, grinning like a member of the royal family performing their public duty, seemed to be loving all his sketchy replies.

But then, puckering her lips, and looking upward she proclaimed, "I'm normally so good at memorising all the Irish who are knighted each year. I simply don't understand how I missed out on you." She glared into his glasses. "Actually, what year were you knighted?" Immediately, she followed up her problematic question with one even more problematic. "Who else was knighted that year?"

Damn, damn, damn, Doocey inwardly shrieked. *What the f am I going to say?*

"Ghastly, isn't it, that they haven't yet found Harriet Nolan," the Ambassador casually but loudly intervened.

Doocey gazed up at him with pretend puzzlement and secret extreme gratitude.

"Oh, sorry, Sir Cornelius, I forgot that with you living in the UK, you may not have been following the story. The missing woman is the wife of a Mr Markus R. Nolan who Kenneth here is best friends with."

"I wouldn't have said we were best friends," Mr Tidd irritably pointed out.

"No that's right," Mrs Tidd weighed in.

"Any idea what happened to her?" Doocey asked of the Ambassador.

"According to the rumours," he replied, in a lowered voice, "the Irish police think Mr Nolan murdered her—though I personally would find that very hard to believe."

"Well, it wouldn't at all surprise me," Mr Tidd said, taking a sip of champagne. "You haven't known the man as long as I have, Ambassador. He has a filthy temper."

Some best friend you are, Doocey silently remarked. *No loyalty whatsoever, but please do carry on, my good chap.*

"I hadn't realised," the Ambassador said in a whisper.

"Oh yes," Mr Tidd affirmed with pride, seeming to enjoy being able to share the inside story with two men so high up in the British realm.

Tidd smiled, showing off his magnificently decayed teeth. "I remember in our earlier days of playing cricket together how Nolan would get tremendously worked up. He would have given several referees bloody noses, had I not managed to drag him away."

The Ambassador's eyes widened. "That does surprise me . . ."

"I suppose sport is one thing," Doocey interjected, "We can all get carried away on the sports field." He paused, thinking, *Not that I would really know considering I never played any sport.* "*One* would think, however," he resumed, "that murdering your wife is an altogether different matter."

Mr Tidd leaned in, "Well . . . I suppose there is that . . . but the thing is . . . the poor chap does have a lot of mental scars." He gave a glance about as if to check for anybody listening. "You see, Nolan confided in me about what happened with his brother Richie."

After more glances about for potential eavesdroppers, he continued. "With just a year between him and Richie, they were the best of childhood friends. They shared every waking moment, every happy-go-lucky day, although Nolan was adamant his elder brother excelled him in every respect. He professed him to be much more handsome, much more intelligent, much sportier, much kinder. Also unlike him, Richie had been very close to his father."

Tidd heaved a heavy sigh. "At the age of just eleven, the boy fell ill as a result of contracting a deadly strain of meningitis. Nolan said it all happened so hellishly quickly. He was taken out of school and rushed to his brother's hospital bedside to watch him die."

Tidd gave a slow sideward shake of his head. "After that, Nolan maintained family life turned darker. His father and he became more and more distant. Mr Nolan senior, this practical-minded millionaire had wanted Markus to follow him into the business world and give up on what he called 'all his writing nonsense,' certain, from the very beginning, that his son would never make it as a writer. Poor Markus did not even have his mother to turn to as she collapsed into a deep depression."

Another slow shake of his head. "Nolan became more introverted, more untrusting and that's when he said his compulsive behaviour began. Having witnessed his brother die of a bacterial infection, the sight of a speck of dirt came to terrify him and in consequence, he told me, how his bedroom became cleaner than a hospital operating theatre. His way, I suppose, of attempting to give some order to what had proven to be a dangerous, unpredictable world."

Tidd itched at one of his gigantic eyebrows. "Nolan's obsession with cleanliness, like this rampant, venomous weed, grew and grew. Hence, the reason for him gutting Nolan Manor. Furniture, statues, paintings, tapestries, wallpapers, rugs—possessions his late father had painstakingly procured at bargain basement prices—all had to go. And all because of his fanatic obsession with cleanliness." Mr Tidd fell silent as if pondering his own words.

The Ambassador chipped in, "And along with all that . . . I hear Mr Nolan was having marital difficulties."

"Oh . . ." Doocey uttered as if intrigued whilst thinking, *Fair fecks to you Ambassador—you are doing a great job as my secret sidekick.*

Rebecca Tidd now excitedly took the bait. "Yes, apparently Harriet Nolan was seeing other men." Seeming to become so excited by the thought of what she was about to disclose next, her eyes became gigantic and she actually began to tremble as if the most explosive piece of gossip of all was travelling up through her body, about to torpedo out her mouth. At length, she breathlessly exclaimed, "I heard she was seeing two other men at once. Two men at the same time. Or even three if you counted her husband. Imagine that!"

"Damn fool to hitch up with her in the first place," Mr Tidd scoffed. "I warned him from the start about her being a money grabber. I mean to say, why would a young, good-looking girl like that marry a man of his age?"

A nasty case of the kettle and the pot, Doocey thought because even through his subpar eyes, Tidd's own wife looked to be a good twenty years younger than him. She also could be classified as marginally pretty whereas, with his bushy eyebrows and filthy teeth, Mr Tidd fell majorly into the ugly camp.

The Ambassador went on to introduce Doocey to several other of Nolan's similarly disloyal friends who largely repeated what the Tidds had said. Nolan had a traumatic past, a dangerous temper, was likely capable of physical violence and had marriage troubles. Though none of them had heard about Mrs Nolan having affairs with two other men or even just the one.

Doocey found that two hours had passed weirdly quickly. The moment he'd stepped into the embassy, time, after all, hadn't ground to a hellish halt. He even reckoned—to his disbelief—that he might be enjoying himself a little, and then, of course, he had to go and walk into a waiter causing a silver tray to launch into the air. People wildly screamed in horror as top-class caviar showered down upon them.

At that point, six glasses of champagne in, he surmised that it was best to call it a night.

With morning light streaming from the edges of his bedroom curtains, Doocey, doing battle with a hell of a hangover headache, struggled to mentally sift through what he'd learnt from the previous night's events or "Operation Nutcracker."

He thought it very sad, the story he'd heard of Nolan's brother dying as just a boy and that the origins of the man's OCD behaviour lay in this traumatic event.

Of potentially more use to his investigations were Mrs Tidd's claims that Harriet Nolan might have been seeing two men at the same time. If he presumed that Murphy, the gardener, was one of the two . . . that left another man to be tracked down. A mystery man he'd no idea how to locate or much less whether the fella would be of any assistance whatsoever in finding Harriet Nolan. Just to make things a little more impossible, he also needed to find this gent within two weeks because that's how long he now had until Ryan kicked his little arse off the case.

He worried too that the story of Mrs Nolan seeing two men at the same time might only be a figment of Mrs Tidd's gossipy imagination because when he'd discreetly asked, she hadn't been able to supply any names. He would've expected that she'd be able to at least name the Nolans' gardener, Murphy, as one of the two. The Nolans' other supposed friends hadn't been able to supply any names either, or even back up Mrs Tidd's two-man story.

Though it might just be that Harriet Nolan had the cop-on to try as much as possible to keep the backstabbing Tidds and their cohort in the dark about her love life.

Doocey ticked off in his mind, the other people he'd interviewed to date in his efforts to learn more about Nolan and his disappeared wife: the doctor, the housekeeper, and Mrs Nolan's best friend—that wagon Powell. Leaving only two people he wanted to speak with, ahead of speaking with Nolan himself: the gardener, Frank Murphy and Nolan's blind daughter, Jennifer. He was wary though about interviewing those two before first interviewing Nolan himself. Fearing Nolan might be annoyed to hear (which he surely would do if not from Murphy, definitely from his daughter) that some scruffy little detective had been asking questions behind his back, trying to rake up dirt on him.

There was no avoiding it then. The time had come for him to talk with Nolan. But what if he wouldn't talk? What if he directed him to his solicitor? Where would that leave him? "Up the bloody swanny," as Ber would later that morning put it, that's where it would leave him. "Cause nothing you've come up with so far is anywhere near strong enough to convict Nolan of murdering his wife or even proves that she has been murdered."

Ber, he knew, was of course right. His best chance of solving the case—like even the assistant commissioner had recognised—would come from interviewing Nolan and—and all going well—catching him out. Everything up to this point, like with a play, had really only been Act One—the build-up—and it remained to be seen if there would be an Act Two, where the real action should happen.

TEN

DRIVING UP ITS TREE-LINED AVENUE, Nolan Manor on the horizon looked like your ordinary historical mansion: ornate stone façade, sash windows and oversized front door. But as Doocey knew from the photos the forensics team had taken, and what Nelly Boyle and Tyson Tidd had described, the house's interior was a very different story.

Nolan Manor had been purchased by the deceased Mr Nolan senior—Mick Nolan. From what Doocey had read in newspaper archives, the man's reputation as being a corrupt builder seemed to be well-founded, even if he never served any jail time. There were so many allegations of Mick Nolan bribing politicians and planning officials that Doocey had been forced to conclude in Mick's case there was no smoke without fire or even a whole forest fire of smoke.

Doocey reckoned that the mere fact that Mick Nolan bought himself a British-built manor house on its own huge estate also pointed to the type of character he'd been. The poor Irish boy who'd done good and wanted all the world to know. Styling himself on the stereotypical British Lord of the Manor, even if the Republic of Ireland hadn't been a part of the British empire for well over a century.

Doocey would bet that Mick's only surviving child, Markus R. Nolan, as someone who'd grown up with a silver spoon stuck firmly in his mouth, even more personified the haughty Lord of the Manor. Someone who never did a real day's work in his life—the very type of entitled individual that made Doocey's skin crawl.

Memories of his Great Aunt Vee or Great Aunt B as he'd secretly renamed her, popped into his head. Nolan Manor, from the outside, also reminded him of Eyre Court, Great Aunt B's house. When Auntie B got truly desperate for her obnoxious child, Benjamin, to have company of his own age, she'd invite him to visit. As a young boy, Doocey had been awestruck by Eyre Court's massive size, making him feel as small as a field mouse and Great Aunt B also seemed to view him as little more than vermin.

She would make condescending comments about his coarse country accent, about how poorly he dressed, about his lack of social etiquette, about his very existence—constantly comparing him with her 'gifted' privately educated, athletic son. "Stand next to Benjamin," she'd command, and with glee entering her voice, trumpet, "Oh Benjamin is two heads taller. That is a surprise." Or, "Can any of you two boys tell me what number I'd get if I multiplied nine by nine by nine? No, it's not 88 Shamie . . . you silly boy. Excellent, Benjamin, 729."

Doocey had, however, let all of her vitriol fly over his head, just taking enjoyment from eating all her fancy food and playing with Benjamin's expensive toys.

A few years back, he'd been surprised to receive a visit from Great Aunt B who, having fallen foul of the taxman, had been reduced to living in a tiny caravan. She had been looking for or more demanding a favour from him. That as a serving detective, he would use his influence to have drug-dealing charges against her precious Benjamin dismissed.

"Oh, you silly, silly woman," he had responded, echoing how she used to love referring to him as: 'you silly boy.' "Surely you must know that it would be totally inappropriate for me to interfere and thwart the proper workings of the judicial system."

As he drew ever nearer the huge Nolan Manor, he found himself hoping that Markus R. Nolan would be just as arrogant an idiot as Great Aunt B. It would make his task so much easier.

He parked in front of the house—where there was enough space for a hundred cars. After giving his jammed driver's door a third good shove with his weak shoulder, it opened, and he literally fell out.

Even after getting back to his feet, his embarrassment continued, as he now noticed how close he'd parked to a large, ornate flower pot. If he'd gone another few millimetres forward, his front bumper would've surely toppled the pot and its red geraniums, and maybe it was just his wonky eyes, but the thing even already looked a bit lopsided.

He considered hopping back into his car to reverse a bit. What, though, if Markus R. Nolan was looking out from within, and what if the motion of reversing his Ford caused the bloody flower pot to keel over? That would be a disaster entirely.

Deciding to forget about the whole humiliating situation for the moment, he walked on, towards the house, but had only taken a few steps when some protruding pebbles sent him flying and he just about managed to save himself from falling onto his face. He straightened himself up. *God, what an entrance!*

The sound of pebbles crunching beneath his boyish-sized feet blended with the screams of seagulls overhead as he drew ever closer to the house's monstrous silhouette. He pressed a grubby finger on the sparkling door-bell button and within seconds the enormous front door swung open.

Doocey gazed up at the man standing before him, who, going by the photographs he'd seen, had to be Markus R. Nolan. Yet there was a niggling note of doubt in his mind because since he'd started seeing that tiny bit of fog, he was coming to doubt everything he saw. "Mr … Nolan?" he ventured.

"Yes," came the curt reply.

"Oh, good afternoon, Mr Nolan," he brightly continued, fumbling for his detective ID. "My name is Detective Shamie Doocey. I'm helping with the investigation into your wife's disappearance. Can I come in?"

For some moments, Nolan scrutinised both Doocey and his ID. No doubt asking himself, *Could this person truly be a detective?*

With a slow nod, he eventually—and incredibly—said, "Yes, do please come in."

Doocey gave a glance past Nolan into his vast hallway, and as if about to propose marriage, got down on one knee. "I'll just take off my shoes first. I wouldn't want to get dirt on your immaculate white marble floors."

In his stripy socks—a toe sticking through the left one—he stepped inside, into not at all your typical historical house interior. None of your dark-painted walls or masses of antique furniture or the stench of damp-ness. More like walking into this vast, airy, modern museum with one exception. This particular museum seemed to have been burgled of all its colourful artworks. "God," Doocey exclaimed, looking about at all the whiteness, "this is all very . . ." He paused, searching for another word besides white. "All very modern."

Nolan, sounding a little like a jaded tour guide, fed up with having to repeat the same thing to every halfwit tourist who stepped in off the street, began into abrupt explanations. "Years ago, after my father's death, I updated the old place. As you see, my tastes lean more towards minimalism."

Doocey reckoned Nolan's minimalist tastes also carried through to the man's appearance. No fussy tweed jackets and neck cravats for this would-be lord of the manor. Dressed as he was in a tailored black suit and the whitest of shirts, buttoned right to the top.

How Nolan was dressed, coupled with his full-on shaven head, blackish eyes, tall and broad stature, would mean he could easily pass for a nightclub doorman. Given his posh accent, however, it would most likely be a very exclusive nightclub. He looked young and strong enough for the job too—despite Doocey knowing him to be sixty-seven. He could easily envisage him hoisting some brawler on the dance floor up by their designer collar to toss them out onto the street.

He trailed Nolan into a large room at the front of the house that Doocey suspected, in a previous life, might have been a ballroom. The room's many windows looked out to the vast pebbled driveway where he'd so badly parked. Beyond that pebbled driveway were acres of regimentally neat gardens and in the far distance, a frenzied sea.

Doocey gave some long glances about the gigantic room which appeared severely under-furnished. There were only two leather sofas and a glass coffee table—adrift in a sea of oak floorboards. Nolan indicated for him to take a seat as he sat down on the sofa opposite. Doocey zipped open his anorak to reveal a faded grey suit jacket, a rumpled shirt, and a sagging paisley tie.

After checking all of his many pockets, he fished out a notebook and a clear plastic pen with a mangled top. Not that Doocey was genuinely one for notebooks and writing things down. He relied more on mental notes, and with years of practice, he reckoned he'd become fairly good at remembering people's exact words.

The notebook and pen he'd just unfurled were essentially only props. To make it look like there was some kind of method to his madness. As in he was properly documenting witness testimony and also not just firing out random questions—off the top of his messy-haired head.

Doocey gazed across at Nolan and he was struck by how composed he seemed. Sitting there, seemingly examining his lengthy fingernails for any traces of dirt. He would have expected a man whose wife was missing to be more shaken up.

Yet his gut, the same gut that was telling him shortly before this that Nolan was unquestionably a murderer, was annoyingly now just a tiny bit more doubtful. Could it even be possible that Dickson might just be right about Nolan having nothing to do with his wife's disappearance? That she had, after all, just accidentally fallen into the sea or thrown herself in and drowned. *God, what a nightmare that would be! If Dickson was right all along.* Though Doocey was in a major moral tizzy about how to feel. Because it wasn't right, was it, to hope, just for his own selfish detective ambitions, that a man had murdered his wife.

"I know, Detective Dickson took your original statement with regards to your wife's disappearance and has followed up with you since," Doocey said, glancing at his opened notebook.

"Still, if you wouldn't mind, I'd like to quickly run through that statement with you again. Just to get the sequence of events clear in my own head. Would you be okay with that?" and he had to stop himself from adding "Your Lordship" which had already wormed its way into his brain as his secret nickname for Nolan.

He hoped that he'd sounded casual. Like whether or not the man agreed to talk with him was no big deal. When really, it was the biggest deal in the world or at least in his world. It'd be so brilliant if the fecker would let him question him though he feared, more than ever, that Nolan was never going to be so stupid as to do that.

"Look Detective, let me be frank," Nolan suddenly began. "At this point, I believe Harriet is dead. It seems obvious to me that she slipped from the cliff path she'd been walking along and drowned." He bowed his head, momentarily falling silent.

Doocey could already hear inside his head what he reckoned *His Lordship* was about to say next. '*What therefore would be the point in going through my original statement again—unless you think she didn't drown and I murdered her.*'

Nolan raised his head. "However, as Harriet's body has not come ashore, I realise there's no proof that she drowned, and you have your job to do—to rule out any other possibilities. Therefore, I'm fine with going through my original statement. If you believe it will help."

Doocey, employing mental elbow grease to maintain an indifferent expression and tone, said, "That's much appreciated." He'd not expected it to be this easy to get Nolan to talk to him but his joy was short-lived as a new disheartening thought sprang up. By now Nolan would've had plenty of time to come up with lies to explain away those more suspicious parts of his original statement. Maybe he would even opt for outright denials that he'd ever said such and such.

Doocey flicked to a random notebook page of illegible writing. "According to my notes," he began, "your wife, Harriet, on Tuesday, the 15th of May at approximately 5:00 p.m. left the house here to bring Rupert, her white Icelandic sheepdog, for their usual cliff walk as far as an abandoned lighthouse. There and back would normally take them . . . let me see . . . forty-five minutes. You'd spotted her leaving from your library, where you'd been doing some writing. The weather at the time was extremely stormy. Your wife was wearing a blue raincoat, black jeans, and brown boots. It also looks like she took her house keys and her car key because these were later found to be missing. You also assumed she had her mobile on her because she never went anywhere without it."

He paused, and doing his best impersonation of a professional poker player's placid face, asked, "Now, have I got all that right?"

"Yes," Nolan replied in such a relaxed and free way that a weak-kneed Doocey had to resist the urge to ask him to repeat himself, even though he—ninety-nine percent knew—he'd heard him perfectly clearly. "Can I just go back to how you'd been writing in your library?" he managed to ask instead. "I understand that you write crime fiction?"

"Yes, that's correct," Nolan replied, sounding defensive.

"You're an actual crime writer, that's fantastic," Doocey exclaimed and proceeded to ask another question that he already knew the answer to: "Have you had many books published?"

"No."

"Oh, I see," he continued with a backward jolt of the head. "Is it that you've only taken up the old writing recently?"

"No. I've been writing since a very young age."

"It's more of a hobby? You're not interested in getting published?"

Nolan leaned sideways. "No, I would very much like to be published," he replied, with more than a whiff of irritation. "It's just the publishing world doesn't always recognise or understand great talent when they encounter it."

"Oh, I see . . ." Doocey said, pressing a hand to his forehead. "God . . . you must've great determination to keep on trying."

"I do," Nolan said, now sounding properly vexed.

"Well fair play to you," Doocey acknowledged and reverted to apparently reading from his notebook. "When Harriet hadn't arrived back by 7 p.m., you went to look for her. About a kilometre up the path, you found her dog, ah . . . Rupert . . . in a distressed state, clawing at the top of a dizzying cliff. With how stormy the day was, you feared the worst. You even bent down over the cliff edge but saw no sign of your wife, only waves pounding the rocks, far below."

Doocey flicked to a new page of scribbles. "You then rang the emergency services. As you waited for them to arrive, you tried ringing your wife's mobile but it went to voicemail. Thirteen minutes later the Coast Guard helicopter arrived on the scene, joined shortly afterwards by two lifeboats. But despite intensive sea searches at the time and in the intervening weeks, Harriet's body hasn't been found." Resting his notebook on his lap, Doocey glared across at Nolan. "Can I just check with you again, if I've got all that correct—or am I missing anything?"

Without the slightest hesitation, Nolan replied, "I think that appears to be the bones of it."

Bloody brilliant, Doocey thought, the knees now totally gone on him. The fecker was sticking with his flawed first statement, and what a clumsy way to have confirmed it. Surely as a writer, he could've come up with a less inappropriate phrase than *'the bones of it.' Although, he must be a really bad writer, despite his delusions of greatness, to be writing for his entire life without ever managing to get published.*

Gnawing the top of his already well-mutilated pen, Doocey mumbled, "You know a few things about what you say happened don't quite make sense to me." He gazed out at a colossal tree in full leaf which he was seeing as this misty green cloud. However, so caught up was he in playing mind games with Nolan, it hardly registered with him that worryingly he wasn't seeing the tree at all clearly,

"Perhaps, it would be useful to talk through whatever doesn't make sense to you," Nolan said. "See if I can't clarify matters."

Turning back to face Nolan, Doocey said, all casually, "You know that's probably not a bad idea."

ELEVEN

SCREWING UP HIS FACE, DOOCEY went on, "Thinking back to that Tuesday, it was truly a terrible day with wind and rain. I can't help but wonder . . . why on earth Harriet would've ventured out in such horrendous weather."

"There's no mystery whatsoever there, Detective," Nolan replied so rapidly that he might be a participant in a quick-fire quiz. "My wife is devoted to her dog and his well-being. Come rain, hail or whatever inclement weather, Rupert had to get his walk."

"Oh, I see," Doocey said deliberately flatly. "That makes more sense to me now, except . . ."

"Except?"

"Well, I'm a little confused about why your wife would've chosen such a dangerous route to walk her dog, given the stormy conditions of the day." He paused for an explanation but none was forthcoming. "I've walked that cliff path myself, a couple of times at this stage," Doocey went on. "I have to say, it scared the devil out of me. In many parts, it goes right to the verge." He enacted a shiver of trepidation before continuing. "The height of those cliffs is crazy . . . and anytime I've walked them, the weather has been lovely and calm. Nothing like the wild weather on the Tuesday Harriet disappeared. I can't understand for the life of me why your wife didn't take a more inland route." He gave a prolonged glance out one of the floor-to-ceiling windows. "Especially when there looks to be no shortage of lovely countryside—well away from the sea—around here."

"Evidently, Harriet thought she could handle it. She had walked that cliff path, probably a thousand times before, in all sorts of weather."

"That's a good point," Doocey acknowledged. Scribbling into his notebook as he muttered Nolan's words back to him, "She'd walked that cliff path a thousand times . . . in all sorts of weather." Then, appending in a lower voice, "Yet—*strangely*—only ran into trouble this one time."

Nolan cleared his throat. "I have to say, of course, that it was unwise of Harriet to choose the cliff path, but to quote Socrates, '*The only true wisdom is in knowing one knows nothing.*'"

Doocey looked up from his notebook with a deliberate expression of awe. "God that's brilliant, absolutely brilliant, Mr Nolan. I wish I had your brains—to be able to recite quotes off the cuff like that."

Nolan remained silent.

Doocey went back to his notebook and underlined some scribbles. "Oh yes . . . I wondered why Harriet would have taken her car key when she was only going for a walk. I mean, fair enough that she took her house keys, to let herself back in—but why her car key?"

"Oh, that's an easy one to explain. Her car key, or that is her car fob, was attached to her bunch of house keys. Therefore, she could not take one without taking the other."

"Unless she removed the car fob," Doocey contradicted.

"Why would she do that? It was more convenient that she kept them together. To prevent, when she was going out, her forgetting to take one of them." He half chuckled. "And I'm afraid my wife was rather prone to such forgetfulness. Harriet could be . . . well . . . for want of a better word . . . a little *scatty*." He half chuckled again. "It's also not as if the addition of a car fob was some huge, extra weight for her to haul about."

Doocey gave a few nods. "Well, that seems to nicely clear that one up. Now let's see what else was niggling at me," he briskly went on, once more pretending to consult his notebook. "Oh, that's right, I wrote here: 'What would I do if I was worried about where my Mrs *(my fictional Mrs)* had got to?'"

He proceeded to answer his own question. "Well, the first thing I think I'd do would be to give her a call on her mobile. Normally, there'd be a very simple explanation about why she'd gone off the radar. Say like her having bumped into some old chum, got chatting and lost all track of time." He grinned. "As happens a lot."

Doocey's grin died, and he held up a finger as if threatening his host with a minuscule blade. "But you, Mr Nolan, didn't ring your wife—not straight away at least." He whisked back through his notebook, coming to stare at a page of chaotic writing. "In your original statement, you said that you presumed Harriet had her phone on her person. That she never went anywhere without it." Looking up, he asked, "Why then did you not call her?"

Nolan swept a hand over his naked head. "I was worried I wouldn't have been able to get through to Harriet because her mobile would likely not have a signal down at the cliffs. Phone reception in these parts is dreadfully sporadic. Quite honestly—neither did I think I had time for dilly-dallying about, trying to get through on the phone to her."

He eyed Doocey cautiously for a long second. "I know this is going to sound strange, but I also had this peculiar feeling. A premonition, if you will—of something being wrong. I can't really explain it. I only can think it had something to do with the dreadful weather of the day. Before I'd ventured out to look for Harriet, the wind had begun to beat so savagely. I would have sworn—at any second—the library windows were going to come crashing in upon me."

Doocey began rooting at an inside anorak pocket and ultimately removed what looked like an oversized toy phone. "Well . . . that's a strange one . . . because I made a call back to the station, last time I was down at the cliffs . . . and I had no problems at all with reception."

Nolan returned a wry smile. "Why don't you try ringing the station now? See if you still have no issues."

Doocey stared down at his phone as if pondering Nolan's suggestion when really he was more checking if he could see clearly enough to dial the station's number without needing to put the phone too close to his eyes. "Okay so . . ." he said at last. "Let's give it a go."

When he finally peeled the phone from his ear, he exclaimed, "You're right! No signal."

Nolan stretched out his hands in an 'I told you so' fashion. "The house's three-foot stone walls are yet a further hindrance. To get reception, we normally have to go outdoors but even then, there is the difficulty of the proximity of the mountains."

"*Janey Mac* . . . that's bad, needing to go outside to make a phone call,"

Doocey said with a pained expression which morphed into one of confusion. "But why wouldn't you use the landline instead?"

"Because we don't have a landline," Nolan said gruffly as if feeling that Doocey already had to have known this (which he did). "Over the years, we've petitioned various phone companies for one. They all, however, declined, saying the necessary infrastructure would be too cost-prohibitive given how isolated Nolan Manor is, and the fact that we are only a single residence. Therefore, we are forced to rely on using mobile phones but unfortunately, as I've explained the reception is dreadful."

"But, even if it means stepping outside, eventually you do get a signal?"

"Yes, typically," Nolan sourly conceded.

Doocey looked down at the sock that had his big toe sticking out of it and muttered, "That's very strange . . ."

"What's very strange?"

The detective looked up again. A startled expression on his face, almost as if he'd forgotten there was someone else in the room with him. "Oh . . . it's just that Harriet's phone records, on the Tuesday, the day you reported her missing, show she never made a single call. Not one."

"I don't see why you think that especially strange," Nolan calmly countered.

Doocey cocked up his chin. "Don't you?"

"No, as you cited, the weather was wretched that day. I therefore presume Harriet wouldn't have wanted to stand outside, in the driving rain, for the sake of making a phone call. Or perhaps, exasperating the usual reception problems, the high winds may have knocked out a phone mast."

Doocey raised a stumpy finger. "That could be it! I'd better write that one down too. You know, I think it's you, Mr Nolan, that should've been the detective. The way your brain can come up with all these explanations so quickly is truly extraordinary."

Nolan gave an exaggerated smirk. "It's all simply common sense."

Doocey became much more animated, swaying from side to side in his chair as if a clock pendulum. "Well, I can tell you, I've met very few people who seem to have as much common sense as you. Very few." He stopped swaying and stared fixedly at Nolan for some moments before adding, "I'd say it's more to do with your crime writing. Needing to be able to think like a detective." *Or even like a murderer?* "Wouldn't you say?"

Only getting a "Perhaps" in reply, Doocey moved on. "On the Monday, the day before she disappeared, I understand Harriet had gone shopping and you were playing in a cricket match."

"Yes, that's right."

"Where did she go shopping? Was it to that posh place, Richmond Shopping Centre, by any chance?"

"Yes, as it happens, I believe it was."

Doocey made a mental reminder to have Ber get her hands on any CCTV footage from Richmond Shopping Centre to verify if Harriet Nolan had really gone there. He slapped his knee. "My Mrs is mad for that place too. You should see all the bags she lands home with." He gave a shake of his head. "I suppose yours is the same?"

"Yes . . . Harriet rather tends to be a big shopper," Nolan said tentatively as if suspecting some ulterior motive to the un-PC line of questioning, which of course there was.

As at that very moment, Doocey was wondering whether he might've caught Nolan out on a lie but for now he decided to move to his next question. "Had Harriet been in good form lately?" he asked and gripped the side of his glasses to shield against the sun pouring in through the fecking huge windows. The laser-like beams of light made the blasted fog in his eyes much more distracting.

Nolan looked momentarily mystified. "Well . . . now that I think back, recently Harriet seemed a little glum." Then an abrupt pause. "Is the sun bothering you, Detective? Shall I pull down a blind?"

"Oh no," Doocey said with a shaky smile, "It's fine." He cleared his throat. "You say your wife was feeling a little glum recently. Do you think she could've been feeling that way on the Tuesday she went missing?"

"Possibly—but Harriet was rather a master at hiding her true emotions."

Lowering his voice, Doocey said, "I hate raising this . . . but you don't think, do you, that she might have taken her own life?"

Nolan examined the knuckles of his right hand. "I suppose, regrettably . . . I can't deny that being a possibility."

"Did she ever talk about the subject?"

"Well . . . indirectly. Occasionally she'd make some disturbing comment. Wonder aloud with a great sigh, for instance, as to the point of it all. I remember her recently describing what sounded to me very much like panic attacks and her blacking out." Nolan looked suddenly distraught. "Gosh, Detective, you don't actually think my wife took her own life?"

"No," Doocey murmured, flicking through his notebook. "No, I don't think that at all, but in these types of situations, I'm obliged to ask . . . as a matter of routine."

Nolan threw back his head. "You seem terribly confident that Harriet did not take her own life . . ."

"Yes, I am, and would you like to know why?"

Nolan shrugged as if in substitution for the words, *Yeah, why not?*

"Well, it's very simple really. You see, I don't think a woman contemplating suicide would've brought along her dog. Particularly with the way you said Harriet adored hers so much. She'd hardly be so cruel to leave poor Rupert out in a storm. All alone."

"No, I suppose not . . . Though of course, if she were considering taking her life, one assumes she may not have been thinking straight. Furthermore, it may have only been a spur-of-the-moment, irrational decision."

The room turned murky as outside the troublesome sun disappeared behind a cloaking cloud.

"Yes . . . I suppose there's that . . . Though . . . would she not have left some sort of note?"

Nolan scrunched one dark eye shut. "Possibly, Harriet feared that if she were to have left a suicide note, I would blame myself. Perhaps, she thought it would be kinder to have me believe her death was accidental."

"Well, there you go again, Mr Nolan. I never thought about it from that angle. I guess we can't rule out suicide as a possibility." He repeatedly rotated his badly chewed pen. "Can I ask, when you noticed your wife feeling down, did you try to get her to see someone? Say like a doctor."

"Yes, many times," Nolan heatedly replied. Then the heat in his voice dwindled, "But regrettably Harriet suffered from this great fear of doctors though I never could get her to confide to me where this fear originated." Nolan placed a hand to his heart, "I truly did my level best to persuade her to seek help but to no avail." He inhaled deeply. "I therefore had to be content with attempting to cheer her up. Attempting to convince her things weren't as black as she imagined them."

"I see," Doocey said, sensing Nolan's sincerity. His claim that his wife had a fear of doctors also tallied with what her best friend, that cow Powell, had said about doctors terrifying Harriet because, as a child, she'd been abused by one—something, if Nolan was to be believed, she had kept from him. He went on aloud, "Your wife wasn't on any medication, was she? No anti-depressants?

"No."

"I think those are all my questions," Doocey said, standing up, only for a second later to sit back down again. "Oh yes, I almost forgot to ask you about your security cameras."

Nolan returned him a disbelieving *yeah right* kind of expression as if already having judged that the detective wasn't one for such forgetfulness, and if that was what he was thinking, he was bang on.

Doocey had nearly thought of nothing else but those security cameras since learning from Dickson's investigation file that they were located all over Nolan Manor, both inside and outside. There was never then the least chance that he wasn't going to ask about them. Their footage could prove crucial to finding out what really happened to Harriet Nolan. Maybe the footage would even show if she'd been murdered by her husband. Doocey looked down at his notebook and after a few seconds back to Nolan. "I believe, your father, originally arranged to have the security cameras put in?"

"Yes, when Nolan Manor had been stuffed full of so-called antiques—notwithstanding that the majority of which were cheap replicas—the company that insured the house had nevertheless insisted on the installation of the security cameras. That's one of the ugly black things over there."

He raised a finger to the far-right corner and Doocey gawked to where he pointed. Then said as a question, "Our forensic people reported that all the cameras were switched off?"

Nolan sat up a little taller. "That's correct. With the house largely divested of all its two-bit antiques, the insurance requirement no longer pertained that the cameras be operational."

The formalness of Nolan's words struck Doocey. They sounded like those of a cagey defence solicitor, and he wondered if they'd been rehearsed in advance.

Nolan continued, less formally, "To be honest, having the dreadful things switched on also made me feel rather uncomfortable. Like I was being constantly watched—as if one were a prisoner in one's own home."

Doocey stood up again. "Would you mind if I take a look upstairs . . . at Harriet's and your bedroom?"

"I don't understand why any further inspections should be necessary," Nolan snapped, also having got to his feet. "Especially, when those forensic people of yours spent so long snooping about. Is there something, in particular, you need to see?"

Doocey silently answered. *Well . . . it's more a case of there being something I'm hoping not to see.*

TWELVE

"OH, IT'S NOT REALLY AN inspection," Doocey mumbled aloud, but his attention seemed focused on his anorak cuff. He began scraping at some sort of crispy brown matter, causing Nolan to shudder in disgust. Just the kind of reaction the detective had been hoping for even if he did feel terrible about using Nolan's cleanliness OCD to deliberately torment him, but as Nolan seemed to be such a cool-headed liar, he needed some way to unnerve him.

Still scraping away, Doocey continued, "I'll only be a minute, and as I'm sure you'll appreciate our forensic people needed to be thorough."

"Yes," Nolan said, keeping his gaze lofty as if to avoid seeing any more of Doocey's vile antics, "whilst one can appreciate that—one would've thought, however, their time might have been better spent at the location where my wife actually disappeared. That is to say, down at the cliffs, rather than going about swabbing every surface in my home."

"Maybe so," Doocey murmured, still occupied by his cuff. "That said . . . God only knows what clues they might've found in the house, here." He looked up to cast Nolan a quizzical look. "Suppose, for example, they found a trace of blood."

Nolan bellowed, "What do you mean—a trace of blood?"

After a long pause, Doocey elaborated, "Well, what if, for instance, your wife had some sort of a fall in the house and hit her head? Remember how you were telling me there about how she'd been having what you reckoned might be blackouts?"

Nolan chose not to respond.

"Say Harriet experienced another one of those blackouts and fell, that could give us a good indicator about what might have happened to her." He paused interrogatively but Nolan stayed silent. "Down at the cliffs she might have had a follow-on blackout," he continued, "and, *Lord help us*, fell into the sea."

"I see," Nolan said acidly. "And did your people actually recover any trace of blood?"

"Oh, I'm afraid they're still working on the samples they took away, so it's too early to say." This was a lie, of course, because as Doocey knew damned well, the results of any forensic testing conducted had long since come back and were contained in Dickson's investigation file.

Though going by the current conversation, Dickson must not have discussed them with Nolan. However, Doocey wondered if this had been the wrong strategy on the dope's part. Whether it might be worth bringing Nolan up to speed about some odd things in the forensic reports. Maybe it would be a good idea just to suddenly blurt them all out. Try using the element of surprise to trip *His Lordship* up.

Nolan said, "Strange, I would have imagined that blood should be quite straightforward a substance to identify and not take weeks to do so."

Doocey shuffled about. "I'll have to bow to your knowledge on that one, Mr Nolan. I'm not that up on the science end of things myself." *Now, are you going to let me go upstairs or not?*

After taking a deep breath, Nolan muttered, "Let's get this over with." He stomped out into the main hall, and at the bottom of the huge marble staircase, he held out an arm for Doocey to hurry on and catch up, much like a frustrated parent directing a distracted child.

Doocey's attention, however, seemed to be again elsewhere. "I can't get over how huge this place is." He stopped to gaze upwards as if he might be singling out stars in the night sky and had all the time in the world. At length, he chuckled. "What my Mrs wouldn't give for a house like this!"

Nolan heatedly replied, "If your wife only knew all the effort that went into the upkeep of such a giant old pile, I promise you she wouldn't be so keen."

Doocey chuckled again. "Yeah, no doubt you're right there. She complains enough already about all the housework to be done in our little terrace. God only knows what she'd be like with this massive baby."

"How long have you been married?" Nolan asked, half smiling.

"Oh, about eighteen years now."

His Lordship shot a protracted stare at Doocey's left hand as if to silently ask, *Where's the wedding ring?*

Feeling the weight of the stare, Doocey fidgeted—positive Nolan knew fine well that Mrs Shamie Doocey was only a fictional creation. A fictional creation to encourage *His Lordship* to open up to him. To have him believe that he too knew what it was like to be the put-upon husband. That they were—after all—in the same married boat.

"I hate wearing blasted rings," he explained, determined not to let Nolan have the satisfaction of knowing he'd caught him out in a lie.

At a much slower pace than Nolan, Doocey followed behind, hating the steep incline of the marble staircase. A dangerous staircase for someone with bad sight though ideal for someone intent on murder—one good push from the top would nicely dispose of their victim.

Doocey made it to the upstairs hallway, and even though Nolan was waiting impatiently for him outside an open bedroom door, he failed to go to him. Instead, he ambled over to an object that stood out as a rarity given the stark décor of Nolan Manor—a photograph. A photograph with an entire vast white wall to itself and was of the Nolans on their wedding day or so Doocey had first presumed.

Now, he started to doubt, again, his faulty eyes. He worried that he might not be looking at the newlywed Mr and Mrs Nolan but some other couple entirely. The thought of Nolan mortifyingly pointing out his mistake already making his face flush.

He took a step closer to the photo and told himself to cop on; it had to be of them. The only picture Nolan had hanging on his wall was hardly going to be of another couple on their big day. "Ahh, you and Harriet when you got married," he now exclaimed in excited tones. "My! Harriet looks so beautiful." Or even 'stunning' or the 'perfect blonde bombshell' to quote journalists' descriptions.

"Yes," Nolan acknowledged, coming to stand beside him, and sounding more relaxed than before. "I've often admired how radiant Harriet looks in that picture. As if she were the exquisite creation of some master Renaissance artist—at any moment about to step free of her golden frame."

"If I remember correctly, you were sixty when you married, and Harriet would've been thirty. So there are thirty years between you?"

Nolan's face hardened, but he gave no reply.

"You've been married seven years. That would make you sixty-seven now and Harriet thirty-seven?"

Nolan said, "Very good Detective. Glad to see there's nothing wrong with your simple arithmetic."

Doocey ignored the snide aside and said again how beautiful Harriet looked.

Nolan emitted a sigh of irritation and looked Doocey in the eye. "I know what you're thinking, Detective. Why would a gorgeous young woman like Harriet, an ex-glamour model for Pete's sake, who had her pick of handsome young men, take on a crumbling ruin like me? Other than for my money as all my stuffy friends had presumed. However, Harriet wasn't like that and to hell with what my stuffy friends or anybody else for that matter might think. Only I knew the real—the complex—Harriet."

His voice grew in passion. "The person who had worked two jobs to pay for her mother's medical bills. The person who for three years had tried to make a go of her first marriage—despite the almost daily beatings from her thug of a first husband. The person who despite outward confident appearances was an innately shy, intellectual individual. Harriet would turn pink just watching a romantic movie. Yes, she might have had a forte for such frivolities as shopping but equally, she had a forte for the arts. She adored classical music, adored the theatre, adored art."

Nolan released another sigh, now gazing into the eyes of his wife on their wedding day. "Harriet was the only person who truly believed in me. Believed in me as a writer. She was my soulmate." He fell silent.

The passion that had been in the man's voice made it so tough for Doocey not to believe that he hadn't genuinely loved his wife. In turn, this made him feel even stronger that he had not murdered her. Doocey again consulted his notebook, and after a suitable pause, continued at pace as if in a hurry to get what he had to read—read out.

"Oh, I forgot to check . . . I understand Harriet was an only child and her parents, Peadar and Peggy Reilly are both deceased. Her closest surviving blood relative is an aunt, a Bridgie Reilly, but Harriet had lost touch with her in recent years."

"Yes, that's all correct," Nolan confirmed.

Doocey looked up from his notebook, "I'm afraid we've had no luck—so far—in tracing Aunt Bridgie."

"I can well imagine how difficult it can be to find some people," Nolan said, and placing a hand on the detective's back, he steered him onward into a bedroom.

"Someone likes pink," Doocey exclaimed as he pocketed his notebook and squinted at the room's walls, painted in a dust pink, with the carpet in the same colour. Adding with an exaggerated sniff, "I think it even smells of pink roses in here."

With Nolan watching on, Doocey strode over to a bedside cabinet, slid open its one drawer and took a quick look inside—before closing it again. Strolling around to a matching cabinet on the other side of the bed, he did the same. Catching Nolan's eye, he quizzed, "Was Harriet one for writing down her thoughts? Did she happen to keep a diary?"

"No," Nolan replied in a tone that to Doocey's ear sounded altogether too categorical, as if he were lying. So he decided he might as well have a go at lying back.

"The only thing is . . . when someone goes missing, it's standard procedure to go through their banking transactions and it looks like your wife, last December, bought herself a diary for this current year. Any idea where that diary has got to?"

"No, none," Nolan replied, again all too categorically.

Then much more hurriedly, as if a brilliant—get out of jail—explanation had just occurred to him, added, "Have you considered that Harriet may have purchased the diary as a gift for a friend? You say she bought it in December—so perhaps as a Christmas present."

Doocey pressed a hand to the side of his head. "Well, you know . . . now that you say it . . . that just might be it," whilst thinking, *you had to give the swine credit for so quickly coming up with such good lies.*

He proceeded—multiple times—to pace around the vast four-poster bed, surveying the floor as if he'd lost a valuable possession. Coming to a standstill, he peered into a walk-in wardrobe and gave a little whistle. "Boy, this is some size. It's as big as any clothes shop." Stepping inside, he frisked a hand across woollen coats, glittering ball gowns, several white silk scarfs, and rows of high heels. Meanwhile, Nolan had taken to staring out a window at a cloudy sky. In due course, Doocey shouted out to him, "Did you notice any of your wife's clothes missing?"

"No," Nolan said, coming to stand at the entrance of the walk-in wardrobe.

Doocey looked at him with a raised eyebrow. "Not even a blue raincoat or a pair of black jeans or a pair of brown boots?"

A few moments of silence followed, during which Nolan seemed to be pondering *what the hell the fool was on about now*. Then enlightenment seemed to strike. "Oh, yes . . . but had I not last seen Harriet wearing those items, I'm afraid I would never have been able to tell they were missing. She just has so many clothes."

"Indeed, she does," Doocey said, hauling out one hanger after another to inspect the labels of individual garments. Making sure not to hold them too close to his glasses, more afraid than ever of Nolan copping there was something up with his eyes.

"Can't find anything in your size, Detective?"

"No, Mr Nolan, it's not that," he glumly replied, and as he stared hard at the inside collar of a priestly black blouse, added, "It's just that this wardrobe has me confused."

"How so?"

Doocey's voice took on a more confident air. "Remember, how we were talking about your wife being a big shopper? Always coming home with lots of purchases."

"Yes, and what's your point?"

"Well, it's just with her going shopping at Richmond Shopping Centre the day before she went missing, I would have expected to find some new clothes purchases in here with their tags attached but there aren't any. Neither are there any shopping bags in here or that I spotted out there."

Nolan gave a cursory scan of the wardrobe and then around the rest of the bedroom. "No . . . you seem to be correct." He paused. "I can only therefore assume if Harriet made any purchases, she must have immediately disposed of the shopping bags and labels."

"That's what she must've done alright," Doocey murmured, emerging from the wardrobe.

Nolan walked back out into the hall but his visitor stayed put in the bedroom, looking in at the walk-in wardrobe, pretending to be once again bewildered.

"Something else Detective?" Nolan called from the doorway.

"Oh, it's probably nothing but I'm just noticing now how this wardrobe only seems to have women's clothes. Where's all your stuff?"

"My clothes are in my room," Nolan irritably informed.

"Oh, you and your wife have separate rooms?"

"Yes—and I'd be very surprised if your forensic pals, who have been into every last nook and cranny of the house, hadn't already made you aware of this."

"You know . . ." Doocey said, looking up to the bedroom ceiling, "I think . . . I remember something in one of their reports, alright, about seeing a wardrobe full of black suits and white shirts in a separate room." He looked to his host. "Like what you're wearing."

"Yes," Nolan said. "Similar as it seems to yourself, I'm not one for fashion. I stick to wearing a classic black suit and white shirt." He fixed Doocey with a condescending stare. "Though of course, I do make sure to have fresh ones for every single day."

"Good man, yourself," Doocey said back with the biggest of riling smiles his jaw would stretch to.

When he stopped smiling, his tone became reticent. "If it's not too much of a personal question for me to ask . . ." He looked to the floor before gazing up at an impatient-looking Nolan and continuing. "I was wondering . . . what's the reason for the separate rooms?"

Nolan scratched behind his ear for several seconds before a hint of a smile appeared at the corners of his lips. "Regrettably, I'm a terrible snorer," he said at last.

"Me too," Doocey shot back with a little laugh. "Though thankfully, the Mrs hasn't banished me to the spare room—just yet."

Sauntering across the hallway, Doocey peered in through an open doorway and was very surprised by what he saw—considering Nolan's liking for white walls—a bedroom of clashing colours. The bedspread was a garish green colour, the carpet an orangey brown, and the armchair a bright purple.

"Whose room is this?" he asked aloud though already fairly certain that it had to be Jennifer Nolan's room which would explain the clashing colours. As a blind person, her priority wouldn't be that things matched seeing as she couldn't see colour. She would be more interested in how things felt. Ergo the smooth silky green material of the bedspread, the—sink your feet into—orangey brown, woollen carpet and the velvety purple armchair.

"My daughter, Jennifer, uses this room when on the very odd occasion she decides to stay over," Nolan confirmed. "She has an apartment in Dublin."

"Oh, very good, and I understand Jennifer is blind . . .?"

"Yes, she is," Nolan snarled, seeming to have taken offence that Doocey had even dared to bring up the topic of her blindness. "Nevertheless, Jennifer is a very contented and fulfilled person," he continued, "She's a remarkably talented singer and is well on the way to being one of the best sopranos Ireland has ever produced."

"That's really fantastic," Doocey hurriedly rejoined, genuinely not having intended to cause any offence. Because though he'd yet to meet Jennifer, even from what he had heard about her from Nolan's ex-housekeeper and just now from Nolan, he could not help but already admire her. Like his own mother, and he hoped like himself, it seemed that Jennifer Nolan was not one for sitting around feeling sorry for herself. She made the best of the fecking hand she'd been dealt.

Thinking about it, he could understand Nolan's tetchiness too on the subject of his daughter's blindness. Probably sick to death of people's pitying reactions, like, "Ah she's blind, the poor thing." Doocey remembered his mother often telling him of instances of people who'd been stood right in front of her, making similar comments to each other, as if assuming that her not being able to see that well also meant she wasn't able to hear well either or worse, hadn't even the capacity to understand them. "You must be extremely proud," Doocey added.

"I am."

"Your daughter wasn't in the house the Tuesday your wife went missing?"

"No. Jennifer very much values her independence. As I said, she only stays over very occasionally and she's got her own place. She also tours a lot."

"Before your wife went missing," Doocey persisted, "when had Jennifer stayed here last?"

"Oh, I would say . . . well over a month previous."

"On the day Harriet went missing, only you and she had been staying in the house?"

Nolan expelled a huff. "Yes. I went through all this with the first detective, I think he happened to be called Dickson. By the way, where's he disappeared off to?"

"Oh, he's gone nowhere," Doocey said and hell-for-leather proceeded to his next question. "You don't have a housekeeper?"

"No."

"You used to have one though?"

He pretended to read from his notebook. "A Mrs Nelly Boyle who left your employment a few months back."

"Yes," Nolan snapped. "I'm not sure why it is that you need to repeat questions that, as I say, I've already provided answers for."

"Oh, it's just that I like to check information first-hand."

Nolan released a weary sigh which Doocey chose to ignore.

"It must be hard having to make do without a housekeeper. I mean, in a house this size. You must really miss having Mrs Boyle around."

"Not particularly," Nolan replied. "The woman was a terrible housekeeper and I'd been hoping to find someone much better. Before all this upset, I'd been doing interviews for the post." He paused. "It's frightfully tricky though to find a competent housekeeper these days."

"I can imagine," Doocey said mechanically, not looking up from his notebook. "You have a gardener though—don't you? A Frank Murphy."

"Yes."

"Was he here on the Tuesday your wife went missing?"

The tone of Nolan's voice became more irritable. "No, as I already told your colleague, Mondays and Tuesdays are his days off."

"Grand," Doocey nonchalantly responded but was thinking, *How fecking convenient.* "Does Mr Murphy live on the grounds of Nolan Manor?"

A dog began barking.

"No," Nolan replied, having to yell to be heard over the background disturbance.

Doocey now too, raised his voice though he would really prefer not to do so. He always felt himself getting embarrassed whenever cornered into speaking loudly. He reckoned it complicatedly went back to his school days, and being chased by bullies around the yard, and having to scream like a baby for the teacher to rescue him.

"I've it in my notes that Mr Murphy has access to a cabin at the back of the house. Does he ever stay overnight there?"

The dog stopped barking. *Wouldn't you know it!*

"I would say it's more akin to a small garden shed than a cabin but regardless of how you label it, Murphy purely uses the place for his meals and—no—doesn't sleep there."

"Is he about today?"

"No. He's gone camping for a few days—to the wilds of Connemara."

"Would you have a phone number for him?"

"No. Actually . . . I do not believe he owns a mobile. He's rather one of those new-age hippie sorts. The kind who shuns modern technologies."

"Not to worry . . . I'm sure, I'll track him down."

The dog began howling again, and in this loud, chirpy voice, Doocey said, "Oh, that must be Rupert I hear." Putting his ear against the door opposite, he asked, "Do you mind if I take a gander? I've never seen an Icelandic sheepdog before."

"If you wish, but I'd be careful. The animal has a nasty side. He's bitten me in the past."

"I'll only have a quick peep," Doocey replied as he edged the door open, just wide enough to slither himself inside.

"Don't say—I didn't warn you," Nolan called after him.

Doocey re-emerged, a minute or so later, cradling in his arms a huge chalky-white dog but owing to the detective's smallness, it more looked like he was cradling a great polar bear. "I've never come across a more beautiful creature," he remarked, rubbing his cheek into the dog's back. "He feels identical to cotton wool." Taking a large sniff, he added, "He smells so good too—like a field of flowers."

"That will be owing to the special shampoo Harriet uses to wash him," Nolan explained. Adding in a scoffing tone, "Nothing but the best for that animal."

"Well, she does a great job. His coat is spotless, not a smidgen of dirt." Another one of Doocey's confused looks ensued but for the moment no follow-up question.

After returning Rupert to his very own swanky bedroom, Doocey announced that he'd better be getting going. As he followed Nolan's lead down the perilous marble staircase, he gripped its handrail so tightly that his knuckles turned white.

At the front door, Doocey picked up one of his shoes and stared pensively at its muddy sole.

When almost a minute had passed and he was still studying the shoe, Nolan exclaimed, "What's wrong now?"

"Oh, I'm sure it's nothing at all . . . I was just thinking about your Rupert."

"Yes—what about the animal?"

"Well, I was just thinking how he must have been fierce dirty from being left out in the storm after Harriet had gone missing."

Raising the muddied bottom of his shoe right up to the face of a horrified-looking Nolan, who'd automatically jerked backwards, he continued, "I mean to say, look at the state of this. All that mud is from when I last strolled down to the cliffs, and that wasn't nearly as wet a day. The mud that Tuesday must've been terrible altogether."

"Yes, it was," Nolan said, swiftly opening his front door. "The dog—not unsurprisingly then—had been absolutely filthy—so I naturally gave him a thorough wash."

"Ahh, I see . . . that makes sense," Doocey said. He smiled and waving a finger, teased, "You even took the trouble to use the special shampoo your wife had bought so that he'd smell all nice."

After finally taking his leave of Nolan and once he'd sat into his car, Doocey patted his chest, to double-check that what he'd stolen from Nolan Manor was there, hidden away in an inside anorak pocket. Reassured to feel its bulk, even though he didn't know yet why he'd taken the risk of stealing the item. He just had this feeling that the thing might come in handy at some future point.

He started the engine and began reversing. Then disaster. The movement of his Ford caused the bloody flower pot that he'd parked too close to (and that he'd totally forgotten about) to topple with a noisy thud. He yanked up his handbrake and swung his driver's door open, expecting at any second to hear Nolan come charging out.

With a herculean fecking effort Doocey managed to straighten back up the giant flower pot which now had a big crack running down one side, and scooped in most of the scattered soil before squashing in the red geraniums.

Then—foot to the pedal—he sped off, praying Nolan hadn't been standing at a window, watching everything. After jetting out the gates of Nolan Manor, Doocey parked up again, feeling he needed a nice walk and a soothing bit of sea air to calm himself down. Plus, it should be a good way of getting his thoughts straight about what he'd just heard from Nolan, and hopefully, even a bit of inspiration might strike.

He headed towards the whispering sea, cutting across this grassy area, until he came onto the cliff path that Harriet Nolan had allegedly fallen from. The sound of the sea, no longer a whisper but a thunderous holler.

He'd only walked for another minute when he felt the twist of his right foot where the path unexpectedly dipped. "Feck it anyway," he burst out, bending down to rub his tender ankle, and thinking back to his earlier stumble outside Nolan Manor. *God, what was happening to him?* Yet he still didn't want to admit to himself that these two stumbles in quick succession had any connection to his sight issues—wanting to believe it to be just his usual clumsiness.

He collapsed down on a grassy bank, only for briar bushes he had not really noticed to prick into his back, and he felt the trickle of blood. Above the racket of the unrelenting sea, he wondered again if Harriet Nolan had been telling the truth when she'd told her doctor that she'd got those bruises to her neck from falling onto briar bushes. Maybe, even from falling onto the very same briar bushes that had just injured him.

He stood up and started to limp back to his car, still mad as hell at his supposed awkwardness. Overhead a bundle of—about to burst—clouds crept after him. So much for going for a walk to calm himself down. He felt more frazzled than ever. No chance now of being able to think straight, or for inspiration to strike.

But—just as he sat back into his driver's seat—a glorious flash of inspiration did strike, and he experienced a swell of excitement rising within him as fat raindrops began to fall. He released the handbrake and sped off, but within minutes was tapping on the brake to slow down a bit, telling himself to calm the feck down since what he was thinking of might not even exist, or, if it existed, might prove to be of no use whatsoever. *Or could just prove to be crucial.*

As he drove along at a reduced speed, with his car wipers whizzing, his doubts grew all the stronger that the potentially key piece of evidence existed—because surely if it had existed, Dickson would have already gotten his hands on it.

Although, with how convinced Dickson had been that Harriet Nolan hadn't been murdered, just maybe the dummy never bothered his incompetent arse to check.

THIRTEEN

DOOCEY PULLED INTO A PETROL station, a few kilometres up the road from Nolan Manor. On exiting his car, he looked upwards at a huge sign and smiled on reading the forecourt shop's name: *'On the Run.'* As if literally a sign from above, encouraging him to keep going—that he'd the murderer 'on the run.'

For a few more moments he stood gawping upwards, looking for something, before rushing into the shop. Twenty minutes later, Doocey re-emerged, carrying two small boxes, proof that the basis of his flash of inspiration—incredibly—existed in reality.

One box contained CCTV footage of inside the shop and the other contained footage from outside, and it was this outside footage that he was most interested in. Interested because—as the shop manager had shown him on a monitor behind the sweet counter—the camera on the roof that pointed to the forecourt pumps—fantastically—had in the background the only road into Nolan Manor in frame; the footage should then show every vehicle that entered and exited Nolan Manor on the day Harriet Nolan was reported missing, as well as in the days before and after.

He would be interested in seeing one vehicle in particular, Nolan's SUV. Because sticking to the assumption that he'd murdered his wife, he would've had to dispose of her body and he only had two options when it came to this.

One, dispose of the body on the lands of his huge isolated estate or in the surrounding sea (which Doocey thought was the most likely option as it meant less risk of him being seen). Two, go somewhere else to dispose of the body, meaning he'd have to drive past the petrol station.

Doocey sat into his car, placed the CCTV boxes on his passenger seat, and got out his phone to ring his mother, to debrief her on how his meeting with Nolan had gone.

As he expected, she straightaway wanted to know if he'd now a better idea of whether the crime writer had murdered his wife. A question that should be easy enough to answer 'yes' to, going by all the gaps and inconsistencies in Nolan's account of events. Yet, that earlier inkling of doubt about him being guilty persisted and maybe even was getting stronger. "I'm still not sure," was how Doocey finally answered. "I'll need to do more digging."

"Oh … right," his mother replied, in a tone steeped with disappointment.

No doubt thinking that had she been in his detective shoes she'd have definitely known by now if Nolan was guilty or not.

Their conversation moved to talking about his mother's latest big passion, darts. Her visually impaired team had gone to play a match against the local pub's team, captained by the pub owner Paddy—this chubby, friendly man who always had a smile plastered on his face. Although according to Mrs Doocey, Paddy and his darts team had been altogether too friendly. She felt as if they hadn't played nearly at their best. That they had been just throwing them, 'the poor blind people' games out of pity.

"So I ordered my team to lay down their darts," she explained. "And I told Paddy there was no point in us playing on, seeing as how his team were just letting us win. They might as well just gift us the silver cup. That we didn't want their bloody pity. That we'd rather lose or win fair and square, and with that, we all marched out."

On getting back to the station, Doocey asked Ber to come with him into interview room 2C and similar to his mother's reaction, she seemed less than impressed with what she heard of how his interview with Nolan had gone.

"Even after spending all that time with him—you're still not sure if he murdered her?" she'd asked in an accusatory way.

"Yeah . . . I'm just not sure," he repeated and as a distraction tactic, quickly passed her over the box with the external petrol station CCTV footage, and after shyly asking if she could review it, they talked through what she should look out for.

Less than two hours later, Ber came over to Doocey's desk to report that she'd spotted something "extremely interesting" on the CCTV, not concerning Nolan or his disappeared wife, but concerning their gardener. This very clever discovery by Ber made Doocey more anxious than ever to speak with Frank Murphy.

FOURTEEN

AFTER THE CLIMB UP THE steep path behind Nolan Manor, Doocey paused to catch his breath before giving two polite knocks on the cabin door. He shivered. The lunchtime sky overhead, a slab of icy grey.

The door in front of him swung open, and he found himself gazing up at a man wearing a luminous green vest, a man built like a professional wrestler. One tiny punch from this gent, Doocey was sure, would smash his glasses into a million pieces and in the process smash his entire face.

"Yeah," *Mr Muscles* snarled.

Provoked to do so by the ignorant greeting, Doocey, for no other reason than to annoy, leisurely perused notebook pages, pleased to feel the oaf's irritation radiating like a scorching sun down upon him.

"Ahh . . . yes," he finally exclaimed and looked up. "Are you Frank Murphy, Mr Nolan's gardener?"

"If I am, what's it to you?"

"I'm Detective Doocey—"

With thumbs hooked around his cowboy-buckle belt, Murphy scoffed, "You're a detective? Pull the other one!"

This compelled Doocey to yank out his official ID. After gaping—at length—at the said ID, the gardener gruffly apologised for not believing him to be a detective, and in a feeble attempt to excuse his behaviour, explained how there were always salespeople calling. "Mr Nolan isn't home," Murphy further explained. "He's gone for lunch to his private members club on Saint Stephen's Green. He said he'd be back at three."

"Oh, that's fine, I wanted to have a quick chat with yourself, anyway. Do you mind if I come in for a minute?"

Not giving Murphy a chance to object, Doocey edged past him. The cabin inside was deceptively spacious. He reckoned it might even be bigger than his own poky apartment. A far cry from the shoe-boxy garden shed that Nolan's descriptions had conjured up in his mind, although, compared to the massive footprint of Nolan Manor, he could understand why *His Lordship* might think the cabin minuscule. He liked too how the weighty wooden logs out of which the cabin had been constructed smelt like they'd only been freshly felled from the forest.

Doocey ambled over to a plastic yellow table, on which was a red mug, emitting the scent of some sort of herbal tea, maybe nettle. On the floor, to the right of the table, he observed a damp towel draped over what seemed to be seriously heavy dumbbells.

A slightly ajar door to an inner room also caught his attention—and what might be a camp bed. He wondered with irritation if a person without his sight issues could have easily told if it was a bed or not. Doocey plucked out a plastic chair. A chair which was the same dandelion yellow as the table it had been hiding beneath and which, like a dandelion, seemed to weigh nothing. As he sat himself down, fresh annoyance swept over Murphy's face.

"I have a lot of work to be getting on with," the gardener said, plopping himself down onto a matching chair that looked comically teeny for a man his size and which Doocey reckoned was in real danger—*and wouldn't that just serve him right*—of collapsing beneath the fecker, especially with it only been made of plastic and being the weight of a weed. Murphy elaborated, "Mr Nolan needs some hedging trimmed."

"Oh, very good," Doocey said in an indifferent tone as he flicked through his notebook. "Now let me see, you weren't working the Tuesday, Mrs Nolan went missing?"

"No, I am off on Mondays and Tuesdays."

Doocey looked up from his notebook and gaped, open-mouthed, at Murphy as if he'd just seen a burly ghost. "God, those are some arm muscles you've got. You must do a lot of training?"

Murphy's serious expression lightened a little. "Yeah, I try to work out every day."

"Every single day. That's some commitment!"

Murphy's mouth showed the trace of a smile of pride.

"I know," Doocey continued, "you said you weren't working the day Mrs Nolan went missing, but might you have been here in the cabin, doing some weights?" He gave a long deliberate gaze across to the dumbbells.

"Nope," Murphy said and Doocey got the strong feeling that he was lying.

"Would you ever sleep the odd night here at all?"

Another unconvincing, "Nope."

The detective let out a low cry of pain, squeezing his right knee. "Damn leg freezes up when I sit," he said, standing up and hobbling across to the cabin's inner door which with an elbow—he not so furtively—attempted to nudge a bit more open.

"Having a good snoop?" Murphy hollered and proceeded to sip some of his nettle tea.

"I thought you said you never stayed here overnight. What's the bed for then?"

The gardener folded his beefy arms, concealing his entire chest behind them. "Just for the odd nap, when I'm on lunch," he muttered. "I don't stay over."

"I see . . ." Doocey said in a dubious tone, before asking, "What was Mrs Nolan like as a person?"

Murphy gave him a startled look, seemingly surprised at the sudden change in direction of questioning. "I don't know her that well," he said at last. "Mr Nolan is the one who gives me my orders about what needs doing in the gardens."

"Is he a nice boss?"

"He's alright . . ." Murphy said, but in such a wintry way as to strongly suggest that Nolan was far from '*alright*.'

"How long have you been working here?"

"About a year."

Doocey strolled over to the cabin window. "I have to say you keep the gardens in magnificent shape. Every blade of grass is millimetre-perfect." He made his observation with an air of total confidence, a confidence not coming from what he was actually seeing out the window, which was very little, as right now, the fog in his eyes was particularly bad. No, it came from his earlier close-up inspection of the lawns. He'd even gone so far as to get down on his knees to try to better see the said millimetre-perfect blades of grass.

Murphy appended, "Mr Nolan likes everything to be extremely neat and tidy."

Doocey silently noted the gardener's use of the word "extremely." It tied back to what he'd heard from his aunt, Nelly Boyle, going on about Nolan's OCD. "You have a fantastic view from up here," he commented aloud. *If I could only bloody well make it out properly.* "You can see all the comings and goings of the house."

Behind him, he heard Murphy repositioning his dodgy chair before answering. "Mr Nolan doesn't pay me to look out windows."

Ignoring Murphy's little rebuke, Doocey asked, "What's that small black shed down there for?" The same shed that, on his way up to the cabin, he'd taken the time to go into.

A worry wrinkle appeared on Murphy's forehead as if he was wondering why the scruffy clown should ask about that shed in particular. "That's where I keep the lawnmower and the other gardening bits and bobs."

"Like spades," Doocey said, swinging back around—to again face Murphy.

The gardener seemed unable to speak for several seconds before finally he repeated in a disoriented voice, "Yeah . . . like . . . spades."

"Have you seen Mr Nolan remove any spade lately?"

"No . . . but he wouldn't need to. I'm the one who does any digging in the gardens that needs doing."

Doocey resumed gazing out the window. "I wonder is there any truth in those rumours about Mrs Nolan having affairs?"

"I heard nothing like that," Murphy replied—a little too quickly.

"That surprises me," Doocey said, swerving around, causing the gardener to sit bolt upright. "With you working here for a year."

Murphy sniffed. "I mind my own business." Then standing up, he strode over to the cabin's door to the outside and opening it, said, "Sorry not to be of any help."

Doocey thought, *cheeky asshole,* but with a smile, peering up at Murphy, he sunnily declared, "Not at all. You've been much more helpful than you think."

Doocey stepped outside, with the big gardener staying put at the doorway. The sky the same icy grey. "Oh, by the way, Mr Murphy, where's it that you do live?"

"In Blackwood with my parents. Me and my fiancée are saving up for our own place."

"Oh, you've got a fiancée? And Blackwood you say? That's a fair old spin."

"It's not so bad, I can do it in half an hour."

"Half an hour, that's good going. What route do you take? Do you go past that petrol station at the crossroads?"

"Yeah . . ." Murphy replied in this slow, confused tone as if wondering why he even needed to ask this when there was only one road into Nolan Manor, or at least only the one driveable road, and the petrol station was located at the side of that road. Meaning there would be no way for him to avoid passing it.

With an apologetic shrug of his shoulders, Doocey clarified, "Sorry, that was probably a stupid question. I don't know the area. What type of car do you drive?"

"I haven't got a car. I have a motorbike."

"Oh, brilliant. Do you mind if I have a look? I have a thing for motorbikes."

Murphy grunted something unintelligible in response, then swiftly stepped outside, and headed for the back of the cabin. Chasing after him, Doocey thought, *You sneaky fecker, keeping your motorbike at the back so Nolan wouldn't be able to spot from the house whether you'd left for the day or not.*

Catching up to Murphy, Doocey noticed for the first time how the gardener seemed to be limping. "Hurt your foot?" he called out.

Murphy stopped for a second and muttered, "It's nothing."

At the rear of the cabin, the gardener came to a halt beside an unimpressive, rusty blue motorbike, parked alongside a black bench.

"Aw, a lovely vintage one," Doocey said, petting the motorbike as if it were an adorable puppy. At length, he got out his notebook and hovered his chewed pen over a blank page. "Can I take your mobile number—just in case I need to contact you again?"

"I don't have a phone," the gardener replied with an air of smug satisfaction.

Doocey recalled what Nolan had said about Murphy being this sort of new-age hippie, someone who shunned modern technologies. But still, he pressed, "No mobile?"

"Nope." Murphy cheerily re-confirmed. "Life is much more peaceful without the annoying things."

"Fair play," Doocey acknowledged, and putting his notebook and pen away, he rubbed his hand along the motorbike's patched-up leather seat. Abruptly, he looked up at Murphy. "Frank, is there any particular reason you're lying to me today?" Murphy swung out his powerful arms, causing Doocey to work overtime at appearing unflustered. "I'm not lying," he growled. "I don't know what you're on about!"

"I think you do Frank," Doocey said mildly and moved his gaze back to the motorbike. "Because I know for definite that you don't return home to Blackwood, to your parent's house, every evening. What's more, I know for definite that you were here the day Mr Nolan reported his wife missing."

"That's bull, pure bull. I told you . . . I wasn't here."

"But . . . I know you were . . . You see, the CCTV footage we got from the petrol station down the road never showed you leaving Nolan Manor on your motorbike. So we know you were here on the day Mr Nolan reported his wife missing and even for the two days before that."

The gardener's sculpted face became drawn and Doocey prayed that what Ber had been so clever to spot on the CCTV, or that is not spot on the CCTV—Murphy's motorbike not leaving Nolan Manor—was about to reap rewards—big time.

Though he'd found it truly mindboggling that Dickson—the pure donkey—must not have bothered or even thought of searching the cabin, leaving the crazy situation to arise that as he was having Nolan Manor searched, millimetre by millimetre, by a big forensics team, Murphy was hiding out in the cabin.

"You saw something, didn't you?" Doocey accused, pacing about on the spot so that his legs, which were as unstable as those of a string puppet, wouldn't be so noticeable.

"I saw nothing," he yelled back. "How many more times do I've to tell you? I wasn't here!"

"Have it your way Mr Murphy, but if I were you, I'd have a careful think. Withholding evidence in a potential murder case is a very serious matter.

Or even worse again, you don't want me thinking you'd something to do with Harriet Nolan's disappearance. Now do you?"

Doocey began to stroll away, but had only taken a few steps when he swung back round to Murphy, "Have a careful think, Frank, now, won't you?"

With the odd stumble, Doocey made it back to his Ford, and finding there to be still no sign of Nolan's black Volvo, he decided to hang on for him. *Sure, I have an update for His Lordship, don't I?* He laughed softly.

Once seated inside his car, Doocey gave a call to his mother who had some news of her own. Her partially sighted darts team had a rematch with Paddy's darts team and, though Paddy's had beat them, she was happy with how her team played and happy that Paddy's hadn't tried again to just let 'the poor blind people' win.

When he finally got a chance to tell her about his questioning of Murphy, she didn't seem all that interested as she'd gone back to being certain that Nolan killed his wife.

For a bit of fun, he attempted to wind her up a little. "You don't think Murphy could've killed her, do you?" he asked all innocently.

"No, not at all," she snapped back. "Sure, what motive would he have had?"

"I told you . . . I think . . . how according to that Powell one, he was having an affair with Harriet Nolan? Maybe they had a huge fight and he killed her by accident. He might have gone berserk because she wouldn't leave Nolan."

"I still don't see it."

"Why would he lie about not staying over in the cabin, though?" Doocey persisted.

His mother released a deep breath down the phone. "I suppose he could have done it, but I'd still bet my last cent on Nolan being your murderer. I'd say Murphy is lying about not being around because he just wants to keep out of it all." Her voice grew stronger. "He doesn't want his boss to find out that he has been having an affair with his wife and end up losing his job. Didn't you say too—that he has a fiancée? Or God knows, maybe he did see something and he's scared that if he opens his mouth, Nolan will come after him."

His mother's latter lines of thought, surprisingly, impressed Doocey. He hadn't said anything to Murphy about knowing he'd been carrying on with Mrs Nolan because he'd been worried that would cause him to clam up and go all defensive. He'd reasoned, precisely like his mother had reasoned, that the gardener would be bricking it about losing his job, and probably bricking it even more about the chances of losing his fiancée.

He next gave a call to Ber, who was not shy in telling him how she'd thought he'd been wrong, seeing as how he'd "got feck all out of Murphy," not to have entirely gone for the jugular. "Considering you're coming to the end of the third week of the four, Ryan gave you," she'd further expounded, "it's not as if you've time to be pussy-footing about." She fell silent for a second. "Then again, you could be completely wasting your time on Murphy, because he might not have seen a damned thing."

After finishing his call with Ber, Doocey wondered if she might be right about Murphy not having 'seen a damned thing' and whether his time might be better spent further interrogating Nolan.

By confronting him with those original forensic results, which to say the least, were odd, he might be able to squeeze something important out of *His Lordship*, maybe even a clue about where to find his wife's body. Doocey checked his watch, five to three, and Murphy had said Nolan was due back at three. Not long to wait then.

FIFTEEN

"Hello there!" Doocey chirpily called out as he slammed the driver's door of his car shut behind him and sauntered across to a grimacing Mr Nolan, who'd just emerged from his Volvo.

"How can I help you today, Detective?"

As if he'd not heard the question, Doocey turned his back on Nolan and gazed towards the crimson sea on the horizon, and the slowly sinking sun. "I've to say, this is a spectacular place." He swung back around to face Nolan, "A really spectacular place. Do you own much of the land around here?"

Nolan tartly replied, "Almost—as far as the eye can see."

"Whoa!" Doocey exclaimed, his head turning every which way. "You own all this? Would you mind me asking, how many acres that would come to?"

"In the region of three thousand. Now Detective, I really must be getting on."

"Three thousand acres!" he repeated with a low whistle, eyeing what appeared to him to be misty mountains. With his gaze returning to Nolan, he added, "That's some amount of land to have to look after."

"I actually rent about a third of it to local farmers," Nolan impatiently explained, "and they are the ones who keep that maintained. The rest is a bogland wilderness. Not suitable for agriculture."

Doocey gave a couple of nods. "I'd say . . . it would be good for hunting though. Yeah?"

"Yes . . . I suppose . . ."

"Do you do a bit of hunting yourself?"

"Not recently. When my father was alive, I used to go hunting a lot with him but it was always his passion—not mine."

The image of a younger Nolan sporting a burgundy jacket, perched high up on a black horse, surrounded by barking hounds, entered Doocey's head. This younger Nolan though looked fed up as if he was being forced by his father into slaughtering innocent foxes. Doocey's misty gaze returning to the misty mountains, he suggested, "You'd know the terrain around here pretty well?"

"Yes, I suppose so." Nolan adjusted his fully tied-up shirt collar.

"You'd know all the good hiding places?"

Nolan pushed his broad shoulders back. "What are you trying to suggest?"

Doocey fidgeted, "I only mean, you'd know, like, where the foxes would be hiding."

His Lordship gave a silent toss of his large head which said as clearly as any words that he didn't believe the clarification for a second.

Doocey again stared leisurely in the direction of the sea before abruptly looking over to his right. "I drove in that way, turning in at the crossroads where the petrol station is. I wondered if I kept on driving past the house," he now turned to look to his left, "where would the road take me?"

Nolan blew out an exasperated breath. "It comes to a dead end two kilometres on."

"Oh, I see," Doocey said, sticking a little knuckle in his mouth. "It's like a private road then—only servicing Nolan Manor?"

"Yes, I suppose so . . . but there's nothing to stop anybody using it."

Nolan gave an elongated stare to the simple white face of his watch.

Not taking the hint, Doocey asked, "Are there no other connecting roads?"

"No."

"It's only that I thought I might have seen another side road. Over to the right there?" He pointed towards where he thought the road should be, the road that at this moment he could not make out but knew was there because he'd walked up a bit of it.

"Oh, I wouldn't categorise that as a proper road. Rather a mere bog . . . road . . . In days gone by, locals with their donkeys used such trail-like roads to cart turf in from the mountains for heating their thatched cottages in winter. These days, with turf cutting no longer permitted for environmental reasons, they are now redundant—and certainly not drivable. Not unless you'd some banger of a vehicle that you didn't mind obliterating." He gave a complicit glance to Doocey's battered-looking Ford. He turned to his left and pointed. "There's another one, over there."

After pretending to see this second bog road, Doocey eyed Nolan's black SUV. "I'd say though a machine like that would be a match for any road, no matter how rough."

"Oh, but I'd never dream about driving my *Volvo* on anything other than a suitable surface."

Doocey pointed to his right." I assume the car parked over there must be your wife's."

"Well spotted," Nolan said, sounding as if his reserves of patience had been well and truly drained.

Doocey headed over to the red BMW, strolling around the car. The sound of his worn-out shoes crunching pebbles breached a tense silence. Peeping in at its ivory leather interior, he declared, "That's one beautiful car, and it looks brand new."

Nolan, who'd followed him over to the BMW, with a sigh, acknowledged, "Yes it's only a few months old."

"How much would a beauty like this set you back?"

"Somewhere in the ballpark of a hundred thousand."

"A hundred thousand euros!" Doocey breathlessly exclaimed. "Gosh . . . I'd say you would buy a hundred of my car for that kind of money."

"Possibly even a thousand," Nolan said dryly. After a pause adding, "My wife was well overdue a change of motor. Before this car, she'd been driving a ten-year-old little hatchback." He took a step towards the house "Now, I really must get on."

Doocey cast him a sideways glance, "I believe our forensic people examined both vehicles." He got his notebook out. "Yeah, and I think I made a note of their preliminary findings which I have to say were puzzling. Yeah, fairly fecking puzzling."

Nolan came to stand right next to Doocey—who deliberately made him wait as he turned over one random notebook page of awful writing after another. "Why is it you can never find things when you go looking for them?" he mumbled.

A minute later, snapping his notebook shut, he gawped up at Nolan and said, "Wait until you see, as soon as I get back to the station, I'll find that note. Anyways, I won't delay you any further."

"Don't be silly. Take a proper look."

"But I thought you were in a hurry?"

"No . . . a few minutes won't make a difference."

"Okay, if you're sure . . . you don't mind holding on. Let me take another look." Only for a matter of mere seconds later, to burst out, "Well what do you know? There's the note now."

"Fantastic!"

"Now let's see what my forensic colleagues had to say. Well, the good news is that the tests on your Volvo came back absolutely clear. Nothing unusual there, whatsoever."

On hearing this, Nolan nodded with gusto, colour returning to his face.

Doocey continued, "As a matter of fact, they couldn't get over the immaculate state of your vehicle. Not one smidgen of dirt. Even the tyres were sparkling." Doocey paused to see if any explanation might be forthcoming.

Nolan gave a stiff shrug. "What can I say, but one likes to drive a clean vehicle, and my Volvo had its usual thorough wash just the Monday evening before Harriet went missing." Adding, as if an afterthought, "The power washer, I use, is excellent."

"Oh, you clean your car yourself?"

"Yes. Regrettably, I have yet to find a valet service that does a truly thorough job."

Doocey pushed up an eyebrow. "Well, how clean you managed to get it—is a real credit to you. It was exactly the same story when it came to your house, Nolan Manor. They couldn't believe how spotless you got it. Especially for such a big property and with you being currently without a housekeeper." Again, he paused, looking to Nolan for some sort of explanation.

"Well, what can I say there, either? Only that one also likes to keep a clean home."

"Well, it's really incredible how clean you manage to get things." He looked again at his notebook. "When it came to Harriet's car, well, the only odd thing they found there was this small oil stain on the back seat."

He looked up at Nolan. "I suppose you've no idea where that might have come from?"

"No . . . none."

Grasping his, almost non-existent, chin—Doocey further explained, "We checked if the car had been in the garage recently and it hadn't which is hardly surprising. I wouldn't have expected a vehicle so new to be giving any mechanical trouble."

He went quiet, leaving it for Nolan to break the silence.

"I'm afraid, Detective, as I say, I've no idea how any spot of oil got there."

"Not to worry," Doocey said and went back to his notebook, murmuring, "Sure it's only a tiny speck of oil, it's probably not important anyway." *Or maybe it might be the most important clue of all.*

Doocey redirected his gaze to Nolan. "There, of course, was also what else they found, the part that makes it all so fecking puzzling." Looking to the ground, as if embarrassed, he muttered, "I'm sure though it's nothing."

Nolan seemed to go into a state of paralysis.

Doocey went on, "No, I won't go bothering you with that—when it has to be nothing."

Nolan swiftly came back to life. "Not at all," he enthusiastically encouraged. "Perhaps, I can clear up whatever it is for you."

Doocey fell quiet again as if carefully thinking the offer over before finally replying. "Oh . . . alright . . . You see, forensics have this amazing dog called Max, a black Labrador retriever. He's supposed to be a beautiful-looking animal but I hear he's a real devil for jumping up on people." He gave a little chuckle and continued in a more serious voice. "The dog is specially trained to detect the scent emitted by a decomposing body. I think they call it *'the scent of death.'* It's incredible how powerful a dog's sense of smell is. Would you believe they've ten thousand times a better sense of smell than us humans?"

"How fascinating," Nolan said flatly, caressing the tied top button of his shirt. "Did the dog detect something?"

"Ah yes," Doocey said, glancing back to Nolan's Volvo. "Poor old Max gave a positive reaction to *the scent of death* in the boot of your Volvo."

A shocked expression came over Nolan's face. For a long moment—speechless. "Well . . ." he finally fumbled, "the . . . dog . . . has to have been mistaken."

"Yeah," Doocey replied in the most casual way and after a deliberately lengthy pause further elaborated. "We came to that conclusion too, seeing as how our Max also detected the scent of death in the boot of your wife's BMW."

Nolan emitted a slight gasp. "There you go . . ."

Doocey fiddled with his glasses. "The dog's handler, Mary, thinks Max might have got confused. She thinks the poor old devil might have got the scent of death in one vehicle and somehow thought it had been in the two."

He cast Nolan a searching stare, but Nolan showed no reaction. "Or probably there never had been any scent of death," Doocey continued. *Like Dickson—going by his file notes—had been so adamant to believe. Who knows, maybe the idiot might've been right—for once.* "Poor Max is getting on in years," he continued aloud. "Mary says they'll have to retire him soon." He consigned his notebook to an inside anorak pocket before announcing, "I better be going."

Nolan took a step towards him. "Detective, I have to say that I'm more than a little concerned at the tenor of your questions thus far. You don't seriously think I'm somehow involved in my wife's disappearance?"

"Ahh now . . . What would make you think that? No, I'm sure it's like what you reckoned happened. Your wife was probably just swept out to sea and once her body comes ashore, everything will be cleared up. We'll be able to prove once and for all that her death was accidental."

He patted his anorak, "There's one tiny bit of good news on that front. You see, I've consulted with a Professor Farina, who's an oceanographer. You know, one of those people who are experts in tidal patterns and she maintains it's an absolute cert that Harriet's body will—any day now—wash ashore." He put his hands up in surrender as if Nolan was pointing a gun at him. "But please don't ask me anything about the technicalities of how she can be so sure . . . something to do with the tides being a certain way the evening Harriet went missing . . . It's all too complicated for a simple mind like mine. That's what she says though, it's an absolute certainty."

Nolan sighed heavily. "It would be good, at least, to have her body back, and get some crumb of closure."

"Well . . . as I say, Professor Farina is very confident. That's—of course—if your wife fell into the sea . . . in the first place."

Doocey left a deliberately long silence, which Nolan chose not to fill. "I mean, who's to say she's not still alive? Maybe for whatever reason, she just needed some time away."

Nolan muttered under his breath, "I only wish . . . I could believe that."

Doocey strolled over to his Ford and wrenched his dented driver's door open, but did not sit in. Instead, he stood gazing over the car's roof towards the sea.

Obviously having had quite enough of the scruffy detective's antics for one day, Nolan commenced walking back to his house. However, he'd only taken a few brisk steps when he heard Doocey's voice once more.

"You know, I really can't get over your determination."

Nolan swinging back round, asked sharply, "What are you talking about now?"

"I mean your determination . . . when it comes to your writing," he replied, all innocently. "To never get published but to keep on trying, again and again."

"I suppose everybody has their dreams, their passions," Nolan fired back and without any further comment, swiftly disappeared into Nolan Manor, shutting its enormous door behind him with a bang. However, Nolan had not slammed his door shut on the woman who turned up at his doorstep the very next day. Though, given what apparently went on to happen, he might have been much wiser to have done so.

Sixteen

The following evening, at half past five, a woman in a distressed state walked into Blackstones Garda Station and was ferried by Ber up to interview room 2C on the second floor. Ber then went to tell Doocey about how "some smelly old drunk one" was saying she'd 'vital new information about Harriet Nolan's disappearance.'

But as soon as Doocey entered meeting room 2C, the woman waved a hand of protest. "I asked to speak to the detective in charge of the Harriet Nolan investigation."

"That's me," Doocey said, putting a hand to his mouth—to shield himself from her smell of stale sweat and booze.

"Oh!" she exclaimed, leaning her head to the side, eyes narrowed in puzzlement.

Doocey took a seat, getting even more of a nose full of her disgusting stench. Now closer to her, he also noticed ingrained dirt in her hands and rips in her jade-coloured jacket. She could pass for being in her seventies but he guessed her to be a lot younger than this. He would find that he'd guessed right because, when he checked up later, he discovered she was only in her fifties.

Continuing to look unconvinced, the woman asked, "You're sure you're a detective . . . the detective in charge of the Harriet Nolan case?"

Doocey, who'd been opening up his notebook, lost his concentration for a split second, and the pen he'd been clasping with his mouth clattered off the table onto the floor. He stood up to do a visual sweep (as best he could) of the grey carpet but had no luck in spotting the damned pen. He got down onto his knees to search under the table, trying to avoid looking directly at the woman's black and blue legs.

Suddenly, giving him a right fright, he saw an upside-down head gawking over at him and the woman blaring, "Your pen is there beside the leg of your chair."

"Oh, thanks," Doocey said, reaching his hand out for the chair leg he thought she was on about.

"No, not that one!" she blared even louder. "No, no . . . not that one either!"

Finally, he felt his fingertips touch the pen and clutching hold of it, he resumed his seat.

The woman opposite chastised, "My God, man, I think you badly need to get your eyes tested."

Doocey took a few inner breaths, trying to slow his galloping heart, and asked in a purposely calm tone, "Can I have your name?"

"My name is Bridgie Reilly, I'm Harriet's aunt," she grumpily declared, and it was a declaration that Doocey scarcely believed even if he knew Harriet Nolan's maiden name to be Reilly and even more to the point, knew they had been trying to trace an aunt of hers by the name of Bridgie Reilly.

It was just incredible to think that a woman as attractive as Harriet Nolan (even if he'd only seen photos of her) could be related to someone so revolting. Though, he wondered if, maybe before years of neglecting herself, Auntie Bridgie might too have been a stunner. His inner voice—turning suddenly fecking poetic—imbued: *An erstwhile rose, shrivelled and withered by life's harsh weather.*

"Oh . . . you're Harriet's Aunt . . . very good," he said aloud, striving to keep the surprise out of his voice. "We've been looking for you?"

He waited for an explanation about her whereabouts, but none seemed to be forthcoming, until finally Reilly relented with a defensive, "I've been away."

Doocey reckoned that "being away" equated to her lying drunk on some Dublin backstreet corner. He recalled too what Nolan had said when he'd told him of the trouble they were having in tracing his wife's aunt, '*I can well imagine how difficult it can be to find some people.*'

Doocey, deciding to waste no more time on the matter, asked, "Were you and Harriet close?"

With her eyes watering, Reilly whispered, "Very much so. I loved her with all my soul. I was the only family she'd left."

Doocey made a mental note of how she was talking about her niece in the past tense.

Reilly pulled out a dirty handkerchief and blew hard into it. "God knows . . . it might be just as well that my brother, poor Peadar, is dead, not to have his heart broken to bits by all of this."

Doocey, after an empathetic pause, said, "I believe you have some new information concerning your niece's disappearance."

"Yes, I do," she replied in an angry tone that matched with her facial expression. "I know exactly what happened to her. Harriet was murdered."

The words made Doocey—probably like the woman sitting across from him mostly felt—feel all inebriated inside but he cautioned himself to sober up. Too early yet to be getting carried away. "How do you know this?" he mildly inquired.

Reilly thrust her seated body forward. "I know it because that animal of a husband of hers told me he killed her. I've just been to see him."

"Mr Nolan confessed to you?"

"Yeah."

"Tell me exactly what he said."

Reilly cocked her blackened chin into the air. "He said, he and Harriet had got into a scuffle, and she'd accidentally fallen, hitting her head against a wall in Nolan Manor."

Doocey took a few seconds to control his breathing before asking, "What did he do with the body?"

"The evil monster said that he threw . . . my beautiful niece . . . into the sea."

"Mr Nolan just confessed all this to you?"

"Yes," she said warily as if she knew her story sounded seriously suspect.

Doocey put a hand to his forehead, feeling as if the first thuds of a vindictive hangover were hitting. "Do you think Mr Nolan might have been a bit drunk or something?" he asked and silently added, *like yourself.*

"I don't think so . . ." she slowly answered. "I'd say it's more to do with him not being able to handle the strain of the awful thing he's done. That he needed to tell someone. Even before he confessed, I got the feeling something was not right with him. I've always been very good at reading people and spotting when someone's hiding something."

As she peered unblinkingly into his eyes, Doocey felt his insides twist with anxiety as he wondered if she'd already clocked what it was . . . he was hiding. He speedily asked, "Was there anybody else around to witness the confession?"

"No."

"Were you and Mr Nolan very close?"

Reilly glowered back at him, seeming to have taken offence at the question, and Doocey clarified, "It's only that I'm assuming that the two of you must have been very close—for him to have chosen you to be the person he confided in."

"No, not really," she snorted.

"You and he didn't get on?"

She jerked her head. "No. If you must know, I thought him all wrong for Harriet. For crying out loud . . . the age of him. He could've been her grandfather."

"Can I ask . . . if the two of you didn't get on . . . why you went to see him today?"

Her face quivered with more anger. "What are you on about? Sure of course I was going to see him. I needed to know what happened to Harriet. And when I'd only just found out she was missing."

Doocey rose to his feet and said, "If you'll excuse me for a moment." Down the corridor, he got out his mobile and, concentrating hard, managed to dial the right number. Returning to the interview room, a few minutes later, he explained to Reilly how he'd phoned Nolan.

"What did the brute say?" she asked with venom. "I suppose he denied it."

"Yes . . ." Doocey replied, taking out his notebook to pretend to read from it. "He said that you were quote, *'Just probably drunk out of your head as usual and imagining all sorts.'*"

Reilly thumped down hard on the interview table. "The cheek of him. I'm not the slightest bit drunk."

When the table had stopped shaking, Doocey asked, "Would you be okay then with doing a quick blood test for us? Just to confirm there's no alcohol in your system."

Reilly's ragged face knotted with rage, "Why the hell should I have to take a blood test? I'm not the murderer here."

Doocey nodded firmly. "I understand, Miss Reilly. Really, I do. But if we have the clean blood test, we can show that you were sober as a judge and Nolan's barrister won't be able to argue in court that you'd drink on you."

She went silent for a minute before speaking again, her voice calmer. "I might have taken a small glass or two of brandy from him." She scowled, "I don't see where the harm in that is—when I'd just found out that my beautiful niece was missing. Anybody would need a drink for that sort of a shock."

"I totally understand," Doocey said soothingly. "Though probably best not to risk the blood test for the moment . . ."

"Is that it then? You're just going to let him get away with it."

"No, not at all. I can assure you our investigations are ongoing."

Reilly bolted to her feet. "Listen here, Mr Magoo. You've had plenty enough time to investigate, and you haven't found Harriet. I want to speak with a real detective. One who can bloody see." Her voice transformed into a roar, "Get me a real detective."

"No problem at all," Doocey replied, deliberately pleasantly. "I'll just pop out to get you one of those."

After two hours, Bridgie got fed up of waiting for her *real detective*. Exactly as Doocey had predicted, given there was only so long an alcoholic could go without their next drink.

"I'm telling the truth . . . he did confess," Reilly yelled as she was being escorted by Doocey out of the station.

"Yes, I know," he replied, sounding fully sincere, whilst thinking: *If only I really did know.* Especially now that he was into the last four days of the four weeks, Ryan had given him to investigate. All he supposed he could do was to keep putting Nolan under pressure and hope for some sort of breakthrough . . . a breakthrough that might even come when he next went to see him, armed with a series of suspicious photographs.

SEVENTEEN

O N OPENING HIS FRONT DOOR to see Doocey, Nolan burst out, "I really hope you're not here about more ludicrous lies Harriet's Aunt has been filling your head with . . . As I explained to you on the telephone yesterday, the woman is a drunkard and not to be believed—"

"Oh don't worry . . . I'm not here because of her. No, I just wanted to give you an update."

"Oh really . . . an update!" Nolan sceptically exclaimed but relented to allowing him in.

They proceeded into the usual vast room at the front of the house, and as Nolan remained standing, so did Doocey, who now began gazing out of one of the room's tall windows, seemingly lost in thought. Nolan, looking like he wanted to give the detective a violent shake, asked sharply, "What's your update?"

"Oh . . . yes," Doocey said, turning back to face him. "Well, it's just that I checked out your theory with the phone company."

Nolan stretched back his head. "What're you talking about?"

"Remember your theory about why Harriet never used her mobile, the Tuesday she went missing? How you thought the storm could have knocked out a mast and there mightn't have been any reception. Don't you remember?"

"I think . . . I vaguely recall mentioning something of the sort . . ."

"Anyway, Mr Nolan, the phone companies said that they'd no record of any mast outages within the radius of Nolan Manor that Tuesday."

"Oh really."

"Yeah, and even without checking with them—I'm such a fool—I should have realised this myself." *And I did realise it.*

"Should you?"

"Yes, because how would you have been able to ring the emergency services if the phone lines were down?"

Nolan inhaled deeply. "Perhaps then . . . Harriet simply had some technical issue with her phone. Possibly, for whatever reason, it would not switch on."

Bypassing this new theory of Nolan's, Doocey said, "We also checked the CCTV cameras of that petrol station at the crossroads." He paused for a moment, sensing with delight that *His Lordship* seemed taken aback by this new piece of information. "I think it's called, *On the Run,*" he eagerly elaborated. "You know it, don't you?"

Nolan snarled, "Of course, I damned well know it. How could I possibly not? Given that it's located on the only road into my home, and when I drive past it nearly every day."

Doocey calmly reached into an inside anorak pocket and removed a bundle of photographs, before continuing. "The footage shows Harriet's red BMW passing by at noon on the Monday, headed away from Nolan Manor and going by again at about 4:00 p.m. on her return journey home." With a shaky hand, he passed two photographs over to Nolan, explaining, "Those two images, which we printed from the CCTV, show this."

After giving Nolan time to look at both of the photographs, he added, "Sorry, I know they're not great quality and how with the windscreen reflections and the camera angle, you can't even make out that it's Harriet driving." Although Doocey had feared that it might just be his bad sight that was stopping him from seeing who was driving, so in advance, he'd treble-checked with Ber, who had better than twenty-twenty vision, that you really couldn't spot who was in the driver's seat. Yet, he still feared that Nolan would contest the point. Inside his head he could already hear him challenging: *What on earth are you talking about? It's perfectly clear that Harriet is driving.*

With Nolan keeping silent for a long time, Doocey continued in a firmer voice. "I think though we can be fairly sure they show your wife's BMW. Wouldn't you agree?"

"Yes, it looks like Harriet's car," Nolan said, giving him back the photos, only for Doocey to hand him two more.

"These other two show your Volvo leaving at 7:30 a.m. on the same Monday to go to your cricket match and returning around 4:30 p.m."

Doocey handed over yet two further photos. "Those show your Volvo driving away from Nolan Manor, again on the Monday, at a quarter past seven in the evening, and driving back at ten past nine, that same evening."

For what seemed to Doocey like ages, Nolan carefully studied these last two photographs. As with the others, the reflections on the windscreen together with the unhelpful camera angle made it impossible to see who was inside the vehicle. Nolan was still scrutinising the two photographs when Doocey interjected, "Do you mind me asking, where you were going to that Monday evening?"

He replied sharply, "Simply to call in on my daughter." His tone mellowing a little, he further clarified, "I visit her a lot. It's more convenient, as obviously Jennifer can't drive and neither are there any public transport options to bring her here."

"How long is the drive to Jennifer's? I think I remember you saying she lived in Dublin."

"Yes, she lives close to the city centre and I usually get to her apartment in about forty-five minutes."

Doocey nodded. "Meaning the journey there and back would have taken you ninety minutes. And according to the petrol station footage you were away for less than two hours in total. So you would have only spent about half an hour with Jennifer?"

"Yes," Nolan confirmed. "It was a short visit. My daughter had been doing a lot of singing rehearsals and felt rather tired."

He clenched his perfectly straight teeth. "I'm not sure, Detective, why you're so interested in what happened the day before my wife went missing, on the Monday. Shouldn't you be concentrating on the actual day of her disappearance? Unless you think I'm lying about her having gone missing on the Tuesday?"

"Oh, it's purely standard investigative procedure," Doocey hurriedly reassured, "that we fully account for the movements of missing persons and those connected with them in the days leading up to their disappearance." The sound of him tapping a foot on a floorboard echoed around the vast room. "Also," he continued in a low confidential voice, "there oddly doesn't seem to be any CCTV for the Tuesday. Harriet doesn't appear to have driven anywhere that day. Or for that matter, neither do you seem to have. Any particular reason for this?"

Nolan quick-fired back, in a bad-tempered tone, "I would have expected the reason to be obvious from our previous conversations. You know very well about the inclement weather of that Tuesday. Accordingly, I did not fancy venturing anywhere in such beastly conditions. I can only assume also, though I never even thought it necessary to question her on the subject, that Harriet was of a like mind."

Doocey wrinkled up his button nose. "Yet, Harriet did *venture* out and without the shelter of a car—to walk Rupert?"

"Yes, yes, but that's different. As I told you previously, no matter the weather, that cossetted creature had to get his walk."

"Grand . . ." Doocey said under his breath, seeming preoccupied with yet another photo. "There's something else too," he went on, looking at Nolan. "On your return home from your cricket match, on the Monday— do you remember seeing a cyclist? This would have been on the road into Nolan Manor, past the petrol station."

Gazing out a window, Nolan said, "Yes . . . I think I may have."

"Male or female?"

He turned back to Doocey. "I think the cyclist was a man but I can't be certain . . . I barely had time to notice their existence." He gave a little apologetic half-smile. "I do tend to drive rather fast, and if I recall correctly, the gentleman was cycling on the opposite side of the road. Why do you ask?"

"Oh, it's only that I'd be interested in speaking with him," Doocey replied, deciding to be deliberately evasive. He now handed Nolan over the photo of the cyclist in question or more accurately a photo of a silhouetted figure on a bike, against a bright blue sky. Doocey eyed Nolan through greasy glasses. "As you see from the time and date in the corner, the CCTV image was captured at 4:20 p.m., on the 15th and it looks to show a man cycling away from Nolan Manor. This seems to fit with you spotting a cyclist on the opposite side of the road as you travelled home from your cricket match. I know you can't make out the face, but I suppose you've no idea who our friend here might be?"

Nolan burst out irritably, "The date on this photo is Monday, the 14th not Tuesday, the 15th and my cricket match also occurred on the Monday.

"Oh yes . . . you're right . . . I meant the 14th . . . my mistake." Doocey felt his face redden and redden. He rushed back to his original question, "You don't know who the cyclist might be?"

"No . . . I can't say that I recognise the person, but as you point out, you can't even see the face in this photograph."

Doocey thought he detected this strange undercurrent to Nolan's answer, almost as if he were lying and did recognise the cyclist. "You know, a few things baffle me about that photo," he continued. "Can you spot anything, yourself?"

Nolan took another look. "I'm afraid . . . I can't. As I say, it simply seems like someone, a man, out for a cycle."

Receiving back the cyclist photograph from Nolan, Doocey stared hard at it, biting into one of his teeny knuckles at the same time. "It's just the way he's dressed struck me as odd. He seems to be wearing long, loose trousers—and don't cyclists normally wear all that tight gear? It also looks like, doesn't it, that he's wearing a suit jacket? I'd bet too those are ordinary shoes he's got on and not those special cycling ones."

Taking another look at the photograph that was being held out to him, Nolan just shrugged and Doocey got that feeling again, even stronger, that *His Lordship* knew—perfectly well—the identity of the silhouetted figure . . . and that maybe he'd calculated it might suit his purposes better to play dumb. Leave the cyclist as a potential unidentified suspect so as to take a bit of heat off himself as the only main suspect.

"Maybe the gent isn't one of those professional cyclists," Doocey went on. "Maybe he's just some ordinary Joe who's not big into cycling and only fancied a quick spin. Didn't bother dressing up in all the cycling paraphernalia or never even owned any—to start with." He pressed his hand to his forehead. "The only thing is . . . for that kind of Amateur Joe, he has got a very professional-looking bike with those drop handlebars and skinny wheels."

Nolan put a finger to the tied top button of his shirt. "I take your points, Detective, but I'm afraid I'm not in any position to enlighten you." His voice—so chirpy—that Doocey felt as if he were privately finding his interest in the cyclist to be '*most amusing*.'

Doocey returned all the photographs to his inside anorak pocket, except for one. "The strangest thing of all," he said, staring at the cyclist photograph in his hand, "is that although we can see the guy heading away at 4:30 p.m. on the Monday, there isn't any footage of him going in the other direction, heading towards Nolan Manor."

Nolan did not attempt to comment.

Looking to the vast oak floor, Doocey said in a doubtful tone of voice, "Though, I suppose . . . considering the hours and hours of CCTV footage reviewed, it would be easy enough to miss a few seconds of him cycling past the petrol station, for the first time." But in truth, knowing Ber's thoroughness, he very much doubted this. "Or maybe, he went cross country—down that bog road, I asked you about before." He feigned an expression of excitement at this thought, only for a moment later to feign one of disappointment. "No, that can't be it either. I'm forgetting about the type of bike he was riding and as you explained before, the terrible condition of those bog roads." Once more, Doocey held out the cyclist photograph in front of Nolan. "No . . . the thin tyres on his bike wouldn't be fit for such a bad road. He'd have a puncture before pedalling a yard."

Nolan maintained his silence. "You wouldn't happen to own a bike yourself, Mr Nolan?"

"No, I certainly wouldn't. I must have been a boy of eleven when I last rode a bike." He gave a sourly grunt. "I very much hope you're not suggesting, in some convoluted fashion, that I'm that cyclist?"

"No, not at all," Doocey replied with a vigorous shake of his head. "Sure, the image isn't clear enough for me to say such a thing. How could it even be you anyway—when, at the same time, you were in your Volvo, driving home?" *Unless you'd an accomplice.* "As I said," he continued aloud, "I was just all fecking confused about how we were able to see this fella cycling away from Nolan Manor but not cycling towards it. I thought then he might've taken the bike from the house here. That's all."

"Well, as I say, Detective, I don't own any bicycles."

Doocey squeezed one side of his glasses, looking to be thinking intensely, and muttered, "I'll circulate this photo to the media and hopefully our cyclist friend will come forward."

In turn, Doocey requested Ber to arrange for the said circulation of the photo, and she grudgingly obliged, though not before telling him how she thought it a complete bloody waste of time considering the image was of such poor quality. She reckoned it would be a miracle if anybody recognised themselves as being the cyclist and even more of a massive miracle if such a person came forward within the three full days they'd left on the case. Though he said nothing, Doocey secretly could not agree more. It was past time then that he started to make things happen.

Eighteen

"If you don't mind, I won't come in," Doocey said in answer to an invite Nolan hadn't given. "The wife is expecting me home." A gust of wind caught a clump of his hair and also seemed to catch all his attention.

"What is it today, Detective?" Nolan broke in.

Doocey got out his notebook and turned over some of its dog-eared pages. "Well, what it is Mr Nolan, was that I wanted to check something with you. You see at this point—we've reviewed your wife's phone records in detail." He felt a pang of guilt at his use of the word 'we' knowing it had been Ber—alone—who'd done any reviewing. He continued, "There's only one mobile number that your wife regularly rang and took calls from, we can't account for."

He raised his head to look at Nolan. "Of course, we've tried phoning the number but it doesn't seem to be any longer in service and with it being a prepaid mobile, we've no way of tracing its owner." He showed Nolan the notebook page where he'd written down the telephone number in his best writing and asked, "I was wondering if you recognised it at all?"

Nolan took a few seconds to study the number before answering, "It doesn't look familiar."

"The thing is," Doocey said, staring hard at his notebook, "Harriet rang this mobile an awful lot. It also seems to be the last number she rang."

Using a single finger, he pressed his glasses to his face, mouthing, "There's something else that's even more suspicious."

Nolan huffed, "What are you talking about now?"

Doocey's tone grew grave. "Mr Nolan, Harriet never went to Richmond Shopping Centre . . . the day before she disappeared—like you said she had."

"How do you know this?"

"We know it," Doocey replied, "because we *(as in Ber)* checked the shopping centre's CCTV. As you're probably aware . . . there are cameras at the barriers into and out of their car park that record every vehicle registration number but there wasn't a trace of your wife's reg number for the Monday . . . Not a trace."

"Well, that's where Harriet told me she was going. She must have changed her mind or possibly she went to another shopping centre."

Doocey rubbed his forehead. "You might be right . . ." he muttered and seemed to disappear into his own world. Forcing Nolan to eventually ask, "Was that everything, Detective?"

Doocey gave a jerk as if someone had just snuck up on him and shouted boo. "Oh . . . the only other thing was . . . just to let you know that I was chatting with Professor Farina again. You know that lady I was telling you about who is an expert in tidal patterns? Anyways, she's very confused. She just can't understand why Harriet's body hasn't washed ashore by now."

He paused, and pretending to read the disappointment in Nolan's face added, "Please try not to be disheartened, we won't give up. In fact, I was down there at the cliffs earlier myself, looking to see if—" He came to a sudden halt as if he'd just remembered something. "Do you go down there much yourself—to look?" he finally asked.

"Not really," Nolan mumbled.

"Yeah, that's what I was thinking cause in all the times I've been down at those cliffs, I never came across you."

Nolan inhaled deeply. "I just find it too upsetting. I'm sure you can understand?"

"I think I understand, alright," Doocey said in a jeering way. He sighed. "I best be getting home. The wife will be going ballistic."

Nolan moved to close the door and Doocey headed for his car but abruptly swung back around—magician style—holding up a plastic bag, containing some soggy white fabric.

"Oh, by the way, I found this scarf down at the cliffs. I don't think it's your wife's, but I thought it best to double-check with yourself, just on the off chance."

He handed over the bag with the scarf to a surprised-looking Nolan, whose surprise seemed to grow the more he looked. Finally declaring, "This scarf very much looks like one of Harriet's."

"Really," Doocey excitedly responded, but his excitement seemed to almost instantly dissipate, and his voice became more doubtful. "Are you sure though? Didn't you say your wife owned so many clothes—you couldn't tell if any were missing?"

"Yes, but I do know the style of clothing Harriet buys, and in recent times, I'd seen her wear plenty of similar white scarfs. I see too, by the label, it's from a favourite designer brand of hers."

Doocey took back possession of the plastic bag and moved it up to within millimetres of his glasses. "How very clever of you to notice that tiny little tag." *What a stupid thing to do and to say,* he then immediately thought. *Are you trying to show him how blind you are—or what?*

"Heavens—you don't mean to say you hadn't already spotted the label?" Nolan gravely questioned. "How very concerning!"

Doocey's heart gave a scared shudder, but he still managed to muster a reply. "Label or no label," he fired back, "I still don't think this scarf can possibly be Harriet's."

"Do you not?"

"No, I don't, and in your statement, you never mentioned anything about her wearing a white scarf."

He opened up his notebook and picked out a random page of illegible scribbles. "You said your wife was wearing a blue raincoat but nothing about a scarf."

"Yes, but who's to say she wasn't wearing a scarf beneath that blue raincoat."

"Oh, I see," Doocey said, looking skywards. "I never thought of that." Casting a confused gaze in Nolan's direction, he placed one hand on the crown of his head. "So, this scarf must've unwrapped itself from around Harriet's neck and freed itself from under her raincoat to become the only item of her clothing to wash ashore."

Not commenting, Nolan steadfastly held his hands behind his back as if they were handcuffed there.

"But even if Harriet had been wearing a scarf," Doocey resumed, holding up the plastic bag, "this can't be it."

Nolan clinched his chin and said in a sarcastic tone, "Can it not?"

"No . . ." he confirmed with a firm shake of the head. "Because do you remember that spot where you found your wife's dog? At the edge of one of the cliffs."

Nolan gave a gruff nod.

"Well, I came across this scarf on the rocks, at the bottom of that very same cliff."

Nolan's eyes narrowed. "I'm not following your logic, Detective. I would think the scarf being found at the place where Harriet most likely fell into the sea only strengthens the argument that it's hers."

"I suppose that's what you might think at first, alright," Doocey said, staring accusatively up at Nolan. His lips tightened into a frown. "Except our Garda search teams minutely scoured that seashore for weeks without finding anything and it's unlikely they'd have missed it. Meaning the scarf must have been swept out to sea."

Doocey paced about in a half-circle, the sound of shifting pebbles beneath his feet. "Though it must've been swept very far out, otherwise it would have arrived onshore long before this. Plus, if it had gone so far out . . . what are the chances that it would arrive back at the exact spot where it first entered the water and in such great shape? I'm no expert when it comes to the behaviour of the sea, but common sense tells me there wouldn't be a hope in hell of that happening. It would be just too unbelievable. Do you not agree?"

"Well like yourself, Detective, I'm no expert in such matters either."

Doocey hid his mouth with one hand. "No, but as a crime writer, I thought it might have been fairly obvious to you."

Nolan chose to make no reply.

A sceptical Ber also thought the whole situation of the scarf suddenly washing ashore and Doocey just happening to find it, to be also unbelievable in the extreme. However, as the events of the following day would show, unbelievable things could sometimes happen.

NINETEEN

Doocey reckoned you'd never have guessed from his smart appearance and calm demeanour that the man now sat across from him in interview room 2C was unhinged. Jack Hanson was one of those people he would hear Dickson refer to as 'nutjobs.' People so off the rails that they would imagine themselves to be involved in every big case they saw reported in the media.

Doocey even wondered if Dickson might be behind this Hanson fella showing up. The bitter so-and-so would only be delighted to have him wasting the last two days that he'd left on the Nolan case, courtesy of *Mr Wacko*, going around in crazy circles.

He removed some pages from a manila folder, he'd brought with him, and after pretending to speed read them, looked up and declared, "I need to advise you, Mr Hanson, that this interview is being recorded." He eyed the camera in the corner of the room that he couldn't properly see. "Are you okay with that?"

"Yeah of course, but I've honestly no idea what I'm doing here."

Sure, you don't, Doocey thought, as he caught a whiff of booze on the man's breath and it was still only morning.

Hanson shot him a broad smile, "By the way, I like your specs. Very retro."

Doocey felt himself turning into a fecking tomato. Just not used to compliments on any scale. As if he hadn't heard, he said formally, "If you don't mind, I'd like to confirm some preliminary details."

Hanson gave a devil-may-care shrug.

"You're 48?"

"Yes, that's right. Getting old."

Doocey bit into his teeny knuckle. "Aren't we all, aren't we all . . . What's your occupation?"

"I'm in car sales."

"Full-time?"

"Yeah," Hanson answered and chuckled. "I'd say even more than full-time, seeing as how I average seventy hours a week."

"Like it?" Doocey asked, scribbling notes, and trying not to let his surprise show through that someone unhinged could hold down a full-time job.

"Love it. I'm good with people."

"Are you married?"

"Yes, for twenty years." Then came a frown, and he murmured, "But we've recently separated."

"I see, and any children?"

"We have a sixteen-year-old son, Keith."

"Very good," Doocey acknowledged with a nod, and removing the single page contained in his manila folder, he passed it across to Hanson who, on reading it, turned the colour of death.

"That there is the reason we've asked you to come in to see us," Doocey elaborated. "What have you to say about it?"

For some moments Hanson was as still as an ice sculpture before letting out this great gushing sigh. "I don't know what to say . . . Someone's idea of a joke . . . I presume."

Doocey took back possession of the page which was a printout of a very short email and pretended to read aloud, though he was really going off memory, the email's one typed sentence: *"My name is Jack Hanson and I want you to know that I murdered Harriet Nolan."* He looked to the man opposite. "Hmm, it doesn't read like much of a joke to me."

"Well, all I can tell you is that I never wrote it," and there was this unmistakable trace of fear in his voice.

His denials dumbfounded Doocey who'd been expecting him—in true wacko fashion—to be jumping up onto the table, demanding credit for a crime he never committed. So, just in case, he asked, "Did you know Harriet Nolan?"

"Yes," Hanson replied, and the detective's mindset clicked into an altogether more serious gear.

"Look Detective, I don't want to hide anything from you. I've been having an affair with Harriet."

"When did you see her last?"

"We spent a little while together in my apartment on the 14th of May."

Doocey felt himself go all twisty inside. Mrs Tidd had been right, after all, about Harriet Nolan seeing two men at once: Murphy and this Hanson lad. Penelope Powell also said that Mrs Nolan had been seeing a married man before Murphy but it looked like her friend hadn't really stopped seeing him. Mrs Nolan had probably been too embarrassed to admit she was fornicating with two men at the same time, so she'd just lied to Powell.

"On the day before Mrs Nolan disappeared, you were with her?" Doocey asked, with an exaggerated air of suspicion. *Harriet Nolan had gone to see you and not shopping like she'd told her husband.*

"Yeah . . . but only for a little while . . . in the afternoon."

"Can you remember what time she arrived at your apartment and left again?"

"She called over just before one o'clock. I remember that because I'd been working a half-day and I'd just got in. She left at three o'clock. She wanted to be home before Nolan got back from his cricket match."

Hanson looked at Doocey with frightened eyes. "Listen, just because me and Harriet were seeing each other, that doesn't mean that I've anything to do with her disappearance."

"Of course not," Doocey said but his words deliberately lacked even a smidgen of conviction.

"Seriously, I'd never hurt anybody."

"Of course not," Doocey repeated, but again without conviction. "You mentioned that you recently separated from your wife. Was your affair with Mrs Nolan the reason?"

"Yeah," Hanson replied, tightly folding his arms. "Though me seeing Harriet was only meant to be a bit of fun, a bit of excitement. I never intended to leave Annabell, but when she found out, she gave me the old heave-ho."

He began itching at his tight hair and as if predicting the obvious and awkward question that was bound to soon come, explained, "I never came forward to speak with you because I didn't want my affair with Harriet coming out in the media. I wanted to avoid upsetting my wife and son, any further." Hanson's tone of voice became firmer. "And my get-together with Harriet on the 14th hadn't anything to do with her disappearance. Seeing as how I'd read in the newspapers that she went missing on the 15th. I'd read too that she was supposed to have accidentally fallen from a cliff path. It had nothing—*then*—to do with me."

Choosing not to respond, for now, to the argument Hanson was making as to his innocence, Doocey asked, "Did you happen to use a prepaid mobile when contacting Mrs Nolan?"

Hanson started to fidget. "Yeah . . . I was afraid my wife might see the calls to Harriet on my regular phone."

"Do you still have that prepaid mobile?"

"No," he abruptly answered and looking jittery, added, "It broke . . . I let it fall . . . so I binned it."

Very convenient, Doocey silently quipped. Hanson's prepaid mobile had to be a match with that unidentified number Harriet Nolan had regularly rung and it couldn't be Murphy's because the hippie didn't even possess a phone.

Doocey flicked through his notebook until he came to the page where, in his best writing, he'd written that unidentified number down to show to Nolan. Holding up his notebook for Hanson to see the number, he asked, "Was that the number of the mobile you'd been using?"

"Yes, that was its number," he replied with a tiny nod.

Doocey moved to yet another topic. "In the weeks before her disappearance, had you noticed any injuries to Mrs Nolan's neck?"

Hanson replied slowly, "Yeah . . . I had."

"How did she get those injuries?"

"She'd tripped when out walking and fell onto some briars."

Doocey felt a painful pang of frustration at how Hanson had so swiftly and so cruelly, albeit unwittingly, just obliterated a precious lead. Harriet Nolan's pompous doctor had been wrong then about her husband having beaten her up.

Doocey glared down at the email printout. "You're sticking with your story that you never wrote this confession?"

"Hand on heart," Hanson vowed and even placed his left hand on the part of his chest where his ticker should be. "I swear—I don't know anything about that email."

"That's your email address though, *Jack.Hanson1*, isn't it?"

"Yeah, but someone must have hacked into my account because I never wrote that email. You have to believe me!"

He repeated his mantra of innocence, several times more, but then something strange happened. The confidence in his tone suddenly started to go—as if a punctured balloon losing air. Until finally, he stopped protesting altogether. As Doocey waited to hear what Hanson would say next, he caught again that whiff of drink on his breath and wondered if what the car salesman was about to say would match with the spine-tingling scenario that had just popped into his own head. *What if Hanson had really written the email, but because he was blotto drunk at the time, he'd totally forgotten doing so? And now, having just remembered he'd written it, had he realised the game was up?*

TWENTY

That evening, seated in the oversized sitting room of Nolan Manor, Doocey asked, "Have you ever heard of a man called Jack Hanson?"

Nolan shook his head. "No. Why?"

"Well, before I explain, I think I'd better warn you to be prepared for a bit of a shock."

"Go on . . ."

"The thing is . . . this Mr Hanson looks to have been having an affair with your wife. That's where Harriet had really been going on the Monday, to see him, and not to Richmond Shopping Centre as she told you."

Nolan bowed his head.

"I'm sorry," Doocey said, lowering his voice. "You didn't know?"

Nolan rubbed his paper-smooth chin. "I suppose, I had my suspicions."

Doocey reached into an anorak pocket to unearth a folded piece of paper which he handed to Nolan.

"What's this?"

"It's a confession."

"A confession?"

"Yes, a confession," Doocey repeated, gesturing for him to take a look.

Nolan promptly unfolded the paper and silently read: *My name is Jack Hanson and I want you to know that I murdered Harriet Nolan.*

Doocey said, "You look shocked," even though he couldn't truly tell.

"Is this genuine?"

Doocey stroked the side of his face. "Yes, I would say the person who wrote the confession is genuine." Taking back the printout, he continued. "At first, I thought it a hoax. I mean . . . if you murdered someone, you're not going to write to the Gardaí telling them you'd murdered them, now, are you?"

"I wouldn't know as I've never murdered anybody."

"No, but say you had, you wouldn't write to the Gardaí, would you?"

"No, I suppose one wouldn't but who's to say that we're dealing with a sane individual."

"A good point. Except this Jack Hanson seems very much with it to me."

"You mean to say . . . you've got hold of the fellow."

"Yes."

"And you say—he's sane?"

"As far as we can tell."

Nolan rested a hand on the top of his shiny head and glanced out a window at a row of trees with a thousand crossed branches. "Let me see—if I can get this clear," he continued, re-establishing eye contact. "You've managed to locate a man by the name of Jack Hanson who claims to have been having an affair with Harriet and furthermore claims to have murdered her. You also say the chap is perfectly sane, perfectly compos mentis."

"Well . . ." Doocey hesitantly replied. "There's a bit more to it than that. I best explain what else I found out."

Anybody watching Doocey, some hours earlier, shuffling up one driveway after another might have mistaken him for some bothersome door-to-door salesman. It was only though that he couldn't properly see the door numbers—which he told himself were just unusually small—unless he got right up close to them.

At long last, he found the one he was after and pressing the doorbell of number eighty-two, he took a few steps back. He was standing outside a large, handsome two-storey house which looked out onto a pretty park. An attractive lady came to the door. Her long, dark chocolate-coloured hair glowed from the light flooding in from outside. Doocey sensed a calmness, an easiness to her, like a rippling woodland river. "Mrs Hanson," he said, looking into her hazel eyes, "Detective Doocey, I phoned earlier."

"Oh yes, please do come in," she said with a smile that, from the blurry bit he could make out of it, didn't strike him as one of those sceptical type smiles he normally got whenever he introduced himself as a detective.

They proceeded through a gloomy hallway into a large bright room, with patio doors leading out into a decked garden. Hung over a cream-coloured mantelpiece was a simple gold mirror reflecting photos on surrounding walls, and on a blue corner sofa, a teenage boy curled up into a ball.

"This is my son, Keith," Annabell Hanson informed in a bad-tempered tone, causing the boy to sit up straight.

The boy had his mother's dark chocolate-coloured hair and her hazel-coloured eyes. He wore a discoloured white tee shirt with jeans, and gooseberry green runners that Doocey suspected were the source of a tiny scent of sweat.

Mrs Hanson gestured for Doocey to take a seat on a large leather armchair and offered him tea or coffee, before sitting down on the sofa alongside her son.

Sensing the boy's rigid apprehension, Doocey thought it best—less cruel—to quickly get on with what he'd come to do: get the confirmation he needed, straight from the horse's mouth or more like straight from the colt's mouth. "Keith, can I just confirm that what your mum told me earlier on the phone is true, that you are the one who wrote the email saying your dad murdered Harriet Nolan?"

Head bowed, the teenager made no reply until his mother prompted sharply, "Answer the man," and in a whisper, her son grunted back, "Yeah."

"Just tell me why you wrote it?"

Once again, there was a delay in his answering, and as each silent second ticked away, his face grew redder. Finally, and seeming to be on the verge of tears, he huffily muttered, "I wrote it because Dad left us and he wouldn't stay even though Mam asked."

Doocey repeated the boy's words slowly inside his head and then announced aloud, "Okay Keith, that's all I needed to check."

With that, Mrs Hanson signalled for her son to leave the room.

Having finished telling Nolan about his visit to see Mrs Hanson and her son Keith, Doocey fell silent. Nolan glanced at the email printout in his hand, before questioning in an irked voice, "Did you believe the boy about him writing this?"

"Oh yes," Doocey replied with a firm nod. "Because you see, Hanson's wife—Annabell—a lovely woman . . . after her son had left the room separately confirmed it to me. She explained how Keith had been so angry with her father for leaving them for Harriet Nolan, especially after she'd offered to take him back. Because up to this, she'd thought their lengthy marriage had been a happy one and was hoping they could work things out. Although, in the earlier years, when her husband's drinking had gotten a bit out of control, he'd sometimes become violent. But he'd attended Alcoholics Anonymous and stopped drinking and, after that, he never laid a drunken hand on her again."

Doocey scratched the side of his head. "No, I'm fairly certain it was the son and not Jack Hanson himself who wrote the email. You see Keith had been staying over in his dad's apartment and had borrowed Mr Hanson's computer tablet, as he usually would, to play online chess. Plus, Hanson says he hadn't signed out of his email so it would have been easy for Keith to have sent the confession."

Doocey pressed at the back of his head. "Like I mentioned before, if Jack Hanson had got away with murder, I can't see how he would be so crazy to go writing a confession. Not unless his conscience got to him and he just had to own up but that doesn't seem to have been the case here."

Doocey said. "What's more, on the Tuesday your wife went missing, we've confirmed that Jack Hanson had been in London, from 7 a.m., at a sales conference and it was after midnight when his flight arrived back in Dublin." Behind his glasses, Doocey's eyes grew a shade brighter. "He then has an airtight alibi."

Clutching the email printout by a corner as if it had transformed into something contaminated that he would prefer no longer to be touching, Nolan leaned forward and dropped it onto Doocey's lap, who after some protracted refolding, returned the piece of paper to his anorak pocket.

Nolan leaned back into his sofa. "Forgive me Detective, but if you've ruled Hanson out as a suspect, I don't see the point of your visit here today."

"Well, Mr Nolan, I simply wanted to make sure you were up to speed with the situation. Just in case any of it got into the newspapers. I wanted to put your mind at ease that we'd fully followed up on the matter. That's all."

Nolan jolted to his feet and snapped, "Don't take me for a fool!" His words were said with such anger that Doocey automatically flinched, fearing a flooring right-hook was headed his way. "You wanted to gauge my reaction," Nolan shrieked. "Hence, the real purpose of your visit here today."

"Not at all," Doocey lied, conscious that Nolan was exactly right. If *His Lordship* had a big problem in believing Jack Hanson could be his wife's murderer, which seemed to be the case, that might be another good indicator of his guilt.

Doocey faltered out of Nolan Manor into dazzling sunshine, hardly able to see a thing, but he carried blindly on, hoping he was headed towards his car. Just like he would blindly keep going forward with his investigations, hoping he was headed towards a solution, and his next/last step in that regard would be to interview Nolan's daughter, someone who could prove to be a crucial witness despite her blindness, and someone Ber had been nagging him to interview long before this, even threatening, "If you don't interview her soon, I'll do it myself."

But on his drive home, as he continued to do battle with the blinding sun, Doocey had a slight change of mind.

Twenty-One

"Oh, Good Morning," Doocey cheerfully greeted a grumpy-looking Nolan who'd just opened his front door to him and provocatively waited for a "good morning" back but when none came, explained, "I'm looking to have a quick chat with your daughter, I just need to get her address from you."

Nolan, looking seriously livid, burst out, "Now really, I don't see why you should need to go pestering a helpless blind girl."

That's a huge change of tune, Doocey pondered, remembering how Nolan had previously spoken of his daughter as this very successful opera singer who highly valued her independence but now, all of a sudden, she was a *'helpless blind girl!'*

"I'm sorry," he went on aloud, "but I need to cover off all the angles. I promise I'll be as sensitive as possible."

Nolan bowed his head and releasing a long sigh, said, "Detective, you had best come in. There are some matters I need to get off my chest."

Doocey trailed silently after Nolan, his thoughts filled with excited anticipation about what exactly these matters were that *His Lordship* needed to get off his chest. This time around, Nolan led him into a different room than usual. "My oh my, now this is what you call a library," Doocey exclaimed, his seeming astonishment causing him to slow right down. However, in reality, he was only wanting to give his ever-slowing eyes time to adjust to the gloominess of the huge room. Suddenly, a thunderous crash and

Doocey felt as if a trap door were opening in slow motion beneath his feet as he realised what he'd done. "I'm so sorry," he said, getting down on his knees to frantically scoop up blue and white porcelain pieces.

A silent Nolan strode over to where the detective had knelt and Doocey really did fear his Lordship was about to give him an almighty, avenging kick up the arse. He was gobsmacked then to see Nolan also get down on his knees, to start gathering up the smaller fragments that he kept missing until all the debris had been deposited onto a side table. A side table that mere moments before had hosted an extravagant oriental vase.

"I must've brushed off it," Doocey said, getting to his feet. "I'll pay to have it repaired."

"I dare say it's beyond repair," Nolan icily replied.

"I'll replace it then . . . Was it valuable?"

"Upwards of two hundred thousand euros."

"Two hundred thousand euros! You're not serious?"

"Yes, I am," he confirmed in a dour tone of voice. "It was an extremely rare Chinese piece that my father purchased."

Doocey bowed his head, wondering how he was ever going to pay him back two hundred grand. It would take him the rest of his life. Then he heard Nolan giggling. Giggling like a madman.

"I'm so delighted that you knocked it over," he said, still half giggling. "I loathed the vulgar thing and with it being so delicate and intricate it was an absolute nightmare to dust. I was constantly petrified that it would fall apart in my hands."

He squeezed his neck. "With it being so valuable—ironically—it gave rise to problems in disposing of it. Whereas I had no difficulty finding buyers for the rest of the replica antiques and bric-a-brac my father had bought to clutter up the house, I found it impossible to find a buyer for the vase or at least one prepared to pay a fair price. I tried auctioning it but it failed to make its reserve on three separate occasions. I therefore had resigned myself to keeping it until market conditions improved."

He started to giggle again. "Now I won't have to wait . . . and I can look forward to receiving a two-hundred-thousand-euro cheque in the post from the insurance company. I'm so thrilled."

Doocey's spirits shot back up. He smiled at Nolan. "Well . . . I'm glad to have been of some service."

They made their way over to two leather armchairs, and they both sat down. Doocey noted to himself how uncomfortably close the chairs were to each other but reckoned it would be rude to do anything about it.

However, Nolan had no such rudeness qualms and promptly moved his chair back to substantially increase the distance between them, and after a tense silence, he began to speak. "I fear I may have misled you about the real state of my marriage." He looked downwards. "The fact that Harriet and I slept in separate rooms wasn't simply owing to my snoring."

He stopped speaking as if expecting this disclosure to invoke a big reaction. Doocey, though, only gave a tiny nod. Nolan, looking uneasy, seemed to clench up a little. "You see, our marriage, recently, had been rather rocky. As you've discovered, Harriet was seeing other men." He rotated his platinum wedding ring. "I realise, of course, it looks terrible that I kept this from you . . . I was just terrified that if you knew we were having marital problems, you'd start thinking I had something to do with Harriet's disappearance, and you seemed so suspicious of me already."

"Ah, I wouldn't be over-worrying yourself on that front," Doocey reassured in a relaxed voice. "There's no crime in being stuck in an unhappy marriage. Sure, there's many the man in the same situation." He smiled. "Even myself sometimes." He repeatedly tapped his badly shaven chin with a finger. "I'm sure too, you would have worked things out. You see, I believe you still had feelings for Harriet."

Nolan frowned and gave a doubtful shake of his shiny head. But Doocey kept blithely going on with the argument he was making. "I would even go so far as to say that you were still in love with her. Sure, why else would you've only recently bought Harriet an expensive new motor?"

Nolan silently seemed to count the long fingers of his left hand before he finally replied. "Whatever the state of our marriage, I wouldn't see Harriet without a decent car."

"No, I'm sure you wouldn't. Yet, I'd bet you could buy a lot of other *decent cars* for a fraction of the hundred thousand euros you spent."

"Yes, most probably. I'm afraid though, one can regrettably get caught up with prestige and what others may think. I wouldn't feel it to be appropriate for my lady wife to be seen driving around in some bargain basement banger."

"Now, don't be trying to fecking kid me," Doocey said, leaning over to give Nolan a joke punch on the knee. An action that invoked a look of abhorrence on *His Lordship's* face. "I know fine well it hadn't a thing to do with prestige," he continued. "Sure, before Harriet got her new *Bimmer*, didn't you tell me she drove around in a modest ten-year-old hatchback?" He chuckled. "No . . . I know fine well why you bought her such an expensive car."

After several seconds of taut silence, Doocey finally elaborated, "You bought Harriet that car because—deep down—you still were madly in love with her." Getting no response, he added in this reassuring-sounding voice, "Mr Nolan, as I said, you don't need to be one bit nervous. Most marriages go through their rough stretches."

"Well, whilst that's reassuring to hear," Nolan, after a long silence, declared, "I'm afraid there's more . . . I need to tell you. I did such a silly thing."

Showing no reaction, Doocey suggested, "Why don't you tell me all about it? I'm sure you'll feel much better once you get whatever it is out of your system."

After a few dramatic twists of his substantial shoulders, Nolan relented. "Remember how your forensic people remarked on the spotlessness of my Volvo?"

Doocey gave a slow nod.

"Well, that's because I'd only cleaned it on the Wednesday morning."

A puzzled expression came over Doocey's face. "Do you mean the Wednesday morning after the Tuesday Harriet disappeared?"

Nolan rubbed at his brow. "Yes—and I know it looks so suspicious. Washing my car the very morning after my wife has gone missing."

"Why do it then?"

"I really can't tell you. I suppose I wasn't thinking straight and wanted to keep myself busy by doing some cleaning."

Doocey nodded. "Is there anything else you'd like to tell me?"

"No, nothing more comes to mind."

Doocey stood up, "Well . . . if that's everything, I must be getting going."

Nolan, now too, rose to his feet and rubbing his clean-shaven jaw, said, "I feared that if I told you all this, you might very well arrest me."

"Not at all," Doocey soothingly reassured. "Don't worry. I'm not going to do anything as stupid as that." He strolled alongside Nolan, past the pile of broken vase pieces, out of the gloomy library. "As I said, being in an unhappy marriage is no crime and sure, washing your jalopy isn't a crime either." Reaching the front door, he looked up at Nolan. "Sure, aren't we all *OCD* when it comes to different things?" *You see, I know about your OCD and your plan to later pull that out of the bag as your defence.* He went on aloud, "I hope our little chat here has set your mind at ease."

"Yes . . . yes, very much so," an unnerved-looking Nolan replied.

"Oh, I almost forgot," Doocey exclaimed, getting out his notebook and pen. "Can I get your daughter's address?" *Even though I have it already.*

Nolan replied with a growl, "1 Grand Canal Dock, Dublin 4."

Doocey jotted the address into his notebook. Then appended, "I best get Jennifer's telephone number off you too—so I can give her a ring to let her know I'm on my way."

Twenty-Two

Doocey was sitting at his desk, reading an email, when Dickson sneaked up behind him and whispered, "Am I right in thinking this is your last day messing about on the Nolan case?"

"Yeah . . . I think so . . . Ed," Doocey replied in his best chilled-out voice.

Dickson's whole fat body shuddered as if Doocey daring to use his first name had sent a shock wave right through him.

"Well . . . I can't tell you how much I'm looking forward to having you back reporting to me." Then with a muddled look on his face, he gave a contradictory clarification, "Though, as I warned you before, there probably won't be a vacancy for you. We seem to be getting on fine without you. I really don't know what you used to do Doocey any—"

He suddenly fell silent midsentence, and Doocey felt nauseating butterflies swarm inside his stomach, realising what the donkey had spotted—for a second time.

Dickson started up again, raising his voice even louder so that everybody on the station floor would hear. "I see you still haven't managed to get your computer sorted. The size of that text man! You could read it from the moon! God! I'll have to send you on a computer course to teach you the basics."

Naughton, living up to his reputation as Dickson's number one lickarse, shouted across to him, "Sir, I wonder is there something wrong with his sight?"

"That's a good point, Tony, I hadn't thought of that." He turned back to Doocey to question, "When are you due to do your next medical?"

"Next week."

"Next week," Dickson repeated and started to laugh. "Oh, that's just perfect timing, I'll be really looking forward to seeing if you pass the eye test part because I reckon it will be a damn miracle if you do."

More nauseating butterflies swarmed inside Doocey's stomach as, later that afternoon, he tapped on Jennifer Nolan's apartment door. She was his last hope of a big breakthrough before he met with Ryan the following morning.

Of course, he knew full well, he should've questioned her long before this, but it was as if some subliminal force had been holding him back. Though, he realised too that it might not be that much of a subliminal force. It might be simply down to his admiration for how Jennifer Nolan had courageously overcome her blindness to find singing success, and how that reminded him of his mother's courage. He hoped then—with all his heart—that she'd nothing to do with her stepmother's disappearance.

Jennifer Nolan opened the door and after Doocey introduced himself, she invited him inside, and he saw that her bright, spacious apartment had magnificent views of Dublin's Docklands. Magnificent views, he mused, that the apartment's owner would never see, and he felt grateful for the sight he had himself, however imperfect.

The layout of the apartment was open plan and accommodated a galley kitchen, a pale wood table with pale wood chairs, a grey sofa with a matching armchair. The walls were plain white and the floorboards were bleached white. All very calm compared to the strong, clashing colours of her bedroom back in Nolan Manor, leading Doocey to surmise that the apartment had come already furnished.

Jennifer made her way over to sit on the sofa, leaving a strong scent of citrusy perfume in her wake. Doocey admiring how deftly she navigated her world of darkness. Sitting down on the grey armchair, he stared for a second across at his slightly out-of-focus host and thought, *My eyes are a hundred percent getting worse.* She was wearing a black blouse and blue jeans, and though, a sturdy, broad-shouldered girl, at the same time, he perceived a delicateness to her. "I understand you're a singer?" he said aloud.

"Yes," she replied in a silky-smooth voice, "singing is my life."

"It's great to have a passion," Doocey commented back and went to get out his notebook and pen, those props he used to reassure his interviewees of him being some bit professional but then decided not to bother. Considering how this particular interviewee was blind—she would never be any the wiser.

"Now, Ms Nolan—I won't delay you," he continued, in a business-like voice. "I just have a few questions."

"That's fine, and please call me Jennifer."

"Okay, thanks . . . Jennifer. Your Dad told me you weren't staying with him the Tuesday, Harriet went missing."

"That's right."

Clocking the anxiety in her voice, Doocey said, almost in a whisper, "There's no need to be nervous." An intervention that led to a thin smile appearing on her face. "Before Harriet's disappearance, when had you stayed in Nolan Manor last?"

The strong line of her jaw melted a little, "I can't remember exactly . . . but at least a month beforehand."

"Your Dad said that he came to see you the evening before Harriet went missing, that would have been Monday, May the 14th. However, he said he only stayed for about half an hour."

"Yes, I wasn't very good company—exhausted from rehearsing frantically for an upcoming performance."

"How was your dad's own mood that evening?"

She jerked her large shoulders. "He seemed to be in his usual good spirits."

"By any chance . . . can you recall your last conversation with Harriet?"

After a marked delay, Jennifer Nolan replied, "I can't honestly remember . . . We hardly spoke."

"Any particular reason?"

Her face darkened and she said acidly, "Because Harriet was the cause of Dad breaking up with Mum."

A fair enough reason, Doocey considered and asked aloud, "Were there ever any arguments between the two of you?"

"Very occasionally, I mostly tried to avoid her." She half laughed, "It's easy enough to avoid people when you're blind."

Doocey half laughed back but kept to the same topic. "Whenever the two of you argued, what were the arguments about?"

Jennifer growled back her reply. "They were about her seeing other men, behind Dad's back."

"How did you know this?"

"I used to hear her on her phone, making plans."

"Did you tell your dad?"

"Yeah . . . but he didn't want to know."

"Did you ever get into a physical fight with Harriet?"

She wriggled herself more upright. "No."

Doocey sensed some hesitation. Some doubt in her tone. "What about your dad and Harriet? Did they ever argue?"

Jennifer bent her head to the side and swept a hand over her hair, as if thinking hard how best to answer and said weakly, "Hardly ever."

"I'm sorry to ask you this, but you don't think your dad could've harmed Harriet, do you?"

"No, absolutely not."

After a few more meek questions that yielded nothing useful, Doocey left Jennifer Nolan in peace. Because—despite his certain knowledge that she'd just lied to him—he hadn't the heart to go trying to scare the young lady into telling him the truth by coming the heavy with her—not that he reckoned he'd make much of a heavy, anyways.

He exited the apartment lift into the quarter light of the underground car park that reeked of petrol fumes, stumbled his way over to the entrance barrier, and squinted up at a CCTV camera—the footage of which he'd got Ber to examine and that initially seemed to corroborate Nolan's testimony that he'd paid a visit to his daughter on the evening of Monday the 14th of May—the evening before his wife supposedly vanished.

The footage showed his SUV driving into the car park where Doocey now stood—except that sitting alongside Nolan, in the passenger seat, had been his daughter. Nolan's vehicle departed half an hour later, though this time with an empty passenger seat.

Doocey recalled how carefully Nolan had studied that petrol station CCTV photo of him driving away from Nolan Manor on the evening of Monday the 14th and he was sure he now knew why. He'd wanted to be positive that the photo wasn't clear enough to reveal that his daughter had been travelling with him.

Leaving him free to tell his half-true, half-false story. True: he'd gone to Jennifer's apartment. False: he hadn't gone there to visit her but to bring her home. He must not have remembered or known about the CCTV cameras in his daughter's car park—or maybe, he hoped it would never get to a situation where they would come into play.

Doocey, though, had this irking suspicion that it all mightn't be as menacing as it looked on the surface. It might still even be true that Harriet Nolan had been accidentally swept out to sea and that Nolan had lied about Jennifer not having recently stayed over in Nolan Manor purely to protect her: shield her from potentially becoming a suspect when it came out that she hated her mother-in-law's guts, to shield her singing career from as much adverse publicity as possible.

Except Doocey, of course, saw a glaring and fatal chink in that harmless enough rationale. If Harriet Nolan went missing from Nolan Manor on the Tuesday, and if Mr Nolan brought Jennifer back to her apartment the day before, as the CCTV seemed to show—why would he have been so worried about his daughter becoming a suspect? It wasn't as if she'd even been staying over at Nolan Manor on the day her mother-in-law had gone missing.

What though if Harriet Nolan hadn't gone missing on the Tuesday but something happened to her on the Monday? What if, for instance, Jennifer had heard her dad murder her? Then becoming frightened that his daughter would break down under interrogation or that again she would become a suspect herself, Mr Nolan judged it safer to say she hadn't been there.

Back in his apartment, Doocey rang his mother and told her about how his questioning of Jennifer Nolan had gone and what the car park CCTV had revealed. He felt a little more reassured, given the poor job he reckoned he'd done in interviewing Jennifer, that his mother thought the girl had to be entirely innocent, or at the very worst might be covering for her father.

Doocey next phoned Ber and his raised spirits were not to stay raised for long as she gave out hell to him for not having asked Jennifer straight out—and especially with this being his last day on the investigation—why she was lying.

Doocey had finally mumbled in reply, "Ahh I thought . . . there was no

TWENTY-THREE

IN THE GARDAÍ HEADQUARTERS UNDERGROUND car park, Doocey switched off his Ford's engine and let out a guttural sigh. The never-ending drive from his apartment had been brutal. The fog in his eyes—*wouldn't you know it*—was extra bad today. Not helped by getting no sleep from worrying about whether things were going to go a disaster with Ryan or helped by that morning's dazzling sun—its glare making it almost impossible for him to read the traffic lights.

In the end, he'd had to resort to waiting to hear a beep from the car behind to know the lights had gone green, and he could safely proceed. However, as this asshole driving a silver Jaguar had most recently demonstrated, some drivers weren't happy just to beep you the once but had to keep blaring their horns, even when you'd pulled off.

He feverishly checked his watch—positive he was late. *God*, Ryan was going to murder him! But to his surprise, he found he was a little bit early. He closed his eyes and relaxed back into his ripped car seat, running through in his head, for one final time, how he was going to play things.

Fifteen minutes later, he stepped inside an empty lift and eventually locating the button for the top floor, the doors slid shut. At close range, he inspected himself in the lift mirror and forced a finger through his heavily gelled hair. Concluding that the grey suit, white shirt, purple tie, and slip-on shoes that he'd purchased, especially for the occasion, had been worth the money.

need for me to go arguing with the girl seeing as we've already collected enough evidence against Nolan."

"Arrah, will you go away out of that!" Ber shot back. And how could he blame her for not believing him? When he didn't even believe himself. The truth being, he wasn't at all sure he'd got enough evidence to convict Nolan and, even more worryingly, he wasn't even sure any more that the man had murdered his wife.

Thanks to his stubborn intransigence, however, he was lumbered with this frustrating feeling of the road to success not fecking taken. If he'd only been ruthless enough to call Jennifer Nolan out on her lies, he might well have ended up getting that one piece of indisputable evidence Ryan demanded. Instead, heading into the hungry lion's den, his survival solely depended on his powers of persuasion—and whether he had the *gift of the gab.*

After Ryan's PA, Frances Horan, checked to see if the assistant commissioner was ready to see him, Doocey, doing his best imitation of an assured professional who'd everything in hand—despite his fecking new shoes squeaking all the way—strode into Ryan's office.

But he hadn't even made it to taking a seat when Ryan let roar, "What's wrong with your damned sight?"

Doocey stopped on the spot, feeling all his life's energy leave his body. Somehow, he managed to speak. "There's . . . nothing . . . wrong with it . . . why do you ask, Sir?" he said, forcing himself to smile. He inched forward—that fake assured stride of his already abandoned. Now it was more the petrified walk of a man about to step off the edge of a skyscraper.

Ryan, looking his impeccable self, dressed today in a black suit with a red tie, whisked through papers on his desk, muttering, "That was me—in the silver *Jag*—beeping you at the lights."

Doocey managed to fake an odd-sounding laugh. His legs beginning to give way—he sat his mortified arse down. "Sorry about that Sir, my old crock of a car is causing me fierce trouble—it keeps on stalling."

Behind Ryan's back, a wall of windows looked out on a chaotic muddle of buildings and, somewhere in amongst them, the faint chug of a departing train. The assistant commissioner grunted, "You need to get yourself a decent car, man."

"You're right," Doocey agreed, feeling his heart begin to beat again. "I definitely will have to, Sir."

"Anyway . . . enough about your blasted car—tell me what you've come up with on the Nolan case?"

Doocey obediently obliged, though he hated every moment of it. He felt like an unknown artist being pressurised into showing a half-completed painting, only expecting to receive aggressive feedback from his supercritical audience like, 'What the hell is that supposed to be?' or 'You're never going to make anything out of that rubbish.'

He finished explaining the potential evidence he'd amassed—even going so far as to honestly detail any flaws, as he saw them, in that evidence.

About a minute later, Ryan put down the gold pen he'd been fervently taking notes with. He'd reminded Doocey of a little boy, rushing to finish copying his homework from the class swat before the teacher marched in. "As I see it," he then proclaimed, reading from his notes, "these are the key pieces of evidence against Nolan you've come up with." After proceeding to read out his summary of all the said pieces of evidence, Ryan raised his gaze from his notepad to declare, "It seems on the face of it to be a decent list."

"Yes, I think so too," Doocey eagerly agreed.

"But you do know the problem?"

Doocey faked a perplexed shrug, knowing—all too well—the obvious *problem* he was on about.

"It's all circumstantial. There's nothing there to definitively prove Nolan murdered his wife or to disprove she committed suicide or just accidentally drowned."

Doocey pretended to be speechless.

Ryan released a frustrated sigh and began explaining in some random order of his own, all the flaws in the evidence, as if he'd detected every single one for himself, and hadn't just heard them from Doocey. "Having no alibi, for example, does not mean someone's a murderer. If it did, my being home alone last night would make me one. You're not to go spreading this around . . . but I wouldn't say my marriage is the happiest either. And like Nolan, I wouldn't want my Mrs to file for divorce and scoop half of what I own. Do you see what I'm getting at? Even an innocent person can have a motive for murder."

Doocey nodded.

"Nolan not calling his wife's mobile to check she was okay is damned strange alright but in moments of stress, we can all react differently. It could also be like he told you, just to do with problems with the phone reception. Those same reception problems might also explain why Harriet Nolan never used her phone on the day she disappeared, or her phone was broken or something . . ."

Doocey nodded again.

"I agree it is surprising at this stage that her body has not yet washed ashore, as your expert in tidal patterns predicted it would. Experts though can be wrong and who's to say the body wasn't swept far out to sea by a wayward wave or wasn't eaten up by a shark or whale or whatever."

Outside, the dazzling sun slunk out from behind a tall building and Doocey was glad to lose complete sight of Ryan's stupid face, but unfortunately, he continued to hear his stupid voice—persisting to repeat everything back.

"The bruises to Mrs Nolan's neck, a month before her disappearance, would be majorly significant had she told her doctor she'd been attacked by her husband, but she didn't. She told him that she'd got them from accidentally falling on briar bushes. Plus, one of the fella's she'd been seeing . . ." He checked his notepad, "Jack Hanson . . . said that's how she got them too."

He looked down at his notes again for his next point (or that is to repeat one of the points Doocey had already made). "As for Nolan buying his wife's silence with a new car, he might have bought her that BMW for any reason."

Doocey gave a robotic nod.

"The surfacing of that white scarf looks very dodgy. Most likely Nolan was the one that threw it into the sea for you to find, but there's no chance of us ever being able to prove that. So, it's not worth a damn."

Hearing Ryan's swift dismissal of the scarf, as not being of any real importance, came as a giant hammer blow to Doocey.

Now he realised the huge risk he'd taken had been a total waste of time, and he'd felt horrible about doing it from the start. The first time he'd resorted to such underhanded tactics. But he'd reasoned he had no other choice.

He'd been running out of time, and with nothing concrete—no physical piece of evidence—to present to Ryan, he had needed to start to make things happen meaning he'd been the one and not Nolan who'd thrown the scarf into the sea, having previously pinched it from Harriet Nolan's walk-in wardrobe, and then gone on to lie about just happening to find it washed ashore down at the cliffs.

Sadly, however, all his scheming with the scarf had, as Ryan put it, turned out not to be 'worth a damn.' Because even though he seemed to have convinced the assistant commissioner that he was putting Nolan under so much pressure—that the man had resorted to planting fake evidence, it was clear now that this would not be enough, as he'd hoped it would be, to persuade his stupid superior into letting him have more time to investigate.

"Washing your Jeep, the morning after your wife disappears," Ryan continued, "well that is even more suspicious. However, I'd say Nolan would get away with it in court based on his obsessive-compulsive disorder."

He paused for a slight breather. *It must be hard work, this repeating everything back.* "Then there's the gardener Murphy. He might be lying just because he doesn't want Nolan finding out that he's staying over in the cabin without Nolan's permission, and we don't know if he saw anything."

Doocey continued to hold his tongue.

"As for Nolan's alleged confession to the aunt, we can't rely on that because of the woman's drinking and there were no other witnesses. Plus, the woman . . . what's her name again . . . yeah . . . Bridgie Reilly . . . has a long-standing grudge against Nolan. She never wanted her niece marrying the old git in the first place."

Ryan turned to the next page of his notepad. "With regards to Nolan lying about his daughter not being home, I don't see any major significance in that. He's probably just trying to protect her and her singing career." He looked Doocey in the eye. "Sure, the girl's also blind so she can't have anything to do with it."

Doocey registered that this last remark from the assistant commissioner was the first insight—albeit a very ignorant and prejudiced one—that wasn't a repeat back of something he'd just told him. However, it still wasn't even an original insight on his part because most likely Ryan had robbed it from a fellow idiot—Dickson—who'd been thinking along the same lines. Doocey recalled that one-liner file note of Dickson's deeming Jennifer Hanson to be innocent purely because of her blindness. There had been, however, as he'd previously looked up on the internet, incidents of blind people convicted of physical assault and even murder.

Ryan sighed. "What you've come up with is all circumstantial." He sighed again. "It's disappointing that you couldn't deliver me anything concrete when I stuck out my neck so much to get you on the case. I don't think many others in my position would have given you such a great opportunity to prove yourself."

"No," Doocey agreed, sounding like a timid teenager who'd just received a lecture from his father for totalling the family car. "I'm so sorry I wasn't able to have done better . . . and I'm extremely grateful for . . . the opportunity."

Ryan gave a kind of snarl and after waving a hand for Doocey to be on his way, he turned his attention to documentation on his desk. *That was it then.* His time on his first big case was done and—going by those threats from Dickson about his old job not being there to go back to and him *'really looking forward'* to seeing if he would pass the sight part of his medical—his entire detective career was done too.

TWENTY-FOUR

A MINUTE LATER, RYAN LOOKED UP from his papers, and fury flashed across his face on seeing Doocey hadn't left his office and had only got as far as the unopened door. "What is it?" he snapped.

"Well . . . it's just something is puzzling me about the Nolan case." Staring down at the dark floor, he continued in a tentative voice, "Though, it's probably nothing . . ."

"Spit it out man . . . spit it out . . ."

"Well . . ." Doocey began. "It's just that your brilliant feedback there got me thinking about the case differently."

"Yep," Ryan replied, sounding not one bit dubious that his feedback would be described as "brilliant" or that it could inspire fresh thinking on an underling's part.

Doocey continued, "You got me wondering about Nolan's stupidness. He had to have known that we were going to be suspicious about his account of his wife's disappearance. I mean, who goes walking their dog along a cliff edge in the middle of a serious storm?"

Ryan rested his handsome chin in his hand. Doocey took his silence as a green light to continue with what he'd rehearsed to say. "When I saw Nolan last, he was also so keen to highlight that he and Mrs Nolan were having marriage troubles. But why would he go emphasising a motive for wanting his wife gone?"

Doocey adjusted his tie and felt the slight dampness from an earlier tea spillage. "And if his marriage was in the doldrums—he could hardly think we'd believe he ventured out into a storm to search for a wife, it looked like, he would only be too glad to be rid of. Wouldn't it suit him perfectly if she'd fallen off the edge of a cliff? Saving him from a costly divorce."

He inhaled some air through his nose. "However, I don't think his marriage really was in trouble. According to Nelly Boyle, his ex-housekeeper, who was no fan of his, he and his wife got on great together. Although, Boyle reckoned it was all a show for her benefit. I doubt that . . . though. There's no way they'd be able to keep such a show going for so many years."

He inched closer to Ryan's desk. "Or why would they even care anyway about what Boyle thought? She was just an employee and someone Nolan hadn't the least bit of respect for. Remember how I told you about him saying she was a 'terrible housekeeper.' Plus, Jennifer Nolan also said her father and Harriet never argued."

Doocey frowned dramatically. "I know what you are going to say, Sir . . . *What about his wife's affairs with other men?* Though maybe with him being so much older than his wife, Nolan was not that bothered about those affairs. Powell, Mrs Nolan's best friend, also thought that."

He took another small step towards his old chair. "Nolan also seems to be getting stupider. Because what if he truly fessed up about murdering Mrs Nolan to her aunt? And why own up to having washed his motor, the morning after his wife had gone missing? Surely, he'd have realised how suspicious that looked. Why not just stick to his original story that he'd washed it in the days before, and we'd never have been any the wiser? Why—"

"Okay, okay," Ryan said, raising a hand and leaning back into his velvety chair.

"I get the idea of how stupid Nolan looks to have been and presumably—you don't think he really could be so stupid?"

"No Sir, I don't. Here's a man who spends his days writing crime novels (*however bad*) and can quote Greek philosophers and who's superbly able to think on his feet."

Ryan fiercely shook his head from side to side. "But don't you damn well see?"

Doocey acted out a puzzled stare. *God, it was hard work getting the dimwit to understand.*

In an act of true irony, Ryan squeezed his eyes shut in obvious frustration at Doocey's apparent denseness. Then, letting himself see again, at least physically, the assistant commissioner declared, "Nolan is playing us for fools." He gave a hard slap to his ornate oak desk. "As I explained to you, everything we've got on him is circumstantial. It's not worth a damn. He could dismiss every bit of it by saying, 'Why would I be that stupid?'"

Doocey cut in, "Gosh Sir, I think I see what you're saying. He's setting us up. That's why he fessed up to washing his motor and everything else."

Ryan let out a sarcastic laugh. "At last—*hip-hip hooray*—you're getting it. After he makes us look like goons in court, he figures we'll leave him be."

"That's exactly it, Sir . . . A bit of a risky strategy but that must be exactly it."

Ryan's eyes narrowed and as if the thought was entirely his own, said, "He's taking a bit of a risk, though."

"How do you mean, Sir?" and, as he asked the question, Doocey imagined how enjoyable it would be, using a hammer, to knock Ryan's incredibly white teeth out, one at a time.

The assistant commissioner now finally waved an irritable hand for Doocey to resume his old seat.

"Nolan knows," Ryan continued in an impatient tone, "that we haven't found a body or got any physical evidence. So why is he incriminating himself? Or even talking to us? Getting himself in trouble."

Doocey glared out the windows behind Ryan's back, half seeing piles of golden clouds drifting over Dublin city. "Gosh, I never looked at it like that," he excitedly replied, leaning forward in his chair. "That puts a whole different slant on matters. Sorry for being so slow here, Sir, but if I'm understanding correctly, you think Nolan is painting himself as the prime suspect to protect someone else?" Not wanting to give Ryan any time to incorrectly contradict him, he rushed on. "Ah, it all makes more sense now, Nolan has to be covering for his daughter. That's why he lied about her not being home. She must be the real killer."

Striving more than ever to head off dumb interventions from the assistant commissioner, he further picked up the pace. "I think, I'm following you now," he said, staring up at the ceiling, "I never truly considered a blind girl could be a murderer." He returned his gaze to Ryan. "I'm not—though—going to say you're wrong, Sir. Jennifer Nolan is a very strongly built girl. She could've been standing close to Mrs Nolan and have given her a push and her mother-in-law might have hit her head on say a wall—fatally. Actually . . . very much like the way Nolan told Harriet's Aunt, if we were to believe her, that his wife had died. Yeah, it might've happened as simple as that."

An irksome silence settled as he waited for Ryan to catch up. Until, the look of total mystification on the assistant commissioner's symmetrical face faded as he said in an imploring tone, "It's possible though . . . Jennifer could have killed her? She had the motive, she hated the woman, and it would explain why Nolan would want to portray himself as the main suspect. To stop us going after his daughter."

"Yes Sir, those are excellent points." *My fecking excellent points!*

"The only thing I can't understand," Ryan continued, "is why Nolan went to all the trouble of covering up for the girl in the first place. I'm sure a good defence barrister would be able to make a feasible case that she'd been provoked and never intended to commit murder. Given her blindness, I can't imagine her getting more than a year or so in prison—if any custodial sentence at all."

Doocey held back from enlightening the thicko as to what he reckoned were the very obvious reasons why Nolan felt he needed to cover up for his daughter: let Ryan think that his "big brain" had made yet another crucial breakthrough.

For what felt like hours, the assistant commissioner firmly pressed a hand to his forehead as Doocey repeatedly asked himself, *How dim could someone be?*

Suddenly Ryan sprang back to life and burst out, "I have it." Falling silent, he looked to Doocey and smiled, seeming to relish the opportunity to keep a subordinate in apparent suspense. "Even if Nolan's daughter avoided going to prison," Ryan at last resumed, "the bad publicity around the whole episode would be bound to put the kibosh on her singing career. I can't imagine many record labels wanting to sign up a murderer." He laughed to himself. "It's no wonder Nolan wanted to cover it all up."

About bloody time, Doocey thought but said aloud as if dumbstruck, "That has to be it. Shit! That's it."

Ryan drummed fingers on his fancy desk. "The problem again, though, is how we prove any of it."

Doocey grinned inside on hearing the asshole using once more the word "we" as if he truly believed they might be working together as a genuine team.

"Maybe Sir, proving it won't be so hard, now that it looks like there were two of them involved. Don't they say too that a secret is almost impossible to keep when more than one person knows it? There might even be a third person in on this secret if the gardener, Murphy, witnessed something. Chipping away at all three, I'm sure—I can get through to the truth."

For a few long seconds, the assistant commissioner gazed down at his desk as if the answer to his dilemma of what to do next was written there. When he ultimately looked up, it was to tell Doocey to step out of his office for a few minutes and to close the door after him.

On summoning Doocey back in, Ryan announced before he'd given him the chance to sit down again. "Okay, I put a call through to the commissioner, and now that I've steered you onto the right path, he's okay with me giving you one final week to work the case. After that, if you haven't come up with something in terms of evidence that would stand up in court and secure a conviction, I've promised the case goes straight back to Dickson. The commissioner isn't going to agree to any further extensions. Are we clear on this?"

"Yes Sir, crystal clear," Doocey said, giving the only answer he knew Ryan wanted to hear and would accept, even if he considered a week to be a ridiculous amount of extra time to come up with something major.

When he phoned Ber to let her know how his meeting went with Ryan, she had also even used the word 'ridiculous.' "Come on," she'd blared, "does he seriously expect you to solve the thing in a week—that's bloody ridiculous."

He wondered what her reaction would be if she knew there was a huge chance of things getting a lot more ridiculous, seeing as how his work medical was scheduled for the following morning. He might not then even have a week to wrap up the Nolan case but less than a miserly twenty-four hours.

He'd his strong suspicions that Ber had to have already sussed that something was up with his sight but likely was not aware of how serious the situation was—that his sight was so bad that there was a good chance of him failing his medical.

He got the feeling too that she wasn't interested in raising the subject of his sight with him, not because she didn't care, but because she considered it to be too much of a personal matter for her to go asking about. It was funny, Doocey thought, that even the usually very direct Ber had certain red lines she would not cross when it came to her directness.

As he sat into his car to drive back to the station, he wondered again if there was any way for him to reschedule his medical. But concluded as he'd concluded a hundred times before this that there wasn't. Especially not now that Dickson, thanks to that lickarse Naughton's prompting, was suspicious of there being something up with his sight. If he rescheduled, alarm bells would start to go off.

Plus, Doocey reckoned doing the medical now might not be such a terrible thing, after all. Better to get it over and done with before his sight got too bad (as he feared it might do) and he had his best chance of passing.

Another positive was that the doctor who conducted the annual medicals, Doctor Burke, was this kind-hearted old chap with a reputation for letting things slip under his relaxed radar. Maybe then he'd let him off not being able to read as far down the eye chart as he usually could.

Now, an even more wonderful possibility occurred to him, dancing like a mad thing about in his head. That by some massive miracle he might just be able to get the Nolan case wrapped up in the less than twenty-four hours remaining before his medical exam. Ryan would then be so delighted with him that he wouldn't care about any bad eyesight results and let him stay on being a detective. As if some wheel of fortune was spinning in his favour to bring this dream of his to fruition, on his arrival at the station he found that someone he'd already interviewed was waiting to see him and had important new information to disclose.

TWENTY-FIVE

ACROSS THE SCRATCHED TABLE OF interview room 2C, Jack Hanson cast Doocey a nervous look. "I suppose you're wondering why I've come back in to see you."

"I was a bit . . . alright," Doocey replied with a half-smile.

"Well . . . there's something that I thought you should know for your investigations into Harriet's disappearance." Hanson slightly bowed his head. "Though . . . even now . . . I'm not sure if I should say anything . . ." He paused as if waiting to be persuaded.

"It's vital, Mr Hanson, that you share any information you have. Even the tiniest detail might be enough to help us find her."

Hanson put his hand—as if it were a lid—over his mouth and after demonstrating marked reluctance for a few more moments, said, "It's to do with Jennifer Nolan."

"Oh . . . what about her?"

"Well, it's about how she and Harriet weren't getting on."

"They weren't getting on—really?"

"No . . . hadn't you heard?"

Doocey gave a sideways shake of his head.

"Yeah," Hanson continued, "they were always at each other's throats. Even though, of course, Harriet felt sorry for the girl on account of her blindness. But she found out that Jennifer had been eavesdropping in on her private calls and reporting back to her father."

Hanson put both hands to his temples as if going through some inner crisis, before regaining his composure. "I suppose trying to get her own back, Harriet started saying these daft things on our calls, for Jennifer to hear."

He hung his head low like an innocent schoolboy scared of fully snitching on his bold friend but finally managed to go on. "In front of Jennifer, she'd ring me up to say how great I'd been in bed . . . That kind of silly stuff. Just to rattle the girl's cage a little. I didn't think she meant any real harm."

Hanson paused, maybe hoping Doocey would say how he—of course—understood that no harm was ever intended. However, on only receiving a frosty stare, he continued. "Anyhow, this day, about a month before she went missing, Harriet was on the phone to me when she whispered, 'Jennifer is listening—I'll sort her.' Then she started into the slagging, saying how hard it must be to be both ugly and blind and how poor Jennifer would've no chance of getting any, and all this super nasty stuff."

Hanson scratched the back of his ear. "Before I got a chance to tell Harriet to put a sock in it, she started screaming, and I heard her phone falling to the floor. It never went dead though. I could still hear everything—Harriet screaming her head off." He shifted in his chair. "Panicked, I shouted down the line, 'Harriet are you okay? Are you okay? What's going on?' It was terrifying. I felt so helpless. Then, thank God, I heard the yells from Mr Nolan."

Hanson took a breather. "Harriet told me later how Jennifer had been deliberately trying to push her down the main stairs of Nolan Manor. She swore she'd be dead only that Mr Nolan came to her rescue."

He rubbed at his chin. "That's how she really got those bruises to her neck, you were asking me about. They were so bad that she had to go to see a doctor about them, and Harriet so hates doctors." He bowed his head again. "Not wanting to get Jennifer into trouble with the law, she only told her doctor that story about tripping onto briar bushes." Hanson stopped speaking, having apparently said all he had to say.

"That's very useful information, Mr Hanson, but why not come forward to tell us all this when Mrs Nolan first disappeared? Or why lie to me about her neck injuries being the result of an accidental fall?"

The pace of Hanson's speech became rushed as if he'd been expecting these exact questions and could not wait to get out his rehearsed answers. "Well, like I already explained, according to what I'd read in the papers,

Harriet had been out walking with her dog when she was accidentally swept out to sea. There was no mention of Jennifer being involved, and I saw no point in stirring things up."

"You never suspected that the story about her out walking along the cliffs might have only been made up? That Mr Nolan might be covering for his daughter?"

Hanson's face took on a pained look and his voice became higher. "But that's exactly why I came back in to see you, today. The idea that Nolan might be protecting Jennifer just struck me. I feel so stupid for not having thought of it before. You probably think me a complete fool?"

Doocey just smiled and asked, "Do you happen to own a race bike?"

"No . . ." Hanson warily replied as if wondering what a race bike had to do with anything.

Doocey got no sleep that night from going between thinking about what Hanson had told him and whether his sight was up to passing his work medical, the following day.

Twenty-six

Doocey sat alone in the narrow, overheated waiting room of the usual Health Centre where the work medicals were done. He stared unseeingly at the muted television on the wall which was switched to a 24-hour news channel, showing breaking news pictures of the devastation of the latest earthquake to strike the world, earlier that morning. He reminded himself that he would get through the medical fine but as every agonising second ticked down—he grew more and more unconvinced.

He heard a door opening and his name being called but it wasn't the semi-comforting voice of Doctor Burke that he'd been expecting to hear. This voice was female and sounded Eastern European. The new doctor introduced herself as Doctor Nowak and in answer to Doocey's question as to the whereabouts of Doctor Burke, she coldly explained in one word, as if she didn't appreciate being asked about her predecessor, "Retired." This news made Doocey feel like bursting into tears. No more kind-hearted, old Doctor Burke. No more of him letting things slip under his relaxed radar.

Nowak, a pretty but serious young woman, he guessed to be in her mid-twenties, went through the medical questionnaire he'd completed, much more forensically than Doctor Burke would've ever done. Doing various tests to verify the truthfulness of his answers. Testing his hearing, blood pressure, heart rate, lung capacity etc. In the fullness of time, she got to the part of the medical he'd been dreading. "You wear glasses?" she interrogated, as if she were only discovering this because he'd ticked 'yes' to wearing glasses on the questionnaire and hadn't noticed that he'd been wearing them right in front of her the entire time.

"Oh, yes," Doocey responded with a giggle. "There's no escaping getting old."

"Okay, let's see how your vision is, with and without the glasses," she said, simultaneously flicking a switch to light up an eye chart in the distance.

Looking at the chart, Doocey felt his heart rattle his ribs—horrified by how little of the letters he was able to make out. He told himself to stay calm. His eyes might only have dried up again. Like with what happened that time with Doctor Bullock. He blinked furiously and tilted his head every which way, but none of it improved matters. All it achieved was to cause Nowak to give him stunned stares. *What was even the point of having got those damned injections?* Though irritatingly he remembered the eye consultant, White, had said he would have good days of seeing and bad ones so maybe this was just one of the bad days—a very fecking bad one.

Left with no alternative, he read out the letters on the farthest down line that he could see—that wasn't very far down at all—and definitely not far enough down to pass the medical.

"Anything, from the lines below?" Nowak asked, and Doocey definitely thought he detected an underlying note of shock as if she were inwardly questioning, *How on earth is it possible for a serving detective to be this blind?*

"I think my eyes are just a bit tired," he said with a fake smile. "I haven't been getting much sleep," he waffled on. "You see, I've been working on this big case for Assistant Commissioner Ryan."

"Oh really," Nowak said mechanically as she continued making notes. "You can't read any further down even with wearing your glasses?"

"No . . ." Doocey conceded, sensing this Doctor Nowak was the closest thing you'd get to a human robot. And, of course, when asked to read the eye chart with his glasses off, he saw even fewer letters.

"If you don't mind holding on, Detective Doocey, I just need to step out for a moment," Nowak said, and almost ran to the door, shutting it after her, with a bang.

Doocey imagined her, in the coming seconds, scrambling for some red telephone. The red telephone they used to alert the powers that be that someone had flopped their medical big time.

That's it then. The final, fecking curtain. He thought about making a run for it—before things got any worse. Though how could things get any worse? It seemed though that they could. Because when Nowak, a few minutes later, marched back in, she was accompanied by some gent whose skin was whiter than his doctor's coat and who Doocey reckoned would make a very good Dracula.

The man curtly introduced himself, with a slight German accent, as Mr Kepler—the Health Centre's resident eye consultant. Then he got immediately down to business, shining a bright torch thingamajig at him, to examine the backs of his eyes.

"Have you noticed any deterioration in your vision recently?" he sternly asked.

"No," Doocey replied, determined to play dumb.

Kepler shook his head, and Doocey got a whiff of his bad vampire breath. "Most unusual," he hissed. "As I'm seeing significant degeneration. I would have expected you to experience a drop off in your vision, perhaps seeing a kind of fog?"

"No . . . nothing like that," Doocey lied again.

Kepler and Nowak headed out into the corridor to have a private word—their voices too low for Doocey to hear.

A few minutes later, Nowak returned alone, and consulting her notes said, "You mentioned that you are working on a case for Assistant Commissioner Ryan. Correct?"

"Yes . . ?" Doocey said hesitantly, cursing himself for being so stupid to ever have mentioned Ryan's name. Now, the report confirming he'd failed his medical would be winging its way directly to him. Though even if this didn't happen, a copy would be definitely—as happened every year—going to Dickson.

As he exited the scorching hot stillness of the medical centre into the relatively fresh air of the loud street outside, he wondered how long the process would take. Normally, with how slow the wheels of Garda bureaucracy turned—months would pass before he got his medical results back. He'd bet though those wheels of bureaucracy spun a hell of a lot faster when someone failed a medical so badly as he had. Best case scenario, he had a couple of days, maybe two or three at the most, before he got ordered either by Ryan or Dickson to finish up.

But what if you were able to solve the Nolan case in those two or three days? Ryan then, as you'd been thinking before, might sort something out for you. Let you stay on being a detective. And you might as well have a go at solving it in whatever little time you've left. It's not as if you've anything else to do or anything more to lose.

Getting into his car, he got out his mobile to phone Ber, to tell her his medical went fine and about his next plan of action which mainly involved directly calling people out on their lies. Ber's reaction to this being, "Well about bloody time."

Twenty-seven

THE FOLLOWING DAY, AS HE was walking up to Murphy's cabin at the back of Nolan Manor, Doocey tripped and went flying, head over heels. Getting to his feet and dusting himself down, he strove to shove from his mind worries about his sight, and that failed medical. Telling himself that he'd shortly have buckets of time for worrying—after he'd officially got the sack.

On hearing movement inside the cabin, Doocey heaved a sigh of relief. Based on his latest horrible luck, he feared Murphy might have done a bunk. He knocked on the cabin door twice and waited a minute. He was about to give a third louder knock, when the door creaked open, and his eyes, with their—freshly vouched-for—diminished abilities, struggled to fathom how Murphy had changed so drastically.

However, on hearing the words, "Hello there," his ears made sense of the situation first. Murphy looked so unrecognisable because the man standing before him wasn't Murphy, and whilst he might be around the same age and height as the missing gardener—there the similarities ended in terms of him being his twin, not unless he was his very ugly unidentical twin. This fella had a big bouncing belly and a nose that even Pinocchio would consider on the long side.

Doocey got out his detective ID and introduced himself. In turn, the stranger gave his name as Ned O'Malley and explained how he was Nolan's new gardener, prompting Doocey to grumpily ask what had happened to Murphy.

And after doing some manoeuvres of his mouth, as if to get his false teeth in the right position to speak, he answered, "Mr Nolan says he emigrated to Australia."

"When?"

O'Malley rubbed the bottom of his prolific nose. "I'm not sure . . . but I started here the day before yesterday."

Though feeling like he'd just been repeatedly stabbed through the heart, Doocey attempted to compose himself and managed to sputter out his next question. "Do you know where Mr Nolan is? He doesn't seem to be home, and I wanted to have a word."

An hour and a bit later, Doocey pressed a golden doorbell button, twice. As he waited, his mind's eye imagined the stereotypical scene inside. Pompous rich men sitting in winged armchairs, sipping brandy, talking twaddle.

The door opened, and this prim and proper-looking man stood glaring at him. Glaring at this tiny, clownish character with the mad hair and goofy glasses, togged out in a raggedy anorak. Taking a repulsed step back, the man pronounced, "I'm afraid this is a private members' club. We're not open to the general public."

Or The Great Unwashed, Doocey silently substituted. Retrieving his official ID, he snapped aloud, "Yes, I'm aware of all that but I'm a detective, and I'd like to speak with one of your members, a Mr Nolan."

Mr Prim tersely ushered him in and ordered that he wait in an empty, oak-panelled room, where a coal fire threw out intense heat. A minute later, the sound of footsteps rapping off parquet flooring, and judging by the loudness and speed of those footsteps, Doocey took it that *His Lordship* wasn't going to be at all happy to see him.

"Yes?" Nolan almost yelled from the doorway, making it clear as fecking day that he was in no mood to go sitting down for a long chat. "What is it this time?"

"Oh, good afternoon, Mr Nolan," Doocey cheerfully responded and deliberately remained seated. "I have to say, I like the look of this place." He relaxed back into the soft leather of his chair. "Aah . . . that's comfy. You know . . . I wouldn't mind joining a place like this myself—to get some peace from the Missus. Is it very hard to become a member?"

Nolan's scowl intensified. "Is there something in particular you want?"

"Oh yes, there is, Mr Nolan," Doocey said, sitting forward again. "What … I suppose I want to know … is why you lied to me about your daughter?"

Nolan looked momentarily taken aback before finding his words. "I haven't the slightest idea what you're talking about."

"You lied to me about Jennifer staying over in Nolan Manor."

Nolan's whole body tilted backwards as if he'd been pushed. A look of pure fury on his face. Doocey could virtually feel the heat of anger seeping from him, almost as much as the heat seeping from the room's coal fire.

"You said that she hadn't been staying over in the days up to your wife going missing," Doocey elaborated. "You claimed it had been weeks since she'd stayed over last. But we've CCTV footage from Jennifer's apartment complex showing you driving her back there from Nolan Manor, just the evening before you reported your wife missing."

Looking dazed, Nolan rubbed at his bare head, and Doocey, seeking a figurative knock-out punch, hit him again. "Jennifer killed Harriet, didn't she? You're covering up for her."

"That's a preposterous accusation," Nolan thundered back. "Utterly preposterous!" He fluxed about in agitation, like a ship caught in a deadly storm.

"No, I don't think it is preposterous at all, Mr Nolan. You see, Jack Hanson, who, as I told you, had been seeing Harriet, has now come forward to testify that Jennifer severely assaulted her, only a month before she went missing."

"What?" Nolan shrieked. Then as if thinking he must have misheard, asked, "This Hanson person actually said that Jennifer physically attacked Harriet?"

"Yes."

Nolan began to shout. "That's a lie. A complete lie."

"Your wife's doctor also confirmed that at about the same time Harriet visited him to have severe bruising to her neck treated. Bruising consistent with a physical assault. Were you aware of those injuries?"

"No …" Nolan said slowly, his voice dropping. "I never knew about any injuries or that Harriet went to see a doctor."

He fell silent as if he were trying to remember back.

However, Doocey reckoned Nolan's strained trip down memory lane had to be an act on his part. Surely, if his daughter had physically attacked

Harriet, either she or his wife would have confided in him. Then Nolan asked what Doocey considered to be a very astute question. "Did Harriet actually say to her doctor that she'd been attacked?"

"No. She only said she'd accidentally fallen against briar bushes."

Doocey felt uneasy about being so candid. That he might be letting slip too much to Nolan. But on the verge of being sacked—he judged he hadn't time for slow caution. With Nolan seemingly rendered speechless, he continued, "However, Hanson said Harriet had been on the phone to him when it all happened, and knowing that Jennifer was listening, started saying these nasty things about your daughter. Apparently, she was fed up with Jennifer eavesdropping in on her phone conversations and grassing to you."

Doocey unearthed his notebook to read something out, or that is to pretend to read something out, seeing as his sight wasn't good enough at this particular moment in time to do any real reading—not unless that is, he held the notebook right up to his eyes. He felt his face already burning up at the words forming on the tip of his tongue. *But to feck with disgust and embarrassment!* At this point, he needed to do whatever it took to get Nolan to crack. "Hanson said that Harriet had teased Jennifer about how, quote: *'Hard it must be, to be both ugly and blind and how she'd have no chance of getting any . . .'"*

Nolan squeezed a fist to his forehead and when he removed it, the pure white imprint of knuckles remained.

Hoping, at any second, the barricades of Nolan's defences were about to collapse and that the truth of what became of his wife would be revealed, Doocey pressed on. "He says, he heard Jennifer trying to push Harriet down the main stairs of Nolan Manor and heard you dragging your daughter away."

Nolan mumbled, "I don't know why the man would tell such a pack of revolting lies." His voice rose in volume. "Have you forgotten my daughter is blind? How could a blind girl attack anyone?"

Doocey's whole body twitched and he said timidly, "I'm afraid there have been documented cases of blind people physically attacking and even murdering others."

After a few seconds of stillness, Nolan came back to life with renewed rage as if a sleeping dragon awakened by the poke of a stick in the eye. "I've had quite enough of your antics, continually coming to my home to harass me, and now coming here. Well, no more."

The veins of Nolan's forehead visibly throbbed. Whisking out a skinny wallet, he forced a business card into Doocey's hand. "These are my solicitor's contact details. From here on in, kindly address all your idiotic questions and unfounded allegations to them."

Doocey felt his entire body droop as that small confident part of him died. His tactics had tremendously backfired.

For some seconds Nolan looked at him, almost pityingly, but in an instant snapped back into his previous state of outrage. "Do you understand?" he blared. "You're to go through my solicitors. You're not to come anywhere near Jennifer or me."

Once more there was the clatter of loud footsteps on parquet flooring as Nolan took his leave, and within a minute, *Mr Prim* had returned to brusquely usher Doocey out as if he were a human broom brushing out onto the street a piece of embarrassing dirt.

Doocey crossed the road to Saint Stephen's Green and trudged around the perimeter of the park's large pond, desperately trying to think what the feck to do next. However, with each step he took, it felt as if he were sinking deeper and deeper into the pond's dark waters.

He'd truly been so stupid. He should've made better use of all his opportunities. His mind conjured up an image of Nolan as a fed-up farmer getting out his gun to let fire at this brazen little bird who'd been constantly coming back to nibble his crops—crops that his survival depended on.

He held up the business card Nolan had given him to his glasses—so close that it touched them—and just about managed to make out: 'Fredrick R. Scott & Co.' His spirits lowered another niggly notch. Scott & Co. were the best defence solicitors in the country, famed for keeping their wealthy as hell, and usually, guilty as hell, clients out of prison.

Doocey felt full sure that those well-spoken solicitors at Scott & Co. wouldn't deem there to be the slightest possibility of Nolan or his daughter being charged with anything. The evidence against them, even with Hanson's new testimony incriminating Jennifer, was just way too weak to secure any sort of a conviction.

Now, any cursed chance of marshalling any more substantial evidence from Nolan and his daughter had vanished. All he'd be getting from this point onwards, via Scott & Co., would be, "Our clients have no comment to make."

On his return to the station, Ber was having none of Doocey's defeatist attitude, maintaining that Nolan warning him off and Murphy doing a runner were just "setbacks." Then giving one of her customary kicks to his swivel chair, she declared, "You just need to keep ploughing on."

Although—of course—Ber had still no idea that he'd failed his medical and was due to be getting the sack at any second now, so he'd run out of time to do any more 'ploughing on.'

Not that he reckoned having any more time would make a difference anyhow. Now that Nolan and his daughter were refusing to talk to him and Murphy was gone—all his main leads had been severed. He might as well face it—his investigation into Harriet Nolan's disappearance was over, as was his entire pathetic detective career. Doocey went to bed that night, a broken man.

TWENTY-EIGHT

Doocey awoke the next morning a few minutes before his work alarm went off, but he stayed in bed. His eyes were killing him; they needed rest, and he wasn't sure what would be the point of going into the station when he'd no leads to follow up. Unless he just fancied going in to be sacked because he felt sure that today had to be the day, Ryan and Dickson got to hear about his failed medical.

He was even surprised that the assistant commissioner had not already been on the blower to give him his fecking marching orders. But maybe he'd calculated, for the sake of a few days—better to hold off giving him the sack until the extra week he'd granted him was fully up. Ryan would wait until they were due to meet in person, and only after milking him for anything new he'd discovered, would he then give him the sack.

At ten past nine, Doocey sat himself up in his bed—to ring Ber, an idea having just popped into his head. He wondered if by utilising her slick computer skills, she could track down Murphy's exact whereabouts but considering the massive size of Australia, he didn't much fancy her chances.

After finishing his call with her, he rested his head again on his pillow, trying to forget about the AWOL gardener and to think of some other line of inquiry that might supply a critical breakthrough. However, lying there with his eyes closed, his stubborn mind just refused to move away from the subject of Murphy and why he'd fled.

Maybe, as his mother had speculated after he'd told her about him doing a runner, that the fecker had truly been in love with Harriet Nolan? Meaning, he couldn't stomach working a minute longer for the man who he believed murdered her.

Or, had Nolan clocked that his gardener had seen something incriminating? So, he'd packed him off to the other side of the world with a "you'd better keep your mouth shut" suitcase of cash. Might Murphy even have feared he was going to be Nolan's next victim?

On the other hand, there might not be anything sinister at all to him suddenly upping sticks. Maybe, like the thousands of other Irish who emigrated there every year, he simply fancied a new start in sunny Oz.

He wondered if Murphy's fiancée had gone with him or whether they'd broken up and even if that could be the reason for him skedaddling.

Defeated, Doocey rolled over onto his other side. Whatever Murphy's reasons for leaving, what did it matter? He'd gone and had taken with him his last hope of solving the case.

At half-past eleven, Doocey was still in bed when his phone started to ring and he just about summoned up enough energy to answer it, only to hear Ber excitedly proclaim, "Murphy hasn't left the country. According to his tax employment records, he's got a new job working for a *Green Acres Garden Centre* on the Blessington Road."

Lazarus style, Doocey hopped out of bed and joyfully exclaimed, "Great work Ber." He threw on his old suit and anorak and drove (erratically) straight to *Green Acres Garden Centre*. He'd no bother finding the place because providentially it was on the Blessington Road which was a road he took when going from his apartment to work and on the way back, so he'd driven past it tons of times.

He pulled into a car park of what, from the outside, looked more like a large steel warehouse than a garden centre. The name *Green Acres*, crudely sprayed across its rusty front in shaky luminous yellow letters. Inside was equally unimpressive, with scruffy plants strewn everywhere and a shop assistant—who looked to be catching forty winks—slouched over her till. He chose not to wake her up to ask where he could find Murphy, afraid if given any sort of advanced warning of his presence, the gardener would scarper . . . *best to try sneaking up on him.*

As Doocey frantically looked about for someone bearing the woolliest resemblance to Murphy, he still wasn't sure as to the right tactic to take with him. Should he try the direct, aggressive approach to get him to cough up what he knew? That though would risk a dire rerun of what happened with Nolan. Murphy could also easily say, 'Speak to my solicitor.'

It might be best to try a more subtle approach; just keep applying the pressure, keep turning up at Murphy's new workplace, and wait for him to gradually crack. Except, of course, that kind of cat-and-mouse strategy required a major amount of something he had very little of—fecking time.

After he must've walked nearly every inch of the gone-to-seed garden centre, without finding Murphy, Doocey began to tense up, fearing Ber's recon was only codswallop. That Murphy genuinely had hopped on a plane to Australia.

He marched up to the shop assistant at the till who managed to straighten up a little and drowsily relay how Murphy was "out back" and pointed a limp finger to where she meant.

Doocey smiled to himself, thinking how he liked that this particular "outback" was in good old Ireland. He proceeded through a squeaky door that opened to an outdoor plant area where—after more wandering about—he located his target. Murphy was standing at a workbench, repotting some blue flowers that looked to be on their last legs. "Ah, there you are Frank," he sunnily called out. "How's the new job going for you?"

Seeming at once to be both dumbfounded and disgusted to see the scruffy little detective, Murphy snarled back, "I don't have time for talking to you. I need to get on with this."

He gave the bottom of a pot the slightest whack of his hand to unfree its plant and the smell of rotting roots filled the air.

Doocey carried on in an upbeat tone. "That's no problem at all. We'll have plenty of time for talking when I bring you into the station tomorrow. I'm just waiting on the paperwork for the arrest warrant to be rubberstamped." He smiled broadly at a motionless Murphy. "No, I'm only here today because I just wanted to double-check you really hadn't left the country."

"What're you on about?" Murphy exclaimed, slamming down the empty terracotta pot in his hand, causing it to crack in half. "Arrest me for what? I've done nothing."

Even though Doocey felt sure that the mammoth gardener was on the verge of knocking his little lights out, he tried to keep his voice calm. "Well, we'll be charging you with withholding information to start with . . ."

Murphy enacted, in slow motion, a mocking laugh. "Ha . . . ha . . . ha. Very fricking funny." He dialled down the scorn in his voice a smidge. "I told you . . . I don't know anything about Mrs Nolan's disappearance. I wasn't bloody there!"

"But we know for definite that you were there. Don't you remember? We've got the CCTV footage from the petrol station."

Murphy went quiet for several seconds before giving a shrug of what looked to be resignation. "Okay, okay, I might have stayed over in the cabin, but I saw nothing. I was asleep."

You were asleep, were you? Doocey inwardly questioned. *But how would you know that whatever happened took place at night?* "I think you had to have seen something, Frank," he said aloud. "Why else would you finish up working in Nolan Manor?" Murphy tossed his head back and as if after the silent count of three, said, "I just fancied a change."

"I find that hard to believe," Doocey disagreed, giving exaggerated glances at his surroundings. Even through his forgiving eyes, *Green Acres Garden Centre* resembled a kip. "This place doesn't exactly seem like a promotion. I'm sure taking care of the gardens of a manor house had to be much more enjoyable and prestigious employment. Why also lie to Nolan about going to Australia?"

For a few seconds, Murphy looked to be stumped. "Because . . ." he finally began but Doocey immediately cut him off.

"Ah don't bother, Frank. I've had enough of your bullshit. Anyhow—Nolan isn't going to be best pleased when he hears you lied to him about going to Australia and when I tell him you were staying over in the cabin. He's bound to suspect you saw something."

Doocey took a step forward. "For your own safety, Frank, it's best if you tell me what you know."

Murphy became very animated. "I'm not afraid of him, and like I've told you a hundred times—I know nothing."

"Suit yourself," Doocey said, strolling away. Turning back to the gardener after only a few steps. "Oh, one last thing, Frank. I know you were having an affair with Harriet Nolan . . . and I'm afraid . . . I'm going to have to let some journalist mates of mine know all about it."

Murphy started to growl like some ferocious, cornered animal, but Doocey kept talking, "If I were you, I'd make sure—pronto—to have a chat with your fiancée." He frowned. "Unless you're happy for the poor girl to read in the newspapers all about how you were carrying on with Mrs Nolan behind her back."

Murphy squeezed his hands into fists and moved within millimetres of Doocey, and threatened through gritted teeth, "Listen to me you six-eyed little fart . . ."

Stepping out of the gardener's furious shadow, Doocey said coolly, "You'd better keep that nasty temper under wraps. Otherwise, we might start believing you're the one who murdered Harriet."

He eyed Murphy for some moments. "Now, I can see that this is upsetting you. That me arresting you is going to cause you a lot of grief."

Doocey paused and looked up into Murphy's anguished face. "It doesn't have to be like that Frank. I don't have to arrest you tomorrow, or for that matter, ever arrest you or tell my journalist mates a thing. Your fiancée need never find out you were doing the dirt on her." He lowered his voice a fraction. "You see I'm certain at this point that Harriet Nolan is dead, and all I want from you is a little help in finding her remains. After that, we'll leave you be. We'll easily be able to charge Nolan once we've recovered the body."

The gardener furrowed the palm of his hand down across his chiselled-like face. Encouraged that Murphy seemed to be at least thinking over what he was putting to him, Doocey pushed on. "Are you just going to let Nolan get away with killing Harriet? Come on Frank, I know you cared for her a great deal."

Murphy groaned, "I don't want to get involved in any of this."

Doocey grabbed Murphy's overdeveloped wrist. "I'll keep your name out of it."

"You promise?"

"Yes . . ." he vowed, giving a squeeze of Murphy's wrist, "just tell me what you saw."

Murphy, with hardly any effort, pulled his wrist free. "If I do, that will be the end of it? You won't bother me again?"

Doocey felt the first quivers of relief. *Progress at fecking last.* "That's right, I will never bother you again," he vowed aloud, not giving a toss what he'd to say to get the weight-lifting weasel to talk.

Murphy pointed with his head for them to move right to the very back of the outdoor area. Presumably not wanting to risk being overheard by the rare customer or more likely another staff member. As he trailed after Murphy, this manic voice inside his head shouted out, *This is it—finally your big break.*

TWENTY-NINE

"**O**KAY, OKAY," MURPHY SAID, CHECKING one last time that nobody else was within earshot. He began speaking at lightning speed as if trying to get everything, he'd to tell, out without the need to take a breath. "You were right about me sometimes staying overnight in the cabin at the back of Nolan Manor and about me seeing Mrs Nolan—Harriet. But it was only a fling . . . nothing serious."

Now, where have I heard that one before, Doocey silently teased.

"We'd arranged to meet on the Monday night, at nine in the cabin—"

Doocey interrupted, "That'd be Monday, the 14th of May. The night before Nolan reported her missing?"

"Yeah . . ."

"Okay, carry on."

"She never showed up in the end. I knew she was home though. I'd spotted her car parked outside the house."

"Weren't you worried?"

"Not really. I just thought she hadn't been able to get away. That sometimes happened, and like I told you before, I don't have a phone so Harriet couldn't ring me. I just passed the time doing some weights instead." He ran a massive hand through his dark hair. "Before heading to bed though . . . I took one last peep out the cabin window, and that is when I saw him, coming out from the back of the house."

Doocey held his breath. It felt like he was tiptoeing across a frozen sea, and the next step he took would determine whether the ice broke—would determine his salvation.

Murphy continued, "Nolan drove his SUV around to the rear of Nolan Manor, parking it near the back door. Then he went back into the house and when he came out again, he was carrying something in his arms. Something very large and heavy—because he was staggering under its weight, and he was struggling to get it into the boot of his Volvo."

Murphy's voice wobbled, "Straightaway, I'd this bad feeling . . . even though I was too far away to see exactly. This bad feeling that what he'd put in the boot of his SUV was a body. Harriet's body. I thought too I'd spotted what looked to me like a woman's limp hand hanging down."

Murphy closed his eyes for a moment and shook his head.

"Right," Doocey prompted, striving to keep the rising tide of excitement within him at bay. "What happened next?"

"I kept on watching from inside, and I think I remember Nolan looking up towards the cabin once or twice, but I'm sure he never spotted me. You see, I never switched on any lights at night, in case he'd cop that I was staying over in the cabin."

"Very smart of you," Doocey acknowledged.

"I saw him walk up to that small tool shed you asked me about and he took out a spade. I kept watching until he drove off, and I saw the lights of his Volvo turn up onto the bog road."

Murphy stopped speaking. A worry wrinkle appeared on his forehead as if he knew Doocey would think his thrilling testimony had ended in a calamitous anticlimax. Which was exactly the case as at that very moment the detective was thinking, *It's not enough.* His mind's eye conjured up the thousands of acres of barren bogland that would need to be scoured. No doubt, OCD Nolan would've also done a first-class job of hiding any trace of a grave.

He could well imagine him, after having buried the body, meticulously slotting heather-topped sods, he'd set aside, tightly into position—making it impossible to tell with the naked eye (as in a properly functioning naked eye) that a body lay buried beneath. He doubted ground radar would be of any use either when deployed on such a vast area. There'd be all sorts of debris hidden within the bog, from ancient tree trunks to animal carcasses. All of which would result in a flood of false readings.

Specially trained sniffer dogs would probably be the only option, but there again, if Nolan had buried the body deep enough, they'd never pick up on a scent. Harriet Nolan's final resting place seemed fated to remain a secret forever.

Of course, he'd still got Murphy as an eye witness, but if forced to make an official statement, he felt positive, the two-timing rat would deny it all, to protect his chances with his fiancée, or out of fear of retaliation from Nolan. Though, even if Murphy could be coerced to take to the witness stand, Nolan's defence team would likely argue that the gardener was only lying as he'd a vendetta against his former boss, the man married to the woman he'd coveted and who he mistakenly had believed to have murdered her.

As Doocey continued to wallow in his 'so close and yet so far' hard luck, Murphy calmly announced, "For whatever mad reason, I followed after him."

The detective burst into spontaneous, crazed laughter. The gardener hadn't been anxious that he'd seen too little, but that he'd seen too much. Doocey snappily stopped laughing and asked himself, *What the f are you at?* The last thing he wanted to do was to show his huge relief because that might spook Murphy. Trigger him to think about the hugeness of his testimony. Trigger him to doubt whether he was doing the right thing by fully ratting on such a rich, and consequently powerful, man as Nolan.

The gardener glared at him, and in the brutal silence, Doocey dared not speak. Finally, Murphy continued, and Doocey breathed an inward sigh of relief, determined, from here on in, to keep his, all over the shop, emotions in check.

"I raced cross country to where Nolan looked to be headed, keeping low, afraid of being seen." He squeezed the back of his muscular neck. "The night was very bright on account of this massive full moon. I watched him park up, carry the body down into a valley, and begin digging a grave close to a dolmen."

The word dolmen instantly brought to mind for Doocey age-old memories of a school field trip and his favourite teacher, Mr McHale, standing in the shadow of this gigantic structure—or at least gigantic through the eyes of an eight-year-old—simply constructed from three standing stones, each at least seven feet tall, and resting horizontally on top of them, an even bigger capping stone. Mr McHale had imparted how such dolmens were thought to mark the sites of prehistoric burial chambers.

"That's everything I know," Murphy curtly concluded. "I swear—and I'm only telling you all this because I can't stand to see Nolan, the piece of trash, getting away with killing her. Harriet was such a nice person."

Too thrilled to speak, Doocey shook Murphy's hand. However, their awkward handshake had no sooner ceased, when, like a runaway train, this horrible thought crashed through all his joy. *What if Nolan had* spotted Murphy on the night, especially with that bright moon, he'd mentioned? Or more recently, might've clocked Murphy had seen him, after becoming suspicious about why his gardener would suddenly up and leave his employment. He asked aloud, "It must've taken Nolan a good while to dig the grave and fill it back in?"

Murphy nodded, "Yeah—ages."

"And you waited until he'd finished?"

"Yep. I was scared that if I moved, he'd spot me. Like I said, it was a very bright night."

"You're sure that during all that time he definitely didn't see you?"

"Yeah . . . I'm . . . sure," Murphy said falteringly.

Doocey frowned and followed up, "You're positive?"

Murphy returned an anxious look as if considering whether or not to unburden himself of some concern. "Well . . . there's one tiny thing," he said at last. "Just as I'd started to run back to the cabin, I twisted my ankle, and I let out this tiny yell."

"Did Nolan hear?"

"No . . . I don't think so. You see . . .at that stage . . .he'd already sat into his motor . . ."

"You don't sound too sure," Doocey whipped back, now recalling how Murphy had been limping the first time he'd met him. *Just effing fantastic,* he thought. If Nolan copped, he'd been seen, he would—afterwards—have dug the body back up and reburied it . . . God knows where.

"No, no, I'm sure I got away with it," Murphy continued much more confidently, causing Doocey to start to hope again. The gardener's voice became more excited. Almost as if he were a pleased-as-punch little boy who knew with certainty that he'd the right answer to the difficult puzzle set by the teacher. "I lay down flat on the ground, well-screened by long heather, and Nolan never got back out of his Volvo. He just drove off and I lay there hidden for another good ten minutes to make certain, he'd gone. When I made it back to the cabin, I saw his SUV parked up and all was quiet. So—yeah—I'm certain he never spotted me."

Doocey found Murphy's assurances seductively alluring. He was bizarrely reminded of the time he'd fallen in love with this gorgeous house being sold by an estate agent named Lilly. The same sweetly lying Lilly who vowed that even as an irredeemable bachelor, the house's four huge bedrooms wouldn't be wasted on him or neither would its field of a family garden. What real difference did it make either that the property price blew his budget to smithereens when, as Lilly repeatedly liked to remind, "Sure isn't life short."

Doocey looked to Murphy to ask, "The next day, did you notice anything peculiar about Nolan's behaviour?"

"No," Murphy snapped. "Because the next day was a Tuesday, and like I told you already, I don't work Tuesdays. Like I also told you, Nolan never knew I stayed overnight in the cabin. *So—no—I saw* nothing because I didn't dare poke my nose outside the cabin." He looked around again for customers or other staff. "And if I chanced trying to go home to my parents' house, I worried he'd hear my motorbike."

And Doocey thought again about what a donkey Dickson had been not to have the cabin searched because if he had done so, they might have found Murphy hiding out there and everything could've been so different.

"Even so," Doocey said aloud, "I'm sure you might have had the odd curious glance out the cabin window?"

"Well yeah . . ." Murphy conceded. "But all I saw was Nolan cleaning his motor, and if I hadn't known what he'd been up to the night before—I wouldn't have thought that to be anything out of the ordinary. He was forever cleaning that Volvo of his."

After falling silent for some seconds, he piped up again. "Oh, and . . . of course . . . later in the evening, I noticed a lot of commotion down at the cliffs, and the lights of cars coming and going, and even a helicopter. I'd wondered what the hell was going on."

Murphy's tone became bitter. "I even thought that Nolan might've had the decency, after murdering Harriet, to throw himself off the cliffs. Only to discover later that the evil, scum of the earth was pretending Harriet had been swept out to sea."

There was silence for a few seconds as Murphy waited for Doocey—who seemed to be lost in thought—to speak.

"A month before Harriet disappeared," Doocey resumed, "she went to see her doctor about bruises to her neck. Did you know this?"

Murphy nodded, "Yeah . . . I'd noticed the bruises. They were bad enough."

"How had she got them?"

"Well, she told me that she'd slipped into some briar bushes or something. But now I think she was just lying, and Nolan must've attacked her."

Doocey nodded, and zipping up his anorak said, deliberately casually, as if taking it for granted that Murphy would have no problem in agreeing to what he would propose next. "I'll need you to come along to show me exactly where you saw Nolan burying Harriet's remains."

Murphy almost bounced with rage. "I'm going fricking nowhere!" he exclaimed through gritted teeth and punched the air. "Don't you remember we had a deal? I tell you what I saw—and you—leave me the hell alone! Nolan's not stupid. If he sees or hears about me going up to those mountains with you, he'll know I shopped him in. Anyhow, haven't I already told you exactly where he buried the body? Up the bog road, beside the shagging dolmen!"

Okay, asshole, don't have a stroke, Doocey silently intervened. Anyhow, Murphy probably wouldn't have been able to point out the precise burial spot as, by now, new growths of heather would've likely covered any tiny traces of the ground ever having been disturbed.

However, Doocey still reckoned—even if it was on his lonesome—that it would still be well worth his while to pay a visit to those mountains at the back of Nolan Manor—to see if Murphy's story had substance, by checking for a dolmen and even with how bad his sight had got, he reckoned he should still be able to spot something so large as a dolmen. And, of course, if he discovered Murphy had been lying and there was no dolmen—well . . . he'd be paying the lying toe-rag another visit.

THIRTY

SHORTLY BEFORE COMING TO NOLAN Manor, Doocey turned onto the
bog road that he hoped, if Murphy was telling the truth, should be
the road Nolan had driven up, to secretly bury his wife. Instantly, he felt
himself being hurled every which way as his poor old Ford got subsumed
by one massive crater of a pothole after another.

At last—and grateful just to be breathing—he reached the summit.
He emerged from his Ford, amazed that the old boneshaker seemed to
be still in one piece, and stumbled down into a valley where he longed,
with all thirty trillion shaken-up cells in his body, that he'd discover a
dolmen.

An hour or so later, Doocey made it back up to his car, but not without a hell of a struggle on account of how gloomy it had got and how
treacherously bumpy the bog was underfoot. Even walking at a turtle's
pace, several times he'd managed to go flying, mud splattering all over his
face and clothes. On top of this, for the last never-ending minutes of his
ordeal, the heavens had spitefully opened up.

Now, sitting in his driver's seat, resembling a dirty, drenched dog, he
waited a few minutes to get his breath back before ringing Ryan, still not
sure if the maggot had or hadn't yet heard about his failed medical. The
dialling tone ended and he heard the voice of Ryan's PA, Frances Horan.
Doocey explained how he'd a big update regarding the Nolan case and
after a couple of seconds of classical hold music, Horan informed,

"Putting you through now Detective." The rain lashing down on his car roof almost drowned out Horan's saccharine voice.

Then the sound of the phone being grabbed from her and Ryan was on the line, "Hello there Doocey. I believe you have a big update regarding the Nolan case." His tone upbeat and excited. Not the slightest hint of him being pissed off, having just discovered that the detective he'd brought in over the head of the commissioner's first cousin, was half-blind.

On hearing what he had got Murphy to tell him, Ryan burst into giddy congratulations. More evidence, at least in Doocey's mind, that his failed medical had not yet landed on Ryan's desk. The assistant commissioner's tone turning more cautious, he asked, "Do we know for certain that there is a dolmen up in those mountains?"

"Yes Sir, it's there alright. I drove up to make sure, and I've just sat back into my car."

An image of the dolmen flashed through Doocey's head: three huge vertical standing stones holding up a horizontal capping stone as if this great lopsided stone table with a missing leg, four giant, bluey-grey, stones coming together to form one structure, peculiarly, just like the four main pieces of his investigation seemed to be coming together to form the structure of an answer as to what had become of Harriet Nolan. The first standing stone represented Nolan's testimony, the second his daughter's, and the third Jack Hanson's, and the capping stone, making sense of it all, being what Murphy had witnessed.

"Any sign of a grave?" Ryan followed up.

"Not that I see Sir, but I'd expect, by now, for it to be well grown over."

Doocey, sensing Ryan's disappointment, hurriedly added, "I'd say though, the old ground radar should easily show up the precise burial spot."

"You're certain Murphy is telling the truth? You know yourself, once we start excavating the site, it will be hard to keep it from the media."

Especially when—like the self-promoting sleeveen you are—you'll be sure to tip them off so you can sweep up all the credit. "Yeah, I'm sure Sir," he answered aloud. "I can't see any reason for him to lie."

"Well, if you're sure then that's good enough for me. I'll organise the search for first light."

Next, Doocey rang Ber to tell her the great news, but they were not long into their conversation when he started to feel his first misgiving. Because even though Ber had been delighted to hear that he'd got Murphy to crack, this hadn't stopped her from asking some unsettling questions and posing some unsettling scenarios.

She just could not understand why he hadn't said anything to Ryan about Murphy having twisted his leg and the real possibility that Nolan had heard him call out in pain. Why hadn't he forewarned the assistant commissioner that Nolan, realising he'd been seen by Murphy, might have later dug up his wife's body and buried it somewhere else? Why too had he said so confidently that the ground radar would easily locate it?

How come, Ber had wanted to know, he was such an expert in ground radar when he'd never even been involved in a case where it had to be used? And, of course, he wasn't a bloody expert. What if, like along the lines he'd been thinking before, the radar started showing up all sorts of useless debris? Making it impossible to come up with a conclusive reading.

He grabbed hold of some of his wet hair and squeezed it tight, causing water to stream onto his face. If they found nothing—when all of Ryan's media buddies would be there watching hawk-eyed on—it would be an absolute PR disaster. The assistant commissioner would go ballistic. No way then would he be doing any favours for the shabby, half-blind, nitwit of a detective who was responsible for so diabolically embarrassing him.

Next morning, Doocey chanced his life again by turning up the treacherous bog road, he'd just about managed to drive up the day before. The car's engine immediately began to roar. Petrol fumes filled his lungs.

During the night, he'd heard ferocious rain lash his apartment window, and obviously that ferocious rain must have been widespread—judging by the amount of muck now spewing up on his windscreen. Yet even this morning, the weather gods were not playing ball; they had sent as a replacement to the downpour—this thick fog.

Bad enough having fog already inside his eyes, Doocey had irritably reflected, without adding more of the cursed stuff from outside. Considering how little of the road ahead of him he could see, he had reckoned that he nearly might as well drive with his eyes shut.

What he actually ended up doing though was just to drive painfully slowly, to the point that he feared being overtaken by a brisk-paced pedestrian. In one way, however, his excruciatingly slow headway didn't bother him too much. It meant less time waiting around, as an anxious wreck, at the dig site—where everybody would be watching and pre-judging him.

Near the mountain top, he awkwardly parked alongside an assortment of Garda vehicles. Seconds later, he exited his car like a bow-legged drunk and stumbled onwards, fighting hard to stop his whiplashed body from throwing up an earlier breakfast of black tea and burnt toast.

Within a matter of seconds, he found himself enveloped by the blinding wet fog. However, with how the ground was jolting him along, he presumed he was headed in the right direction . . . downhill into the valley of the dolmen.

Then again, he might be straying into the wrong valley entirely. *God*, he inwardly panicked, it would be so mortifying if any of his fellow colleagues spotted him—this idiot lost in the fog. The idiot who was supposed to be a detective and what's more was the reason for them all being there—likely wasting their time.

To his almighty relief, he stumbled upon a trail of muddy machine tracks which he faithfully followed until some promising sounds came to his ear. Stumbling onwards, the hum of an engine grew louder, and he began seeing glimpses of things: a large bright orange shape moving and smaller clusters of bright yellow, enough glimpses for him to paint a good approximation of the unfolding action. A mini orange digger excavating, Gardaí in high-vis yellow jackets looking on, and in the background, presumably the dolmen.

An icy shiver ran down his back as he saw, in the distance, a blurry figure approach. As the figure drew closer, he heard a man's voice call out, "Hello there Shamie." However, with the fog inside his eyes joining forces with the fog outside, he still could not identify the man's face but fortunately his ears were able to identify the voice—the distinctive country accent of Detective Don Scanlan.

For a short while, many years back, the two of them had worked out of the same station and Scanlan was one of a handful of colleagues who Doocey had any real time for. He was an extremely capable individual, and had it not been for his straight-talking and honest nature, Doocey reckoned that Scanlan could've gone right to the slimy top of his profession.

Suddenly, Scanlan broke into a run, looking as if he'd some thrilling news to impart. And as he came right up to him, Doocey blurrily saw that beneath his red woollen cap and coffee-coloured coat, Scanlan remained the scarily tall and scarily thin man he'd remembered him to be.

"Your timing is bang on. It looks like we've come up trumps where the digger is at work," he excitedly exclaimed as he forcefully shook Doocey's hand.

And Doocey, so overtaken with rising exhilaration, did not even automatically flinch at the feel of the man's skeletal fingers.

Scanlan took back his bony hand and began nodding. "A hundred percent there's something there. The radar gave a very strong reading in just that one spot."

Doocey managed a smile. His momentary joy of believing Harriet Nolan's body had already been found, swept away like a wisp of smoke in the wind. All the same—things were looking very promising. Just a little more patience—required. As if Mother Nature was doing her best to keep his spirits raised, the brightest of blue skies battled its way through the fecking fog.

Scanlan and Doocey began catching up on the good old detective days as they peered down to the activity in the valley below. The digger's thrusting arm only removed the tiniest lumps of earth. Presumably—to minimise the risk of inflicting damage to any human remains.

Scanlan, reverting to the present moment, asked, "Did you hear the dolmen down there is supposed to be called The Lacken Dolmen?"

Lacken, Doocey silently repeated, and his heart quickened on account of how the Irish word sounded so much like the English word *lacking. Was it an ill omen?* Would the dig underway be found 'lacking' when it came to a body being discovered?

He answered aloud, "No, I hadn't heard that."

"Yeah, the lad driving the digger told me. He's big into his history."

A long silence ensued, during which Doocey felt as if the very mountain beneath his feet had come to be weighing unbearably on his shoulders. *Was there a body buried down in that valley or was there not?* Soon everything would be clear. Gloriously or catastrophically clear.

The brilliant blue sky started emerging much speedier now as if someone with this colossal cloth had been told to get a move on. The last remaining patches of stubborn fog were being rapidly scrubbed away in readiness for the big reveal. Doocey asked aloud, "Is himself here?"

"Nope," Scanlan replied, pursing his razor-thin lips, automatically clocking that Doocey had been talking about Ryan.

"That's surprising?"

Scanlan smiled. "Oh, don't worry . . . he told me to ring him the second we found anything."

He pointed towards two men in civilian clothing who were standing near the digger, one with a camera strapped around his long rubbery neck. "He's sent those two lads," Scanlan elaborated, "a journalist and photographer from *The Echo*, so he must think we're on to a winner."

He smiled again. "Right now, he's probably only a few minutes away, sitting in a TV satellite van, having his television makeup done, waiting for our call, ready to jet in with a camera crew in tow—"

A roar of "hold it" coming from the dig site interrupted him, and a Garda held his hand up high and straight as if it were a red flag. "Looks like they've found something," Scanlan yelled, already rushing forward.

THIRTY-ONE

Doocey didn't chase after Scanlan, down to the dig site. His stomach was still not the best from that roller-coaster drive up the bog road and he reckoned the sight and smell of a decayed corpse, at close quarters, could trigger him to throw up.

A Garda carrying a spade manoeuvred himself into the would-be grave. The growl of the digger's engine dying and an unsettling silence. A circle of Gardaí formed, their heads bent downwards, waiting to see the gruesomeness their colleague's spade would reveal. The whole stunned world seemed to be holding its breath, and then low mumbles were to be heard as the circle of Gardaí began to fragment. *The shocking sight must be too much for them.*

The burly digger driver extended his hand and hoisted his colleague up from the depths of the bog. For a few seconds more, Scanlan, doing a good imitation of a lopsided telephone pole, stood staring down at presumably Harriet Nolan's corpse. In slow, hesitant strides, he began walking back towards Doocey. Coming to stand beside him, in this forced casual tone, he explained, "No luck yet I'm afraid . . . just a dead fox."

Doocey's legs nearly gave way with the shock and though rendered speechless, he managed a weak nod.

Scanlan's words ricocheted inside his head, '*No luck yet I'm afraid . . . just a dead fox.*' Painfully aware that his old comrade's use of the word 'yet' was only a kindness. A way of letting him down gently.

He recalled that earlier comment of his. *'The radar gave a very strong reading in just that one spot.'* Not several spots, but 'just that one spot.' No "yet" then about it.

Suddenly he felt it so hard to breathe, almost as if Scanlan had that second wrapped his skeletal fingers around his neck and was strangling him. What's more, with exquisitely bad timing, the spiteful sun had now arrived to shine like this massive mortifying spotlight down upon the effing fox. Groups of guards huddled together and though Doocey's eyes weren't up to making out their facial expressions, he felt their annoyance and heard their sneering whispers, making him wish he were a thousand kilometres away.

"It's amazing how well the bog has preserved that old fox," Scanlan continued. "That's why the reading came up so strong. It's even got all its orange fur."

"That's amazing, alright," Doocey said, though he already knew all about the bog's powers of preservation even if, admittedly, he'd forgotten that he knew. Ages ago, he'd gone to the bog bodies exhibition at the National Museum of Ireland. There he'd seen how ancient men, women, and children, although stained black from being buried in the bog for thousands of years, managed to retain a lot of their skin and hair. The bog acting like this colossal cold room in keeping the dead preserved. *None of that "dust to dust" lark of your standard graveyard . . .* With the word 'graveyard' swirling through his thoughts, he remembered how his mother had been on about that Slovakian serial killer who buried his victims in other people's graves.

Tapping Scanlan on his bony arm, he asked, "Would you mind getting them, Don, to dig down another bit?" As there was a delay in Scanlan answering, Doocey further explained, "Just in case Nolan used the fox as a decoy and buried the body underneath."

"Sure, we can do that," Scanlan said in a pessimistic tone that twinned with Doocey's growing inner pessimism as it dawned on him that Murphy hadn't mentioned anything about there being a fox.

Twenty minutes later, Scanlan joined him again and relayed the news that after digging down considerably deeper, they still hadn't found any human remains.

However, in the meantime, another possible explanation had occurred to Doocey. Just as he had worried before: what if Nolan, knowing he'd been spotted by Murphy, had later dug the body back up to rebury it somewhere else? Replacing his wife's body with the fox. To make it look like, if the grave was ever discovered, it had just been dug to bury some dead animal.

But Scanlan quickly poured icy water on this alternative scenario. Explaining how the fox they'd dug up looked to be a very ancient animal and probably had been in the ground for a few hundred years.

Having refused for a third time the *Echo* journalist's pleas for an interview, Doocey made a stumbling run for his car. *God, what a laugh the newspapers were going to have at them digging up some ancient fox.* But, of course, Ryan wouldn't be laughing.

Doocey had only sat into his car when he received a call from the assistant commissioner's PA to icily inform that Ryan wanted to see him in his office the following day. Doocey squeezed his eyes shut and felt hot tears stream down his cheeks.

As the bog road, once more, transformed his car into a rollercoaster cart, he went quickly from feeling sorry for himself to feeling mad as hell. Mad as hell, of course, at one person. It was time to pay Murphy—the lying scoundrel—another visit.

Stomping his sodden shoe down heavy on the accelerator, he drove at what, considering the disastrous state of the bog road together with the disastrous state of his sight, could only be described as a suicidal speed. His manic brain, however, couldn't care less, focused on only one thing— finding out why the gardener had lied.

Maybe he'd been too quick to discount Murphy as Harriet Nolan's murderer. What if he really had one hell of an argy-bargy with the woman and had ended up accidentally killing her? But why make up some story about having seen Nolan burying his wife beside a dolmen? For what was he going to say now when Harriet Nolan's corpse wasn't found?

Coming to a screeching halt, mere inches from the front door of the ramshackle *Green Acres* Garden Centre, Doocey bolted from his car. After some false sightings, he located Murphy, again, in the outdoor plant area, and—in a few choice sentences—explained the situation: how they'd found no trace of Harriet Nolan's corpse.

"Well, you mustn't have searched in the proper place," the gardener blared back, tossing aside this big bag that he'd been holding as if it had been filled with airy popcorn and not heavy-duty rocks. "Did you not—like I told you—search in front of the damned dolmen?"

"Yes, we did," Doocey replied, trying to keep his voice calm.

Murphy punched the palm of his hand. "Well, you must not have fricking searched it right because that's where he buried her. Near the dolmen, that's where he fricking buried her."

"No, it was a very thorough search," Doocey replied, not raising his voice. "We used ground-penetrating radar. If a body had been buried there, it would have shown up."

Murphy paced about in a manic state. "I just don't understand this. He buried her there. I swear . . . I saw him burying her."

He grew stiller and, after a silence, said in a low voice, "He must have seen me." His voice grew stronger. "Yeah, that's what must've happened. He must've seen or heard me when I twisted my foot that time." Murphy's voice quietened again, and he said sluggishly, as if part of him was reliving the exact moment. "I thought he'd not spotted me, but he must have, and later moved the body." He began to shout hysterically. "He moved the body! He moved the body!"

"If the body were moved," Doocey explained, repeating what Scanlan had confirmed to him when he'd suggested the same thing, "the ground radar would have shown up the empty grave but there was no empty grave."

"Well, your radar mustn't be bloody working because he buried her there, I swear, he buried her there and afterwards moved her."

Getting back into his car, Doocey phoned Ber—though he hated having to do it—to let her know how terrible things had gone—and like him, she was peeved off as hell with Murphy and neither could she understand why he'd lied.

Next morning, Doocey unlocked his post-box, located just inside the front door of his apartment building, and removed a copy of the Irish Echo and blurrily read—with heart-stopping horror—its massive, main headline: TRULY BLIND INCOMPETENCE. Directly underneath the headline, a fuzzy picture of that cursed fox.

Back inside his apartment, Doocey threw himself down on a sofa and gazed blurrily again at the headline: TRULY BLIND INCOMPETENCE. That word 'blind' caused every part of him to tremble. It was even worse than he'd been fearing. Because not only was it the hilarious story of the dim detective who'd dug up the dead fox but it looked to be, the even more hilarious still, story of the dim and—wait for it, 'blind' detective who'd dug up the dead fox.

The secret of his sight problems had been made public. It was all over. Somehow that damned journalist had found out. Some rat, maybe in the medical centre, must've made a nice few quid by leaking the results of his failed medical. He'd need to phone his mother before she made it out of bed and got to read her copy of *The Echo* which every morning also got shoved into her post-box.

With the aid of a magnifying glass, because the article text below the fox picture was so much smaller than the text of the main headline, he just about managed to decipher what was being said.

The deceased fox pictured is the closest—it seems—the Gardaí have come to finding Mrs Harriet Nolan who was reported missing by her husband, Mr Markus R. Nolan, on the 15th of May. She had purportedly failed to return home from taking her dog for a walk along a cliff path, close to the family home of Nolan Manor.

The discovery of the dead fox came about after a major search operation in the mountains surrounding Nolan Manor, close to a stone dolmen.

In an exclusive interview with the Irish Echo, Mr Nolan described the Garda investigation thus far into his wife's disappearance as "truly blind incompetence."

He went on to say how he firmly believed that the Gardaí were continuing to absurdly follow wrong lines of inquiry and were preposterously targeting him as a suspect.

He further elaborated, "It remains my firm conviction that no foul play was involved in my wife's disappearance. On a stormy day, she simply slipped and fell from a cliff path and ended up, very tragically, being swept out to sea. The antics of the police are ludicrous. One wonders how many more dolmens they are going to dig around?"

The story continued on the inside pages but more or less just repeated what had been said in the opening paragraphs with no mention that the detective overseeing the search couldn't see properly. "Well, that's something at least," Doocey muttered aloud, beginning to breathe a bit. The journalist hadn't managed to get hold of his medical file. He could delay for another bit telling his mother about his sight problems.

Despite his poor strained eyes, pleading with him not to do so, he reread, again aided by his trusty magnifying glass, those paragraphs on the newspaper's front page, sensing, though he was fecked if he knew why, that they contained some sort of a clue.

After four rereads, however, he could still not unscramble any clue and with his jaded eyes now refusing to cooperate in reading another blurry word, he flung the paper and his magnifying glass aside.

There's nothing damned well there! He inwardly raged. *You're just pathetically clutching for invisible fecking straws.* He headed back to bed, only certain of one thing. In a matter of hours, Ryan would be giving him the boot.

THIRTY-TWO

"You've got me into some hell of a mess here," Ryan said, glancing down at the newspaper headline, 'TRULY BLIND INCOMPETENCE.' I'll be lucky if I don't lose my job over you." That was how the assistant commissioner, sitting behind his titanic desk, began their meeting.

"I'm sorry, Sir," Doocey beseeched. "I just don't know why Nolan's gardener, Murphy, lied to me."

"Oh, really! You don't know why he lied to you? Well . . . allow . . . me to enlighten you." Ryan shot him a long sarcastic smile, just in case he hadn't copped his over-the-top sarcastic tone. "Detective Dickson has already followed up with Murphy *and surprise, surprise* he's denying that he ever told you anything about seeing Nolan burying his wife's body. All he claims to have told you . . . was how lately he'd noticed that his former boss liked going for walks out to a dolmen near to his house. Nothing else."

Dickson was back on the case, Doocey's brain silently processed, *and good old Murphy had U-turned on everything. The gutless yellow-belly liar. He'd even come up with a decent enough cover story to take the heat off himself.*

"It's obvious to Detective Dickson and obvious to me what happened here," Ryan continued. "Realising you were rapidly running out of time, you went with some mad hunch that Nolan buried his wife beside some godforsaken dolmen, he had recently taken up visiting. But knowing, I'd never authorise a full search and excavation—just based on some stupid hunch of yours—you fed me a pack of lies to persuade me."

"That's not true . . ." Doocey attempted to argue back but Ryan cut him off.

"Just shut it. What would you know about the truth? When you've been lying to me all along. And don't even bother with the confused face. I remember very clearly asking you at our last meeting, after what I'd witnessed of your disastrous driving, whether there was something up with your sight. But you lied to me and told me some bullshit about your car stalling."

Ryan shook his head. "Then this morning, I receive this." He picked up some stapled-together papers and waved them in front of Doocey. "Your failed medical—showing you to be as blind as a blasted hen in the night." Ryan scoffed. "Wait until the commissioner hears about this. How I'd the *bright* idea of replacing his cousin for a detective who can't even see properly. You even had me believing your dribble about a blind girl being a murderer." He shook his head again. "God, this is all career-ending stuff."

Doocey stayed quiet—not seeing any point in arguing back. He could say that his sight was fine, that his eyes had just been tired on the day of the medical, but Ryan would only then frogmarch him off to do another eye test which would show him up to be lying, yet again.

Ryan rubbed a hand across his smooth forehead and said wearily, "I'm passing the investigation back to Ed Dickson."

Tell me something I don't already know, Doocey silently quipped.

Ryan continued speaking, "Naturally, with you being near effing blind—you'll have to resign. HR will handle that process, which probably will take a few weeks but, in the meantime, you're suspended. But just to be bloody clear, you won't be coming back. Your useless detective days are behind you."

After exiting Ryan's office, Doocey drove to Blackstones station to clear out his desk and just about managed to get there in one piece, despite some close calls with other cars and a bin truck, and of course, as he was walking into his work cubicle, Dickson would have to instantly spot him. Gone any slim chance there ever had been of him sneaking quietly in and out for his last time.

Dickson was stood at Tony Naughton's desk, just across the ways from his partitioned-off desk. Doocey hadn't even packed a single belonging before the dumbass was already mouthing loudly off. "Didn't I tell you there was something up with Doocey's sight, Tony?" Dickson almost shouted. He held up his copy of the Irish Echo and slapped its front page. "This just goes to prove it! I mean it's bad, very bad, isn't it, when you can't tell the difference between a fox and a human being? What a blind idiot!"

"Yeah, what an idiot," Naughton echoed.

Then the two of them and everybody seated around started into piss-your-pants laughter. When the laughter died down, Dickson continued mouthing off. "Why Ryan put him on the case in the first place—I'll never know."

Again, Naughton duly responded with his usual top-class sucking up. "Now, you've got to clean up *his* mess. It's a joke!"

Dickson let out a long-suffering sigh and said, "Oh, don't I know it."

Ten minutes later, a smiling Doocey, just to show the pair of idiots hadn't got to him, waved over to them as he sauntered out of the station for the last time, carrying with him a shoe box of his personal belongings. But neither Dickson nor Naughton, still so caught up in spewing out vitriol, even noticed him leaving. *Some detectives, you are!*

He'd intended to say his goodbyes to Ber in person, but she hadn't been at her desk and when he rang her later on her mobile, she explained she'd taken the day off. She had correctly predicted Ryan would sack him and Dickson would be put back on the case and she didn't then fancy going into the station to have Dickson and Naughton poke fun at her too.

After his call to Ber, Doocey rang his mother. And still fearing she would want to take over his life and even demand he go live with her, if he mentioned a word about his failing sight, he continued to pretend everything was hunky-dory. As far as she was concerned, his sight was fine, and he was still a detective. And as for that worrying story, she'd read in that morning's newspaper about them digging up a fox, well that was all just part of the bigger plan, he reassured her, to keep the pressure on Nolan.

In subsequent calls to her, he would go on to lie that Ryan, because of the supposed good progress he'd made, had asked him to continue working in the background on the Nolan case. Which he didn't consider to be that big a lie, seeing as how all of his time genuinely was spent, cooped up in his apartment, ruminating about what really happened to Harriet Nolan.

In the days to follow, besides his telephone chats with his mother, his other slight bit of human interaction came from telephone calls from Ber whose only real update, which came as no surprise, was that she'd heard that Dickson was on the brink of closing the Nolan case off as a tragic accident.

It almost physically hurt, the desire Doocey felt to yet solve Harriet Nolan's disappearance. To have his revenge on Dickson and Ryan, but most importantly to prove to his mother that he was a proper detective, capable of solving a big case. However, after days spent churning everything over and over in his mind, new answers refused to come.

Feeling like he badly needed a change of scene before he literally started climbing the walls of his apartment, Doocey decided he'd head West, to see his mother. He'd pretend he'd blagged a few days off work. As 4 p.m. came around, the usual time he phoned to check in on her, he speed-dialled his mother's number and felt this warm glow around his heart at the prospect of telling her he'd be coming to visit. She'd be so thrilled.

As he waited to hear his mother's voice, he smiled to himself, picturing her, kit out in one of her pink tracksuits, making her increasingly slow journey from the fireside to the phone out in the porch. After several more unanswered rings, he began to feel a flutter of foreboding. *He had checked with her, hadn't he? That he'd be ringing at this time. 'I'll give you a call tomorrow at four as usual . . .' he'd promised, and she'd said that would be fine, she'd be home. God, had something happened? Some sort of accident? A tumble? Was she at that second stretched out on the floor in agony?*

He proceeded to give himself a little lecture for getting worked up over nothing. She must have only lost track of time which had often happened before. She was probably just outside in the garden again, wrestling with weeds or down the pub playing darts.

Some seconds later, the phone cut itself off and because that initial uneasy inkling of his remained, Doocey decided, just to be on the safe side, to give Harry Fogarty a call. Harry was the nearest neighbour and had a spare key to his mother's. After Doocey had explained the situation,

Harry promised to head off straight away to check everything was fine and promised he'd get Mrs Doocey to call Shamie back.

Though Harry's and his mother's houses were only a stone's throw away, Doocey expected it would take a fair bit of time to get that promised call back—given that Harry was well over eighty and needed a walking stick. However, he hadn't reckoned on it taking a full fifty minutes. He tried calling Harry again but got no answer.

After another twenty minutes of hearing nothing, he chanced ringing his mother's phone again. When this time round, he got an engaged tone, he felt so relieved though more than slightly irritated. She must not have heard the phone ringing the first time and now, was on another call . . . probably to her favourite bingo pal, Maggie Clancey, who'd talk the hind legs off the biggest of donkeys.

His mother, no doubt, would be so wrapped up in conversation that it would go totally over her blue-rinsed head that Harry was stood there waiting for her to fecking finish up. He smiled, imagining her, after finally putting down the phone, making Harry have a cup of tea, and pumping him for all the latest local gossip.

Suddenly this startling sound: his mobile was ringing and he could just about make out that it was his mother's number. Pressing the answer key, he exclaimed, "Do you know you frightened the life out of me, Mam?"

To his surprise, a man's voice replied and Doocey gave a little chuckle, "Oh it's you, Harry, I thought it was herself. Did she keep you talking?"

"I'm sorry," Harry whispered back, sounding close to tears.

Doocey's voice became panicked. "What is it? Has Mam fallen? Is she badly hurt?"

A long pause followed before Harry spoke again, in a slow, sombre voice, "Your . . . mother . . . has . . . passed away. I'm so sorry . . . Shamie."

"No," Doocey exclaimed, "That can't be right. Ring for Doctor O'Neill, she must only be sleeping."

But Harry explained that Doctor O'Neill had already arrived. He'd phoned for him immediately and in his panic, Harry must've left the phone off the hook, accounting for the engaged tone.

His mother had gone for one of her normal afternoon naps, never to reawaken. A massive heart attack, the doctor had said. The audiobook she'd been listening to, *The Murder of Roger Ackroyd*, had been playing when Harry had found her.

Doocey returned to Mayo to organise the funeral, not that he'd much organising to do as the local undertaker, together with Harry and the other neighbours, had it all in hand and his mother had even left very specific written instructions about how she wanted her sending off to go.

She wanted it to be a celebration and if anybody was seen shedding a single tear, she demanded they be kicked out of the church. Everybody was to wear the brightest of bright clothes and a strict ban applied to the wearing of black.

Any choir singing or the playing of any melancholy music was also strictly forbidden. The "music" instead was to come courtesy of the three remaining members of the Old Iron Maidens and Mrs Doocey had apologised in advance for inflicting them on the congregation and recommended having a good supply of earplugs, which genuinely did turn out to be a real godsend.

Father Musgrave, this hippy priest who liked to wear jeans and t-shirts and who was a favourite of his mother's, in his eulogy reflected on how Mrs Doocey loved trying new things and was not one for giving up. He too had often heard her speak the mantra she genuinely lived her life by: 'If you're not growing, you're dying.'

As the mass concluded and the loud, chronically out-of-tune Old Iron Maidens played them out with the renowned but totally inappropriate heavy metal song, 'Welcome to Hell,' Doocey thought about how he would miss his mother so much and especially the way she'd always believed in him.

Wearing this outrageously loud Hawaiian shirt that he'd purchased especially for the funeral, he trailed his mother's coffin, which had her three darts glued onto its wicker lid, out of the church, and watched it being manoeuvred into the hearse. He continued to stand there, as his hand got shaken by a long succession of people whose faces passed by too quickly for him to recognise. After the burial, sandwiches and drinks were served—*where else*—but in *Paddy's Pub*.

Unable to bear how lonely the house, he'd grown up in, felt without his mother, Doocey hot-footed it (via train) back to Dublin. Before leaving, he left spare keys to the house with Sean and some other trusted neighbours who promised they would regularly check all was okay with the place and switch on the heating to keep any dampness at bay.

Though considering, he was living so far away, in Dublin, and probably would only rarely come back to visit, it occurred to Doocey that it probably made better sense—especially from a financial perspective—if he were to sell the house and the small bit of surrounding farmland (currently rented out to a neighbour whose sheep grazed on it). Yet he just couldn't bring himself to sell the home that he'd grown up in. To sell the house that contained so many priceless memories.

It was not long after arriving back to his apartment in Dublin that something crazy started to happen. He began hearing—loud and fecking clear—his mother's full-of-life voice, telling him how she still believed in him. Telling him she knew he still had what it took to solve the Nolan case. Telling him to get off his sorry little arse and get on with it.

He duly tried with all his heart and soul to honour her wishes, going back over everything, really applying mental elbow grease, but to no avail. Until slumped on his sofa, not knowing whether it to be day or night, he fumbled for the television remote in a desperate attempt to distract himself from a complete mental breakdown. Though he didn't even bother with the effort of looking at the screen, his eyes just felt too tired to attempt to decipher blurred images.

Some French-sounding scientist was describing the proven telepathic powers of twins and cue Doocey's great moment of unexpected inspiration. Drifting like a slow majestic sailboat, mysteriously—magnificently—into the suddenly calm waters of his mind. Leaving in its wake the certainty that, at last, he understood why they'd only found a dead fox and not Harriet Nolan's remains.

He now understood why Murphy had been telling the truth, and it had been so simple, so shamefully simple. Nolan had even pointed it out to him and in that, 'Blind Incompetence,' newspaper article, he'd given him yet another giant clue.

Doocey ran to retrieve his laptop, did an internet search, and straining to read the results (even though he'd zoomed up the text to the max) he managed to find what he'd been hoping to find. Or almost what he'd been hoping to find because there was only that one little part that he literally disliked the sound of.

He hauled the dusty sitting room curtains back. Early morning sunshine warmed his face and soul. Within two minutes, he was in his car speeding towards Nolan Manor, but he hadn't gone a kilometre when doubts, like shards of glass, cut through the flimsy flesh of his excitement. *You'll see, it's not simple at all,* an inner voice warned. *It's just that you've gone and lost your bleedin marbles. The only thing simple is bloody well you.*

THIRTY-THREE

Doocey hurtled forward until he came to be stood breathless in front of what—miraculously—he'd been praying to find. He stretched out the palm of his hand and was happy—no, *ecstatic*—to feel the cold, coarse surface against his skin. It hadn't only been demented wishful thinking on his part. It truly had been so simple all along.

Down in this other valley, where he now stood—there was a second dolmen: the dolmen his hand now touched, the dolmen Murphy had been on about from the start. Murphy obviously hadn't known there were two dolmens, in close vicinity of each other, in the mountains near Nolan Manor.

Neither would Doocey have expected the gardener to have known. His dominion were the gardens of Nolan Manor and not the surrounding countryside. Probably, the night he'd followed after Nolan had been his first time out in those mountains.

Doocey fully blamed himself. He should've thought to clarify with Murphy exactly which bog road he'd been on about. Not presume, for no good reason, that it had to be the first one you came across when driving to Nolan Manor. Nolan had also spoken of there being another bog road. He even had the audacity to attempt to point it out to him. *But I'd been too blind to see, and too stupid to remember.*

It had been his cursed luck to find the Lacken Dolmen up that first bog road. Because once he'd found it, his euphoric brain had proclaimed "job done" and switched itself off. There wasn't a chance of him then thinking that if you drove past the gates of Nolan Manor you came to that second bog road. The second bog road that astonishingly led to a second dolmen. He reckoned though, it ought not to have been all that astonishing. Not when every corner of Ireland had oodles of dolmens. Any leprechaun-hatted tourist would even know that.

Also seeing as how dolmens were supposed to demarcate ancient burial sites, it made total practical sense, at least in his mind, that they were going to be found close together, like how members of a family might wish to be buried close to each other in the same cemetery.

It had been the French Scientist talking on the television about telepathic twins that'd finally sparked his stalled brain to life: made him wonder for the first time if there might be a twin or second dolmen.

A speedy internet search (well as speedy as it could be with the text massively enlarged to facilitate his poor sight) of "dolmens near Nolan Manor" had indeed revealed the existence of a second dolmen, called "Easca."

"Easca," was a name he instantly disliked—as he'd taken an instant dislike to the first dolmen being called Lacken. That name had sounded so close to the word "lacking" which seemed to forebode—and rightly so as it turned out—a "lack" of anything being found. In a similar vein, "Easca," as Doocey knew from his rudimentary knowledge of the Irish language or his Gaelic—ominously—was the Irish word for "easy." Causing him to fear that his solution to the entire puzzle was way too "easy."

In measured steps, he began surveying the ground surrounding the second dolmen for a potential grave but soon wondered why he was bothering to waste his time. Given the height of the heather—not to mention his bad sight—he reckoned he'd have a better chance of spotting that proverbial haystack needle, in pitch darkness.

Nevertheless, he carried on with his hopeless endeavour, consoling himself that at least he was getting a bit of badly needed fresh air and exercise, but his tired eyes soon forced him to take a break and, as those eyes rejuvenated a little, he noticed the unusualness of the rock he'd chosen to sit on. It was this brilliant white colour and much larger than the other rocks about the place, which almost looked like tiny grey pebbles in comparison. But most mind-bending of all, the ground surrounding the large white rock didn't look right—even to his un-right eyes.

He got down on his knees for a closer look, gawking at what very much resembled messy spade marks in the skewed shape of a grave. He wiped some sweat from his short brow, absolutely amazed that it appeared he'd beaten every odd.

Waves of joy washed over him as he pictured himself storming into Ryan's office, yelling, "I've found where Harriet Nolan is buried. Really, this time I have!" Boy, would he take pleasure in making the creep grovel! Then he instantly felt ashamed of himself—rejoicing at the confirmation of the death of a fellow human being. Rejoicing in confirmation of a woman's murder.

In a flash, he went from feeling totally disgusted at himself for being so callous to being totally disgusted at himself for being so stupid. With damp heather soaking its way through his trouser knees, it now miserably dawned on Doocey that the messy spade marks were all wrong.

That white rock seemed wrong too. Murphy hadn't said anything about seeing Nolan placing a big white rock over his wife's secret grave. Although he might just have forgotten to mention it, or Nolan might have gone back at some point to put the rock there—as a makeshift headstone.

The towering dolmen in the background caught his blurry eye and he had this flickering feeling of it too being wrong. It was different from the first dolmen though, for the life of him, he couldn't figure out why. Its giant stones looked more or less the same size as those of the Lacken dolmen and they'd the same bluey-grey colour.

Still on his knees, he closed his aching eyes. When he opened them again, he ran to check if what he'd just seen inside his head matched with reality and it did. The first dolmen had reminded Doocey of this huge, lopsided stone table with a missing leg, but this second dolmen was not lopsided. Why? Well, simply because it had all four of its legs: four standing stones holding up its horizontal capping stone.

It was funny in a strange way because he'd thought the original dolmen had fitted perfectly with representing his investigations, but he now wondered if fate, by way of this new five-stoned dolmen, was dropping him a hint about there being a piece of the jigsaw he'd missed. Something crucial that had yet to fully reveal itself.

He rested a tiny thumb, in turn, on each of the four massive standing stones and reassigned the four labels he'd assigned to the four stones of the first dolmen.

The first and second stones of this newly discovered dolmen, representations of Nolan's and his daughter's testimonies. The third a representation of Jack Hanson's testimony and the fourth what Murphy had witnessed.

However, there existed that all-important fifth capping stone, connecting the four standing stones. He thought again about how he had taken for granted that there was only the one dolmen, wondering what else he might have overlooked or not bothered to have checked.

One thing or that is one person immediately sprang to mind: that unidentified cyclist captured on the petrol CCTV, cycling away from Nolan Manor. Doocey having this crazy hunch itching inside him that like with the fifth capping stone, that cyclist would tie everything together, if only he could identify him. More crazily still, he felt sure, he would soon be in a position to do just that. In the present moment—however—he was more concerned with not making an ass of himself for a second time which was why he now marched back to his car and drove away.

After a whirlwind visit to the nearest hardware shop, he turned his car around to head back to the second dolmen, and as he'd done earlier, he drove past the first bog road, and past the gates of Nolan Manor to turn up onto the second bog road.

He proceeded at an arthritic snail's pace as this bog road like the other was in a treacherous condition. Finally, Doocey parked near to the top of the mountain, and emerged from his Ford—looking a sickly green colour—retrieved his newly purchased spade from the boot and strode into the valley of the second dolmen.

Just about managing to find, despite its substantial size, that white rock again which potentially served as an unofficial headstone. He dragged the rock aside and straightened his spade, its shiny steel shimmering in the sunlight, and began to dig. However, at that moment, ice-cold realism set in, freezing him into stillness.

Even if a body lay buried beneath his feet which he was beginning to very much doubt, he reckoned, he might as well leave it there because his mind had now skipped to the future, envisaging how things were inevitably going to play out and he didn't like what he was seeing. Yes, when he told Ryan he'd found Harriet Nolan, the assistant commissioner would be, no doubt, over the fecking moon with him. Yet, no matter his delight,

Ryan was never going to be loony enough to give him—with his sight problems—his old job back.

Though he probably would take him back on a very short-term basis, and when he'd pumped everything out of him about the Nolan case and took all the credit for solving it—he would sack him again. The only person to truly benefit from him finding Harriet Nolan would then be Ryan, who, off the back of him gobbling up all the good publicity from him allegedly having cracked the case, would probably get himself promoted to commissioner.

Doocey's grouchy voice of reason now interjected, questioning why the feck he was getting himself so morally hot and bothered when—didn't he know damn well—he wouldn't be finding a body. On foot of the failed dig at the other dolmen, Nolan would've realised that he'd been seen burying his wife and wouldn't have needed to use too much additional brain power to figure out that the person who saw him had to be Murphy, so before the real dolmen—The Easca Dolmen—was discovered and a second dig organised, he'd hurriedly reburied the body somewhere else . . . somewhere it would never be found.

Those fresh spade marks then were because the body had only recently been dug up. However, purely for the sake of proving himself right about the grave being empty, Doocey pressed his spade into the bog, inwardly hearing as he did so, Nolan laughing his bald head off at him.

As he dug deeper, it came to him that he was wrong about Ryan being the only one to benefit if he were to dig up a body. He'd weirdly forgotten that finding Harriet Nolan would prove to himself and his departed mother that he was capable of solving a big case. Finally, he would prove he was a proper detective.

As he continued to dig, the soil came away freely—way too bloody freely—more evidence of the ground being recently disturbed.

He felt a sheen of sweat cover every inch of his body. A rain droplet plopped onto a knuckle and he looked up to see swirling black clouds closing in. Within seconds, rain hammered down. In his spent mind, Doocey heard Dickson taunting, '*Digging in the drenching rain, the blind idiot has completely lost it.*'

Enveloped in a muddy five-foot deep hole and with the point of total exhaustion in the distant past, Doocey awkwardly collapsed onto his back. The thought crisscrossed his brain whether he ought not to stay put there—permanently—saving somebody the bother of digging a new grave for someone as shit as him.

With the biggest effort of his life, he staggered to his feet and vowed that he'd only dig down one more damned foot. To be fully certain there was nothing, and that, one hundred and ten percent, would be it.

He scooped out four more spadefuls and then . . . the soil wasn't coming away so easily any longer. His spade touched something spongy, and he heard himself swallow.

As if to put the pox on him experiencing any joy at making it across the finishing line, a variant of an old, demoralising thought hit him. Nolan on digging up the body would never be so stupid as to go leaving the clear clue of an empty grave. He likely had flung in something, probably an animal carcass, and on a three-thousand-acre estate, there were bound to be plenty of those scattered about the place, perhaps a dead deer or badger or maybe—just as a nice vindictive touch—another fox.

THIRTY-FOUR

After a scalding shower and despite all his earlier inner bravado and justifications for not doing so, Doocey rang Ryan's office and asked his PA, Frances Horan, if he might speak with the assistant commissioner. After putting him on hold for a short moment, Horan, in a frozen fish tone of voice, informed, "The assistant commissioner isn't available."

"Not to worry," Doocey cheerfully responded. "Would you mind passing on a message? Just that I've found Harriet Nolan's remains."

Horan shrieked back, "You've found Harriet Nolan's remains?"

Two seconds later, Ryan's voice, "Is this true? Have you genuinely found her?"

"Yes," Doocey calmly replied. "But before I tell you where she's buried, I want to have your word that you will put me back on the case and after I've wrapped the thing up, you'll let me stay working—say like as a consultative detective—no matter what issues I've with my sight."

"Now, come on . . . be reasonable—"

Doocey cut him off, "Those are my terms, and I think I'm being more than reasonable . . . and of course, Sir—officially—you'd be the one in charge of the case, doing all the media." *Stealing all the glory. Because unlike with Dickson who never let you share—even with you being his boss—a single ray of the limelight after he'd solved some easy-peasy big case, I'm prepared to let you have all the acclaim. Then you'll finally have a glittering big, complicated case to adorn your CV. A case you can lie about having solved all by yourself in your interview for commissioner.*

Ryan switched to silent mode for a good minute before speaking again. "Well, I suppose something can be arranged . . ."

"So, I've your word that I can come back to work the Nolan case and that I can stay working as a consultative detective no matter what issues I've with my sight?"

"Well . . ."

"Do I have your word, *yes* or *no*?"

"Okay, okay, *yes* you have my word."

"Oh . . . just one last small thing. I want Ber Willson back on the case with me. Is that okay too?"

"Yes, yes," Ryan snapped, sounding as if speaking through gritted teeth.

At first light, Doocey oversaw the removal of Harriet Nolan's corpse for an autopsy. It hadn't come as any great surprise to him that what Mrs Nolan had been wearing—a short-sleeved pink dress and high-heels with glittery straps—didn't at all match with her husband's descriptions of how she'd been dressed when he'd last seen her.

Nolan had obviously only said she'd been sporting a blue raincoat, black jeans, and brown boots, to fit with the story he'd been peddling. It's not as if he could've said his wife walked out into a raging storm wearing only a summery dress and high heels, as in the outfit that she'd been wearing the previous sunny day. Also recovered with the body was a small handbag, containing Mrs Nolan's wallet, phone, and keys.

When later that afternoon, he entered Blackstones Garda Station, Doocey's heart galloped with excitement at being back in his old workplace and started to gallop all the more as he made a beeline for Dickson's office.

Just as a startled Dickson looked up from his desk to see him standing there, Doocey announced very loudly, hoping for everybody in the station to hear, "I don't know if you've heard Ed . . . but we've found Harriet Nolan's body, secretly buried in mountains near Nolan Manor. Proving she did not accidentally drown or kill herself as you'd stupidly thought all along." He smirked. "You're the only blind idiot around here."

Not waiting for a response, Doocey made his exit, nearly taking Dickson's glass office door off its hinges with the ear-splitting slam he gave it. Everybody on the floor, with surprise written large on their faces, watched him march—head held high—back to his old desk.

From that point onwards, Doocey didn't see sight nor sound of Dickson who was permanently hauled up in his office with the door shut and all the blinds down.

Two days later, with the post-mortem results back, Doocey paid another visit to Nolan. Resulting in *His Lordship*, through his barely open front door, barking out to him: "I thought I made myself perfectly clear last time we met, that should you have any more idiotic questions, you were to speak to my solicitor."

"Oh, you made that *perfectly* clear alright," Doocey replied in a sarcastic tone. "I'm afraid though . . . things have moved on—now that we've found your wife's body."

"What?" Nolan gasped, fully opening his front door.

Doocey squinted. "You didn't know?"

"No . . . Where did you find her?"

"Over that way," Doocey said pointing. "Up that bog road, near to a dolmen called Easca."

Doocey moved closer to him. "Sorry that this is coming as such a shock to you, but with all the comings and goings of Garda vehicles, I thought you might have suspected something was up."

Nolan stayed silent.

"Now that your wife's body has been found," Doocey resumed, "I've got a few more questions for you."

"I suppose then . . . you had better come in," Nolan replied, standing to the side.

"Sorry, but this time round, you'll need to come with me to the station. At this point in proceedings, we'll need to formally interview you."

Nolan took a step back. "And what if *one* were to refuse to go with you?"

"Well . . . I'm afraid . . . if that were to happen . . . I'd just have to arrest *one*," Doocey answered, with a mocking emphasis on the word one.

"Very well," Nolan growled, "I'll come along, but first I need to make a quick telephone call to my daughter . . . to let her know what's happening. I'd planned to visit her this morning."

A good fifteen minutes later, he re-emerged from the house, and

Doocey mused how *His Lordship's* 'quick call' had turned out to be a lengthy enough one.

Just as Nolan had finished locking his front door, Doocey fished from one of his anorak's large side pockets a see-through plastic bag containing a set of keys and a car fob which were all attached to a pink keyring, and holding the bag up in front of Nolan, explained, "We found these with your wife's body. Do you recognise them?"

After giving the bag with the keys a good eyeballing, Nolan replied, "They look to be Harriet's, judging by the BMW fob, and I seem to recognise the keyring."

"Do you mind if I double-check?" Doocey asked, glancing towards the red Bimmer.

Nolan returned a shrug of indifference.

The detective got out a set of clear latex gloves and elaborated, "I'll just pop these on first. Don't want to cause any contamination to the evidence."

After needing to hand Nolan the plastic bag with its contents to hold, Doocey eventually managed to get the gloves on. As soon as he pressed the fob's unlock button, the sound of the car's doors clicking open. "Looks like they're hers alright," he said, and after pressing the fob's relock button, he turned his gaze back to Nolan. "Just to be sure, I'll check that one of these other keys is for your front door."

Nolan let out a lengthy sigh of irritation as if to signal that he didn't see why Doocey should needed to check the front door key. Since the detective had already established the car fob belonged to his wife, it was obvious that the other keys on the pink keyring were hers as well.

But ignoring the lengthy sigh from Nolan, Doocey elbowed past him, and using his fingers to feel for the keyhole, tried each key, but without any apparent success. "Strange, that none of these seem to fit," he said at last, "It looks as if your wife's front door key is missing. Any idea where it might have got to?"

"No. None whatsoever," Nolan replied, and seeming to have run out of patience with Doocey, started briskly walking to his Volvo, giving a cursory look across to the woman sitting in the driver's seat of Doocey's car.

Ryan had insisted that if he was going to bloody well let Doocey bring Nolan in—he wasn't to do any of the driving. "The last thing we need," the assistant commissioner had vented, "is you crashing with him in the car. Can you imagine the horrific headlines if that were to happen?" Ryan even suggested an example of such a horrific headline which showed up inside Doocey's head, in huge capital letters: 'BLIND DETECTIVE DRIVES STRAIGHT INTO LAMP POST WITH MURDER SUSPECT ON BOARD.'

Doocey had then asked Ber to drive—telling her that he'd some paperwork to read over on route or that is to pretend to read over.

Doocey returned Harriet Nolan's keys to their plastic bag and placed the bag back into his side anorak pocket. Next, he took off the latex gloves or more tore them off, and stuffed them into his anorak's other side pocket, before running to catch up with Nolan. He waited for Nolan to open the driver's door of his SUV before tapping him on the back. "I'll need you to travel in my car. It's just that there are certain protocols."

"Very well," Nolan snarled, and after slamming his driver's door shut, stomped over to Doocey's Ford, opened a back door, and peered anxiously inside for some long moments. Before proceeding to take from his inside jacket pocket a small packet of disinfectant wipes and, using several of them, he scrubbed ferociously at the back passenger seat. Until finally, he tentatively lowered himself into the car.

Showing *His Lordship* into interview room 2C, and after they were both seated, Doocey asked if Nolan wanted his solicitor to be present and was delighted to hear him reply, "No, I don't think that'll be necessary."

After reading him his rights—though there was no real reading involved seeing as fortunately he knew the formulaic wording off by heart—and after then advising that the interview was being recorded, Doocey got straight to the point.

"Mr Nolan, as I've advised you earlier, we discovered your wife's remains buried in mountains close to your home. Is there anything at this stage you'd like to say about how she might have ended up there?"

"I've simply no idea."

"I must also advise you, Mr Nolan, that as a result of your wife being buried in boggy soil, her remains have been largely preserved."

Just like the bog had preserved that fox and its ancient fur. Doocey's mind flashed back to the sight of Harriet Nolan laid out on the autopsy table. With her pink short-sleeved dress and sparkly shoes, she'd reminded him of a real-life *Sleeping Beauty.* He continued aloud, "So much so that we've been able to extract DNA from beneath her fingernails which we believe belongs to the person who murdered her. Can I then ask if you'd have any issue in volunteering a DNA sample to rule yourself out as a suspect?"

Nolan looked down to his knees for several seconds before raising a docile hand and announcing in a defeated tone of voice, "There will be no need for any of that. I'm prepared to make a full confession. I murdered Harriet."

THIRTY-FIVE

AFTER A WEAK KNOCK ON the interview room door, Ber poked in her red-haired head. "Detective Doocey," she said in a heated whisper, "can I have a quick word?"

Doocey felt fiery anger sweep through him. Furious at being interrupted at such a crucial moment, but like a bucket of cold water acting to somewhat quench the flames of his ire, the thought struck him that whatever Ber had to say must also be crucial or otherwise she would not have interrupted, when he'd expressly told her—he wasn't to be disturbed. Excusing himself, he exited the meeting room, closing its door tightly behind him, and listened as Ber excitedly explained, "Nolan's daughter is here and she says she knows who really killed her stepmother."

Doocey went to Jennifer Nolan, leading her into another shabby interview room on the ground floor, and once he'd assisted her in taking a seat, he sat down opposite—and asked across the grey table between them, "Are you okay with us recording this interview?"

"Yes, yes," she snapped back. "I don't care about any of that."

"I need to also ask if you'd like to have a solicitor present."

"No, no. I don't want any solicitor. Is my father here? He rang to say you'd come for him."

"Yes, he's in another—"

She interjected, "Did he tell you he killed Harriet?" Her voice brimmed with emotion. "Because if he did, he's lying." Tears began to trickle down her cheeks.

"How can you know that?" Doocey quizzed.

With the palm of a hand, she wiped her unseeing eyes. "Because . . . I'm the one who killed her, not him. He's just trying to protect me."

She then got straight into explaining how she'd come to murder Harriet on the afternoon of Monday the 14th of May, the day before Nolan reported his wife missing. She'd overheard her stepmother on the phone again to one of her 'fancy men.' And after getting into a blazing argument with her about it, she'd pushed her down Nolan Manor's main staircase, to her death.

At least that's what she believed happened. Because no matter how much she tried, she just could not remember pushing Harriet down those stairs. Eventually coming to believe that her unhinged mind—was trying to preserve what little sanity she had left—by stopping her from remembering the terrible thing she'd done.

Not only that, but she'd crazily imagined things happening that couldn't have possibly happened. She'd this false memory of being in her room, rehearsing her vocals—when she'd thought she faintly heard someone coming into the house. Shortly after this, she imagined the doorbell ringing five times but just as she'd made her way to the bottom of the stairs, to check who was there, she almost tripped over something.

"At first, I was confused about what I'd stumbled into. I never imagined it could be a body. I'd entirely blocked it out of my mind that I'd pushed Harriet down the stairs. But when I bent down and smelt her perfume and felt her face, I knew it was her lying there on the floor. I instantly knew too because of the icy coldness of her skin that she was dead."

Tears began to break up her voice. "Then, before I even got a chance to phone for help, Dad burst in and I told him over and over that I hadn't pushed Harriet. That she must have accidentally fallen." She sniffled. "I couldn't, however, explain how I never heard her fall, and normally I've such brilliant hearing. I could only think that I must have been singing very loudly when she'd fallen."

She rubbed a hand across her teary eyes. "I completely understood why Dad didn't believe me, considering how terribly Harriet and I had been getting on. Though I swear, I never physically attacked her before this."

She went on to further explain what had happened next, mainly what actions her father had taken. Actions that Doocey was confident that Nolan would separately go on to describe because even if *His Lordship* stuck to his story (though he very much doubted he would) that he and not his daughter murdered his wife, the actions he took to cover up the murder would remain the same.

When Doocey returned to Nolan to update him on the situation, about how Jennifer was sitting in a downstairs interview room and had confessed to murdering his wife, he reacted with fury.

However, his fury slowly began to subside as it must have dawned on him that 'what was done was done' and that his headstrong daughter would never take her confession back. It was then that Doocey asked, "Why don't you tell me what really happened?"

"Driving home from my cricket match that fateful Monday, in glorious sunshine," Nolan eventually began, "the warnings I was hearing from my car radio of an approaching serious storm were inconceivable. I switched the radio off. My thoughts drifted back to my plans for a relaxing evening, enjoying a favourite book with a bottle of red."

He released a heavy sigh. "Plans torpedoed away by the spine-chilling sight that greeted me on entering my home. At the bottom of its main staircase, Harriet lay sprawled in a disjointed, lifeless fashion with Jennifer crouched over her—sobbing.

"Too shocked to speak, I fell to my knees, shoving my daughter aside. I lifted Harriet's hand to check for a pulse that I knew I would never find. Her hand was already stiff and icy cold. *God damn it*, I thought. *Why the hell had Jennifer not instantly rang me or rang anybody for help?* Still clinging to Harriet's rigid hand, I noticed for the first time the severe wounds to her arms. And I automatically assumed they were from when she'd tried to free herself from Jennifer's clutches."

He inhaled deeply. "My daughter, though, was adamant that she had nothing to do with the injuries or anything to do with Harriet falling down the stairs. She maintained that she must have somehow tripped herself up and fallen. Yet, even with this scenario—she would not admit to having heard Harriet fall. This despite Jennifer's room being right next to the stairs and her bedroom door being open."

He shook his head from side to side. "Moreover, Jennifer has the most astonishing hearing. When we're out in a restaurant, for instance, she can often hear complete conversations that are happening several tables away when I would not be able to catch a solitary syllable. The only excuse that my daughter could concoct for not hearing a thing was that she might have been singing at the dreadful, pivotal moment."

Nolan rotated his platinum wedding ring. "Jennifer swore, too, that the body hadn't been there at ten past three when she'd gone to the kitchen to fix herself a cheese sandwich or on her return upstairs some twenty minutes later. A little while after this, Jennifer thought she remembered hearing Harriet—very quietly—entering the house but had dismissed the idea—unable to believe that my wife could've been so quiet. There hadn't been the usual clatter of her high heels or the sound of her flapping a mass of shopping bags. Then only a matter of a minute or two later, Jennifer maintained the doorbell rang five times in rapid succession. Making her way downstairs to find out who this rude, impatient person could be, it was at this point she claimed to have literally stumbled upon the body."

Nolan's tone grew tetchy. "I didn't believe her about the doorbell ringing multiple times. I thought it to be some feeble attempt on her part to allay blame. Or even more worryingly, that the doorbell had only rung inside her head."

In a more even voice, he continued, "Other than having silently fallen down the stairs of her own accord, the only other explanation Jennifer could concoct was that perhaps Harriet had been murdered in a botched burglary."

Nolan scrunched up his face. "Though Jennifer had no idea as to how the alleged burglar supposedly got into the house, given that all the doors and windows were locked and showed no signs of having been tampered with."

Doocey cut in, "How did you know this?"

"Because on returning home from my cricket match, as usual, I used my front door key to get in, and the door had been locked. Furthermore, in light of Jennifer's burglar hypothesis, I checked to see whether all the house's other doors and windows were also locked and had not been interfered with."

After Doocey gave some little nods of comprehension, Nolan continued.

"Neither could Jennifer explain why the alleged burglar stole nothing, not even the three weighty diamond rings Harriet had been wearing." His voice rose. "Surely, too, if my wife had been confronted by a burglar, she'd have screamed—but Jennifer heard no such screams."

He shook his head. "Therefore, the idea that a burglar was responsible for Harriet's death seemed patent nonsense."

Nolan pressed a hand to his forehead and, after a few seconds, resumed. "Taking more time to look, I saw how severe the wounds to Harriet's arms were. The injuries also looked like they'd been inflicted by human hands and couldn't just be the result of her tumbling down stairs. I demanded, once more, that Jennifer own up to what she'd done, but she persisted with her vehement denials. However, no matter how much my heart longed to believe my darling daughter, my detached logical brain wouldn't permit it."

Nolan's voice brimmed with undeniable emotion. "Cradling Harriet's listless head in my arm, I surveyed Jennifer with an overwhelming sense of sadness. The young lady who'd courageously cast off the shackles of blindness to be on the verge of conquering the opera world—now transformed into this pitiful wretch strewn before me."

Nolan dabbed his eye with a pristine white handkerchief. "And I could have stopped it all from ever having happened—that was the most heartwrenching aspect. I'd been well aware of the bad blood between Jennifer and Harriet, and there had been that huge argument between them, only a month previous. And where had it happened? At the top of the main staircase in Nolan Manor. The very same staircase, at the bottom of which, I had come to find Harriet lain slain."

The level of passion in his voice increased. "Though, I swear, my daughter on that previous occasion had never laid so much as a fingertip on my wife. Nevertheless, the dreadful thought had preyed on my mind, owing to how shaken Harriet had been, that had I not arrived in time, Jennifer might well have ended up hurling her down the stairs."

Nolan's face fell into a heavy frown. "However, I ignored the matter, persuading myself that my daughter could never in reality physically attack Harriet." His voice turned steely, "Nor was I overly concerned at the prospect of being proven wrong on this point. Convinced as I was that, given her blindness, Jennifer posed no real threat. All Harriet would need to do to stay safe going forward was just to keep her distance, something, I felt certain she would need no future prompting in doing, not when, as I say, she'd been so shaken after that earlier incident on the stairs."

Nolan's face took on an even more pained look as if to signal how his mind was dredging up more terrible memories. "I gazed into Harriet's unseeing eyes," he continued, "pondering how devastatingly I'd miscalculated, and further panic exploded in me as my thoughts turned to what would become of Jennifer. Would she be charged with murder and sent to prison? Surely not. The girl was blind after all—and it had only been an accident. A split-second mishap."

Nolan sucked in his bottom lip. "However, given that I, her own father, could not bring myself to believe that to be genuinely the case, I very much doubted a jury of strangers could be convinced of it either. Neither, I predicted, would it have taken much detective work—a chat with my bitter ex-housekeeper, Nelly Boyle, would suffice—to discover that Jennifer and Harriet hadn't been getting on . . . hadn't ever got on. It might easily therefore be portrayed that my daughter intended all along to kill the stepmother she loathed."

He itched his bald head. "More damning still, there were those awful injuries to my wife's arms. Clear evidence to my mind that Harriet had struggled—ferociously—for a very long time to get away from Jennifer. My other huge concern arose from the body being so icily cold. I couldn't see what reasonable argument my daughter could muster for not having immediately dialled for an ambulance or at the very least phoned me."

He leaned in towards the interview table. "Her blindness had never prevented her from picking up a phone before this. The thought tormented me that had she promptly rang for help—Harriet may well have been saved."

Nolan rotated his head multiple times as if needing a mental break, before resuming. "Of course, one scenario occurred to me where it might be argued my daughter's behaviour made seamless sense—if she were to plead insanity. However, such a defence brought the dreadful prospect of Jennifer being incarcerated in some mental institution, perhaps indefinitely. A fate, in my estimation, that would be even more nightmarish than prison."

Doocey gave an unintended nod of agreement.

"It fell to me, therefore, to act. I drove Jennifer to her apartment, desiring it to be believed that she had not been staying over in Nolan Manor. Wanting her to avoid becoming a suspect when I reported Harriet missing.

We agreed for her to lie, to say it had been at least a month since she stayed over last."

He drew breath. "Returning home alone, I got on with the gruesome task of loading Harriet's corpse into my SUV and driving up into the mountains, to secretly bury her. I ended up burying her close to a dolmen which I thought would serve as a useful future yardstick to locating the grave—as I knew I would want to return—to be close to my beautiful wife."

He bent his head. "Worried though that the dolmen might not be enough in itself to find the exact location of the secret grave when heather would have grown up over it, I placed a large white rock to mark its precise position."

Nolan sighed. "With the body secretly buried, all that remained to do was to thoroughly clean the house of any incriminating evidence. And when the storm would arrive the following day, accompanied by Rupert, I'd venture out into it, pretending to look for my wife, and go on to report my fears that after going to walk her dog, Harriet had been swept out to sea."

He pushed back his broad shoulders. "I had felt I was well on the way to convincing that original dull-witted detective who'd interviewed me, Dickson, that Harriet had accidentally drowned or even committed suicide. Although, I hated myself for perpetuating that latter false narrative of Harriet possibly having killed herself. However, I adjudged the living had to take precedence over the dead. I needed to do whatever it took to ensure Jennifer's continuing liberty."

He looked Doocey in the eye. "But, of course, when you took over the investigation, you instantly picked up on so many holes in my version of events. Like my stupid blunder of only thinking to ring Harriet's phone after I'd already rang the emergency services to report her missing."

A crease formed between Nolan's eyes. "Then fearing that you would soon realise Jennifer had killed Harriet, I tried to keep your focus on me, as the main suspect, by further incriminating myself. Confessing that I washed my Volvo the very morning after Harriet had gone missing and wanting you to believe our marriage was in big trouble because of the affairs Harriet was having with other men."

He paused. "Whereas, the truth was, her seeing other men did not really matter to me, knowing as I did that . . . she still loved me and I still loved her."

He very slightly smiled. "Then, assisting greatly with making me look even more guilty, Harriet's Aunt, Bridgie Reilly, came forward to testify that I had confessed."

His slight smile vanished. "Incidentally, I never made any such confession. However, after joining her in a few brandies, I had become a bit emotional and Bridgie, always being a highly perceptive individual, must have realised I was hiding something. I expect she made up the story of me confessing in the desperate hope that it would cause you to come after me—all the more intently."

Nolan relinquished a long breath. "It's good at last to unburden myself of all this. I'm almost glad in a way that you found Harriet's body. I'm glad it's all finally over."

Thirty-six

"Thanks for coming back in, Mr Hanson," Doocey greeted, as he took a seat in interview room 2C opposite the car salesman. Hanson, this afternoon, was wearing a red-checked shirt beneath a navy jumper and his cropped blonde hair blurrily looked to Doocey to be even shorter than last time.

"No problem," Hanson replied. He leaned over the table between them to say, "You can call me Jack."

Doocey gave a smiling nod of acceptance and after rhyming him off his rights, he asked Hanson whether he'd like to have a solicitor present.

"No," he replied. "Sure, what would I need one of those for?"

Doocey edged his head towards his slender right shoulder. "As you probably know, we've now recovered Mrs Nolan's remains."

Hanson sat up a little straighter and with a fingertip touched a twitching bottom lip. "Yeah, I read about it in the papers." He bowed his head and added in a suitably sombre tone, "Such a waste."

Doocey gave him a second before continuing, in low confidential tones. "Going by what you told me before about Jennifer Nolan attacking Harriet, you naturally are an important witness. Do you mind if I run back through a few details with you? Just to make sure I've got everything straight."

"No problem."

"Grand job," Doocey said, turning over notebook pages. "You told me how you'd been seeing Harriet Nolan and having a sexual relationship with her." He looked over to Hanson, seeking confirmation.

"Yeah, that's right."

"You knew Mrs Nolan was married?"

"Yeah."

"Likewise, she knew you were married and had a teenage son?"

Hanson fidgeted. "Yep, but as I said before, we were both only fooling around. There wasn't anything serious going on between us."

Doocey nodded, "In fairness, I remember you clarifying that, alright. Crucially too, you gave some very valuable information about how Jennifer Nolan had assaulted Harriet a month before she disappeared."

"That's right," Hanson said stoutly.

Doocey glared at the man sitting opposite. "Why are you lying to me, Jack?"

Hanson jerked back into his seat as if he'd been fisted in the chest, mouthing breathlessly, "What . . . are . . . you . . . talking about?"

"Well Jack, when I asked your son Keith why he'd written that email saying you murdered Mrs Nolan, he said something very interesting. I made a note of his exact words." He whisked to some random notebook page, pretending to read a quote he'd long since committed to memory: *'Dad left us and he wouldn't stay even though Mam asked.'*"

Hanson showed Doocey the smooth palms of his hands. "I still don't understand?"

"Don't you see Jack? What your son said contradicts what you told me. You said your affair with Mrs Nolan was only ever a bit of fun and that you were never going to leave your wife for her. You, more or less, repeated the same thing just now—that you were both only *'fooling around.'* Yet, you did leave your wife and not because she kicked you out, as you led me to believe. No, listen to what your son said again: *'Dad left us and he wouldn't stay even though Mam asked.'*"

Doocey looked up from his notebook, "I can easily see how the poor lad ended up faking your murder confession. He must've been so angry. Angry in the first place that you were having an affair, and angrier still at you humiliating his mother by not accepting her generous offer to take you back."

Hanson said in a tone of voice that sounded to be fighting hard to come across as unflustered, "Ah Keith's only a kid . . . He's just got things mixed up."

"No, I don't think so," Doocey fired back. "Because your wife, Annabell, confirmed what your son said. She told me how she'd been prepared to give you a second chance, provided you promised to end your affair with Mrs Nolan, but you refused to do so."

Hanson's head dipped. "Fine . . . I admit . . . that I didn't tell you the whole truth about our marriage break-up. To be honest, I didn't think it was anybody else's business but mine and my Annabell's." His head remained dipped. "I recently realised that I'd made a big mistake in leaving Annabell. I hoped that we might patch things up and that's still my hope." He sniffed. "You're right about my son Keith thinking that I had humiliated his mother and I know fine well, myself, I had. That's why I didn't say anything about Annabell's offer to take me back. If I were to go broadcasting it about that she'd been prepared to take me back, even after she knew I'd been with another woman, I was afraid it would be like me rubbing salt into the wounds of her humiliation."

Doocey, choosing not to offer any opinion as to whether he'd bought Hanson's explanation, moved on with his questioning. "Jack, you told me that Harriet called over to your apartment on the afternoon of the 14th of May, just before one o'clock and left around three. This would be the day before she was reported missing. Can you tell me what you got up to after Harriet had left?"

Hanson cast his eyes upwards and after lowering them again, said, "I went running. I'm training for a 50k cross-country race. There's a trail at the back of my apartment that goes up into the Dublin Mountains."

"What time did you get back to your apartment?

"Let me see . . . it must have been about seven that evening."

"Did you see anybody on your run?"

"Not that I remember. It's pretty remote up there." He paused. "Come on . . . Detective! You don't seriously think I'd anything to do with this?"

"Sorry Jack, but these are just questions I'm obliged to ask. You'll be glad to know though, that there's a way you can categorically prove your innocence." Doocey ran a hand through his hair which had the effect of tidying it up a little. "You see, we've recovered some DNA from Harriet's corpse that we believe came from her murderer."

Hanson sat bolt upright as Doocey casually continued. "I don't know if you are aware . . . but the bog is great at preserving things?"

The car salesman offered no answer.

"As Harriet was buried in a boggy area," Doocey continued, "her remains are then very well preserved."

"I'm assuming, Jack, that you'll want to volunteer a DNA sample to clear your name. That it won't be necessary for us to go down the legal route of compelling you to do so?"

After a tense silence, Hanson falteringly replied, "Yeah of . . . course . . . no problem."

"Perfect," Doocey responded, rising to his feet, "I'll just pop out for a moment to get that organised."

Just as he opened the interview room door, he turned back to face Hanson. "Oh, I forgot to say our forensic people will also want to take a look around your apartment, seeing as Mrs Nolan visited there shortly before she disappeared. I assume you're okay with that also?"

After another tense silence, Hanson said, "Yeah, sure. I've nothing to hide."

Three days later, Hanson returned to Blackstones Garda Station and Ber ferried him upstairs to interview room 2C. Shortly afterwards, Doocey joined him there and after some polite reintroductions, he explained to a surprisingly harrowed-looking Hanson how he'd some "very good news" for him.

On hearing this, all the stress on Hanson's face dissipated but only for a moment as Doocey then clarified, "Yes, the very good news is that your wait is over. The DNA results have come back in."

"Oh . . . great . . ." Hanson managed to respond.

"Yeah, the lab only sent them through to us this afternoon, and it seems that the unidentified DNA found on Mrs Nolan's body . . . that we suspect may have come from her murderer . . . is an exact match with yours."

"Well . . . Jack, what have you to say about that?"

THIRTY-SEVEN

Hanson shrugged. "Big deal. That's what I've to say about it. I was sleeping with the woman so there was bound to be traces of my DNA on her."

Doocey shook his head from side to side. "I wouldn't have necessarily said that. No . . . I wouldn't have said that at all . . . considering where we found this particular DNA."

Hanson threw him a muddled look.

"You see, Jack, going by the serious injuries to Mrs Nolan's arms, it looks like she struggled fiercely to escape her murderer, clawing into their skin, leaving traces of their DNA. Or more precisely, your DNA, under her nails."

Hanson thought for a minute before explaining with a crooked grin, "Look, Detective, Harriet, and myself liked our lovemaking rough. We scratched each other all the time. I can show you the marks she made on my back . . . if you'd like."

Doing his best to ignore his face that felt like it had caught fire, Doocey said in a low voice, "Any marks to your back could also be from when Mrs Nolan tried to escape from you."

"Bullshit," Hanson protested, his voice rising to a roar, and Doocey silently remarked, *Bye-bye Mr Charming!* Aloud, he asked, "Why had you to give up drinking, Jack?"

Hanson looked momentarily shocked as if wondering how he knew about that, and then with a defensive shrug, "I just wanted to get healthier?"

"Not then because when you got drunk, you used to beat your wife up?"

Hanson shook his head in disgust as if the question did not merit an answer.

"You are an alcoholic, Jack—aren't you?"

"No, I'm not!" he shouted back.

"But why attend Alcoholics Anonymous meetings if you aren't one?"

Looking stumped by the question, the car salesman eventually replied, "Ah . . . I just went to those to keep Annabell happy."

"Sure, you did," Doocey said with a calculated smirk. "You've also started drinking again. I smelt the drink on your breath that first morning I met you, and I smell it again off you this afternoon."

"I like the odd damned drink," Hanson snapped. "So bloody what! That's not a blasted crime, is it?"

Doocey coolly opened a cardboard folder and removed a photograph which he slid across the table to Hanson. "As you'll see that photo there is of a red BMW. It came from CCTV footage which showed the vehicle driving towards Nolan Manor on the afternoon of May 14th. Do you recognise the car as being Mrs Nolan's?"

As if he might be handling broken glass, Hanson cautiously moved the photograph closer to him. A long minute lingered as he carefully scrutinised the image. "It looks like her motor," he finally answered, "but the picture isn't great."

"Yeah, in fairness, it isn't a great photo, and with all the reflections on the car windscreen, you can't even make out who's driving."

Hanson's brow furrowed. "If it's Harriet's car—sure it has to be her driving it."

"Yeah, that's what I presumed at first too but then I got the thinking that she couldn't have been the one doing the driving."

Hanson shifted in his seat but offered no comment.

"You see by this time—I think Harriet Nolan was already dead." Doocey stared searchingly across at Hanson. "So . . . I think it was you driving her car."

Hanson rolled his deep green eyes. "That's complete nonsense."

"No, I don't think it is nonsense at all. Stick with me, Jack, and I'll tell you exactly why not."

Hanson dropped his head and shook it from side to side but allowed Doocey to continue.

"We know, as you told us yourself that you met up with Harriet on Monday the 14th of May. A day that I reckon was meant to be a very special one for you."

He paused for a quick second to see if Hanson would try to contradict him but no contradiction came.

"It was the date you'd both agreed that Harriet would leave Mr Nolan. You'd even got an apartment for the two of you."

"This is just pure BS," Hanson said, trying to force a laugh.

"No, it's not BS at all, Jack, because luckily for us we recovered Harriet's mobile, and my forensic colleagues have been able to retrieve many very important text messages from it. Such as all those harassing texts you sent Mrs Nolan, putting pressure on her to move in with you, until you finally broke her down and she texted back that she would—as you'd wanted— move in with you on May 14th."

Hanson buried his face in his hands as Doocey unmercifully kept going. "So it was all systems go or at least in your head, only for Harriet to drop the bombshell when she met up with you on the 14th, that she wanted to end things. I can imagine how this must have made you lose it completely—coming on the very day you were to move in together, and after you'd already left your wife and son for her. I reckon by this point—you'd also started drinking again and I'd bet the alcohol in your system sent your temper levels rocketing, entirely. It's easy to see how you went so berserk that you ended up killing her."

Hanson just gave an exaggerated lengthy stare to the heavens.

Doocey continued, "If you wanted to avoid being done for murder and a life prison sentence, you had to figure out what to do and quick. You had to come up with a plan." His tone became more animated. "And fair fecking play to you, Jack, you managed to come up with a very clever one of those. With fessing up and going to prison being off the menu, that left you with only two other options: (a) cover it all up, or (b) blame someone else."

Doocey delivered a drawn-out smirk. "In the end, you never went with either option because, as was the pure genius of your plan—why choose to ride horse 'a' over horse 'b' when you could ride both horses at once?"

He gave some smiling nods as if to signal his admiration of Hanson's cunningness, before resuming. "You knew from Harriet that she and Jennifer didn't get on. You knew too about their latest big blow-up, a month before Harriet went missing because you'd been on the phone with her when it happened and later, she surely would have filled you in on all the details. Told you that, had her husband, Mr Nolan, not come to her rescue, she was certain she would've been dead because Jennifer would've pushed her down the stairs of Nolan Manor."

Doocey sat up straighter. "The crucial point being though—despite how much Harriet was terrified of her doing so, Jennifer never pushed her down any stairs or ever laid a hand on her. She didn't then cause those injuries to Harriet's neck—like you'd falsely claimed."

Hanson covered his eyes with an arm as if protecting himself from oncoming debris.

"I reckon very shortly after this—you'd your own altercation with Harriet, maybe because she'd hinted at wanting to break things off. Your altercation with her though—crucially—got physical, with you inflicting those neck injuries. Injuries consistent with attempted strangulation. Harriet, though, terrified you would cause her more harm, told her doctor only that she'd accidentally fallen into some briar bushes."

Hanson's wrist began to tremble.

Doocey grinned, "I've to say, it was very clever of you to falsely blame those neck injuries on Jennifer."

"I really can't get over any of this . . . you're an absolute raving lunatic," Hanson vented, but Doocey carried on as if he hadn't heard the abuse.

"Coming back to Monday, May the 14th when this time round, you hadn't just injured Harriet but killed her—what were you to do? Well, the first thing you needed was a plan and as I said, you came up with a good one. No—I should say a fecking genius one."

Doocey paused, "I must pay tribute to your intelligence for so quickly being able to think on your murderous feet. My guess though is that you might have already half-thought about what you would do if the worst happened." He gripped an arm of his glasses. "I'd say when you'd attacked Harriet not long before this, causing those serious injuries to her neck and probably coming very near to killing her, it must have gone through your mind what you'd have done if you had actually gone too far and killed her. Or maybe you are even the type of person who enjoys fanta-sising about how they'd get away—scot-free—with a murder."

Doocey studied Hanson's blurry face, "Though, how you came to think it all up, I suppose is academic. It's not as if we can go charging someone for thinking up a crime but, of course, we can charge them, if like you, they go fecking through with it."

Hanson just sniggered.

"You began by bundling Mrs Nolan's body into the boot of her own car," Doocey continued, "and with the boot then full, you'd no choice but to use the back seat for something else. I'll return to what that something else was, in a minute."

Hanson let out a hard laugh and exclaimed, "Ah, come on? This is get-ting totally ridiculous."

Again, Doocey chose to ignore the interruption and coolly carried on. "Driving Harriet's car to Nolan Manor, you got into the house using her front door key and ever so quietly you laid her corpse out in the entrance hall. Positioning it to look like Harriet had been pushed down the main stairs by Jennifer."

Hanson closed his eyes and exclaimed, "This has to be one big crazy joke," and Doocey wondered why he hadn't yet asked for a solicitor. That said, to do so might be an admission that he didn't truly believe it to be all *one big crazy joke.*' Most likely his strategy was just to sit there, denying everything, which would have the additional big advan-tage of allowing him to hear the whole case against him. That way he'd have time to get his lies and defence straight before consulting with a solicitor.

Doocey continued, "You'd have discussed with Harriet the logistics of her walking out on her husband on the 14th of May, a day when Mr Nolan was due to be out, playing cricket. Maybe Harriet had told you, to avoid an ugly confrontation, that she would just leave a letter for her husband explaining how she was leaving him but, of course, having changed her mind, she never wrote any such letter."

Doocey fiddled with his glasses. "She'd also—no doubt—have men-tioned that Jennifer had been staying over in Nolan Manor which was perfect because her being there was essential to your plan. With Jennifer being blind, you must've presumed, even if you were unlucky enough to happen to rub shoulders with her, that she wouldn't be able to tell who you were or what you were up to."

Doocey reached into his folder again and this time pulled out a small, see-through, plastic bag containing keys and a car fob. The same items he'd already shown to Nolan when he'd gone with Ber to bring him in for questioning and when he'd also taken the opportunity to verify that the car fob was for Harriet Nolan's BMW. Dangling the plastic bag in the air with one hand and pointing to its contents with the other, he asked, "Recognise these?"

Hanson stayed silent.

"I'd say you have to recognise them, Jack . . . because they're Harriet's. We found them with her. See, that's the key fob for her Bimmer," Doocey explained, specifically pointing the fob out. "Do you know the funny thing about these other silver keys?" he continued, again pointing them out. "No? Well, I'd of course assumed one of them would open the front door of Nolan Manor but none of them did. Any idea, Jack, where Harriet's front door key might have got to?"

"No," Hanson growled back.

"Ah now come on Jack, you must know where that key is because—*don't you remember?*—you took it when you were leaving Nolan Manor. You needed it to re-lock the front door and were not overly concerned about leaving the clue of a missing key. Because, of course, if things went the way you were orchestrating them to go, none of Harriet's keys would ever be found."

Doocey paused for breath. "After locking the front door to Nolan Manor from outside, you rang the doorbell to get Jennifer to come downstairs—to discover the body—as you made your getaway." He smirked. "Then, with ideal fecking timing from your perspective, before Jennifer had even the chance to phone anybody, Nolan arrives home to discover her knelt over his wife's dead body."

He placed the plastic bag with the keys and car fob, that he'd continued to hold, down onto the interview room table. "You rightly banked on Nolan jumping to the wrong conclusion, that Jennifer had murdered his wife. There would be no way that he could think it had just been an accident, not with all those wounds to Harriet's arms which you had inflicted. Wounds that were clearly visible because due to the beautiful weather of that Monday, Harriet had been wearing a short-sleeved dress."

Hanson avoided eye contact.

"What's more, by this point, the body would've gone cold, leading Nolan to conclude Harriet had been dead for a long time and to believe Jennifer had deliberately not rung for help. It followed that his daughter would not be able to avoid serving a lengthy prison sentence or—just as bad—would be locked up indefinitely in a mental asylum. Nolan had, on the false face of it, only one choice. The choice that your whole clever plan hinged on. He had to cover it all up."

Doocey pulled some of his white hair upward. "Nolan told me of how Harriet believed in him as a crime writer, and I'd say it's likely she would have chatted to you, at some point, about how her husband was very talented and it was just down to random bad luck that he hadn't yet been published. Such insights must have given you confidence he would pick up on the clues that Harriet's death hadn't been accidental and conclude that his daughter had intentionally murdered her. Then do a good job of getting rid of the body as well as coming up with an excellent cover story to explain away his wife's disappearance."

Hanson, at this point, looked on in a dazed, rigid state as if he were a child sitting around a campsite fire, literally scared stiff by the horror story being recounted. Except in this particular horror story, he starred as the murderous monster.

Doocey flicked back through the pages of his notebook to give the impression of checking for some crucial entry. Settling on a random page of notes that might as well be written in an alien language so far as his eyes could decipher them, he turned his gaze back to Hanson. "Right . . . what was next . . . Oh yes . . . having planted Harriet's body, you had to make your getaway, but you couldn't use her BMW again, because this would set Nolan questioning where the car had got to, and likely questioning everything else."

Doocey did a big stretch of his back and released a big, satisfying groan. "Neither could you just set off on foot because you needed to put the maximum distance between you and Nolan Manor before Mr Nolan made it home. And I know you knew what time Nolan's cricket match was due to finish up because you referenced Harriet needing to leave your apartment at 3 p.m. to be back in Nolan Manor before her husband arrived home. And whilst Harriet Nolan did end up leaving your apartment at 3 p.m., very sadly, she did not leave it as a living person, she left it as a dead woman in the boot of her own car."

Doocey performed a smaller stretch of his back and released a smaller groan. "Calculating then that Mr Nolan could show up at any minute," he continued, "you needed to make a speedy escape—but how?" He slid a photograph over to Hanson, explaining, "That is a CCTV image of a heretofore unidentified cyclist cycling away from Nolan Manor on the 14th. I know, like the photo I showed you of Harriet's car, it's not the clearest, but it does look like, doesn't it, that our cyclist friend is male, of a similar build to yourself, and is wearing a suit?"

Hanson gave no reply.

"You too own a bicycle . . . Don't you Jack? Even though you told me you didn't."

"Ah for *eff* sake, are you now saying I'm a murderer because—like millions of other people—I own a bike?"

Sticking to playing deaf, Doocey continued, "Yeah, when our forensic people searched your apartment, they came across your bicycle out on your balcony. I know you can't properly see the particular bike in the photo but you can still tell from its shape that it's a road bike with drop handlebars and skinny wheels. Just like yours."

Hanson shrugged forcefully as if to silently ask, *So what?*

"I mentioned earlier you putting something in the back seat of Harriet's BMW, and that item, of course, was your bicycle. Very smart of you to think of bringing it for your getaway, and it also answers where a little oil stain on the back seat of Harriet's car came from. It answers too why there was only CCTV footage of a cyclist cycling away from Nolan Manor but none of him cycling towards the house."

Doocey cleared his throat. "The silhouetted cyclist also looks to have been wearing a suit, and as a car salesman, you would ordinarily wear one of those. You'd also been working a half-day that Monday. In the panic of the situation, you probably forgot about bringing a change of clothes for cycling back. Or thought you'd no time for that, and you'd be getting rid of the suit you'd been wearing anyway because of the chances of it having blood spatters or other incriminating DNA evidence. All you cared about was being well gone before Nolan got home."

Hanson gave a nervous kind of chuckle, "That's one crazy, crazy story, you've come up with. But where's your evidence for any of it? What have you got but a bit of my DNA that Harriet picked up when we were having rough sex? Nothing else!"

"Harriet's front door key?"

"A missing key. Big damned deal! How can you blame me for her losing her key? Keys go missing every day."

"But how did Harriet let herself into Nolan Manor if she hadn't her front door key?"

"The door must've been unlocked or maybe her psycho stepdaughter let her in. How the hell am I supposed to know? All I know is that keys go missing every day."

"Oh, but did I not say? It's not missing any longer," and Doocey removed from his folder a small clear plastic wallet containing a silver key and held it up for Hanson to see. "Here it is, Jack, and care to hazard a guess where we found it? No? Well, we discovered it in your apartment. Taped over your bedroom door frame."

"This is just crazy, crazy stuff!" Hanson blared. "I never put that key there. You planted it! You're setting me up."

Doocey gave a little grin as if not to deny the accusation, hoping to rile Hanson even more.

Hanson looked up to the ceiling, as if pleading with God to intervene and said in an exasperated voice, "I don't believe you're trying to pin a murder on me over some stupid key."

"You're forgetting about this CCTV image," Doocey said, picking up and waving the picture of the silhouetted cyclist, "showing you cycling away from Nolan Manor?"

"Don't make me laugh! Sure, that photo could be of anybody."

"There's also that oil stain we found on the back seat of Harriet's car, from your bike," Doocey calmly supplemented.

"A dab of oil!" Hanson scoffed. "Ahh . . . come on now? This is absolute craziness! You've got nothing on me."

"I'm afraid we do, Jack," Doocey gravely declared. "You see . . . we found something else in your apartment, something altogether more serious."

Hanson's mouth stretched open.

Doocey continued, "Our forensics teams recovered what seems to be some of Harriet's DNA."

"Are you thick or what?" Hanson—now on his feet—bawled but after a few faltering seconds, flopped back down onto his chair. "I told you me and Harriet were sleeping together! So of course you were going to find her DNA in my apartment."

"But you see," Doocey calmly replied, "this looks to be a very specific type of DNA—a fragment of Mrs Nolan's brain tissue."

"What?" Hanson shrieked. Then after a pause, in a dazed voice, he asked, "You didn't just say, did you, something about finding a piece of Harriet's . . . *brain tissue* . . . in my apartment?"

"I'm afraid I did . . . On your granite fireplace . . . which Harriet must've hit her head off." Doocey fixed his broken eyes on the defeated-looking figure opposite. "Mr Hanson, Jack," he coaxed. "It's up to yourself whether you want to continue to plead your innocence, but I have to tell you that based on all the evidence we've got, there isn't the tiniest fecking doubt in my mind that you're going to be found guilty of murder. I've checked with our forensics people and they said that there's no way Harriet Nolan could've survived an assault so severe that . . . well . . . that resulted in a piece of her brain being found in your apartment."

He frowned. "You might want to think about your family and all the horrible media publicity a murder trial will bring. Your son reading in upsetting detail all about what his dad did. His pals reading all about it too. Best for your sake Jack, for everybody's sake, just to—simply—confess."

THIRTY-EIGHT

AFTER DOOCEY HAD DONE INTERVIEWING Hanson, he got the Nolans to come back into the station and with father and daughter sat across from him in interview room 2C—both looking tense—he gave them the incredible update. He explained how Jack Hanson was the real murderer and the overwhelming evidence against him.

However, notwithstanding the existence of such overwhelming evidence, a stubborn Hanson continued to protest his innocence. Not that Doocey ever truly believed such a crafty character would just say, "I did it."

But regardless of the lack of a confession, Hanson was charged with murder and remanded in custody, pending his trial, which—given the constant backlog in the Irish court system—would be, at a minimum, at least eighteen months away. However, to be fully prepared for his distant day in court, Hanson hired himself a barrister who had a reputation for being the excellent bullshitter. Though, no matter how brilliant a bullshitter Hanson's new barrister might be, Doocey doubted there'd be a hope in hell of him persuading any jury of his client's innocence, not when a piece of the murdered victim's brain had been found in that client's apartment.

When Doocey finished explaining about Hanson to the Nolans, neither of the two spoke for a long time, both seemingly stunned into silence by what they'd just heard. Until—finally—Mr Nolan wrapped an arm around his daughter and whispered, "I'm so sorry darling, I should never have doubted you."

"It's okay Dad," Jennifer Nolan sobbed, "I don't blame you for not believing me when I wasn't even sure myself that I hadn't killed Harriet."

During all the various twists and turns of Doocey's interviews with the Nolans and Hanson, the assistant commissioner had made sure to keep himself well versed as to developments, in readiness to take all the credit.

The fact that Jack Hanson turned out to be the murderer, and not Jennifer Nolan or her father, initially came as a nasty surprise to Ryan and he'd been highly sceptical in believing it could be true—so much so that he'd even briefly considered not stealing the limelight for having solved the case.

But on coming to appreciate the strength of evidence against Hanson, Ryan had a speedy change of mind, realising that the investigation's twists could serve to highlight his own 'stupendous' intelligence in solving the case single-handedly.

Ber was another one who'd needed convincing. After reviewing all the CCTV footage from the *On the Run* petrol station, she became unsure that the silhouetted figure seen cycling away from Nolan Manor really could be Jack Hanson. She feared that if they charged him, something could very well crop up later to prove he was never Harriet Nolan's murderer. Though seeing as how a piece of Harriet Nolan's brain tissue had been found in Hanson's apartment, Doocey managed to eventually convince her of his guilt.

With all the fabulous ensuing media coverage about the solving of the case—no real big surprise—that when the incumbent commissioner retired, Ryan was promoted to the top job and with his promotion in the bag, Doocey gauged it would be a good time to ask him two favours.

The first of which was that Ber would be promoted to take over Dickson's job, meaning a demoted Dickson and all his lackeys would be left reporting up to her. Doocey, with a mischievous smile, reminding Ryan—who was already ensconced in his fancy new commissioner's office—about the high regard Dickson testified to having for Ber. "Remember Sir, how Dickson, when he told you I could have Ber to work with me, had said that he *rated her very highly.* I can't see then why he wouldn't think her promotion well merited."

"That's right, I remember," Ryan said with a chuckle. "So yeah, he can't have any complaints at all. Consider it done. I was planning on demoting the idiot . . . anyway."

Ryan went on to rant about how he'd grown sick to his immaculate teeth of previously having to cower to Dickson's every demand—even though he'd been his direct boss—because if he hadn't, he knew the asshole would've gone straight over his head to his cousin, the former commissioner. However, Ryan was now top dog, and the former commissioner was gone, taking with him any powers Dickson had to dictate to him.

Ber was so delighted with the news of her promotion that she scooped Doocey up into her hefty arms and kissed him, multiple times, on both cheeks. When she finally put him back down, she excitedly exclaimed, "Oh, I can't wait to be Ed Dickson's boss." She smiled maliciously, "I think I'll put him doing my old job. Inputting mileage claims and making sure the canteen has enough tea and coffee and, most importantly, the toilets have enough loo paper."

Doocey's second favour was for the 'obstruction of justice' charges against the Nolans to be dropped. He thought it would be particularly cruel if Jennifer Nolan ended up going to prison, just because of her father mistakenly believing she'd committed a murder. All the crueller given how she'd overcome her blindness to build a successful singing career.

However, Ryan flatly refused to do anything on this particular matter. Arguing that he simply could not ignore the lies that Jennifer and her father had told or the fact that Mr Nolan had secretly buried his wife's body. He could not just quote "sweep things under the carpet," especially Doocey reckoned when those things were supposed evidence of how he, the new commissioner, had been so clever in his solving of the case.

Thankfully then, Nolan's legal team independently went on to negotiate a plea bargain with the State Prosecutor. On the proviso that no charges were brought against his daughter, Mr Nolan was to complete one hundred days of community service as a penalty for the concealment of his wife's corpse.

In fulfilment of that community service, Doocey could well imagine *His Lordship* eagerly volunteering to thoroughly clean the likes of community centres, and given his love of cleaning, he would probably thoroughly enjoy doing it. The hundred days of community service might not then have been such a bad result for Nolan. Although in the context of losing the love of your life, Doocey supposed that no result could really be described as good.

With regards to himself and his wish to stay working as a consultative detective as the assistant commissioner had promised to let him do, things didn't work out so well there. Ryan, as Doocey had feared, found a sneaky way of going back on his word. The new commissioner now ordaining that 'given his sight issues' it was best if he were to work 'exclusively' from home and that he would be in contact when the right case came up for him to investigate or if he preferred, he could arrange for him to receive a very attractive retirement package but Doocey repeated that he wasn't interested in retirement.

When some very long weeks went by without him again hearing from the assistant commissioner, it became obvious to Doocey that the "right case" for him to investigate would just never materialise. For this reason, he capitulated into taking retirement.

On his third day into that retirement, he received a call from Nolan who he'd been hoping to hear from. His Lordship wanted him to come to see him. He wanted to talk to him about something important and apparently preferred not to say what that 'something important' was over the phone.

Doocey then found himself again stepping into the stark white hall of Nolan Manor, and trailing after Nolan who led him into his ornate library. After they were both seated, in the library's leather wing-backed chairs, Nolan asked about how his detective work was going and whether he was investigating any other big cases. His Lordship seemed genuinely shocked to hear about his sight issues and how he'd had to retire early.

Then after a thoughtful pause, Nolan said through a smile, "I suppose one should have guessed you had sight problems. I mean, after you drove into my flower pot and knocked over my father's vase. But somehow, I just thought it to be all part of how you liked to play the clown."

"Well, I wouldn't be too hard on yourself for that," Doocey said with a smile back. "Because you know after a lifetime of practice, I've fairly perfected playing the clown."

Nolan's smile faded and he asked. "How is your sight now?"

"You know it's not too bad at all. I'm still able to get around fine." Doocey chuckled. "Without bumping into too many things. Though driving and reading are a bit dodgier. And these special injections I'm getting, thank God, seem to be stopping my sight from going really bad and my eye consultant is very hopeful of even bigger medical breakthroughs just around the corner." He sat up straighter. "So, I like to believe it won't be long before they're able to cure me fully."

"That's tremendous to hear," Nolan responded, all enthusiastically. "It's so good to see you are maintaining a positive attitude. Any future work plans?"

"Oh, I've something in mind—alright," Doocey said, and added in the same vague way, "but I need to sort something else out first." He looked Nolan in the eye, "Anyways, enough about me . . . What was it you brought me out here to talk about?"

THIRTY-NINE

Nolan studied Doocey for some seconds as if still considering whether he should disclose his reason for summoning him. Finally, he said, "Well . . . I'm thinking . . . of writing a book about your investigation into Harriet's disappearance."

Doocey nodded—not so surprised to hear this—because he'd a feeling that's what Nolan was going to say. Though with how long it had taken him to spit it out, he'd wondered if *His Lordship* had something altogether bigger to tell him—like for instance Jack Hanson hadn't really murdered Mrs Nolan. "Yeah, I can see how it would make a good book," he said aloud, with a grin. "Lots of twists and a surprise ending."

"Yes . . ." Nolan said, looking towards the library floor. "Actually . . . several publishing houses have been in contact, offering deals." He looked up again. "Naturally, I would split any potential sales revenue with you. However, at this point, I'm not at all sure about writing the book. It rather feels like I would be profiting from Harriet's death."

"I don't think she would have seen it that way," Doocey reassured. "Not with how you said she was so supportive of you as a writer. No, I'm sure she would have been all for you writing the book."

Nolan nodded solemnly, a tear in his eye. "Yes, I also rather think that . . . but still . . . it's difficult . . . so very difficult. I'll need to give it some more careful thought. Can I take it though—that in principle—you are okay with the idea and with me interviewing you?"

"Yes, why not."

Twelve lengthy days dragged out before Nolan phoned Doocey to tell him that he'd decided to go ahead with writing the book. They proceeded to talk about the next practical steps and agreed that Doocey would call out to Nolan Manor for several interview sessions and his taxi fares would be paid for by Nolan.

When Doocey re-entered Nolan's gloomy library and sat down on the leather chair that he'd sat on last time, he noticed it had a faint stench of bleach and this vexed the hell out of him. *The git,* he thought, *must have gone, and disinfected the damned thing after my last visit.*

Nolan, sitting across from him in his—no doubt—bleach-free bloody chair, dressed in his standard attire of black suit and white shirt buttoned to the top, set out with forceful hand signals how he would need his "total cooperation, total commitment, and total honesty" because the book had to be "perfect" so he finally could prove—to all those "ignoramuses" who had rejected him down through the years—what a great writer he was.

In deference to what Nolan had asked, or more like pleaded, for him to do—to be *totally honest*—and to start as he meant to go on . . . as it were, Doocey had cut in. "You know, I don't really reckon that you are writing the book for a crowd of anonymous critics or those 'ignoramuses' as you call them but someone closer to home . . ." he had begun. But sensing what he was saying was not going down at all well, not least because of how Nolan had started fidgeting about in his chair as if he'd angry ants in his pants, he thought it best not to finish the point he was making and instead conceded with a manufactured chuckle, "Ahh . . . never mind me . . . I'm probably just talking out of my fecking hat . . ."

"No, please do go on," Nolan encouraged, forcing himself to sit still for a second. "I want you to be open with me."

Doocey shrugged. "Okay . . . Well . . . all I was going to say is that . . . I think when someone is very crazily driven to prove themselves, as I can personally testify, they usually want to prove themselves to someone close to home. In my own case, I wanted to prove myself to my mother, who had always believed me capable of great detective things, and—even now . . . after she has died—I'm still trying to prove myself to her. In your case . . . if you really don't mind me saying . . . I'd bet you always wanted to prove yourself to your father." *The self-made millionaire businessman who Nolan's "friend" Tyson Tidd had referenced. The man who had never believed his son could make it as a writer.* "And even though your Dad's dead now too—I bet you're also still trying to prove yourself to him." He smiled sadly. "We have, at least, that in common with each other—wanting to prove our-selves to a dead parent."

"Thank you for your honesty," Nolan said, but his tone did not sound as if he were the least bit thankful. His tone was that of someone who was livid. Still, Doocey decided, he would continue as he'd started, carry on with being as honest as possible with Nolan in his recollections of his investigations into the murder of his wife, whether *His Lordship* genuinely liked it or not. Easier that than to go tangling himself up in lies and he reckoned, given all the twists and turns of the case, it would be more than hard enough—without adding lies into the mix—for him to describe accu-rately all that had happened. Though this being said, there was just the one point which he decided it would be best to leave right to the very end to tell Nolan the truth about. Anything else that he'd been holding back, however, he was prepared to put on the table—straight away.

Like telling Nolan the truth about the white scarf that had supposedly washed ashore, and how in an attempt 'to make things happen' he'd secretly removed it from his wife's wardrobe and had only pretended to have found it down at the cliffs.

However, this revelation seemed to come as no great shock to *His Lordship* who declared in a dull tone of voice, "Yes, I eventually came to suspect you had to have planted the scarf."

On the other extreme, Nolan seemed especially interested in hearing in detail about one subject in particular—Doocey's sight loss. Maintaining that him talking openly about it and how he would not allow himself to be defeated by such adversity would be a real inspiration to others.

Though Doocey found it painful to talk about the subject, in the end, he was surprised at how much better doing so made him feel. He likened it to when he'd got physio after he'd pulled a muscle in his back. It had been so painful at the time but it resulted in less pain in the long run.

There'd been something else that had surprised him. No—had shocked him, and annoyed the hell out of him. It had happened during one of their final writing sessions. Again, sitting opposite, each other in *His Lordship's* library, Nolan had reached across to a side table and picked up a smallish pink coloured item, which up to that point—maybe not that surprisingly—had gone unnoticed to a visually challenged Doocey, and he held it up as if a barrister in court holding up the key exhibit to the jury.

"This is Harriet's diary," he explained, totally out of the bloody blue. "I hid it from you because I feared it would incriminate Jennifer as Harriet's murderer."

On hearing Nolan explain why he'd supposedly kept the diary hidden, Doocey now felt his stomach seriously go to bits. Because whilst he could perfectly understand Nolan originally hiding the diary based on a fear that it would incriminate his daughter as his wife's murderer, what he didn't understand was why he hadn't just left it hidden forever. Why was he bringing the diary out now? Could the reason be to do with *His Lordship* knowing the shabby, half-blind detective investigating the case had got it all wrong and he was dying to write all about it for his bloody book? Well, his unsettled stomach thought it was, that's for sure.

Nolan had looked down at the pink-covered diary in his hand. "If I may, I would like to read some key extracts."

FORTY

Harriet Nolan's Diary Extracts:

I know nobody will believe me because of the huge age difference between us but I truly do love Markus. People can think that I married him for his money or think whatever. What does it matter when I know the truth? I married Markus because I love him and I love the man more every day.

I know I'm so shallow but I've to admit that I adore being married to someone so wealthy as Markus and the privileged circles this allows me to mix in. Of course, I'm fully aware a snob such as Penelope Powell would treat me like dirt on her designer high heel if I were poor again. I scarcely then dare to think what it says about me that I'm so desperate to be her friend.

Being able to buy nice things also makes me feel better about myself and makes a nice change to how depressed I sometimes get. Markus is so understanding and is forever trying to get me to see someone but the thought of seeing a psychiatrist almost horrifies me as much as seeing a regular doctor.

I've tried so hard to get on with Jennifer but she resents me for having stolen her dad from her mother and perhaps even as being the cause of her Mum's cancer and consequently the cause of her death.

I've come to the sad realisation that she's never going to forgive me and my clumsy attempts at building bridges are only making her hate me all the more. Best that I keep my distance.

It's such a shame because I would've liked to have been friends with Jennifer. I so admire her as a person and for what she has achieved in her singing career, despite her disability. I so love her courageousness. It's a courageousness I believe she got from her father. It's amazing how, after all the setbacks Markus has suffered, he's never given up on his writing dream and I do believe he's a very talented writer. He just needs that one heavenly break. He'll always have my backing.

I've tried my level best to be civil to our housekeeper, Nelly, but with each day that passes, the woman becomes more difficult. She detests taking the tiniest instruction from me. I'm sure she thinks herself better than me—a lowly bin man's daughter. This morning, when I asked her to try dusting my bedroom for a second time (as her first effort had been so dismal) she smiled viciously at me and snarled, "No problem—can't have madam's brothel dusty."

I wouldn't mind but I often come to her defence when Markus goes on the warpath about what a terrible housekeeper she is and she truly is so terrible. A toddler would do a better job. With Markus's cleaning OCD, she drives him bonkers. He swears that she spends most of her time sitting around sipping tea and he has shown me footage from the security cameras of her literally sweeping shovelfuls of dirt under rugs. It's hilarious in some regards.

Despite Nelly's incompetence and rudeness, I can't help but feel sorry for her. She grew up close to my childhood home so I've got a fair idea of her stringent circumstances. She's not had an easy road with her jailbird husband and bringing up seven children practically all by herself.

I feel so terrible carrying on with other men behind Markus's back. There is simply no excuse. Who could blame Nelly Boyle for thinking me a prostitute?

And Markus knows about the affairs because Jennifer, in the past, has told him of overhearing me on the phone, making my illicit arrangements. The girl has such super hearing. I swear she can hear right through the three-foot-thick walls of Nolan Manor.

Markus though just turns a deliberate blind eye and I love him all the more for doing so. I hope he can understand that what I have with these other men is purely a physical thing and it'll never stop me loving him.

I've been seeing this married man, called Jack Hanson, for several months now. He's lovely—but maybe just a bit intense.

I know it's revolting of me but I've now also started carrying on with, of all people, Markus's gardener, Frank. I just can't seem to restrain myself. What is even more disgusting is that I'm continuing to see Jack. Although Jack obviously knows nothing about Frank and vice versa.

Markus berated me this morning for taking Rupert for a walk along the cliff path in such stormy weather. He's such a worrier. God only knows how stressed he'd be if he knew how often I think about jumping off that same cliff path.

The day has come when we finally had to let Nelly go. When she called me "a whore" in front of Markus, I couldn't stop him from sacking her. He said we'd given her ample chances. It was past time to get a proper housekeeper in. That it had been his father who'd originally hired her, not him.

Markus has been interviewing for a new housekeeper, but my prediction, given his OCD, is that finding the perfect candidate is going to be a long arduous process, and I rather think he is enjoying doing all the cleaning himself. Funny!

Frank knows that what's going on between us is nothing serious. He knows I'll never leave Markus and neither does he want to leave his fiancée. I only wish Jack were as relaxed about things. He remains blissfully unaware that I'm also seeing Frank. He's all set for leaving his wife, and us moving in together. I just don't know how to let him down gently. He has got such a terrible temper. I'm scared about what he might do.

I've been getting these dizzy spells where I black out, and I know I should go to see a doctor, but I just can't get past the trauma of what that beast, Doctor Angela Thornton, did to me as a child. I would prefer to brave a swamp of crocodiles than to walk into another doctor's surgery.

Today, I mentioned to Markus about the dizzy spells but he was so caught up with his writing that he only seemed to be half-listening and simply agreed that they were probably just coming from tiredness. I got the impression too that he assumed it might be more a mental than physical thing because he asked if I'd reconsidered talking to a psychiatrist.

Now that I've calmed down about the whole situation and am not as spooked, I'm glad that I hadn't got Markus's full attention, as otherwise he'd have been sure to frogmarch me to see someone.

In the last few days, I haven't had any more dizzy spells. I've been sleeping better too, so as I thought, they just seem to have been down to tiredness. I pray they're gone for good.

I have noticed that Jack has started drinking heavily and his temper has got much worse. Today, on our way to a restaurant for lunch, after having to brake suddenly to avoid rear-ending a learner driver, he went berserk. Exactly like how my horrible first husband would go berserk.

Most worryingly of all, Jack is now fully convinced that we are going to be moving in together and keeps harassing me to leave Markus.

Jennifer, who'd been staying over in Nolan Manor for the weekend, got so mad with me today and I was entirely to blame. She overheard me on the phone with Jack, arranging for us to meet up, which triggered her to start screaming at me. She seemed so big and powerful in comparison to tiny little me and she'd me pinned up against a wall, just at the top of the main staircase, that treacherously steep main staircase of Nolan Manor.

I felt so scared for my life. Had Markus not come to my rescue, I genuinely feared she would've flung me down the stairs. However, Markus insisted I was being ridiculous. That Jennifer would never hurt anyone. That I was letting my imagination run riot.

I finally gave in to Jack's constant badgering and promised I would move in with him on Monday, the 14th of May. However, I should never have done so, and I think the only reason I did was because of how upset I'd been with what had happened with Jennifer. I was not thinking straight and Jack kept insisting that, for my safety, I needed to move in with him ASAP. He's going to go ballistic when I tell him I won't be moving in with him—as he has already left his wife and son and got an apartment for us. He's even forced me to take a key for the apartment.

This morning when I was walking Rupert, I had another dizzy spell. It's so disappointing because I truly thought I'd done with them. I took a nasty stumble and fell onto some briar bushes. My neck was so badly injured that I felt I had no other choice but to see a doctor.

I thought it best though to not tell Markus about the fall. I did not want him fretting and, knowing him, he would not be at all satisfied with me seeing a doctor, just once. He would be sure to have insisted on me attending countless follow-up appointments.

I was so anxious to get through the encounter with Doctor Bullock as speedily as possible, to just have the visible injuries to my neck treated, that I didn't mention how it was dizziness that had caused me to fall. I just said I stumbled. Though he must have sensed I wasn't telling him the full story and ludicrously seemed to think that I'd been attacked by Markus.

I've resolved not to tell Penelope or any of my other friends about my fall, lest they too mistakenly think Markus responsible for my injuries. I'm going to keep wearing neck scarves so they and Markus won't see them.

However, I felt I had no other option, given . . . well . . . our continued intimacy . . . but to tell Frank and Jack the truth. Frank reacted, as I thought he would react, by wanting to make sure I was okay, but not making a big deal about it. As for Jack . . . well, I had a terrible time trying to convince him that Jennifer had not attacked me or that 'for my own safety' I didn't need to move in with him sooner than May 14th.

Jack's drinking is getting even worse and I know it's only a matter of time before he starts becoming violent with me. I've seen it in his eyes. How he's holding himself back. I need to finish it with him and if he does end up hurting me, well perhaps I deserve what I get for having led him on for so long. A black eye would be worth it, at this stage, to be rid of him.

I'm going to end it with Frank too. It's time for me to grow up. Markus is the only man I need.

"That—heartbreakingly—was the last thing Harriet wrote," Nolan said with a sorrowful sigh, closing her pink-covered diary and placing it back on the side table.

"I was wrong then about Hanson causing those injuries to her neck?" Doocey burst out. "She did just get them from tripping onto briar bushes? That's why you kept her diary from me."

Nolan smiled a sad type of smile. "Trust you," he said, "after you got so much correct to home in on the one thing you didn't get quite right."

He pursed his lips. "Neither could you be blamed for not getting it right. Not when the doctor, who had actual sight of the injuries, led you to believe my wife had been physically attacked. And, of course, as we know, Hanson went on to attack Harriet, as she had prophetically written in her diary that she feared he would do."

Back in the present, in what Nolan had explained would be their final interview session for the book, Doocey looked blurrily out a library window as Nolan jotted down some notes.

Nolan stopped writing and gazed down at the notepad on his lap and mumbled, "Okay . . . I think I've now got enough from you to complete the book." Eyeing Doocey, his voice became clearer. "Except, as in all good crime mysteries, there has to be one extra twist."

"Oh . . ." Doocey said in a simultaneously surprised and worried-sounding voice. "What would that be?"

Nolan got to his feet. "Follow me, and I will show you."

Trailing Nolan out of his library, Doocey couldn't clear the insane thought from his head that he was about to meet the real—fully alive—Harriet Nolan.

FORTY-ONE

THEY PROCEEDED INTO A LONG, narrow room that Doocey hadn't been in before and which, to his annoyance—was in near darkness—with its curtains closed and only a trickle of dim light coming from a lamp in the far corner.

"Please take a seat," Nolan said, gesturing to a large sofa that Doocey could scarcely make out—his snail-paced eyes yet to adjust to the room's dimness.

Nolan, after retrieving some item from a coffee table, that Doocey, with the poor light combined with his poor sight, could not manage to identify, joined him on the sofa, although maintaining a considerable distance. It was only when *His Lordship* stretched out an arm that Doocey realised he had picked up a TV remote and that they were sitting in front of a large screen that had been hidden in the gloom but now lit up.

"I lied to you about the house's surveillance cameras being switched off," Nolan let drop in this relaxed voice as if totally unaware of the bombshell such a disclosure was. He scrutinised Doocey for some seconds, "I rather thought you would have picked up on that—given what you relayed back to me as to your conversation with Nelly Boyle." He paused, and after Doocey returned a baffled stare, continued. "Do you not recall how she said that I used the cameras to check up on her?"

Doocey gave a slow nod. "Yes . . . now . . . I remember . . . alright."

"I used to sit in this very room watching her lazing about the place." He shook his head. "You would never believe all the shortcuts the woman took when it came to cleaning." His voice grew serious, "But enough about her."

He pressed another button on the remote and some soundless images began to play and Doocey was glad that his host—rightly knowing he would struggle to properly see the screen—had the understanding to begin describing aloud what was happening. "Here you see me walking into Nolan Manor on Monday the 14th to find my daughter crouched over Harriet," he described, again in that relaxed voice, as if still completely unaware of the incredibleness of his words. "I'll just forward it on a little."

After some seconds, he pressed play again. "Here you see pictures from the external cameras. Oh . . . I should have explained that I've combined the key footage from multiple cameras, positioned inside and outside the house, into the compilation you're watching. Here, I'm leaving Nolan Manor with Jennifer, to take her back to her apartment."

He pressed fast forward and, in due course, the play button again. "This is when I've returned from Jennifer's, and I'm putting my beautiful Harriet in the boot of my Volvo, and I'm driving off to bury her in the mountains."

Hitting pause, Nolan turned to a flabbergasted-looking Doocey. "So at least you know those elements of what I told you are true. Okay . . ." he continued, looking back at the screen. "Now for—the most important part—what happened prior to me walking in and finding Harriet lying dead, with Jennifer crouched over her."

Nolan pressed the rewind button. "If only I'd thought about the cameras earlier," he said, with his gaze remaining on the screen, "things could have been all so different. But after coming home to find my wife dead and feeling convinced that Jennifer had murdered her, my mind was simply scrambled. It had also been months since I'd sacked Nelly Boyle, so I no longer had any reason for checking footage from the security cameras. I'd forgotten that they were even running.

"On the Tuesday evening I reported Harriet missing, your chum Dickson, informed me that the following day, a full forensic examination of Nolan Manor would need to be conducted. He stated this to be 'standard procedure' in a missing person case. The next morning, I'd been down on my knees, doing one last check that I'd thoroughly scrubbed away any speck of blood, when I happened to look up and saw a camera pointing down to the exact spot where Harriet had lain dead."

Nolan squirmed about on the sofa. "At breakneck speed, I stuffed every last piece of security camera footage into a plastic bag which I buried underneath a bushy plant in a distant corner of the gardens. The same spot where I'd already buried another plastic bag containing Harriet's diary, which at that point, I hadn't had time to read. Nor had I any desire to read it, as I did not want—despite her being dead—to intrude on Harriet's privacy."

He heaved a heavy sigh. "However, given Hanson's lies about Jennifer having physically attacked Harriet, I ultimately felt I had no choice but to read the diary to see if it would confirm my suspicions that Hanson was the one with a predilection for physical violence and the one who'd caused those injuries to Harriet's arms."

Doocey continued to not comment because hadn't he, as the apparently gullible eejit he'd been shown up to be, said more than enough.

"With your forensic people due to arrive at any second to go over the house, neither had I time to play the security camera footage. However, I didn't think that ultimately mattered. Positive, at that point, the footage would just be gruesome confirmation that Jennifer had murdered Harriet. My priority . . . as with the diary . . . but even more so—was just to stop you getting hold of it."

Continuing to eye the screen in front of him, Nolan fell silent and pressed play. "Now, we're back to the most monumentally important segment of the footage. The segment of footage showing what occurred before I discovered my daughter crouched over my wife's dead body. There's the front door of Nolan Manor opening and Harriet coming in."

"She was still alive?" Doocey mouthed in a shocked voice. "She never died in Hanson's apartment?"

Nolan, pressing pause on the remote, answered, "Yes, she was still alive."

"I was all wrong?" Doocey asked in a devastated tone of voice.

"No, I would not agree. You see, you were absolutely right about the fundamental point—about Hanson viciously attacking Harriet when she told him she wanted to end things."

As Doocey silently collapsed into himself, Nolan pressed play and explained in a tearful voice, "You can see in this part of the footage, the injuries he inflicted. How my poor darling looks so shaken and is clasping one of her injured arms."

Nolan leaned forward towards the screen. "Here she is making her way upstairs, perhaps to ring to report Hanson's assault. Though knowing my wife's forgiving nature, and going by her diary entries, I suspect she may well never have made any such call. Absurdly counting herself lucky, just to finally have escaped the animal's violent clutches."

He momentarily squeezed his eyes shut as if not wanting to see what was to come. "Now, about a quarter-way up the stairs," he continued, "Harriet puts a hand to her forehead and as her foot seeks out the next step, she stumbles. Falling horribly backwards, her head hits, a terrible number of times, unforgiving marble—one of the hardest surfaces on this earth."

Nolan cleared away tiny tears with a fingertip but was unable to clear the connected distress from his voice. "I wouldn't have expected Jennifer to have heard a thing, given that she'd been rehearsing at the time, no doubt hitting some ear-shatteringly high note." He continued to look, unseeingly, at the television screen—now showing a picture of his wife lying lifeless on the hall floor. "Harriet's fall also happened towards the lower part of the stairs," he went on, "which is a considerable distance from my daughter's room. Nor does it appear that Harriet even screamed. It seems she just fainted off, after experiencing another dizziness spell."

He straightened his back. "I've been reading up on a potential reason for those dizzy spells, and it could be that Harriet had something as simple as an imbalance of the ear. Seemingly, this is a very common condition, easily rectified with some pills. If only she'd confided truthfully with her doctor, he might have identified this as being the real reason for her falling into those briar bushes, and she might be alive today."

He pressed the top of his head down with a hand. "Or before that fall had even happened, if only I'd paid more attention when she'd come to me. Instead of being so caught up in my silly writing. That remains my biggest regret of all. I will forever hold myself accountable for Harriet's eventual death because if I had acted—convinced her to tell me the full truth about her symptoms, things might have turned out differently."

He squeezed the fingers of his right hand into a white-knuckled fist, anger also showing through in his voice. "Yet this does not mean that I'm exonerating Hanson from blame for my wife's death. No, because I don't believe that it was any coincidence that Harriet had that fatal blackout on the same day that *he* attacked her. His attack, I'm certain, acted as a trigger."

Doocey, sounding equally angry, interjected. "I don't understand why you didn't just come forward with this footage earlier. I mean, before Hanson told those lies about Jennifer, and when you already knew I hadn't bought your story about Harriet accidentally drowning."

Nolan replied in a pained voice, "Because I only saw the footage after I'd already secretly buried Harriet's body and had told a glut of lies. If I divulged the truth, it would come out that the only reason I covered up my wife's death was because I thought my daughter had murdered her."

He scratched at his hairless head. "I feared, similar to what you'd hypothesised, such a revelation would wreck Jennifer's reputation and singing career. In all likelihood, she would never have been able to cast off the label of being a suspected murderer. For, if her own father, the person who should know her best, believed her capable of murder—why should say some stranger attending one of her concerts, be expected to think otherwise."

He drew in a deep breath. "The simplest solution would have been for you to believe Harriet had accidentally been swept out to sea." He scratched again at his hairless head. "However, reaching the frustrating realisation that you were never going to leave us be, I actually had been about to come forward with the security camera footage but then Hanson started telling his lies about Jennifer. Leading me to ask why he would lie about my daughter having previously physically attacked Harriet. And only one answer made sense. He had to be the one responsible for those wounds to Harriet's arms. Wounds that he knew, in the event of Harriet's body being found would be clear evidence that she had been savagely attacked before her death."

The pitch of Nolan's voice rose. "The security camera footage also revealed that there were no wounds to Harriet's arms upon her leaving Nolan Manor to go, as we now know, to meet with Hanson. Therefore, Jennifer categorically had nothing to do with causing them. Harriet's diary entries about Hanson's heavy drinking and her fears of him turning violent just further cemented my conviction of his guilt."

Nolan half-punched his thigh. "Therefore, I determined to have my revenge on the beast for attacking Harriet and triggering her death—and for him having tried to frame my daughter, an innocent blind girl, as her murderer."

He frowned. "I had wanted to leave Jennifer out of my bittersweet revenge but she was determined to be involved. Partly because she wanted to get Hanson back for trying to falsely incriminate her but more so for a desire to see justice done for Harriet. Even if she hadn't got on with Harriet, she wanted Hanson punished for having beaten her up—adamant that no woman deserved such treatment. Hence, deciding to give the monster a taste of his own devious medicine, together, we set out to frame him."

Nolan proceeded to explain how he used the 'clues' Doocey's investigation had pinpointed, such as the petrol station CCTV images to concoct a false narrative of Hanson after killing Harriet, having then tried to frame Jennifer for the murder. To make that false narrative much more convincing, Nolan planted, in Hanson's apartment, DNA from Mrs Nolan's remains.

He'd done so by digging up his wife's body, and rubbing a cloth handkerchief to a large open wound at the back of her head, which she'd got from falling down the stairs of Noland Manor. Then he rubbed the handkerchief onto the granite surround of the fireplace in Hanson's apartment, having gained access to the apartment using the spare key Hanson had given Harriet. He'd been shocked to learn that the DNA he'd planted would turn out to contain microscopic fragments of Harriet's brain tissue. The whole task, he swore, of digging up his wife's body and planting the DNA had been so horrendous and he hated himself for doing it. Along with the DNA, he also planted Harriet's front door key to Nolan Manor, in Hanson's apartment.

"Then Jennifer would plant further false clues of her own," Nolan elaborated. "False clues that unlike the ones I'd planted in Hanson's apartment were verbal and not physical in nature—but nevertheless were crucially important in sewing together our fabric of lies. Lying as she did in her recollections of what she'd remembered happening. Lying about having heard the doorbell ring multiple times. To falsely make out this had been Hanson's way of getting her to come downstairs to discover Harriet lying dead. Also lying about how the body had been icy cold so as to suggest Harriet had been dead for a lengthy period which would fit with Hanson having earlier murdered her in his apartment."

Doocey sighed, remembering how Nelly Boyle had testified to Jennifer Nolan being a great actress, having inherited her mother's talent for acting.

Well . . . he reckoned Nelly had been right on that score. So much so that if he were in charge of doling out one of those famous gold statues of the little fella holding a sword, he'd have definitely given one to Jennifer. He heard a voice, with an American accent, announce inside his head: *And the Best Actor Oscar goes to Jennifer Nolan for her performance as the lying stepdaughter.*

"It all seems to make bloody sense now," Doocey declared aloud. He straightened his glasses. "Though aside from all that you've just told me, I really should have known the second you asked me to be interviewed for your book. Because I'd been wondering why the hell you would want to write a book all about how great I'd been in solving your wife's murder."

Not giving Nolan time to respond, he continued, "It was like you were taking a dodgy shortcut. Real life was giving you the book's crime, your wife's death or you could say the plot, as well as your main character, little old shabby me. All that was left for you to do then was to write everything down—something any talentless transcriber could do. How was that supposed to help in achieving your stated goal of proving yourself to be the great crime fiction writer? Because in crime fiction, don't you have to rely on your creative talent to come up with an intriguing crime and an intriguing main character?"

He shook his head from side to side. "But, of course, you never intended the book to be about fecking little old me. It was really to be about you and how great you'd been as this true master of crime mystery in staging the perfect fictional murder. Allowing you to give your writer's finger to all those who'd rejected your work."

Nolan acknowledged, in a shy voice, "Yes that was precisely my plan."

Underneath his messy hair, Doocey's brow furrowed. "I don't understand though, ahead of the book being published, why you would risk telling me what you are up to. Aren't you afraid of me going to Ryan and him stopping your book from ever going on sale? Which, by the way, I'm sure he would easily find some way of doing."

"Not really," Nolan answered with a shrug of his large shoulders. "As I'm not interested in having the book published any longer. I'm writing it purely for me."

He twisted his head around in a circular motion. ""You were so correct to think I felt angry with you when you told me that the only reason

I wanted to write a great book and was so desperate for it to be a critical and publishing success was because I was trying to prove myself to my late father. My chest had burned like I'd swallowed fire." He sat up straighter. "I didn't want to admit you were right. My reason for writing this book and all my other efforts was indeed not to prove some anonymous critics wrong—but to prove my Dad wrong."

Nolan picked out a floorboard to stare at. "Now, I'm beginning to realise, though very belatedly in the day, that I don't need to prove anything to my father or anybody else—be they living or dead."

He bit down on his lip. "Jennifer and I also feel that we should correct matters at this point before Hanson's case goes to trial and a jury inevitably finds him guilty of murder, complicating matters even further. It was never our intention that Hanson should serve a full life sentence for murder. We were just happy to make him fully believe that he faced that nightmarish prospect. However, I want and expect him to be charged with having assaulted Harriet and to serve, hopefully, a very long sentence for that crime."

He peered into Doocey's glasses. "Because you see, I'm going to send the newly appointed Commissioner Ryan a copy of the house camera footage with an explanatory letter, requesting that he drop the charge of murder against Hanson and charge him instead with serious assault. I will explain in the letter that if he fails to comply, I shall be forced to send further copies of the footage to all the national television stations."

Doocey nodded several times as if thinking through all the ramifications of what he'd just heard, and then frowned, "There's only one thing in all this that I still don't get." After a pause, he continued, "If that mysterious cyclist, seen cycling away from Nolan Manor, wasn't Hanson—who the hell was he?"

"Well, I can answer that question also. Because when you showed me the CCTV picture of the cyclist wearing what looked like a suit, I strongly suspected him to be a Mr David Sodwell, an American gentleman, who every few years, holidays in the local area."

He peered into the gloom of his television room as if thinking back. "I only met Sodwell once, about two years ago, but he made a memorable impression on me. An architect by profession, he'd asked if he might have a tour of Nolan Manor. He'd heard from the owner of the guest house he was staying in, how I'd completely modernised its interior."

The hint of a smile appeared on Nolan's face. "The chap had been riding a racing bike on that occasion too and furthermore had been sporting a smart pinstriped suit. When I jovially remarked about him being very formally attired for cycling, he explained how he always liked to dress smartly, no matter the task at hand. His work colleagues had apparently christened him 'Dapper Dave.' He even made a joke about how he wouldn't be seen dead wearing skin-tight cycling shorts. Though at home in America, he normally rode slow city-type bikes and had only borrowed the zippy race bike he was riding from the guesthouse owner's son who was a cycling fanatic."

Nolan gripped the tied top button of his shirt. "I subsequently telephoned Mr Sodwell in America and he casually confirmed that 'yes,' he'd been holidaying in the area in May, and that on the 14th, simply for some sightseeing, had cycled out to Nolan Manor. Again, using a road bike he'd borrowed from the guesthouse owner's son. He was certain that the CCTV image I described of the cyclist taken at 4:20 p.m. had to be of him. The time fitted with when he would have cycled past the *On The Run* Petrol Station, on his way back to his guesthouse."

Doocey. looked to be dying to say something but continued to hold his tongue.

"Sodwell flew home to America the following day and—probably not surprisingly given that he was living on the other side of the Atlantic, nearly 6,000 kilometres away—he said he hadn't heard anything about Harriet's disappearance or your efforts to trace a cyclist." Nolan reached inside his jacket pocket. "He gave me this business card when we met previously. If you give him a call, he'll be able to corroborate what I've told you."

Doocey snapped the business card from Nolan and, without even attempting to read its text, stuffed it into a side anorak pocket. "Even if this Mr Sodwell was the cyclist and not Hanson," he burst out, "that doesn't explain why there is only footage of him cycling away from your house. Where's the footage of him going in the opposite direction, earlier on in the day—headed towards Nolan Manor?"

Nolan gave a smiling nod of the head. "I also quizzed Sodwell on that peculiar point and discovered on his outward journey, he'd popped into the shop of the *On The Run* petrol station, to buy a bottle of water. And in so doing, I presume, he inadvertently circumvented the patch of road that the CCTV overlooked."

Such an explanation had also—though admittedly it had taken some time—already occurred to Doocey which was why he'd eventually got round to asking Ber to review the internal shop CCTV footage from the *On The Run* petrol station. Ber had then spotted for herself, by the timings on the CCTV, that the silhouetted cyclist and the man who'd walked into the petrol station shop to buy himself a bottle of water were the same person, and that the man—crucially—wasn't Jack Hanson.

However Doocey—by emphasising how a piece of Harriet Nolan's brain tissue had been found in Hanson's apartment—had managed, just about, to convince Ber that she was mistaken. That the man who'd come into the shop wasn't the cyclist but just some randomer. That the silhouetted cyclist still had to be Jack Hanson.

Even though he felt terrible for hoodwinking Ber in this way—he thought it was best to keep her in the dark, worried because of her blunt nature that she would inadvertently let the secret cat out of the bag or even not accept that promotion he'd been planning to get Ryan to give her. Ber had just about forgiven him, when he finally fessed up the truth, though she'd given him a joke whack across the head which had sent him flying.

Back in the present moment, Doocey removed a photo from an inside anorak pocket and handed it to Nolan, who seemed so shocked by what the photo showed that he was unable to speak.

Doocey smiled broadly. "Remember when I discovered the real dolmen that you'd buried your wife beside, and how I'd been thinking about the way the capping stone connected all the standing stones? How likewise, I thought the mysterious cyclist might connect all the pillars of my investigation, certain, that if I could just fecking identify him, I would be able to solve the entire case. Well, you see, I was telling the truth."

A still thunderstruck Nolan continued to stare at the photo in his hand, of a man in a pinstripe suit paying for a bottle of water at a shop counter.

Doocey asked, "That is Mr Sodwell, I presume?"

"Yes . . ." Nolan muttered, sounding flabbergasted. "But—"

Doocey cut him off. "Just have a read of the note I wrote at the back of that pic. It should explain everything."

FORTY-TWO

Nolan turned the picture over and slowly read Doocey's note aloud: *Did you really think that I didn't know that you were framing Hanson? I was only ever pretending to half-see.*

He stared at Doocey in disbelief. "You knew all along," he mouthed. "But how?"

"Because when I found where you had buried your wife, there were those fresh spade marks . . . and the only reasonable explanation I could come up with for them being there was that after having secretly buried Harriet, you'd dug her up again. Why though had you done this? Was it because you'd realised Murphy had originally seen where you'd buried her—forcing you to secretly rebury her somewhere else? Well, apparently not, because you never did bury the body somewhere else."

He tapped the back of his scraggly head. "There was also how messy the spade marks were. I reckoned that as the very compulsively neat person I had you down as, you would never have been so messy, unless intentionally so."

He let out a little chuckle. "And not to forget that gigantic white rock you'd used to mark the burial spot when a much smaller and ordinary grey stone would have easily done the job. Neither had Murphy, who'd seen you burying the body, mentioned anything about you hauling a big white rock into place." He pushed himself up straighter on his wingback chair. "So I presumed you had positioned it there later—to make it really easy for me to find the grave because if the grave was easy to find, it would mean it would be quick to find, and time was of the fecking essence."

Another pause. "The reason you'd dug up your wife's body, as you've confirmed just now, was to get what you needed to frame Hanson, and having done this, you wanted me to speedily find the secret grave. You even gave me that clue in the newspaper—to hint that first time round I'd searched at the wrong dolmen: *'One wonders how many more dolmens they are going to dig around . . .'*"

Doocey fiddled with his glasses. "Apart from all this, I also wondered how Hanson could've been such an idiot. I mean to have murdered a woman in his apartment and to stupidly let months go by without cleaning the place of incriminating DNA, even to go holding onto his murder victim's front door key. Now, I mean, come on!" His voice lowered. "And if he was that huge an idiot, there wouldn't be a wax cat in hell's chance of him coming up with such a clever plan as to plant Harriet's corpse in Nolan Manor."

Nolan interjected, "But why pretend you didn't know I was framing Hanson?"

"Because I reckoned my best chance of getting to the real truth of what had happened to your wife was just to let you think that you'd fooled me into believing Hanson had murdered her. I figured that eventually, like with what's just happened, you would tell the truth." He took a deep breath. "I also had no real problem with letting a lying, woman-beating dirtbag like Hanson get a nice scare. Letting him—like you too had wanted—to fully believe he was facing into a life prison sentence."

"But what if you were proven wrong in your belief that Jennifer and I, in the end, would tell you the truth? What if we had just left Hanson to rot in prison, to serve out his life sentence?"

Doocey smiled. "I sensed you or Jennifer would not do that. I doubted you'd have been able to live with yourselves and you even said as much, just a minute ago."

Nolan gave a rigid nod of the head.

"I figured too," Doocey continued, "you'd never have gone through with framing Hanson unless you'd a solid exit plan. You had to have some way of being sure that when you finally fessed up to what truly happened to Harriet, the murder charges against Hanson would be dropped."

Doocey paused, "And you had to be sure that the finger of suspicion would not point right back to Jennifer and yourself. I was convinced then that you had to have some cast-iron evidence to prove Hanson's innocence or partial innocence as well as yours and Jennifer's. And what could be more fecking cast-iron than having footage to show Harriet fell down the stairs of Nolan Manor and hadn't then been murdered in Hanson's apartment."

He gave Nolan a smirk. "Did you really think I hadn't picked up on Nelly Boyle telling me you used the security cameras in Nolan Manor to monitor her? So I knew you'd been lying when you said you never switched them on."

"Gosh," Nolan exclaimed. "You truly had me fooled." His brow furrowed even tighter. "What, though, about the huge personal risk you were taking in sending a man to prison for a murder he technically never committed? What about the possibility of you being prosecuted and going to prison yourself?"

Doocey leaned forward on the sofa. "But you see, I—personally—hadn't sent Hanson to prison. Playing to Ryan's crooked nature, you'll remember that I told him that he could take all the glory for solving the case. And he'd been more than happy to be the one who officially signed off on Hanson being charged with murder."

Nolan slowly nodded.

"Oh, and that reminds me about something else," Doocey continued. "I understand where you are coming from about only writing the book for yourself, but at the same time, I do wish you'd have a rethink about going for publication which as we've talked about, Harriet would have been all for . . ." Doocey smiled. "Plus, I'd love to see Ryan get his comeuppance."

His tone turned business-like. "Here's what I think you should do. Don't give any heads up to Ryan that you've written any book but do go ahead with your plan of sending your letter to him, explaining what truly happened to Harriet, along with a copy of the house security camera footage. To get him to change the murder charge against Hanson to serious assault. And I'd bet Hanson will only be too delighted to fess up to the assault charges—he'll just be relieved not to be going down for murder which with all the evidence against him looked like a foregone conclusion."

Doocey pushed some hair back off his forehead. "Then when that's all done and dusted, go ahead with publishing your book. With it showing Ryan up for the crooked asshole, he is, there'd be no chance of you or Jennifer being hit with any new charges or them coming after me, the ex-partially sighted detective. They won't want any more horrible publicity." He burst into laughter. "Oh, it would be so brilliant to see Ryan get his just deserts."

Nolan smiled. "I'm surprised to hear how much you want to reap revenge on the man—given that—"

Doocey interjected, "Given that he gave me a chance to investigate my first big case . . . That I should then be thankful to him."

Nolan nodded in agreement.

"Well . . . I suppose I'll always be grateful for him letting me have that chance," Doocey continued, "but, at the same time, I can't forgive him for weaselling out of the agreement he made with me, to let me carry on working as a detective. I feel too, it's only right that the Irish public should know the corrupt sort of person they've got in charge of their police force. They deserve better. I was even hoping that following your book's release, Ryan would be forced to resign."

His expression and tone turned serious. "Though seeing as how I've turned the tables by telling you how I knew all along that you had framed Hanson, I can understand why you wouldn't want to go ahead with the book. I probably should have kept my trap shut."

"No, I'm glad you told me the truth. Oh no, that wouldn't be a reason at all for not going for publication. Because in my opinion, you knowing all along would just make a terrific second final twist. Furthermore, I believe I can continue to validly claim to have pulled off the perfect fictional crime as in I fooled the official powers that be, fooled a person no less than the current commissioner, into believing Hanson had committed murder."

"That's very true," Doocey enthusiastically agreed.

And as it would turn out, Ryan was forced to resign when the truth all came out. And Hanson, who having admitted to seriously assaulting Harriet Nolan, just like Doocey had predicted he would, received a lengthy prison sentence.

Back in the here and now, in the semi-darkness of Nolan's television room, a long silence ensued as both men—having covered so much monumental ground together—seemed to be struggling about what to talk about next.

"Tell me this . . ." Doocey piped up at last. "Have you come up with a title for the book?"

"Well, I had been thinking of, *A Good Way to Murder Your Wife*.

Doocey grinned. "It was a good way to murder your wife because you only made it look like she'd been murdered . . . to get payback on Hanson."

"Precisely," Nolan acknowledged. "I do always like when the clue to the entire plot is hiding in plain sight in a book's title."

He frowned. "Although now, I don't think, after all, it would've been the right choice. Any potential buyer of the book on reading that title, *A Good Way to Murder Your Wife*," might reasonably expect that the book they were about to purchase related to the story—my story—of how I supposedly got away with killing my wife. However, I've come to realise the book is more about your story."

Doocey shot him a sceptical smile.

"No, trust me it is," Nolan insisted in a vehement voice. Falling suddenly silent, as if something had just occurred to him, he picked up the photograph of Sodwell and stared again for several long seconds at what Doocey had written on its reverse, before excitedly exclaiming, "You know what you've written here—*I was only ever pretending to half-see*—has given me a new idea for a title. How does *Doocey Half-Sees Whodunnit* sound?"

"Sounds great to me," Doocey, after taking a minute to consider, replied with a smile. "I think it's clever, the different ways it can be read and how, like you were saying there, it has that clue to the whole plot thing going on."

He paused. "You know, I've been thinking," he continued at last, "of going out on my own—becoming a private detective, specialising in unsolved murders." He grinned. "Where there's nothing to see."

Nolan gushed, "That's fantastic to hear, really—"

"Yeah," Doocey said, cutting him off. "The only thing is . . . with the state of my sight . . . I know I won't be able to manage everything by myself. I was wondering then if you'd be interested in helping me out. Maybe, you could even base more books on our investigations?"

A few minutes later, their conversation was interrupted by the blare of a car horn, prompting Doocey to stand up and say his warm goodbyes. On heaving himself into the taxi's back seat, he was greeted with the question, "Where are we headed for, buddy?"

Then, after they'd just pulled out of the gates of Nolan Manor, the taxi driver asked his second, inevitable question. The question every Irish taxi driver (or at least the ones Doocey ever encountered) loved to ask. "What do you do for a living yourself, bud?"

In a confident and proud tone, Doocey answered, "I'm a Detective," and he really couldn't give a damn if your man believed him or not.

"Working on any big cases?" the taxi driver, of course, also wanted to know.

"Yes, as a matter of fact, I've just finished up working on a very big one, and there's going to be a book based on it . . ." Hurriedly adding, "And there'll be more books about other big cases of mine to follow."

M Y NAME IS TOM MCANDREW and I'm an Irish mystery writer. I grew up in a little village (of about twelve houses) on the very edge of the West of Ireland—next stop America. I now live in Dublin with my wife and two children. I have an MA in media studies.

I have written a series of funny (well I hope they're funny) whodunnits which feature a scruffy, oddball detective named Doocey who starts losing his sight just as he's assigned his first big case. Talk about bad timing! And my favourite books to read—probably no big surprise—are cosy mysteries, especially funny ones.

"Sight" as a subject matter has always fascinated me and having had my own fair share of sight issues, I believe it is a subject I can authentically write about. Alongside my writing, I love to do Art which I studied at the National College of Art, Ireland (NCAD).

9 781684 923304